This Private Plot

Books by Alan Beechey

The Oliver Swithin Mysteries
An Embarrassment of Corpses
Murdering Ministers
This Private Plot

(with Gina Teague)
Culture Smart! USA

This Private Plot

An Oliver Swithin Mystery

Alan Beechey

Poisoned Pen Press

Copyright © 2014 by Alan Beechey

First Edition 2014

10 9 8 7 6 5 4 3 2 1

Library of Congress Catalog Card Number: 2014930371

ISBN: 9781464202407   Hardcover
        9781464202421   Trade Paperback

Poisoned Pen Press
6962 E. First Ave., Ste. 103
Scottsdale, AZ 85251
www.poisonedpenpress.com
info@poisonedpenpress.com

Printed in the United States of America

To the memory of my parents: Tom Beechey,
who gave me my sense of humor;
and Lucy Beechey, who gave me a copy of
Agatha Christie's *The Mysterious Affair at Styles*
when I was twelve.

"…it seems to us that the readers who want fiction to be like life are considerably outnumbered by those who would like life to be like fiction."

—Sarah Caudwell
The Sirens Sang of Murder

An old Danish jester named Yorick
Drank a gallon of pure paregoric.
My jokes have been dull,
Said he, but my skull
Will one of these days be historic.

—Ogden Nash
There's Always Another Windmill

Chapter One

"The odd thing about a banana," Oliver Swithin mused as he chased the naked policewoman across the moonlit field, "is not that it's an excellent source of potassium, but that everybody seems to know it is."

A week earlier, he'd been borrowing a book about swans from the library. A passing reader had tapped him on the shoulder and whispered: "A full-grown swan can break a man's arm, you know."

Oliver might have forgotten the incident, but on his way home, a bus passenger had spotted the book poking out of his leather satchel and said the same thing. Later, his housemate Geoffrey Angelwine couldn't resist making a similar comment.

That's when it struck Oliver that he'd never had a conversation about George Washington without somebody piping up: "Did you know he had wooden teeth?" Every time the subject of hedgehogs arose, someone felt compelled to say: "They're covered in fleas, you know." Munch on a celery stalk and you'd inevitably be told that you burn more calories digesting it than you take in from eating it. And how many discussions of sexual orientation had led to the dubious anecdote that Britain had no laws against lesbians because Queen Victoria didn't (or couldn't or wouldn't) believe they existed?

An owl hooted, interrupting his thoughts. At least Oliver guessed it was an owl. It could have been a hedgehog howling at the moon for all he knew about country matters. It was hard to hear anything over his labored breathing. Was that a nettle patch he'd just run through?

Oliver had assumed that he and Effie were only going for a nighttime stroll. But when they'd reached the edge of Synne Common, the tract of scrubland near the Cotswolds village where they were staying, she had swiftly disrobed, bundled her clothes under a holly bush, and, ordering him to "get your kit off," hared off into the darkness. Mesmerized, Oliver undressed and followed, struggling to catch up with his girlfriend's slim outline, silvery-blue in the moonlight, the mass of curly hair fanning out around her head and bouncing wildly as she ran. Pure Botticelli. But he knew that he'd need some serious mental distraction to blot out his awareness that he was stark naked in a public place and it wasn't a dream.

Back to bananas.

Oliver believed that this irresistible urge to educate strangers about swans and bananas and lesbians was a new strain of trivia that he'd identified. No, not trivia. *Anti*-trivia. It was the opposite of conventional trivia, the stuff of board games and pub quizzes.

That kind of trivia, you either knew or you didn't. More likely, you didn't. For example, Effie Strongitharm, like many women, had a pair of faint indentations, set symmetrically on her lower back. (The clear moon might have been bright enough to reveal them now, but Oliver had left his glasses with the rest of his clothes.) And he would have bet that not one person in a hundred knew they had a name—the "dimples of Venus."

But in contrast, Oliver thought, his attention drifting downwards, *everyone* can (and, crucially, does) tell you that the gluteus maximus, the humble buttock, is the largest muscle in the human body. (Well, strictly speaking, it's in joint first place with its counterpart.) "Muscle" couldn't do justice to Effie's fleet derriere, flickering about five yards ahead of him. No need for his glasses to make that out. Perhaps there is a divinity that shapes our ends, he reflected. Or maybe it's the squats.

Did Botticelli do bottoms? Or would it take a sculptor to do full justice to his girlfriend, capturing the way each side approached the Euclidian perfection of the sphere, those gluteal creases each an almost perfect arc? Dear God, they seemed to be smiling at him!

Effie slowed and turned round. Oliver stumbled to a halt, remembering Sir Robert Helpmann's caveat about nude ballet: that not everything stops when the music does.

"What's on your mind?" she asked.

"Solid geometry," he confessed.

Effie nodded. "Serves a girl right for asking."

Oliver sneezed. Fair-haired and English-skinned under the full moon, he felt as conspicuous as a polar bear in a nunnery. In his late twenties, he had so far avoided gathering any spare flesh on his wiry frame, but his physique was still an embarrassing contrast to Effie's lean, athletic build. Her attractive face under the teeming curls, vaguely reminiscent of the young Ginger Rogers, would always score higher out of ten than his own benign features—his chin not quite firm enough, his teeth a touch too prominent, his pale blue eyes always looking as if he had just removed his glasses, even while he was wearing them. Gazing at her blurry form and trying to recover his breath, he was struck again by how grown-up it felt that a whole adult person, with a smirking bottom and everything else that goes with it—most of which was currently on display, since she'd elected to unmask her beauty to the moon—should love him as much as he loved her.

"I still wonder what you see in me," he confessed.

"You know, the number of times my colleagues at the Yard say the same thing, you'd think I could come up with a reason by now."

Oliver's riposte was thwarted by another sneeze.

"So have you guessed where you are?" Effie asked.

"In the middle of bloody Warwickshire, far from my clothes, even farther from my nice warm bed, too far by half from London, and in constant fear of being dive-bombed by bats," he thought, but kept it to himself. The irony had not escaped him that, since his adolescence, he'd lavished many hours of his imagination on female nudity, preferably accompanied by his own. Now that it was an al fresco reality, all he wanted to do was cover up his full Monty and go in search of a nice hot cup of tea. A cloud, which had momentarily slid across the moon, moved on, and the expanse known as Synne Common ensilvered itself moment by moment.

He saw that they had reached the highest point of the Common. In front of them, surrounded by a chain-link fence, was a huge, circular pattern, about 150 feet in diameter, where the top surface of the chalky soil had been scraped away to leave a dozen concentric rings of dark grass, each a yard wide. This landmark was the nearby village of Synne's greatest claim to fame. It was one of England's seven authentic turf mazes, possibly the finest, well documented since the seventeenth century, but called the Shakespeare Race only since the early twentieth, on the grounds that any community within twenty miles of Stratford-upon-Avon needed to claim some Shakespearean connection, no matter how spurious.

Because Synne had been his parents' home for the last ten years, Oliver had seen the Race many times, but its serpentine beauty, monochrome and almost luminous in the glimpses of the moon, was still an impressive sight, despite his fuzzy vision. On the far side of the Race, an ancient tree known as The Synne Oak was reputed to have been the village gibbet.

"Splendid," he said, wiping his nose on his handkerchief. "Although I don't see why we had to take our clothes off first. Can we go back now?"

Effie punched him mischievously in the upper arm. It hurt.

"Back? We haven't even started. We have to do the maze."

"Do the maze?"

"I was talking to your brother Toby."

"Oh dear."

"Toby, as you know, is stuffed full of Shakespearean lore and local traditions. He was telling your Aunt Phoebe and me that it was a custom for young lovers to come up here at midnight on May Day and follow the path of the maze."

"Naked?"

"As nature intended." She paused, narrowing her eyes. "Hang on, where did that handkerchief come from?"

"I stuffed it into my sock."

"You kept your socks on! Oh, Oliver! Here am I, trying to arrange something mystical and life-affirming, and you're turning it into a bad porn movie."

"It's only one sock," he protested. "My hay fever's playing up. I needed somewhere to stash my hankie. And it was the other foot that stepped into what I think was a cowpat."

"Okay, Buster, off with the sock."

"Where shall I put my handkerchief?" He hopped on one foot as he complied.

"Don't tempt me."

Oliver's bare foot landed on a thistle. He cursed briefly.

"My parents have lived in Synne for nearly a decade, but this is the first I've heard of this custom."

Effie sighed. "Oh, come on, Ollie. You've been thoroughly miserable since you got here two days ago. Toby's not around, you're not interested in your mother's village activities, and you never talk to your father. Your Uncle Tim and Aunt Phoebe turned up this evening, and you barely cracked a smile. I thought this might perk you up."

Oliver looked out again over the Shakespeare Race. He knew that it was technically not a maze but a labyrinth: breaks and bridges in the pattern at the cardinal points made it possible to trace a sinuous, half-mile pathway of grass from the starting point, just by the opening in the modern fence, to a round island at the center.

"There's a similar pattern in the tiles of Chartres Cathedral," he said. "Not exactly a steep and thorny way to heaven, but people walk that, too, as an aid to meditation or prayer. They generally keep their clothes on."

"Who said anything about walking?"

Effie began to run along the outer circle of the Race. Oliver followed reluctantly, grateful that the twists and hairpins kept their speed down. He settled into a steady jog, seeking diversion again. Something more effective than buttocks.

Finsbury the Ferret. Yes, good distraction. If he collected more of this pseudo-trivia—he ought to come up with a better name for it—maybe he would have enough material for a book supposedly penned by Finsbury, the nastiest and consequently the most popular character in his Railway Mice series. *Finsbury the Ferret's Guide to What Everybody Knows* would be a suitably cynical theme for the vile creature, and the book would probably sell well to his many adult readers, given that nobody these days seems in a hurry to find out what they *don't* know. It would make a pleasant change from another children's story stuffed with badgers, stoats, pugnacious swans, flea-infested hedgehogs, and the like—always a challenge for their resolutely urban author. Oliver usually limited his visits to his parents' Warwickshire home to a handful of weekends a year. He was staying longer this time because his editor at Tadpole Tomes for Tiny Tots had demanded he do some original research for once instead of leaving it to a team of overworked subeditors to make corrections, such as changing the word "sheep" to "cow" every time he mentioned a dairy farm. "And try to work some zombies into the next book," she'd urged. "Zombies are in."

Oliver hated the countryside. His hay fever had already kicked in. But at least Effie was staying for the duration, taking some overdue leave from Scotland Yard.

They reached the heart of the maze. "Now what?" he asked.

"Well, Oliver C. Swithin," she purred, "we're two young lovers, naked on a grassy knoll, the night is fine, the moon is full, and there's nobody around for miles. What do you think we could do?"

It was clearly a rhetorical question, because she started to show him. Suddenly, she froze. "Did you hear something?" she whispered.

Oliver listened. A slight breeze rustled the leaves of the Synne Oak. A branch groaned, as if carrying a burden. A distant buzz might have been a truck on the motorway, carried miles on the still air.

But there it was. Voices, far off, but getting closer quickly. And fast footsteps muffled in the long grass.

"Oh Lord," Oliver said. "Somebody's coming."

It was too late to scurry back through the opening, and there was no space between the Synne Oak's broad trunk and the fence for them to squeeze into. Their only option was to flatten themselves to the ground. It might just work, as long as the visitors stayed near the entrance.

Two figures came into view, a man and a woman, both at least twice as old as Oliver and Effie, but both running and both apparently naked. To Oliver, they were little more than two out-of-focus white smudges, which merged briefly into one as they paused to embrace.

"And this is some ancient fertility rite?" the man asked. Oliver flinched.

"So young Toby says," replied the woman. "We have to follow the path all the way to the center."

"What do I get if I get there first?"

"The same thing you get if *I* get there first." The woman laughed, and there was further physical contact with a slightly moist soundtrack.

Oliver pushed his mouth as close to Effie's ear as her thick curls permitted. "Oh, my prophetic soul!" he hissed. "My uncle!"

"I know," she whimpered. "That's why I'm not looking."

If Oliver had been wearing his glasses, he could have made out the tall, white-haired figure of his uncle-by-marriage, Tim Mallard, who in his unclothed state looked even younger and fitter for a man in his sixties than he did when dressed for work as a detective superintendent in Scotland Yard's Serious Crime Directorate.

And Effie's immediate boss.

Oliver assumed that the smaller blur was his Aunt Phoebe, Mallard's wife; otherwise her voice and appearance made her indistinguishable from her identical twin sister, Chloe Swithin. Oliver's mother.

The newcomers started to jog around the circumference of the maze. Oliver made his mind up.

"Stay behind me," he said, rising to his feet and screening Effie. She adopted a nymph-surprised-while-bathing pose.

Being an introvert, Oliver always found starting conversations a challenge, but there was nothing in any self-help article he'd ever read that prepared him for attracting the attention of nude relatives in an ancient monument at midnight. Fortunately, his abrupt sneeze solved this problem.

Phoebe came to a halt and screamed. Mallard started like a guilty thing, uttered an expletive, and shielded his wife with his body.

"Who's there?" he demanded. Oliver guessed, to his relief, that his uncle had also discarded his glasses and, fifty feet away, could not see them clearly.

"Uncle Tim, it's me. Oliver, your nephew."

"Oliver?" Mallard repeated, edging nearer, with Phoebe shuffling behind him.

"Don't come any closer—Effie's here, too."

"Effie?" echoed Mallard, as if taking attendance. He squinted into the darkness. "Are you both…?"

"Yes, from top to toe, from head to foot."

Mallard clasped his hands over his groin, like a soccer player in the line of a free kick. "Effie can't see me in my birthday suit," he cried, scandalized.

"I have my eyes closed," Effie assured him. "And you'd better, too. Sir."

"Then I guess I'm the only one who can expose myself," Phoebe called from behind Mallard's back. "Effie's the same sex, Tim's my husband, and Oliver's family."

"I can't see you in the altogether, Aunt Phoebe," Oliver protested. "You look like my mother. It's too Freudian, I wouldn't enjoy it."

There was a silence.

"I have an idea," Effie called out. "Come to the middle of the maze. Keep your eyes down and look for feet."

Mallard and Phoebe shuffled to the maze's grassy center, and then, on Effie's count, the four turned and faced outward on the cardinal points of the compass. There was another long, uncomfortable silence.

"I'm going to kill Toby," Oliver muttered eventually.

"You'll have to join the queue," said Mallard.

"As the actress said to the naked policeman."

"It's a good job for you I can't turn round."

"You're telling me."

"I bet the little bugger was making it all up," sniggered Phoebe. She was the only one enjoying the situation. "It means mischief. I'm surprised he's not up that tree with a flash camera."

Like an old sleeping dog flicking its tail when it hears its name, a long branch of the Synne Oak creaked.

Silence again.

"We can't stand here all night," said Oliver. "How do we get out of this?"

"Look," Effie said, "or rather, don't look, but pay attention. We need one member of each pair to go and retrieve the clothes from wherever they left them. Since the men can't see where they're going, that leaves Phoebe and me. Come on, Phoebe. Boys, you're on your honor to keep your eyes closed for ten seconds."

And Oliver and Mallard found themselves alone.

"A remarkable woman in a crisis," said Mallard, always proud that he had been instrumental in bringing his nephew and his sergeant together. "I assume Effie put you up to this little escapade?"

"It was supposed to cheer me up."

"What should a man do but be merry?" They broke from their north-south orientation and sat down on the low turf island, each doggedly gazing toward the Synne Oak and avoiding eye contact.

"Yes, streaking doesn't sound like your particular brand of lunacy," Mallard continued. "How long have you and Effie been an item? About nine months. And she's already got you leaping around like a trained haddock. To thine own self be true, Oliver."

"Aunt Phoebe made you do it, then?"

"Of course."

The two men laughed, looked at each other briefly, and then hastily returned their attention to the tree.

"Phoebe thought it would enhance my performance," Mallard continued.

Oliver whistled softly. "And you'd think the nipping and eager air would have the opposite effect."

"I mean my performance as an actor. Inspired by your idiot brother's folktales, your aunt thought a nude run around the Shakespeare Race would be like one of those acting exercises that release you from your inhibitions."

"You're not treading the boards again?"

Mallard nodded. "My drama group, the Theydon Bois Thespians, won a contest. The prize is to give one performance of a play by Shakespeare on the stage of the Royal Shakespeare Theatre in Stratford. And since that's just up the road from Synne, we're staying with your parents during the rehearsals. The performance is next Saturday, a week from tomorrow. I don't think you'll see much of me until then."

"I've already seen more than enough of you. What play's the thing?"

"Appropriately enough, *Hamlet*. At least, I think it is. Our director, Humfrey Fingerhood, changes his concept so often that it might be *Cats* by the weekend."

Oliver stood up abruptly and walked toward the Synne Oak. It struck Mallard as a reasonable reaction to any mention of an Andrew Lloyd Webber musical.

"What's the matter?" he called. Oliver didn't answer but stopped on the outer circle of the maze, staring up into the branches of the gallows tree. He beckoned to Mallard, but realizing that his uncle couldn't see him, gave a sharp whistle. Mallard clambered stiffly to his feet.

"I thought I saw something, up in the tree," Oliver said.

"A Cheshire Cat?"

Oliver ignored the comment. He strained his eyes into the darkness.

"There!" he said, pointing. "There's something there, Uncle Tim. Like a sack or a big balloon, caught in the branches. Whatever it is, I don't think it's alive."

"In that case, it can hang there till the morning," said Mallard with a yawn, "when somebody else can take care of it. Maybe it'll fade away and just leave its grin. I wonder what's taking the ladies so long."

He wandered away around the tree. There was an abrupt metallic clatter, followed by several choice curses. Mallard sat up in the long grass beside the fence, disentangling his legs from whatever he'd tripped over, and found himself glaring at an aluminum stepladder.

"Thanks, Uncle Tim, that's just what we need," said Oliver, picking up the lightweight ladder and setting it firmly where he'd been standing. Its top step was about eight feet from the ground, level with the lowest branches of the tree. He glanced down at Mallard. "When you've finished messing around down there, get up and hold the ladder. I don't want to fall arse over Titus Andronicus."

He started up the shaky stepladder. Mallard reluctantly braced himself against the framework. Oliver managed to grab a branch and reached blindly into the leaves for another handhold.

"Uh, Uncle Tim…" he called after a moment, a tremor in his voice. "We have a problem."

Mallard looked up. Oliver's upper body was hidden by foliage.

"What is it?" he asked, sensing the sudden fear in his nephew's voice.

"Who is it, is more to the point. There's a dead body up here."

Mallard's police instincts took over. "Come down," he commanded. "Ollie, come down now. Let me deal with this."

"It's okay, Uncle. I'm fine."

"Are you sure it's dead?"

"It's dead, all right. Cold. A man. Hanged."

"Jesus Christ, Oliver, get down this moment!" Mallard shouted. "Don't touch anything. It's a police matter now." He shook the ladder. "Oliver Swithin, I'm ordering you to return to the ground. I'm moving you on. It's bloody official, sonny!"

There was a pause. Mallard breathed heavily, impotently. Oliver stood on tiptoe, balancing on the highest step.

"Oh no!" he exclaimed.

"What?" Mallard demanded, staring up into the darkness. "Tell me!"

Again, Oliver waited. Then he said, "Hold tight to Exhibit A, Uncle Tim, I'm coming down. I am tame, sir." He descended the ladder cautiously until he could turn around and sit on the top step.

"Well, I hope I shall not look upon his like again," he said, wiping some moisture from his eyes with the heel of his hand. Mallard could not tell if it was sweat or a tear.

"Strangulation does some terrible things to a face," he said.

Oliver wrapped his arms around his knees. "I know him, Uncle Tim."

"What?"

"That's why I needed to see the face. I had my suspicions when I saw what he was wearing. Despite the… changes, the lips, the tongue, I still recognized him. It's Uncle Dennis."

Mallard frowned. "You don't have an Uncle Dennis." Was Oliver hallucinating under the stress?

"Everyone has this Uncle Dennis. Dennis Breedlove. He used to read stories for children on BBC radio. Called himself 'Uncle' Dennis. A worthy pioneer. Retired long ago to write books. Lived in Synne for years. Sorry, that always sounds bad, doesn't it? Little man. Happy. Always wore the same outfit—tweed suit, yellow waistcoat, spotted bow tie. That's why I thought I knew him. Had to see the face, you see. To be sure."

"It's probably a suicide," Mallard said. "Perhaps there's a note—in his pocket, back at his house." He shivered. "We really should leave this to the local plod."

Oliver nodded glumly. He stood up. The stepladder shook and tilted, one of its feet sinking deeper into the soft dirt.

"It's all right, I'm holding it," Mallard called.

"Yes, but who's holding me?"

Oliver tipped sideways. Mallard let go of the ladder, which slammed into the trunk of the oak, and tried to catch his falling nephew. His arms closed around Oliver's waist, his nose going into the young man's navel. The two naked men staggered toward the maze and landed on the soft turf, winded and wrapped in each other's arms, dimly aware that two fully dressed women were watching them curiously.

"Superintendent Mallard," Effie called, as she dropped a bundle of clothes and turned away again. "I wonder if this is a good time to discuss my promotion to Inspector."

Chapter Two

Pry up the staple in the middle pages of the *AA Drivers Atlas to the British Isles* and you may find Synne, a speck of a village sideswiped by the northeastern edge of the Cotswold Hills as they lap up against Shakespeare Country.

Guidebooks to the area have given up trying to explain why the tiny village of some ninety houses should ever have come into existence. Synne was never close enough to the great Fosse Way to have offered a rest stop for foot-weary Romans, nor in later years was it a staging post on the coach route from London to Worcester. It has no historical connection with the Cotswolds wool trade, or the cloth and silk trades, which followed and failed. No healthful spring bubbles up through its limestone. There isn't a working farm within a three-mile radius. The reason for Synne's survival for half a millennium is a complete mystery to most people.

But an isolation that was inconvenient in the past can be a boon today if handled by a canny estate agent. Synne's honey-toned sixteenth-, seventeenth-, and eighteenth-century cottages are now occupied by retired advertising executives, media consultants, and BBC radio producers, once beguiled by the prospect of rural life and now bored to death by its reality. Seven recent arrivals penned opportunistic journals of their first year in the village: five of them were titled *Living in Synne*; the other two were called *A Year in the Cotswolds*; none was published. Meanwhile the born-and-bred Synne-folk they displaced shifted to a clutch of tasteful modern houses just north of the main road, grateful for central heating and windows that close properly at last.

Most of the picturesque older cottages jostle along the main road, particularly where it skirts the long north edge of Synne's triangular village green, inevitably called The Square. It has the shape of the down arrow on an elevator button, pointing due south at nothing in particular.

On the southeast side of the Square is a pair of Georgian houses, handsome but incongruous, the one on the right being the home of Brigadier (retd.) Robert Proudfoot Swithin, DSO, and his wife, Chloe. In front of the house, there's only a shallow flowerbed with a scattering of hollyhocks—a rare example of a flower that Oliver could identify, because he had tried to rhyme them with "bollocks" in a limerick. But to the rear is a deceptively large walled garden, with a generous lawn and, at its center, a massive horse chestnut tree, now covered in blossom.

Effie Strongitharm was spread out serenely on a lounger in a sunny corner of the lawn, wearing a modest black bikini and reading a book. She had chosen to ignore the occasional twitching of curtains at an upper floor window, which she had pinpointed as Toby Swithin's bedroom. She had also decided to ignore the frequent grunts and clatters coming from the tree behind her, caused by the percussive combination of an aluminum stepladder, a steel tape measure, and her boyfriend. But a sneeze followed by a particularly loud crash did make her sit up and glance around. The ladder had fallen. Oliver was not immediately visible, but then two legs in jeans and purple sneakers descended slowly into view from the lowest branches and kicked in mid-air like a frog. Effie turned back to her book and so did not see Oliver drop the remaining six feet to the ground.

He lay flat on his back for a few seconds, then sat up and groped for his eyeglasses. He stood warily, crept up behind Effie, and covered her eyes. "Guess who?"

Effie gave a small gasp of girlish delight. "Johnny Depp!"
Oliver smirked. "You're getting warm."

"I would be if it really was Johnny Depp."

"Oh. Well, it's me, I'm afraid."

Effie lifted her sunglasses and scrutinized him. "Don't I get
two more guesses?"

"Because of that, I'm not going to tell you what I've found out."

"Okay." Effie returned to her book. Oliver perched on the
lounger, dimly aware that he'd just moved himself into check.
He sneezed.

"You don't seem too bothered that we discovered a body last
night," he attempted, wiping his nose.

Effie looked up again. "Naturally, I'm sorry about poor Mr.
Breedlove. But in case you'd forgotten, Ollie, I am on your
uncle's Murder Investigation Team." She leaned toward him and
lowered her voice to a whisper. "I see dead people," she hissed.
Oliver flinched.

"But I see them in London," she continued. "A simple suicide
in Synne is none of my business professionally, and it would
be a complete and utter no-no for the Yard to interfere with a
local investigation."

He was back in the match. "But what if it wasn't a simple
suicide?" he began eagerly. She held up a hand.

"Save it for Tim," she interrupted. "I'm on vacation. I must
be idle."

Mallard might make a better audience, Oliver considered.
His uncle had taken charge the previous evening, dressing
hastily and using his mobile phone to report the discovery of
the body. And then they had waited for half an hour until a
uniformed policeman, fat and scant of breath, trudged up the
path to the Shakespeare Race. Unlike the rural policemen in
detective fiction, Police Constable Ernie Bostar did not secretly
long for the opportunity to impress when he found a Scotland
Yard superintendent within his truncheon's length. In fact he
did not relish any form of work. So he quickly placed a call to

the county detective branch and then, with a grumble or two, took only brief statements from the four witnesses.

They managed to tell their tale without any mention of nudity, and the only detail that intrigued Bostar momentarily was the women's report of spotting a figure on the edge of the Common—a man on foot, robed like a monk, with a hood pulled over his head, who seemed to be scanning the moonlit scrubland from the road. It was this observation, made from behind a convenient gorse bush, that delayed their returning with the men's clothes. But because Breedlove had died at least an hour earlier (based on Mallard's swift appraisal of the dangling body) and a good half-mile from this apparition, Bostar quickly lost interest again. The four slipped away just as the maze was raked by the bucking headlamps of an ambulance, which had taken the barely negotiable car track up to the Race from the far side of the Common.

Their amorous mood spoiled, Oliver and Effie had climbed into bed in Oliver's old bedroom, holding each other and furtively maneuvering so as not to be the owner of the superfluous fourth arm that always gets lain upon when two people cuddle. While waiting for sleep, Oliver was struck by a nagging issue, which had caused him to spend most of Saturday morning recreating the death scene in the Swithins' garden.

He was wondering whether to give Effie the satisfaction of interrupting her again, when he caught sight of his younger brother in an open doorway.

"Toby! Come out here!" Oliver yelled. After a moment's nervous hesitation, Toby complied. Effie reached for a multi-colored wrap on the grass beside her and draped it around her shoulders.

Toby Swithin bore little resemblance to his older brother. Although they were both thin, Oliver was taller. While his hair was blond and floppy, Toby sported a nest of dark waves. Oliver's eyes behind his cheap, wire-framed glasses were blue, like his mother's; Toby, who didn't need glasses, had his father's dark brown eyes and sharp nose, which gave his face a wary intensity. He always looked like he'd just been asked a slightly unnerving question. The overall effect was as if someone had cloned the poet Shelley but tossed in a few otter genes for good measure. Despite the warm day, Toby wore a shapeless white cricket sweater over muddy denims.

"Tobermory Swithin," Oliver pronounced. "Give me one good reason why I shouldn't remove your spleen."

Toby's eyes were on the grass under his feet. He glanced up for a second, took in Effie's bikini-clad state, and quickly looked down again.

"Well, for one thing, my name isn't Tobermory," he muttered. "Just Toby. Not short for anything" He looked up again and tried to meet Effie's eyes. She beamed at him reassuringly. He blushed and glanced away.

"Where were you at twelve o'clock last night?" snapped Oliver. He didn't notice the effect that proximity to his svelte girlfriend seemed to be having on his little brother. In fact, he was pleased that Effie was there. There was little doubt that Toby would shortly be subjected to the notorious Strongitharm Look, Effie's special way of sending her ice-blue gaze deep into an offender's brain, swatting away the defending forces of bravado and self-justification, grabbing the cowering sense of shame by the throat, and plucking it out for all to see, like a still-beating heart. Two seconds of the Look, and Toby would be recalling every embarrassing, scrotum-shrinking moment of his life, including the time Oliver caught him doing bodybuilding poses in the bathroom mirror, dressed only in what he'd supposed was one of their sister's thongs, although it turned out to be their mother's.

"I was in bed," Toby answered, puzzled. "I was late getting back from the dig. Eric Mormal was supposed to give me a ride home, but he did his shift earlier than usual. I had to hitchhike from Stratford to Synne. Why?"

"You didn't stop off at the Common? To see if anyone was doing a midnight run around the Race?"

Toby brightened. "Oh, did Effie tell you about that? It's an interesting piece of Synne folklore, isn't it?"

"I'll not be juggled with," Oliver growled. "And why, for God's sake, did you dangle the bait of falsehood in front of your Aunt Phoebe, of all people?"

"It isn't falsehood," Toby protested. He sniggered suddenly. "I say, she didn't try it, did she? And did she get Uncle Tim to go along, too? Oh gosh, this is priceless! I wish I *had* been there now. That should be on YouTube." He continued to chuckle.

"They weren't the only ones," Oliver said coldly. It was decidedly time for the Strongitharm Look.

Toby stopped laughing abruptly as the implication struck home. He opened his mouth, but the unavoidable mental image of Effie wearing even fewer clothes clearly overwhelmed his powers of speech.

"I think Effie has something to say to you," Oliver continued, and moved to the side to avoid any crossfire. *Look pale and tremble, Tobermory.*

"Toby's right," she said.

"What?"

Effie brandished the thick, black book she had been reading, and Oliver noticed the title on the spine: *Folk Traditions of the Northern Cotswolds.* "It's in here," she continued. "Toby was telling the truth."

"I didn't mean to suggest…" Toby began, but choked again. Effie skewered her sunglasses into her fair ringlets.

"You have nothing to reproach yourself for, Toby dear," she soothed. "You clearly haven't heard yet what put the damper on last night's hijinks, but it had nothing to do with you. Now, Oliver, I think you're the person who has something to say to Toby."

"What?" Oliver said again. *No Look?*

Effie tilted her head. "Don't you owe Toby an apology for being so rude?"

"The hell I do."

"Oliver," she prompted. Damn, she was almost at checkmate. Oliver turned toward Toby, noticing a tall figure framed in the doorway to the house.

"Oh, all right. Toby, I'm sorry I called you a devious, hairy-palmed, weasel-faced troll." He felt Effie's toe jab him in the thigh and continued hastily. "Look, I'd gladly apologize until the cows come home, but Uncle Tim seems to have beaten them to it. Despite your complete innocence, you're well advised to avoid him for the next couple of days. I'd start now."

He nodded over Toby's shoulder. Toby turned to see his uncle glaring at him across the lawn, and without waiting, bolted toward a gate in the garden wall.

"So much for him," said Oliver. "I wonder what he's been doing in his room all morning."

"Binoculars," Effie murmured, swathing the wrap around her torso as Mallard approached. He was wearing an off-white linen suit with an ascot and a dapper Panama hat, which complemented his rakish white moustache.

"Sergeant Strongitharm," said Mallard, removing the hat, "I nearly didn't recognize you with all those clothes on." He fixed his gaze on a single cumulus cloud, adrift in the blue sky.

"Phoebe and I have been at Dennis Breedlove's cottage," he continued, "making a statement to the CID officer in charge of the case. He wants one from you, too. Just a formality. He's Detective Sergeant Culpepper, based in Leek Wootton."

"In that case, I'd better slip into something less comfortable," Effie said. She stood up and handed the book to Oliver. "Be a precious bunny and take this back to your dad's library. I'll meet you by the front door in ten minutes."

Dad? thought Oliver. When had he ever called the brigadier "Dad"?

"Oh, Tim," she added, "Oliver wants to convince you that Uncle Dennis's death was a conspiracy."

She kissed Oliver demurely on the cheek and sashayed away, fully aware that Oliver would be staring after her while Mallard, the perfect gentleman, would be deliberately studying something else.

"Close your mouth, precious bunny," said Mallard, replacing his hat. "So what's this about Uncle Dennis?"

"I don't think he could have killed himself without help."

Mallard checked his watch. "All right, let's hear it," he said with a sigh. "But it's too late to search for traces of extra visitors to the Race. The two of us did a good job of tramping around under the Synne Oak, not to mention that ambulance crew and who knows how many CID busies."

"You don't need that sort of evidence," Oliver answered, setting up the stepladder. "This ladder is the same size as the one we found last night. I borrowed it from the village peeping Tom."

"The village peeping Tom?"

"Yes. Well, one of them anyway. Although the other one prefers the term 'voyeur.' Now watch."

Oliver climbed the ladder, reaching for the blossom-laden branches of the horse chestnut for support, and stood on the top step.

"This is as high as I got last night," he called down. "When I stood on tiptoe, I was face-to-face with Dennis, not a pretty sight under the circumstances. And I could just about touch the knot that tied the rope to a branch."

"So you could easily hang yourself, if it becomes advisable."

"*I* could, yes," Oliver agreed, too enthusiastic to be sidetracked by Mallard's comment. "I'm an inch or two under six feet tall. But Dennis Breedlove was a good six inches shorter than me. It was one of the reasons why children loved him when he was on the radio—they claimed they could tell from his voice that he wasn't much bigger than them."

"So you think Breedlove was too short to reach the branch and tie the rope."

Oliver rattled down the ladder. "Exactly."

"Could he have tossed the rope over the branch and bent it downwards while he tied the knot?"

Oliver shook his head. "It's an oak tree. Not much flexibility in those lower limbs. A bit like old Dennis himself. And even if it did bend, it would surely have stayed bent from the weight of the body. Dennis's feet were floating a good three inches above the top step of the ladder."

"Then he can't have been standing on the ladder when he did the deed. He must have climbed up into the tree to tie the rope."

"In that case, how did he manage to kick the ladder over?"

"Perhaps it fell down when he stepped off it."

Oliver considered this as they wandered out of the tree's shade. "Well, that's possible I suppose. But it still leaves the question of the short rope. It was just a couple of feet from the knot to the noose. Not much of a drop."

"D.S. Culpepper told me the rope was only about eight feet long to start with. Tying a proper hangman's noose would shorten it considerably."

Oliver picked up Effie's book with his thumb and forefinger and absently let it swing. "You'd think if Dennis was going to all this trouble—perfectly tied noose, ancient village gibbet—he'd have some concept of the basic principles of hanging."

"Hanging's a science as well as an art. Suicides rarely get it right. You need a drop at least equal to your height to break your neck, a quick death. Even the public hangman used to have a few failures. Too short a rope, and the poor bugger slowly chokes to death, which is what happened to Uncle Dennis. Too long, on the other hand, and you can decapitate your client. A messy alternative, but at least it's thorough. Ask the French."

"Most people think Jayne Mansfield was decapitated when she died in that car crash. She wasn't. That's a good example of the new trivia I plan to write about."

Mallard closed his eyes, as if in pain. "Oliver, can you focus? I have to get to Stratford for my next rehearsal."

"Sorry. I just think you can answer a lot of questions if you imagine a six-foot-plus man such as yourself tying the noose to the branch first and then lifting Uncle Dennis into it while still standing on the ladder. After all, why would a supposedly suicidal octogenarian carry an eight-foot stepladder all the way up to the Synne Oak on his own and then apparently hang himself by leaping upwards into a dangling noose? Why not just go into the garage and run the car? Why was the last act of his life so complicated?"

"To make a point," said Mallard, "you'd better talk to Culpepper. He may have something to show you."

"Did Dennis leave a note, then?"

"In a way. But he didn't write it himself."

"You're being annoyingly cryptic, Uncle Tim."

Mallard tousled Oliver's hair briefly, as if his nephew were a five-year-old. Oliver didn't resent the gesture. "Go and see Culpepper. You'll understand."

He turned toward the house. Oliver realized he was still holding the book from his father's library. He cut across the lawn to the open French windows of the ground-floor study where Brigadier Swithin kept his collections of cast-iron toy soldiers, which his sons had never been allowed to touch, and books that were mostly about war in the twentieth century, which his sons had never asked to read. Oliver let his eyes adjust to the sudden shade, wondering where his father filed the books on local traditions.

"Who's there?" It was a sharp cry, from the depths of a leather wing chair near the empty fireplace. If Bob Swithin had been dozing over his magazine, he would never have admitted it.

"It's me, Father. Oliver."

He removed the resented reading glasses. His eyes were dark and small, dwarfed by untidy eyebrows, the only hair visible on his glossy head. Oliver was reminded again of his gratitude that male baldness was inherited from the mother's DNA—although he had a nagging feeling this was another example of a fact that was widely known but completely wrong. It did seem to be the case that much of the anti-trivia he was collecting was incorrect. The Victorians didn't cover up the legs of their pianos to disguise their lascivious profile, for example. There's no evidence that Anne Boleyn had six fingers *or* three nipples. And Catherine the Great decidedly did not die while, well…

"Something I can help you with?" asked his father.

"Just returning the book Effie borrowed this morning."

He breathed deeply, as if relieved that the encounter would involve nothing more parental.

"Effie, yes," he said. "Spirited lass. Been courting her for a while now, eh?"

"Nine months. Longest girlfriend ever." The brusque phrasing that Oliver fell into when talking to his father gave the last comment a surreal twist, but he knew it wouldn't register in the brigadier's practical mind.

"Well, don't mess it up then."

"I'll do my best." Oliver was aware that his best had generally failed to meet his father's standards and that, more than anyone, Bob Swithin was glad that his son wrote his children's books under a pseudonym. Bob had never really forgiven Oliver for surpassing him in height at age fourteen.

"Yes, rather fond of Effie. Reminds me a bit of your sister." He referred to his only daughter, Eve, who came between Oliver and Toby in birth order and who was currently in New York. Oliver loved Eve and admired her achievements, so he took the comparison as a compliment, but he'd also noted that his father would create any opportunity to mention his favorite child, whose non-military ambitions offended him less because she was not male. Oliver spotted the gap on the shelves where the black book usually sat.

"Oh, one more thing, Oliver," the brigadier called as his son headed for the door. "This little Breedlove fellow who topped himself last night. Understand from your mother—or it could have been her sister, I wasn't paying that much attention—that you and Timothy were on the scene."

"That's right."

"I knew the old boy, of course—village business, parochial council. Decent enough blighter, could be quite entertaining, if you liked the cut of his jib. Your mother couldn't stomach him. Good conversationalist. Always wore the same outfit. Anyway, I believe he was in your line of business."

"He didn't write children's books, he wrote about them," Oliver informed him pointlessly.

"Not a particular friend of yours, then?"

Dennis Breedlove's erudite and controversial books about children's literature began to appear after he'd moved to Synne thirty years earlier, drawing upon thirty prior years of reading classic stories to children on BBC radio until the institution decided it no longer had time for them or him. The publication of the Railway Mice series had moved Oliver into the same literary circle as Breedlove, and he'd met the old man once or twice at the Sanders, the club for children's authors on Pall Mall, when Breedlove—an honorary member—made one of his rare journeys to London. But last night's encounter with Breedlove's small corpse was the first time Oliver had come face-to-face with him in Synne. Of course, he'd always intended to pay a courtesy call on Uncle Dennis during one of his brief stays with his parents. But somehow that friendly visit had always been squeezed out by other things, including Oliver's self-centered desire to get back to the city as soon as possible.

"Not really a friend, no."

"Ah. No great loss, then." The brigadier picked up his magazine from his lap and put on his reading glasses, signaling that Oliver wasn't meant to take any further comments as an invitation to prolong their conversation. Brigadier Bob always liked having the last word.

"Unpleasant business, hanging," he commented, not looking in Oliver's direction. "I've heard they foul themselves as they come down. And a chap can get a—well, not for mixed company."

"Mixed—?"

"Pistol shot to the temple, that's a man's way."

"Yes, indeed, Father," said Oliver and let himself out of the dim room into the large bright entrance hall, where Effie was waiting for him. She smiled broadly when she saw him, as she always did. If she ever stopped, he thought, the world would end.

Chapter Three

Saturday afternoon

Dennis Breedlove's cottage skulked on a quiet lane that sidled off the main road and led to Synne's Parish church. The old, single-story house had been snarkily stuccoed many years earlier and defiantly patched whenever the local limestone threatened to show through. Small, latticed windows flanked an unusually grand porch with its own slate roof and fussy columns, hidden now by skeins of grape-scented Chinese wisteria. A black sedan was parked in front.

With just enough room between the house and the road for a straggly privet hedge and a terse front garden, there was a marked absence of any springtime color, apart from the wisteria. Even the patchy lawn was partly hidden by a large pile of damp earth carelessly dumped beside the front path. It was clearly an old man's neglected, unweeded garden that grows to seed. Dennis Breedlove's property may have started at his garden gate, but his realm began at the royal blue front door, now standing slightly open. Two full bottles of milk stood by the door, and that morning's *Daily Telegraph* lay on the doormat.

Oliver paused beside the pile of dirt, unconsciously rubbing his thumb across the fingertips of his right hand, before he noticed that Effie had pushed the door open farther and walked in. Privately grateful for her brazenness, he followed, muttering hypocritical protests about trespassing, which masked his guilt that this was his first visit to Breedlove's home.

The chilly space they entered was clearly the heart of the house, with floor-to-ceiling bookshelves lining every wall, and piles of paper mounting like stalagmites from the carpet. There were stacks of notes, magazines, and unsorted books on most surfaces, including the lone sofa. A pile of *Beano* annuals had become an unsteady pedestal for an old, blue Smith Corona typewriter under its plastic cover. Although the papers were untidy, Oliver suspected that they were not disorganized—that their late owner could have told you in an instant where to find any note or publication. Would Uncle Dennis have appointed a literary executor, or would a distant relative just dump all of it, unread, into a recycled-paper sack? Should he volunteer to sort the papers?

There was no sign of the car's owner. Oliver prowled through the room, noting that the volumes of children's literature on the bookshelves were alphabetized. He surreptitiously scanned for copies of his own Railway Mice series, and saw, with another pang of guilt, that Breedlove had the complete set to date under Oliver's "O.C. Blithely" pen name, propped between Elizabeth Beresford's Wombles books and the beginning of several feet of Enid Blyton. He pulled out his most recent best seller, *The Railway Mice and the Vicious Mole*. There was a worrying odor of mildew already in its pages.

Effie wandered over to a heavy oak bureau against the side wall and glanced over some loose papers that had been left on the surface.

"Looking for something, Curly?"

An exceptionally tall, thin, black man wearing a tailored business suit, was still straightening after his entrance through a low inner doorway. He had spoken with a Birmingham accent, and was now staring at Effie with curiosity. The man was of the height that compelled new acquaintances to inform him helplessly that he was very tall and ask him if he played basketball. Oliver guessed that this was Detective Sergeant Culpepper, and he immediately sympathized, because he knew that the offhand greeting had just qualified the lofty policeman for a blast of the Strongitharm Look.

But to his astonishment, Effie merely smiled and advanced toward the newcomer, hand outstretched. *First Toby is spared, now this lanky colossus—was Eff losing her powers?*

She introduced herself. Culpepper looked abashed as he slowly shook her hand. "I assumed you were another of the deceased's nosy-parker neighbors," he apologized. "I had envisaged the famous Superintendent Mallard's trusty sidekick as a much older woman."

"That's perfectly all right. This is the superintendent's nephew, Oliver Swithin." Effie tossed her head in Oliver's direction, sparing him the ordeal of introducing himself to an authority figure, when he tended to develop a nervous lisp. Oliver shook Culpepper's hand, willing himself not to exclaim "You're very tall!"

"This shouldn't take long," Culpepper continued. "Mr. Mallard gave me a good account of the events of last night."

He stepped toward the bureau, stooping to avoid a low beam, and opened a manila folder on the cluttered desktop. He read the Mallards' statements while Oliver and Effie adopted the attitude of airline passengers being quizzed over whether they had packed their own suitcases, nodding solemnly when asked if they agreed with Mallard's crisp narrative, which, like the previous night's statement to Constable Bostar, evaded the issue of nudity. Culpepper concluded with Phoebe's description of the man dressed as a monk spotted on the main road near the edge of the Common. Effie confirmed the observation.

"What do you make of this apparition, Sergeant Culpepper?" Oliver asked. "Did the ladies see a ghost?"

"Not a ghost. A vampire."

"What?"

Culpepper grinned. "That's what they call him, the 'Vampire of Synne.'"

Oliver sneezed.

"Yes, it is a bit dusty in here," Culpepper sympathized. "Let's get some air."

They filed out through the front door, which Culpepper locked behind them, and strolled along the quiet lane toward the parish church, St. Edmund and St. Crispin. Culpepper walked in the middle, taller than Oliver by the same amount that Oliver was taller than Effie. They looked like an Olympic medal ceremony.

"Constable Bostar, the local bobby, filled me in about the Vampire of Synne this morning, before he went on a remarkably extended lunch break," Culpepper told them. "The man you saw last night, Sergeant Strongitharm, is the occupant of Furbelow Hall, that gloomy Jacobean manor house you pass as you drive into the village from the west. He's lived there for a year or so, alone and never leaving the house during the daytime, like a vampire. The villagers see him wandering around after nightfall, always covered from head to foot in a monk's robe and cowl. He never speaks to anyone, and nobody has ever seen his face."

"Are you going to ask this vampire if he saw anything?" asked Oliver. "Armed with garlic and a crucifix, no doubt."

"I've already spoken to him on the telephone. His name's Snopp. Angus Snopp. And he has a perfectly valid reason for living that way, although it's also somewhat tragic."

"May I take a guess?" Oliver asked.

"Go ahead."

"It sounds like he suffers from XP."

"XP?" Effie echoed.

"Xeroderma pigmentosa," Oliver continued. "It's a genetic disorder that basically means any ultraviolet light exposure can lead to skin cancers."

"How do you *know* these things?" she muttered.

"Mr. Swithin's absolutely right," said Culpepper, "although I'd never heard of the condition until Mr. Snopp filled me in this afternoon. People with XP can never go into the sunlight, and can even be affected by the UV light from electric lightbulbs. So a dark, seventeenth-century manor house where he can live by candlelight offers ideal protection. He's had several outbreaks of skin cancer since his childhood, which is why he hides his scarred face, even in moonlight."

"A lonely life," said Effie.

"I get the sense he's accepted his fate. And if he can afford to buy or even lease that kind of property, his condition clearly hasn't affected his finances."

"Did Mr. Snopp notice anything last night?" Oliver asked.

"Well, no sign of Breedlove. Just a couple of cars, tootling along the main road. And a small van, which passed him during the first part of his evening stroll, going rather quickly. He thought he could make out the word 'Cooper' on the side, but there's no local business with that name. Mr. Swithin, you have some knowledge of the locality—have you ever come across a Cooper?"

Oliver ran through the Coopers in his memory—Gary, Henry, Tommy, Gladys, Alice, Minnie, none of them likely to be driving a van through Synne after dark. He shook his head.

"Then it was probably just passing through," Culpepper concluded. "Anyway, Breedlove can't have driven himself to the Shakespeare Race, or the car would still be parked up there."

"Unless he had a chauffeur," Oliver murmured. Culpepper didn't comment.

They had reached the low wall that surrounded the church-yard, with its honor guard of black poplars and the occasional yew. The church itself came into view through the trees, a late perpendicular nave attached to a squat early perpendicular tower, the crenellated base for a spire that was never built. Two people in black cassocks were coming out of the main door. Culpepper halted, as if to maximize the time before the churchgoers would reach them on the lonely road.

"When Phoebe Mallard and I spotted this vampire," Effie said, "he was just standing there, staring across the Common."

"Yes. Snopp was on his way home by then, after a walk that took an hour or so, his daily exercise. He stopped because he thought he saw something. I wasn't going to mention it, because I can't imagine it was relevant to Mr. Breedlove's death."

"But what was it?" Effie persisted. Culpepper assumed a fascination with a stone cherub on an overgrown gravestone.

"He says he saw naked women running among the bushes."

Effie was abruptly silent. The two people had come through the lych-gate and were now approaching them—a white-haired middle-aged man in a clerical collar, and what seemed to be a woman in her thirties with black-framed glasses and a severe bob cut. Oliver rapidly assumed the overly delighted expression that the English always exhibit when meeting members of the clergy.

"Oliver, my dear fellow, I heard you were in town," cried the man, shaking Oliver's hand and assuming the overly delighted expression that the clergy always exhibit when meeting members of their flock. "No chance of seeing you and your young lady in the pew for the morning service tomorrow, I don't suppose? Probably not, eh? You youngsters don't want to be bothered with all this religious mumbo-jumbo, and I can't say I blame you for your better wisdoms, I'm sure."

Using the clergyman's monologue as cover for a private rehearsal, Oliver did a creditable job of introducing the Reverend Gibeon Edwards, vicar of Synne, to his companions in more or less the right order. They were in turn introduced to the other newcomer, revealed as Mrs. Lesbia Weguelin, the church's verger, before Edwards remarked that Culpepper was very tall and asked him if he played basketball.

If you shaved Santa Claus and put him on a treadmill for a year or two, he'd probably shrink down to resemble the ever-genial Reverend Mr. Edwards. The vicar flattered himself on his skill at striking up an immediate rapport with anyone, even the fiercest critics of his calling. This usually took the form of swiftly conceding the other person's point of view—so swiftly, it was often in advance of their saying anything at all. During a teatime chat with Oliver on an earlier visit, Edwards had preemptively pooh-poohed the biblical accounts of the nativity, the resurrection, and most of Jesus's miracles, and then went on to list the many advantages of atheism, all before Oliver had opened his mouth to offer him a toasted tea cake. It was assumed by his parishioners that Edwards didn't actually agree with these heretical positions, but by the time he'd finished ingratiating himself with his opposition—in a talk or in a sermon—he'd usually drifted so far from his own beliefs that there was no room to backtrack. This habit had earned him the nickname of Edwards the Concessor.

The fact that the verger had not flinched when she was introduced suggested to Oliver either that she was a powerful personality who had learned to rise above the discomfiture of an ill-chosen Christian name or that she had no sense of humor. He suspected the latter. After a gruff "hello," Lesbia made no further contributions to the conversation, but Oliver kept glancing at her, wondering if the crisp, flawless blue-black bob was actually a wig—Effie would know—and trying to get some measure of her features behind the thick-rimmed plastic frames, intense burgundy lipstick, and caked-on foundation. He had only the vaguest sense of a certain squareness of jaw and a self-confident nose.

The group headed back toward Breedlove's cottage, Edwards quizzing Culpepper about the likelihood that the late writer's family would want a space in the churchyard, "suicide being no impediment to burial in sacred ground these days, not like that churlish priest in *Hamlet*, wittering on about Ophelia's doubtful death. Indeed the courage of the suicide may well be thought of as an example to us all…was it not Camus who said it was the only truly serious philosophical problem, although I believe he came out against it ultimately, but then so many families choose cremation anyway, so it becomes a moot point, not to mention this new corpse-composting alternative, very interesting, if they take a green outlook, and who's to blame them? Oh, about our stepladder…"

Even the urbane Culpepper was momentarily baffled.

"Stepladder?"

"I heard from Constable Bostar that Dennis used a stepladder when he made his quietus, another *Hamlet* reference, as I'm sure you know, but what a fool I must seem to a young chap like yourself, quoting a man who's been dead and buried these four hundred years. Well, it seems the church stepladder has gone missing. We store it outside the south chancel. Putting two and two together, I was wondering if they might make one and the same, as it were. Will it become Exhibit A, and should we, therefore, purchase a new one, pro tem?"

"I'm not aware that any crime has been committed in Mr. Breedlove's death," said Culpepper, "so if the stepladder turns out to be yours, Vicar, I'll make sure you get it back."

With a flutter of the hands that may have been a blessing or an apology for the Crusades, Edwards and the verger continued along the lane toward the Square while Oliver, Effie, and Culpepper waited beside the black car.

"So before Uncle Dennis carried his stepladder all the way up to the Shakespeare Race," Oliver said, "he had to walk to the church to pick it up. At his age. Not to mention finding a rope."

"He already had the rope," said Culpepper. He unlocked the car and took a plastic bag from a briefcase on the front seat. It contained what looked like a pair of small, wooden maracas, one with a tie-on label. They were the handles of a child's skipping rope.

"As well as his books, Mr. Breedlove collected a few classic children's toys. He kept them in a small display cabinet. The label says this rope is Victorian, possibly used by the girls of the Liddell family at Christ Church in Oxford. Anyway, Breedlove sliced off the handles with his kitchen knife and used the rope to hang himself. It yielded about eight feet."

"Enough to strangle him, but not enough to break his neck," Oliver said.

"I get the sense, Mr. Swithin, that you think I'm missing something here," said Culpepper as he returned the evidence to his car.

"I just think the whole extravaganza seems too much for a man in his eighties. He should be dangling from a beam in his living room, not trudging all the way up to the Synne Oak with an eight-foot stepladder under his arm and Alice in Wonderland's jump-rope in his pocket."

Culpepper looked at Effie, and something clearly passed between them using that sixth or seventh or forty-second sense that was reserved for telepathic transmissions of confidence between English police detectives.

"Let's go back inside," he said.

They stood again among the books and papers in Breedlove's living room, while Oliver repeated the opinion he had given his uncle earlier. Effie listened, clearly weighing her growing interest against the need to avoid encroaching on Culpepper's territory. Culpepper also listened, not looking at Oliver and pulling thoughtfully on his upper lip. When Oliver had finished, he lifted his head.

"Most people I've spoken to describe Breedlove as a likeable chap," he said. "Always genial, good company. The last person to take his own life. One or two were distinctly cooler. You can't delight everybody, I suppose. But his suicide is a puzzle. And I agree with you, sir—the special effort it required is also a puzzle. Perhaps, though, I can supply the missing motivation." He strode across to the large bureau where he'd left his papers.

"My uncle mentioned that you'd found a note," Oliver chipped in. "Was it a suicide note?"

Culpepper didn't reply, but handed him a clear plastic folder that contained a single piece of paper, which once had been folded horizontally into thirds. Oliver and Effie read the text, written in pencil in carefully formed uppercase letters.

DID YOU THINK YOU COULD HIDE YOUR HISTORY? DID YOU THINK THIS WHOLE BLESSED PLOT WOULD BE COVERED UP FOREVER? I KNOW WHAT'S BEEN GOING ON. BUT YOU DON'T WANT OTHERS TO DIG UP THE PAST, DO YOU? SO LET THIS BE OUR LITTLE FAMILY SECRET. I WON'T TELL IF YOU WON'T TELL. ALAS, MY SILENCE ISN'T FREE. THERE WILL BE FURTHER COMMUNICATIONS.

"I found it here, on his desk, as if he'd just opened it," Culpepper told them.

"No envelope?" Effie asked.

Culpepper shook his head. "I checked the wastepaper bins and the dustbin outside. But maybe the paper was slid through the letterbox just like that. Perhaps the blackmailer was scared that we could get a DNA trace from the dried saliva on an envelope."

"Not in these days of self-sealing envelopes," said Effie, "and blackmailers aren't usually worried about the authorities. If they've calculated everything correctly, their victim is going to pay up to keep his secret safe from the world, including the cops."

"Then I'd say there was a serious miscalculation in this case, Sergeant Strongitharm," replied Culpepper. "Whatever 'blessed plot' Breedlove hatched in the past, the merest hint that someone has rumbled it caused him to end it all."

"Please call me Effie," she murmured, and Culpepper remarked in turn that his first name was Simon. "But there was no suicide note from Breedlove?" she asked.

"Not on paper. On the other hand, parading up to the Shakespeare Race, dangling himself from the old village gibbet—it's almost a suicide note in performance."

"I wonder what this 'blessed plot' was," said Oliver, speaking for the first time since reading the blackmail letter. He held onto the folder, eyes constantly scanning the capital letters.

Culpepper shrugged. "We may never know."

"Why? Won't the blackmailer tell us when we arrest him? Or her?"

There was another unspoken communication between Culpepper and Effie. "Arrest him?" she repeated.

"This blackmailer was the cause of Uncle Dennis's death," said Oliver, tapping on the plastic cover of the note that continued to hold his gaze. "How shall this bloody deed be answered?"

"Cause or not, it was unintentional," said Culpepper, gently taking the note from Oliver. "Breedlove's suicide is the last thing the blackmailer wanted. No money to be made from a dead victim."

"Besides," Effie said, resting a hand on Oliver's shoulder, "how can the police trace this blackmailer, now that Breedlove's dead? All we have are the contents of an anonymous letter and a sample of some heavily disguised handwriting."

Oliver was silent, still staring glumly at the letter in Culpepper's grasp. Effie took her hand away.

"Oliver, the person who killed Dennis Breedlove was Dennis Breedlove," said Culpepper. "He took his own life rather than face up to something he'd done in his past. Any police investigation into why he was being targeted for blackmail is bound to turn up some unpleasant truths about your friend. Maybe they're best left buried."

He placed the letter carefully in his manila folder and began to gather up the notes and papers that had escaped across Breedlove's desktop. Oliver closed his eyes, lost in thought.

"Tell you what," Culpepper added, trying to break the tension, "I didn't look behind this bureau for the phantom envelope. Could you help me move it?"

The two men dragged the large, wooden desk several inches from the wall, cockling the well-worn carpet. Culpepper produced a pocket torch and shone it into the space. Among the dust-balls and cobwebs, there sat a bright nest of paper clips, some moldy candy wrappers, and a length of telephone cord. The only piece of paper was a yellowing cutting from a printed book, which had clearly lain behind the bureau for several years. Oliver fished it out. It was a page from an old printed volume of Shakespeare, trimmed tightly around the text so that the play title and even the header showing the Act and Scene were missing. From the character names it seemed to come from one of the *Henry VI* plays. A shame—if it had been *Richard II*, he'd have a link to the blackmail note's "blessed plot" reference. Maybe Breedlove had taped it to the wall above his workplace, but it had lost its stickiness and slid down into the gap?

"No envelope," said Culpepper. "I bet he tore it up and flushed it down the crapper."

Ah, now there's a bit of anti-trivia, thought Oliver. All those eager people who'll tell you that the word "crap" and its variants come from the Victorian eminence Sir Thomas Crapper, supposedly the inventor of the flush toilet. In reality, the vulgarism is far older. The gentleman was never knighted; he was merely the originator of the floating ball cock, and his name is an unfortunate, if risible coincidence. Unless, of course, it had dictated his path in life.

"Can I keep this?" Oliver asked, resurfacing after this momentary meditation. Culpepper nodded.

"Why would you want to?" Effie inquired, sliding the bureau back into place alone.

"I don't know. A souvenir of the sheeted dead, I guess."

They walked out of the house again and paused on the porch while Culpepper locked the bright blue door and positioned a strip of broad yellow tape across the door and its frame. It gave the scene a nautical look, despite the fierce POLICE – DO NOT ENTER message, a welcome splash of color in Breedlove's dismal front garden. Oliver noticed again the mound of damp earth that sat beside the garden path. It was darker than the ground it lay on, and since Oliver could see no corresponding hole, he guessed that it been delivered for some landscaping purpose, now gone with Breedlove to his grave. It reminded Oliver that he'd noticed some caked dirt on his own hands the previous evening, shortly after grabbing onto the swinging body in the tree.

"When Dennis was taken down from the tree, were his clothes dirty?" he asked Culpepper.

"Yes, they were, almost muddy, as if he'd been lying in it. He probably fell down a couple of times on his way across the Common."

Oliver nodded. The damp mound in front of him showed no signs of any collision with a suicidal, eighty-year-old expert on children's literature. But when had it rained last? The dust from the Common, which had swirled off his feet in the shower last night, was lighter in color.

"So these naked women observed by the Vampire of Synne?" Effie began.

"Merely a trick of the light," said Culpepper quickly. "It certainly isn't worth putting into my report, and Superintendent Mallard agrees with me."

"I can see why my uncle took a liking to you, Detective Sergeant Culpepper," said Oliver, shaking hands with the tall policeman.

"Oh well, it never hurts to have friends in high places."

"And vice versa."

Culpepper frowned. "I'm not with you, I'm afraid."

"A little joke…" Oliver began, with a smug smile.

Chapter Four

Saturday afternoon (continued)

Visitors often mistake the tall stone obelisk in the middle of Synne's Square for a war memorial, erected during the spate of numb memorializing that followed the First World War. Unfortunately—or fortunately, depending on your perspective—there wasn't a single villager who'd even joined up to fight the Great War, let alone given his life for King and country. But not to be out-commemorated by the neighboring village of Pigsneye, which had sacrificed half its male population at Passchendaele, the Parish Council of the time erected this monument to the one Synne resident who had gone down on the Titanic in 1912, two years before the war began (or five years before, if you're one of Synne's frequent American tourists).

After the Second World War, which also found Synne unrepresented in the armed forces, the Parish Council discovered that a man born in the village had died in the crash of the Hindenburg in 1937, oddly enough, two years before the war began (or nearly five years before, if you're an American tourist) and his name was duly added to the memorial, conveniently omitting the fact that he had been part of the cabin crew and a keen member of the Nazi Party.

Oliver and Effie were sitting on the steps in front of the obelisk, sharing a stale jam doughnut they'd bought from the village post office across the street. In the afternoon sunlight, the stone cottages facing the Square exhibited a range of shades from cream to pewter, from ivory to amber, spattered with the seasonal primaries of window boxes and hanging baskets of petunias, and, in the case of one house that juts into the road, paint samples from many European car manufacturers.

Signs and displays in the windows added more color, since many of the restless homeowners, unable to abandon their entrepreneurial pasts and desperate for fresh company, had turned front parlors into antique "centres" or estate agencies showing pictures of thatched cottages for sale (of which Synne possessed nearly one) or cramped art galleries for the residents' watercolors of the same buildings. Tourists pausing for refreshment in one of Synne's five tearooms were often baffled to find that their twelve-pounds-fifty didn't just buy them a pot of Earl Grey and a powdery scone, but also a lecture from the proprietor on current trends in conditional variance swaps.

Effie turned and looked at Oliver for several seconds, with a mixture of affection and pity.

"I can't believe you told Simon that he was very tall," she said.

"I was explaining the joke," Oliver bleated. "With Simon, Uncle Tim also has a 'friend in a high place,' as it were."

"I can't take you anywhere," Effie sighed, licking sugar from her fingers. The distant purr of a car engine began to drown out the conversation some rooks were conducting in a nearby hornbeam.

"Tell me something," said Oliver. "How did Culpepper get away with calling you 'Curly'? Why didn't you put him in his place with that magic Look of yours?"

"My what? What on earth are you talking about?" She screwed up the empty paper bag and tossed it into a rubbish bin a few feet away, beside the bus shelter built to celebrate the Festival of Britain in 1951, although Synne had never had a bus service before or since.

The car was louder now, clearly a sports car, clearly being driven too fast for England's meandering country roads. It was approaching from the west.

"No, I chose to give Simon a chance to explain himself," she continued. She smiled contentedly. "It was worth it," she added, remembering the tall detective's compliment.

There was a cinematic squeal of tires and another throaty roar, suggesting that the car had reached the pointless double bend in front of the manor house.

"So I have competition, do I?" said Oliver, pretending to be fascinated by a pigeon that was ambling past them.

Before she could answer—before he knew whether he was going to get an answer—a black Lamborghini sped into view, barely slowing as it hurtled along the stretch of road in front of them, raising clouds of dust and rattling crockery on the small tables outside the tea shops. A small, elderly man stepping out of the post office leaped backwards in alarm and dropped an ice cream cone. Oliver thought he looked vaguely familiar, but not from Synne. The pigeon flew off, affronted. With a shriek of brakes, the car swerved onto the footpath that led to the Swithins' house. The driver gave one more unnecessary prod to the accelerator and then turned the engine off.

"Ben's arrived," said Oliver. He stood up and offered a hand to Effie. She let him pull her to her feet, and then slipped her arms around his waist and kissed him briskly on the chin.

"Are you even slightly jealous?"

"Not a bit," Oliver lied.

"Good. I don't play those games, Ollie. If I ever want someone other than you, you'll be the first to know." She kissed him again, while he registered the fact that she'd said "if" and not "when."

Ben Motley was Oliver's friend and landlord, a photographer whose studio occupied the top floor of the Edwardes Square townhouse they shared with their friends Geoffrey Angelwine and Susie Beamish. Ben oozed his tanned and well-toned body out of the Lamborghini and reached behind the driver's seat for a leather overnight valise and an aluminum case of photographic equipment. He caught sight of Oliver and Effie across the Square and waved delightedly, pulling his sunglasses from his handsome face.

"Tell me again where we're going this evening," Effie asked as they walked toward the house, trying to avoid the broken sticks, bedraggled paper flowers, discarded straw hats, and the occasional shard of a beer bottle left over from the previous morning's May Day event, the annual Beating of the Morris Dancers.

"You and I and Ben and the egregious Toby are having dinner with some old family friends, the Bennets, over at Pigsneye."

"Does Ben know them?"

Oliver spotted her subtext: *Am I the only stranger?*

"No, but Mother let slip that he was staying with us, so Wendy Bennet issued a very insistent invitation. She and her husband have five unmarried daughters, and a famous and famously single fashion photographer is irresistible husband material in these parts."

"Hang on. A family called Bennet? Living in the country?"

"That's right."

"With five unmarried daughters?"

"Er, yes."

"Is this some kind of put-on? Their names aren't Elizabeth, Jane, Mary, Kitty, and whatever that slutty Lolita who runs off with Mr. Wickham was called, are they?"

"No." Oliver cleared his throat. "They're Davina, Catriona, Clarissa, Xanthe, and Lucinda."

"Great. I can see I'm going to fit right in."

She strode ahead to greet Ben. Oliver hung back, using the few extra seconds to recall the text of the blackmail note once again. It was probably the twentieth mental review, with increasing intervals, and he thought he had it by heart.

He didn't agree with Culpepper. Whoever had sent Dennis Breedlove that letter drove the old man to his death. It was the moral equivalent of murder. And if the Warwickshire police couldn't spare the manpower for moral equivalencies, and Scotland Yard was forced by etiquette to sit on his and her hands, then maybe it was up to him to find the murderer.

Did you think you could hide your history? Did you think this whole blessed plot would be covered up forever…?

Chapter Five

Saturday evening

"Thirteen at dinner," sniffed Mrs. Bennet. "I thought we were twelve, six men and six girls. I don't know how I miscalculated."

Oliver knew. The forgotten guest was clearly Effie, since the other six females were all called Bennet, the middle-aged Wendy considering herself as much a "girl" as her five daughters. He glanced behind him, but Effie was still standing by the front door out of earshot, taking in the capacious entrance hall of the Bennets' eighteenth century mansion.

Mrs. Bennet leaned closer. She was almost as tall as he was, with black bobbed hair and abrupt features and wearing a yellow silk sheath that you'd have said was too small for her (although you'd have *thought* that *she* was too big for *it*). "I'm not usually superstitious, Oliver, but we don't want to risk any bad luck tonight, because of Lucinda's engagement."

"Lucinda's getting married?" Oliver was genuinely delighted, because it would reduce the number of Bennet sisters who considered him a potential husband by twenty percent. This was not a flattering distinction; the number of males who fit this target category was, by now, approaching half the population of Europe, including gay men if necessary; but it still required him on these rare occasions to suffer two or three hours of unwelcome flirtation across the dinner table. Or it would have, had Effie not been there. He hoped.

The trip from Synne to Pigsneye was short, even though no English road planner had followed flying crows since the Roman occupation. Effie drove them in her Renault, because Ben's Lamborghini was a two-seater. She seemed to be avoiding any discussion of the approaching dinner.

"What are you working on when you're not shooting semi-naked models?" she had asked Ben, accelerating around a blind corner on the country lane.

"Wallpaper."

"You design wallpaper?"

"I photograph it. Some of my wealthier clients have the most beautiful wallpaper in their homes—William Morris, Alphonse Mucha, much of it original. I want them to see that it can be more striking than the paintings or prints they hang over it. So I take a large-format photograph of the wallpaper and they display it in a frame in front of the real wallpaper."

"But what's to stop them just hanging up an empty frame instead of hiring you?" asked Oliver from the backseat.

Ben sighed. "Because, my dear Ollie, that's not ironic. That's just lazy."

"What's the difference?"

"About £10,000 a session."

Following Oliver's directions, Effie had pulled into a gap in a dense arborvitae hedge. A gravel driveway led eventually to a substantial Georgian mansion where she stopped the car under a porte-cochere. "I smell money," she had muttered. Stepping across the threshold of Bennet Hall, she seemed to shrink slightly and become distracted by the appearance of her shoes. Mr. Bennet, a small man, balding and bespectacled, who always looked as if you were about to speak to him, helped her remove her thin raincoat, exuding nervous hospitality. Oliver had noticed before that Effie, self-assured and fearless when on official police business, was uncomfortable in social settings that contrasted with her own upbringing. At least, he'd always assumed she had a working-class background, although she rarely spoke of her childhood. He'd never met her family.

"So who's Luce's lucky man?" Oliver asked Mrs. Bennet.

"The Honorable Donald Quilt-Hogg, fifth son of the Earl of Yateley. The Honorable Donald is with us tonight. It's an excellent match—not too many potential spouses out there who have all the requirements: just nineteen, a guaranteed virgin, as pure as snow, knows one end of a horse from another, and would look good in a Countess's robes just in case of a regrettable quartet of family tragedies."

"Well, as long as Luce doesn't mind about the cross-dressing." Mrs. Bennet gave what she thought was a girlish giggle.

"I'm describing Lucinda, you rogue, as you well know. It's my heart's desire to see one of my girls marry into the aristocracy."

Oliver thought, "It's your heart's desire to see one of your girls marry full stop." Although the oldest Bennet sister was only twenty-five, that was thirty-nine in debutante years. Lucinda, fresh out of the starting gate at nineteen—he'd assumed Wendy had measured her daughter in years, not hands—was bucking a trend. Still, from what he'd heard about the current finances of the current Lord Yateley (and currency didn't feature much), there was a clear tit for tat in the pairing, no doubt starting with Lucinda's well-heeled father helping to get the Yateley family jewels out of hock in time for the wedding. Never mind the *nouveau,* feel the *riche.*

"And when did the Hon. Don pop the question?" Oliver asked.

Mrs. Bennet lowered her voice still further. "Well, dear, he's not exactly asked her in so many words, which is why we don't want to take any chances with Lady Luck. Lafcadio and I will leave the dining room to you eleven youngsters. I'd join you, but Lafcadio sulks if he's made to dine alone, the brute, and we girls may not see the checkbook for a month."

We girls. Wendy Bennet didn't like to be reminded that there was any generation younger than her own. "My oldest daughter's in her twenties," she would frequently confess with an expression that anticipated your shocked disbelief, and then would look away coyly so she never had to notice that it wasn't forthcoming.

Mr. Bennet was now ushering Effie into the presence of his wife, who managed to force her lower face into a dazzling smile while her eyes skewered the surplus female guest with a malevolent glare. Effie, who had faced down criminal court judges, murderers, and other evildoers, quailed slightly. The senior Bennets withdrew to bully the hired kitchen staff, and the new arrivals were shown into the drawing room.

Once Effie's pupils had adjusted to the blaze of gilded furniture, ormolu clocks, and gold-edged porcelain, she became aware that the settees supported a full hand of Bennet daughters, all staring at her with a mix of curiosity and appraisal. It was unlikely that anyone had ever dared bring the girls' shared plainness to their notice, but that hadn't stopped them devoting much of their time—it would be redundant to call it their "free" time—and much of their father's fortune to grooming and styling. For a quiet dinner at home, the sisters were decked out in bright bracelets, necklaces, and earrings that almost, but not quite, eclipsed the satin and chiffon of their designer gowns. Effie, cool and stunning in the newer of the two dresses she'd brought with her—a blue cotton Monsoon sundress that Oliver had assured her would be adequate for the occasion—felt self-conscious and underdressed.

As Oliver made the introductions, she used her police training to fix which sister was which, noting the color of their dresses and their expensive hairstyles. (Her own mutinous curls had been dragged into a tentative ponytail.) The girls' listless conversation gave her less to work with, with the possible exceptions of Davina, the oldest and least unattractive (dark bob like her mother's, black Valentino), who seemed to have some spark of personality. Unfortunately, not a very pleasant one. Lucinda, the youngest (medium brown hair, long and upswept, caramel Dior) never spoke at all, but gazed with a half-smile at the Honorable Donald Quilt-Hogg. The other sisters gazed frankly at Ben. As Oliver had once commented, Ben didn't so much ooze charm as squirt it.

The same could not be said of the Honorable Donald (Norton & Sons, tweed). He was a tall, well-built young man, with prematurely thinning blondish hair, whose speech was similarly sparse, apart from a sporadic comment that sounded to Effie like "Ah, jolly old honkers!" followed by a throaty chuckle.

Oliver, sensing Effie's discomfort, poured two glasses of white Sauterne from a gold-rimmed cooler on the sideboard and passed one to her without asking. She finished it in two gulps. After an agonizing twenty minutes of desultory small talk about the London Season, the door opened and Toby came in, followed by another young man.

"Sorry I'm late," Toby said. "Eric and I got caught in the theatre traffic."

"Still, better it's us that's 'late' than any of you girls, eh?" said his companion, with a general leer for the room. "Know what I mean?" he added unnecessarily, but the sisters' laughter was apparently genuine. Lucinda whispered an explanation into Quilt-Hogg's ear, and he nodded, muttering his favorite phrase again.

"Oh, Eric," cried Davina, taking the newcomer by the arm, "for Jesu's sake, forbeare. Come and meet the new arrivals."

"At your cervix, dear madam," the young man declared. He was introduced to Quilt-Hogg, Ben, and finally to Effie, to whom he bowed with comic gallantry.

"Nice one, Olls," Eric said, nudging Oliver and indicating Effie with a sideways nod of his head. "Like the hair."

Oliver smiled politely, wishing he had Wendy Bennet's talent for signaling utter contempt at the same time. Eric Mormal (Tesco, black cotton) was an old school friend of Toby's, a lean, pale specter, who looked like a stretched thirteen-year-old, complete with residual acne, a pubic moustache, and a mind permanently in the gutter—not so much for the filth to be found there, but because it was the best place to metaphorically look up women's skirts. He worked for a nearby cooperative farm, but his bliss was to become a full-time rock legend as evidenced by spiky dyed-blond hair, tattoos, and a collection of hoops in his ear that made it look like a shower curtain.

"So who are you fronting now?" Oliver asked, trying to remember what Toby had last told him about Mormal's musical career. "Is it still The Gong Farmers?"

"Nah, we have a new lineup now: we're called 'Mrs. Slocombe's Pussy.'" He tried to toss a stuffed olive into his mouth, without success. It rolled under a sofa.

What was Mormal doing here? Oliver wondered. For girls of the Bennets' micro-class—Orwell would have stuck them in the lower-upper-middle bracket—the provincial dinner party was still the primary *lek*, the gentrified equivalent of the singles bar. No doubt it was at some similar, very soft society event that the Honorable Donald had been strutting his well-tailored but fraying plumage when Lucinda, scenting an aristo, had wafted a few choice pheromones in his direction; thus the Hon. Don was undone. But Eric Mormal was the barrel's scrapings, the living reason why "uncouth" has no antonym. Surely Wendy wasn't this desperate?

Ben had been invited to squeeze onto an unyielding settee between the Bennets' only twins, Clarissa and Catriona (both loose blonde curls, yellow Lanvin and blue LaCroix, respectively) and was asking them politely where he might have seen them before when a young woman in an ill-fitting housemaid's uniform belted a gong beside the fireplace, a fearful summons to the dining room. He got up gratefully from his Bennet sandwich, and the two girls followed silently in his wake.

The customary separation of couples at the dining table didn't seem to apply to Lucinda and the Honorable Donald, presumably so that if the urge to propose came over him during the meal, he could skip the legwork and drop to one knee straight from his chair. Effie, however, was squashed between Quilt-Hogg on her right and Mormal on her left, while Oliver was consigned to the other side of the table. He had squeezed her elbow reassuringly as they entered the dining room. "Just signal if I start to drink the finger-bowl," she had whispered, nervously scanning the ranks of silverware that bordered her tablemat.

"Did you meet Oliver up at Oxford, Effie?" Xanthe Bennet (blond chin-length hair, gray Chanel) ventured from across the table, after they had taken their seats.

"No, but I met him *in* Oxford, once," said Effie with a smile, and immediately watched her witticism sail effortlessly over Xanthe's head. She'd noticed that, among the bling, each girl was wearing a diamond-encrusted pin with the initial of her first name. It wouldn't have surprised her if Xanthe thought it her entire signature.

"So where did you go to college?" Davina now demanded, clearly the chief hostess in her mother's absence.

"Just Hendon."

"Is there a University of Hendon? We don't know it."

"It's the police training establishment, the Peel Centre," Effie explained, as a dish of strangely soapy consommé arrived in front of her. *Spoon*, she thought.

"So what are you?" asked Xanthe, "a Scotland Yard superintendent, like Oliver's uncle?"

"Just a sergeant for now."

"Hey, Olls," called Mormal, between noisy inhalations of the soup, "do you make Effie keep her uniform on? It's the black stockings, innit?"

"Effie's my uncle's principal assistant," Oliver explained, hoping his pride in his girlfriend would cheer her a little. He knew that her role as a guest would keep the Strongitharm Look in check, much as he longed to see Mormal zapped by it. "That means she's a plain-clothes officer."

"How appropriate," murmured Davina with a private smile. Effie eviscerated a dinner roll.

"Well, Effie," said Mormal, patting her on the shoulder, "you can feel my collar any time. And not just my collar, if you know what I mean," he added, winking at Oliver across the table.

"Tragically, I do," Effie muttered, but Mormal wasn't listening. He had jumped to his feet, holding his soup spoon as if it were a microphone.

"And now a little recitation entitled 'She was only the policeman's daughter, but she let the chief inspector…'"

Once again, all the sisters dissolved into indulgent laughter.

"Oh, Eric," chortled Catriona, "you're so *leisure*."

Mormal subsided into his chair at an angle that would let him glimpse down Effie's neckline each time she took a sip of consommé, which, like Mormal, was thick and unwholesome.

"Oliver, what's this we hear about you stumbling over bodies again?" Xanthe demanded. "We've been literally dying to ask you."

"My uncle and I found Dennis Breedlove's body last night," Oliver confirmed. He wanted to learn more about the old man's life, in the hope that it would provide a path to the blackmailer, but this gossipy crowd was surely not the forum.

"Yeah, the word is he hanged himself from the old Synne Oak," Mormal said.

"That's what it looks like."

Mormal smiled. "Got any gory details?"

Davina glared at him fiercely across the table. "Eric, I don't think this is an appropriate subject for a supper party," she said. Her younger sisters let loose little sighs of disappointment.

"I agree," said Toby, who had clearly been told of the death since he had fled the Swithins' home that afternoon. "It's very sad. I liked Mr. Breedlove a lot. I used to visit him. He was always up for a chat about my research."

He seemed to tear up. Oliver noticed Mormal and Davina catch each other's eye again, this time with a faint hint of amusement. He guessed it was some private mockery of Toby's sentiments, a shared cynicism momentarily spanning the class chasm between them, scorning what they saw as unmanly grief, and he despised them for it.

"He seemed such a cheerful little chap," said Catriona. "One felt one could tell him anything. Do you know what drove him to end his life, Oliver?"

Oliver looked at Effie for guidance. She shrugged.

"The police think it was because he'd received a blackmail letter," he said.

"*He* was being blackmailed?" Mormal exclaimed. "What on earth for?"

"I can't imagine." Not here, anyway, Oliver added silently. Davina's eyes stayed on Oliver, across the table.

"Perhaps he couldn't afford to pay," suggested Ben. "And so he knew he would inevitably be exposed."

"Exposed," repeated Mormal, as if he were genetically required to report every potential *double entendre*.

"Exposed," echoed Quilt-Hogg. He pointed at Ben. "It's funny, because he's a photographer," he explained to Lucinda.

"Please," said Davina firmly, "I insist that we change the subject." She sat back as a stuffed artichoke was deposited in her place by the stoic housemaid.

"Oh, Davvy, this is literally the most hair-raising thing that's happened for yonks," Xanthe protested. "All right, we'll respect the late Mr. Breedlove. But let's play a guessing game. What's the one thing that would make each of us commit suicide?"

"I know what would do it for Davina," giggled Catriona. "Being caught with a single hair out of place." She turned to her eldest sister. "Honestly, Davvy, you're so vain. I think if you ever got a run in your tights, you'd shrivel up with humiliation."

"Literally," added Xanthe.

"That's a bit of an exaggeration," said Davina.

"Exaggeration? You even secretly ironed your underwear this afternoon!" said Catriona.

"Why did she do that?" asked Clarissa.

"I think it was because Oliver was coming to dinner," claimed Catriona, with a sly glance at Effie, who felt freshly conscious that her dress had traveled to Synne rolled up in a duffel bag. Oliver, momentarily relieved that the ghastly conversation had drifted from Uncle Dennis toward sisterly teasing, felt the dread return.

"That's astounding," said Clarissa.

"That she was ironing her underwear?"

"No, that Davvy knows how to use an iron."

"She clearly doesn't, because she burned herself. That's how I found out."

Davina glanced ruefully at the pink stripe on the edge of her hand, but Oliver noticed that the move was calculated to show off her golden wristwatch. A Cartier Tank Americaine. Money.

"You're afraid of being baffled, Davina," said Toby genially. "In the Shakespearean sense, that is. In his time, 'baffled' meant publicly embarrassed."

"Really?" replied Davina. "Then I'd have something in common with dear Effie. I hear the police are often baffled."

Effie glared down at her artichoke and took another mouthful of wine.

"Toby, why don't you tell the ladies about the dig you're working on in Stratford," Oliver cut in swiftly.

"Oh, is that part of your research?" Ben asked.

Toby looked at Mormal. "No, it's just an excuse to spend a few weeks in Shakespeare Central, soaking up the atmosphere. There's a small island next to the downstream weir on the Avon. An old Victorian house on it is being demolished. It's standard practice to sift through the dirt whenever there's any rebuilding in the Stratford area, just in case. So a bunch of us from my college agreed to do it, and Eric volunteered to help us in his spare time. But we don't expect to find anything from Shakespeare's time—we're well south of the seventeenth-century part of town and on the opposite side of the river."

"Then what is this research of yours, Toby?" asked Davina. "Educate us."

"It's about the true identity of William Shakespeare. You probably know that many people think Shakespeare didn't write the plays. That the author was really Francis Bacon or the Earl of Oxford or even Christopher Marlowe, whose murder in 1593 must have been faked. What's provoked these theories is our incredulity that the son of a provincial glover—or butcher, according to some sources—with no university education could write dramas that require an intimate knowledge of court intrigue, the law, foreign explorations, Roman history, and so on."

"So you've found yet another candidate?" asked Ben. "Queen Elizabeth the First with no wig and a false moustache? Or is it really that infinite number of monkeys?"

Toby laughed. "No, I believe that the plays were written by William Shakespeare, all right. But this is the odd part. When you look at the very few surviving facts about Shakespeare, the London actor-playwright, and Shakespeare, the Stratford-upon-Avon landowner and businessman, there's no overlap."

"Perhaps he was Ernest in the town and Jack in the country," Oliver said, unable to decide which way his artichoke more resembled a pinecone, in appearance or in taste.

"Ernest and Jack Worthing turned out to be same person. My belief is that Stratford Will and London Will were two different people."

"Because of this lack of evidence?" asked Effie.

"The scanty documentation isn't so unusual in itself. We don't know much about the personal lives of any dramatists of that period. So most research is like Kim's Game. We have to ask what's missing that we'd truly expect to see: the 'pregnant negative.' And what we *don't* have is a single piece of paper written or signed by Stratford Will that lays claim to his being the great London poet and playwright. For example, Stratford Will's notorious last will and testament—the one that leaves his wife the 'second-best bed'—doesn't mention his part ownership in any South Bank theaters. In fact, it doesn't mention any manuscripts or books or unfinished plays or other papers. No, I think London Will is a different William Shakespeare, from somewhere other than Stratford."

The housemaid slipped into the room and began to replace the remains of the artichoke with plates of gray roast beef.

"But just a tick," Catriona protested. "What about Stratford Will's tomb? We were taken there on a school trip once. There's that statue on the church wall that looks just like all those photographs of London Will."

"Aha, that's where history got sidetracked, Cat," Toby remarked, helping himself to overcooked vegetables. "I think that sometime after Stratford Will died in 1616, somebody spotted that he had the same name as a famous London playwright, who may well have died three or four years earlier, going by the dates of his last plays. And thus, with a little jiggery-pokery, the Stratford Shakespeare industry was born, hijacking London Will's fame. Ka-ching!"

"And so we never found the real London Will…" Oliver ventured.

"…because we never knew we had to look for him."

"How deep you are!" said Catriona, leaning across the table and gazing intently into Toby's dark, nervous eyes, which took on an expression of mild panic. Clarissa, beside him, who had tuned out of the conversation five minutes earlier and was wondering instead why Catriona was wearing her own initial pin, took her cue to drop her hand onto Toby's forearm.

"Well, Toby," Davina intervened with a yawn, "it all sounds very brainy, but I'm sure I speak for Effie when I say let's move on to a less taxing subject."

"Then I suppose it's my turn to tell you what I'm working on," Oliver said quickly, observing Effie for signs of an impending Look. He thought about announcing his next planned story in the Railway Mice series, *The Railway Mice and the Frog of the Baskervilles*, but then it occurred to him to try out his idea for the book of common knowledge (which wasn't a bad title, come to think of it). It took several goes to make the Bennets understand he was not talking about regular trivia, known only to cognoscenti, such as that the banana plant is technically a herb, not a tree; nor indeed about obvious information concerning the banana's color, its taste, or (as Mormal persisted in mentioning) its suggestive shape—every fool can tell that. But the banana's reputation as a source of potassium is perfect paradigm of… what *should* he call it?

"Let me think of another example," he said. He fixed his eyes on Mormal and inspiration came. "What's the first odd fact that comes to mind when I say the word 'cockroach'?"

"Cockroaches will be the only survivors of a nuclear war," said Toby instantly. Oliver nodded.

"Most people have heard that, although there doesn't seem to be an atom of truth in it. But, as I'm finding, fact is nowhere near as appealing, or as memorable, as some fictions."

"Effie, you're very quiet," interrupted Davina. "I suppose you're used to that, with such an intelligent boyfriend. Let's tempt you into the conversation. Were you at Royal Ascot this year?"

"Not this year, no," Effie replied sweetly, as she stabbed a soggy Brussels sprout. "And before you ask, you patronizing bitch, not at Henley, or Cowes Week, or the Chelsea frigging Flower Show or any other stopping-off place in the London Season where you inbred oxygen-thieves get a last chance to squander your ill-gotten wealth before the revolution comes and you're all dangling from the lampposts," she added mentally.

"I say," Quilt-Hogg cut in. "Nuclear war—atom of truth. That's jolly good." He chuckled. Lucinda squeezed his hand reassuringly.

The table started to split into smaller conversational clusters, and Effie discovered that if she looked busy with her food, smiled occasionally at nothing in particular, and kept her eyes fixed on the cruet, she could exclude herself from any subgroup that included a Bennet. Apart from a brief exchange with Eric Mormal, who asked her if the "eff" in "Effie" was short for what he thought it was—it wasn't—she managed to get all the way to dessert in splendid isolation. Only Oliver, out of reach, noticed.

"Do you ski?" Quilt-Hogg asked suddenly. Effie turned and realized the question was for her.

"No, I've yet to learn," she said, remembering the Easter school vacations when her more affluent friends jetted off for a week on the bunny slopes of St. Moritz.

"Ah. Sail?" Quilt-Hogg persisted, following some mental checklist for dinner conversations.

"No."

"Shoot?"

"No, I don't like guns." What was next, bungee polo?

"Shame," he went on, clearly permitted to talk about himself after three refusals. "Got a couple of Purdeys, myself."

"I always say there's nothing like a nice pair of Purdeys, eh, Effie?" Mormal cut in. Xanthe and Lucinda giggled. The table was clearly regathering.

"He's so leisure," said Xanthe happily, to nobody in particular.

"Rather," Quilt-Hogg agreed. "One's a bit of an antique. My people gave me the other for my twenty-first birthday. Side-by-side self-opening sidelock. Cost a packet, hundred thou, cleaned out the old man's bank account, but worth the dosh. So you don't use a gun in your job, eh?"

"I've trained in marksmanship."

"Ah. What do you police types use these days?"

"A Glock 17. I've also handled a Smith and Wesson revolver. A .38 model ten."

"Most excellent! Fancy, a couple of rounds from one of those should put the wind up Johnny Foreigner, when he gets above himself."

"I wouldn't know about that," Effie said tactfully. *When the hell can we go home?* she thought. Oh dear God, this wasn't going to be one of those gatherings where the ladies withdraw from the table and leave the men to their cigars and brandy, was it?

"Get the shooters, George!" said Quilt-Hogg suddenly.

"What?"

"That's what they used to say in those old police shows. Most amusing." He adopted what he thought was a Cockney accent. "'Get the shooters, George!'"

"Oh, Donald, you're so frightfully clever," breathed Lucinda. Effie reached for her wineglass.

"Shut it!" cried Mormal, from Effie's left, drawing out the vowels. "They said that too. It's how cops talk. 'Shut it!'"

"Get the shooters, George!"

"Shut it!"

Effie had to speak or she would be forced to grab the two men by their various supplies of hair and slam their heads together into the plate of trifle that had just arrived.

"You all remember what happened to Reg Thigpen, don't you?" she asked.

"Reg Thigpen?" echoed Davina, with some distaste, as if the coarse syllables were coated in brown sauce.

"Undercroft Colliery?" Effie prompted. "Derbyshire? Front page news for a week, about two years ago?" All the women and two of the men at the table were looking at her blankly. She pressed on.

"To remind you then, the government wanted to close the pit, but the miners went on strike to keep it open. Most of the public took the side of the miners, and the more the government dug in, the more popular sentiment began to swing against them. With a general election due, this wasn't good. And then along came Reg Thigpen."

Was this a suitable topic for a Bennet beanfeast? She didn't care anymore.

"Thigpen was a petty criminal from London, just out of jail for the umpteenth time. Years earlier, Oliver's Uncle Tim had arrested him for burglary. Thigpen was an easy recruit for the dodgy bus company that was driving scab workers into and out of the colliery. Every day, the television news showed poor Reg driving slowly through a screaming throng of pickets, while trash and stones were hurled at the bus. The viewing public hated him. Until one day, in the middle of the second week of the strike, bang!"

Some of her audience started.

"The windscreen shatters, and Reg is abruptly the late Reg, a single gunshot right between the eyes."

She paused. The table was hushed.

"We never found the gunman. But the point is that the incident changed public opinion overnight. Reg Thigpen went from being a despised strikebreaker to a tragic victim of out-of-control union thuggery. The strike petered out, the colliery closed, the miners lost their jobs, and the government won the next election on a law-and-order platform. All because of one shot from one gun."

She turned to Quilt-Hogg and smiled. "The British public don't have much taste for guns, Donald. They don't like it when their police officers get the shooters. Not in real life."

Effie took a forkful of trifle, while her audience absorbed the story. Xanthe opened her mouth as if she was going to ask a question, but shut it again.

And then she remembered the tactic that could be used whenever she felt puzzled by something beyond her understanding, when her ignorance might be publicly exposed—that tactic employed by all young English women whose careful breeding and dauntless narcissism are in inverse proportion to their intelligence.

She laughed prettily.

It was a sweet, tinkling laugh, as infectious as a yawn. Her sisters too began to snigger, as if Effie's story had been a joke, a tale to hoodwink and delight them, nothing more than a passing pleasantry. They turned their amusement on their male companions, a strategy that generally charmed their feckless admirers and won them to the ladies' side, isolating the earnest storyteller; although in this case, only two of the men did more than return a strained smile in the face of their hostesses' spiteful merriment.

As new conversations burst around her like fireworks, Effie looked hard at Ben, directly across the table.

"How much have you had to drink?" she asked.

"Just a couple of glasses of wine."

"Good. Because you're driving us home tonight." She drained her glass and reached for a nearby bottle of Riesling.

Chapter Six

Sunday afternoon

"To be…" pondered Hamlet, "or not to."

He turned to the audience. "Be, that is," he clarified. He looked down at the clipboard he was holding.

"The question: Whether 'tis nobler in the—"

He broke off suddenly, as the Junoesque manicurist from Chigwell playing Ophelia launched herself on cue from the wings and barged into him.

"Mind!" Hamlet remonstrated. He cleared his throat. "To suffer the slings and arrows of…" Again he stopped, noticing that Ophelia was now slowly unbuttoning his doublet.

"Outrageous!" Hamlet complained. He glanced at his clipboard again, and frowned. "Humfrey, darling," he called out, shielding his eyes as he looked out beyond the footlights, "I'm fine up to here, but there's something in the next line I really don't follow. Sorry."

The slight figure of Humfrey Fingerhood, director in residence of the Theydon Bois Thespians, rose from the front row and darted toward the stage of the cavernous Royal Shakespeare Theatre. The only other audience member that Sunday afternoon was Oliver, sitting a few rows back, and most of his attention was on the index card in his hand. Fortunately, the house lights were up, so he could read the text of Dennis Breedlove's blackmail note, which he'd jotted down from memory.

Did you think you could hide your history?

Nice line in alliteration, Oliver thought. Accidental? Or does our blackmailer have a literary bent? But "history" must surely mean personal history, something from Breedlove's past that he was intent on keeping a secret.

Did you think this whole blessed plot would be covered up forever?

"This blessed plot." It was a quotation from John of Gaunt's deathbed speech in *Richard II*. A joke, presumably—the "plot" in this case not being a tract of land but some sort of conspiracy or scheme, the "blessed" that most gentle of intensifiers, no doubt a minced oath for "bloody." Or was "blessed" meant literally, to use Xanthe Bennet's favorite word? Was there a religious angle? Was Dennis now or had he ever been a Bible-thumper? Edwards the vicar might be able to shed some light on the dead man's beliefs.

The word "plot" made him turn to the other piece of paper he was holding, the yellowing page of a Shakespeare play from behind Breedlove's desk, trimmed close to the edges of the text. Well, not trimmed—instead of the straight slice of a razor or scissors, its edges were jagged, as if impatiently stabbed out of the book.

Henry the Sixth, Part Two, Act Two, Scene Two. One of London Will's most tiresome scenes. Total backstory. Richard, Duke of York—not the "Now is the winter of our discontent" hunchback baddie but his father—explains at tedious length to a couple of sympathetic earls why he, tracing his heirdom to Edward III's third son, should be King of England instead of the play's eponymous Henry, son of the stirring "Once more unto the breach, dear friends" Henry but runner-up heir to Edward III's *fourth* son. "...and in this private plot be we the first that shall salute our rightful sovereign with honour of his birthright to the crown."

In other words, the Yorkist Jets get ready to rumble with the Lancastrian Sharks.

Apart from the shared reference to a "plot," there was nothing that connected it to the blackmail letter. But did it offer a clue into Uncle Dennis's past? Why had it meant so much to him that he'd gouged the scene from his Collected Works and, presumably, at some time stuck it over his desk? Was it a reminder of some succession issues of his own: a usurped heirdom, a stolen inheritance, a filched family bequest?

On the stage, the actors and Humfrey had been arguing about how you could possibly take arms against a "sea" of troubles, weapons against water. *Idiots.*

Oliver turned back to the index card propped on his left thigh.

I KNOW WHAT'S BEEN GOING ON.

The first entrance of the blackmailer onto the stage of Breedlove's drama. Odd. The wrong tense entirely to refer to something that's supposed to be history. Why not "I know what went on"? Or does the phrase apply to a continuing cover-up?

BUT YOU DON'T WANT OTHERS TO DIG UP THE PAST,
DO YOU?

This was Oliver's lifeline, the single hint that whatever Breedlove's secret might be, it was accessible if you knew where to look. In the old man's past, of course, maybe before he took up residence in Synne. Although Breedlove wasn't universally loved in the village, Oliver had never heard whispers of any scandal or crime. So if Breedlove's sins were public, they must have been committed before he became an author, during his years as a broadcaster at the BBC, an actor turned storyteller; but if private, they were those of a much younger man, a Londoner, a Cambridge graduate, and who knows what else. Oliver had already called some people he knew at the BBC, but they could only be the first links in a chain of contacts that he hoped would take him back to those days in the sixties and seventies, when a "story on the wireless" meant fifteen breathless minutes in front of the radio, not a snippet of vacuous celebrity chat slurped up in a Starbucks Wi-Fi hotspot. As one child famously said, the best thing about a story on the radio is that the pictures are better.

So let this be our little family secret.

A family matter, then. Had Breedlove ever been married? Did he have any children? Not according to the basic reference books or Wikipedia. Or was it the blackmail itself that was presented as a perverted family secret, the blackmailer obscenely claiming the kinship of shared, clandestine knowledge with a man whose Unclehood was universal, more than kith, less than kind?

Or both—maybe the blackmailer was a long-lost family member with a grudge, a black sheep, a skeleton in Dennis's closet, returning to haunt…who? His deadbeat Dad? His unwitting birth father? His wicked uncle? *(And why "his," Ollie, not "her"?)* Hidden history, silenced for a while in a blessed plot, a private plot.

Oliver sneezed. Humfrey, privately glad of the distraction, glared at him.

I won't tell if you won't tell. Alas, my silence isn't free. There will be further communications.

But there won't be now. Dead end.

"Enjoying the play?"

Mallard slid into the seat behind him. Oliver quickly slipped the index card and page into his satchel. The action on the stage had resumed, Humfrey having persuaded Hamlet that Shakespeare was probably thinking of some sort of torpedo or underwater spear gun.

"Humfrey's original idea was to do a silent version," Mallard whispered. "The actors would just mouth the words."

"Dumb show," Oliver commented.

"Indeed. But then he changed his concept and decided that everything in the play happens in Hamlet's imagination."

As if to illustrate, Hamlet had reached the phrase "Ay, there's the rub," and Ophelia was suiting the action to the word, in sweaty haste.

"The murder, the ghost, the incestuous marriage—all in the mind's eye," Mallard added. "Claudius is actually Hamlet's real father, not his uncle."

"So Hamlet thinks he's Claudius's nephew, but he's really his son?"

"And there, but for the grace of God, goes Tim Mallard. Only I'm merely your uncle-in-law, hyphenated."

"Whom do you play?"

"Polonius. I'm also Osric and the gravedigger."

"Is that also essential to Humfrey's interpretation?"

"No, it's because we don't have enough actors in the company. The budget's so tight, we can't even afford a real skull for Yorick in the graveyard scene, just some Styrofoam concoction that's gradually turning into confetti."

"Alas, poor Uncle Tim," muttered Oliver.

Hamlet now got to "with a bare bodkin" and the two men chose to look away.

"Where's Effie?" Mallard asked.

"Out with Ben. He's photographing Cotswold wool churches, and she's carrying his tripod."

"That's what the kids are calling it today, eh?" Mallard looked up at the grunting and sweating on the stage, winced, and began to study his lines in his Penguin edition of the play.

Oliver had welcomed Effie's decision to spend the afternoon with his handsome friend without a flicker of jealousy. It gave him a chance to think about the suicide and her a chance to drive along winding country lanes in a Lamborghini Gallardo, Ben's hesitant reward for her assistance.

Effie would not have been the best company anyway. She was still smarting from her treatment at the ten hands of the Bennet sisters. As they'd driven home from Pigsneye the previous evening, Ben piloting Effie's Renault, Oliver sitting nervously beside him, she had launched into an inebriated recount of all the slights she'd received at the dinner party, delivered from a prone position in the back seat, pausing only to demand they stop so she could be sick in a hedgerow.

"I'm sorry, Ollie," she had slurred as they drove off again, "I know the Bennet harpies are your friends, but really, they're about as much use as a chocolate condom."

"They're not my friends. They're friends of the family. It's not as if I particularly enjoy being thus Bennetted round at these supper parties."

"Don't you mean 'supper potties'?" Effie snapped, copying the Bennets' starchy pronunciation. "Appropriate term 'potties,' considering they serve up shit. I'd sooner eat a crocodile. Potties!" Repeating the word several times seemed to distract her for a second.

"I thought snobettes like that had died out with girdles and rationing," she continued. She assumed a voice that sounded more like the Queen sucking a mint than any of the Bennet girls. "'Oh, Effie, didn't you go to U-ni-ver-si-ty? Then I suppose I'd better talk very slowly.' Well, screw them." She hiccupped.

"They didn't go to university either," Oliver said. "Davina claims an affinity with Oxford because she attended a posh secretarial college near the city. She only lasted two months. She flunked greeting. The others went to an overpriced Swiss finishing school."

"I'd finish them. I'd push them off an Alp." She found her comment amusing and abruptly dissolved into giggles.

"That was funny, Eff," said Ben, speaking for the first time since leaving the Bennets' house. He'd been covering his discomfort at the lovers' quarrel by peering intently through the windshield as he drove, as if terrified that the car's headlights might suddenly illuminate a stegosaurus in the road ahead.

"And as for you," Effie snapped, pulling herself upright and prodding the back of Ben's neck, "what's all this crap about 'haven't I seen you somewhere before'? Isn't that hoary old pickup line permanently retired by now? Call yourself a player, Benjamin Motley?"

"But it was true," Ben protested. "Their faces were familiar. All of them. Don't forget, I do a lot of portrait photography—I have a good memory for faces, and those Bennet faces were, uh, distinctive. I've never shot them myself…"

"Just lend me one of those Purdeys," Effie muttered.

"…but I may have seen them in the 'Bystander' section of *Tatler* or in some other society magazine. Recently. I can't remember where."

He swerved rapidly, as a van overtook them and held a position just a few yards ahead, straddling the middle of the narrow road. The passenger-side window was wound down, and Eric Mormal's naked buttocks emerged from the interior, white and spotty in the Renault's beams. Then the van sped away into the night.

Oliver turned to Ben. "I suppose you're going to say that was a familiar face, too."

Ben frowned. "As a matter of fact…"

Back in Oliver's bedroom, Effie tossed her sundress into a corner and clambered into bed in her white underwear, lying as far from Oliver as she could, her back turned to him.

"Maybe I just don't belong in your privileged world, Ollie," she had said, her voice half stifled by her pillow, long after he thought she had passed out.

"Privileged?" he repeated, staring into the darkness. "I wasn't to the manner born. My father was an army officer all his life. And until she met him, my mother was an impoverished stage performer."

"Are you going to tell me the one about the Actress and the Brigadier? Because I could use a laugh."

He smiled. "He was only a captain then. It's a sweet story. My mother and Aunt Phoebe, being identical twins and also fairly limber, were working for a conjuror. They could do all kinds of teleportation fakes—you know, the same girl disappears from the cramped box on stage and pops up two seconds later in the back of the auditorium. But they could never let the audience know there were two of them, which meant that whenever they were on tour, one sister had to travel in disguise. Well, about thirty years ago, they were part of a Combined Services Entertainment show that came through Cyprus, where Captain Robert Swithin was stationed. The night they met, it was Chloe's turn to take the bow and fraternize with the officers in the mess, while Phoebe had to hide in the hotel room. Otherwise, history could have been very different. Mother and Father got married in a double wedding, with Phoebe and Tim, who'd had a whirlwind romance that still seems to be going on. I arrived on their first wedding anniversary. They bought this old house with their savings and a moderate mortgage when Bob retired. Eve, Toby, and I never went to private schools or anything like that."

"Not even a Fish Swinish-ing school?"

Oliver laughed in the dark at the swinish phrase. "Do you know where the Bennet money comes from? The girls' grandfather patented a particularly effective and disturbingly appetizing laxative. They tend to keep quiet about that."

Effie was silent for a while. "The thing that bothers me, Ollie, is this," she continued sleepily, "when the passion wears off, what will we have to talk about?"

Oliver had slipped from the bed early, leaving her gently snoring, oblivious to the single tolling bell summoning the few churchgoing Synners to St. Edmund and St. Crispin. He started making his phone calls about Dennis Breedlove, apologizing to old college friends with BBC connections or fellow authors from the Sanders Club for disturbing their Sunday morning. Effie had appeared much later, moving cautiously through the kitchen, sucking on a hot and full cup of coffee and allowing him a weak smile of greeting.

He was irritated to hear that he had missed Mallard, whose Jaguar had sped away before breakfast, heading for an all-day rehearsal. So after Effie had left with Ben, he was forced to accept a ride to Stratford with Toby in the Co-op farm delivery van that Eric Mormal drove, squashed onto the front bench between the two men because the rear compartment was full of organic burdock and unable to forget that Mormal had dropped his trousers in the same place twelve hours earlier. They deposited Oliver at the theater before heading off to the dig.

"Neither Effie nor Simon Culpepper think Dennis Breedlove could have been killed by his blackmailer," Oliver said to Mallard. "What do you think?"

Mallard looked up from his book. "Are we back to that? Ollie, Breedlove committed suicide. Didn't Culpepper convince you of that?"

"He convinced me that Uncle Dennis had a motive for taking his life, although there was no suicide note. But I still don't think Dennis could have done it without some assistance."

"Blackmailers aren't murderers. They threaten exposure, not death."

This one is, in my book, Oliver thought. Aloud, he asked, "What if Dennis had threatened to go to the police instead of paying up?"

"Blackmailers assume their victims want to keep their secrets. But just in case, they typically don't reveal their identities until they've hooked their victim. Culpepper showed you that letter. Was there anything that indicated who the writer was?"

"I don't remember."

"No? Then why don't you check that copy you have hidden in your bag."

"Lovely, darlings, lovely," cried Humfrey Fingerhood, leaping from his seat and applauding the post-coital actors lying in a fleshy heap on the stage. "Ophelia, nice baring of your fardels, but put them away now, dear. Now, while watching you, I've had the most wonderful idea. I want to do the whole speech as a PowerPoint presentation…"

Mallard scribbled a name and telephone number on a page in his notebook, which he tore out and handed to Oliver.

"If you want to know about blackmail, call this number," he said, standing up and sidling out of the row.

Chapter Seven

Monday morning

Unlike the aloofness of most classical busts, the famous stone heads outside Wren's Sheldonian Theatre in Oxford—Roman emperors, according to Max Beerbohm, their eyes like pitted olives—glare around with undisguised scorn. And for well over a hundred years, the principal object of their goggling disdain has been St. Basil's College, facing them across Broad Street, snuggled between Trinity College and the New Bodleian Library.

The bells of the city were striking eleven as Oliver strode into the nondescript main entrance to St. Baz's, stepping around a cluster of students who were attempting to disentangle the knotted and combined locks that tethered their bicycles to the college railings. After a brief conversation in the murky porter's lodge with a talking white beard, behind which traces of a human face could just be made out, he scurried around the main quadrangle to an archway in the far corner. Painted on a board was the name Mallard had scribbled down for him: Dr. McCaw. Oliver clumped up the wooden staircase to the third floor and tapped on the double door to Dr. McCaw's room.

A hand immediately shot out, passing him an electric kettle.

"Fill this up in the toilet down the hall, there's a dear. It's just you, is it?"

Oliver confirmed that he was alone, although with a stab of guilt as he recalled Effie's look of surprise when he'd told her that he wouldn't be joining the household jaunt to Warwick Castle because of a business meeting in Oxford. But he knew he couldn't bring her with him or even reveal the true purpose of the outing. Effie had made it clear that she was required to leave the Breedlove case to Simon Culpepper and the Warwickshire CID—a protocol that Mallard clearly shared, although the brief consultation with his uncle the previous day had at least led to today's appointment.

He returned to the room. Dr. Hyacinthe McCaw took the kettle and motioned him to sit down on the room's only sofa. She was a short, sturdy woman, probably in her eighties, wearing a garment that was either a high-quality floral housecoat or a low-quality floral dress. She had a tangle of long, gray curls gathered loosely on top of her head that seemed in permanent danger of slipping off, whether or not they were actually rooted in her scalp. Her eyes were also gray and bright in a pleasant, remarkably unlined face.

"I'm old enough to remember Uncle Dennis on the radio," she said, looking over the text of the blackmailer's letter. "A shame his life had to end this way. There was no suicide note?"

"No."

"Is it possible that the blackmailer got wind of the death and broke into Dennis's home to remove such a note, in case it named him or her?"

"Then he or she would have taken the blackmail letter, too, surely. It was open on the desk, in full view."

Dr. McCaw nodded and reached up to adjust the pile of hair, which was threatening to spill over into her face.

"Well, since this is clearly the first message Dennis received, there's precious little to identify the writer. In my opinion, this was composed by a professional, someone who's blackmailed before. An amateur would get to the demands sooner. So I'd focus on the recipient. What can you tell me about the late Uncle Dennis?"

"He lived a blameless life for thirty years, on his own in a tiny Cotswold village," Oliver said with a shrug.

"Wasn't it Agatha Christie who said there was more evil in a country village than in the whole City of London?" She handed him a mug of tea.

"Then Sir Arthur Conan Doyle beat her to it: 'The lowest and vilest alleys of London do not present a more dreadful record of sin than does the smiling and beautiful countryside.' That's Sherlock, in *The Copper Beeches.*"

"You *are* Tim's nephew," McCaw said, with a smile. "So what about the dreadful record of Synne?"

"If Dennis had misbehaved since he moved to the village, everyone would know. Especially my mother."

"Then you need to go back further. Much further, from the tone of the letter—'history,' 'the past.' What about this 'family secret' reference? Do you know much about his early life, his relatives?"

"I'd imagine the older the secret, the deeper it must be buried."

"It may not be as hard to uncover as you think. Foul deeds will rise. Blackmail victims are often the last people to realize their well-tended secrets are, in fact, common knowledge."

"Then if I'm looking into the dark recesses of Dennis Breedlove's early days, where do you think I should point my flashlight?"

Dr. McCaw thought for a moment.

"Sex," she stated.

"Sex. Why?"

"Because whatever happened in the past still bothered Breedlove to this day, to put it mildly. And sex is the only thing the British fixate on forever. A life of crime? We love a reformed wrong 'un. Financial shenanigans? Name an MP who hasn't fiddled his expenses but still parks his arse on the green leather of the House of Commons. Drugs, alcohol? Everybody adores a reformed hell-raiser. Shame, where is thy blush? No, for the British, sex and blackmail go together like the Lion and the Unicorn. You'll always remember the front-page peccadilloes of John Profumo and that lovely Hugh Grant."

She took a sip of tea. "It doesn't apply to the Europeans," she continued. "They have an adult acceptance of sexual mores. The American attitude to sex, on the other hand, is positively infantile. But the British, as in so many things, are bang in the middle. They stay mired in their adolescence. They can't stop thinking about sex, but they never get it right. That's why the British can be funnier about their sex lives than any other nation."

Oliver took this in, gazing at McCaw's bookshelves. On the subject of the British, she had been disturbingly close to home. Although the room he and Effie were sharing in Synne, sanctified by his mother as Oliver's Room, bore no sentimental value for him, it was still his furtive ambition to carve at least one notch on the figurative bedpost of his late-teenage-years bed. Effie had been in better spirits the previous evening, so Oliver tentatively tried to resume the lovemaking that had been deferred since the Mallards' arrival in the Shakespeare Race, two eventful nights earlier. He was starting to stroke Effie's stomach, wondering whether to let his hand drift north or south, when a vixen's blood-curdling screech from a nearby garden caused him to yell involuntarily, setting off a fit of laughter from Effie that completely destroyed the mood.

Well, there was always tonight. But what role had sex played in Dennis Breedlove's life? Surely none that would cause him, at the age of eighty, to kill himself at the first hint of exposure? And why are Dr. McCaw's books all upside down?

He blinked and looked again. And then he realized they were French books, novels mainly, the lettering on the spine running bottom to top, according to French publishing practice. When scanning a bookshelf, the French reader's head tilts appropriately to the left.

"You like French literature, I see," he remarked, drinking his tea.

A puzzled expression crossed her face. "I should hope so, dear, since I teach it. My mother was French—my first name is pronounced the French way. Nobody gets it the first time."

"But I gathered from my uncle that you're an expert on blackmail," Oliver stammered.

"*C'est bien vrai.*"

"So I assumed you'd be a fellow in Law or maybe a Psychology lecturer, with a specialty in criminology or something."

She shook her head, gazing at him with amusement.

"Then may I ask how you know so much about blackmail?" he persisted.

"Because I'm a blackmailer. Or I used to be, until your uncle arrested me for the first and last time."

"Good heavens!"

"Ah, he didn't mention that? Well, it's ancient history now, of course. Tim Mallard helped me see the error of my ways. Bit of a quid pro quo, you see. Or in my case, fifty quid pro quo, which was how much I was collecting each month from a fellow of Oriel. His shameful lust for one of the more sensitive male undergraduates in his tutorial group turned out, unbeknownst to *moi*, to have played a peripheral role in a particularly tricky murder. Timmy was only an inspector in those days, quite a dashing *flic*, but too fond of his wife, alas. In gratitude for my assistance, he dropped the charges, as long as I promised to go straight."

She took another gulp from the mug of cooling tea. "Rather a pity," she continued. "The pickings had been fat around these parts. Before the Berlin Wall came down, I made several thousand pounds off a nervous New College don whose affection for the Soviet regime had been bruited around the bathhouses for decades."

Oliver smiled, making a mental note to take some revenge upon Mallard for not warning him.

"Still, I was going to retire anyway," McCaw continued.

"Guilty conscience?"

"Dwindling opportunities, *mon cher*. You see, nobody's ashamed of anything these days. When I started, I could hide in the bushes on Hampstead Heath with a torch and a notebook, and come up trumps every time. Today, ambitious young political hopefuls are clamoring for *Private Eye* to find out about their experiments in Eton dormitories, in hopes it'll lead to a cabinet position. Our indiscretions sometimes serve us well. There's a glamour in having a past. The aging pop star on the talk show who announces he's been sober and clean for all of three days now gets a standing ovation, while the poor schmo who's never touched the stuff in his life is dismissed as a prude. Perhaps they're the ones I should target."

There was a hesitant tap on the door. She opened it. A trio of female students was waiting nervously on the landing, clutching essays and textbooks.

"Any last suggestion as to where I start?" Oliver asked her quietly as the young women filed past him into the room.

"Remember the 'family secret,'" she said. "Go to the funeral. Watch the mourners. *A bientôt.*"

Chapter Eight

Tuesday morning

"At least he picked a nice day for it," said Chloe Swithin. She and her son were standing outside the Church of St. Edmund and St. Crispin, half an hour early for Dennis Breedlove's funeral.

"I don't think the weather has much to do with this unseemly rush to put him six feet under," Oliver said, slipping a finger inside his tight shirt collar.

"Oh, there are plenty of countries that would bury a stiff much earlier than this. Especially as you get closer to the equator. It's the heat. They tend to go off sooner."

"Thanks for the mental image."

Oliver had returned from Oxford to discover that the funeral Dr. McCaw had just ordered him to attend was scheduled for the next morning. Detective Sergeant Culpepper had traced Breedlove's only remaining relatives to Hull, and when the vicar had called to them to make arrangements, they had insisted on a quick funeral and burial. Edwards the Concessor's attempt to gain a little more leeway only succeeded in getting the service moved up from Thursday to Tuesday, leaving Oliver no time to fetch his best (and only) suit from London. Forced to rob the sartorial grave that was his old Synne wardrobe, he had come up with a pair of gray flannels and his last school blazer. Toby had lent him a white shirt that was a collar size too small. At least the fashion-conscious Ben wasn't there to despair of him—he had headed back to London earlier that morning.

Oliver had persuaded Chloe to come early and wait with him by the church's Norman doorway. He was following Dr. McCaw's instructions, but he needed his mother's help to identify the mourners.

"Do you think this could be a relative?" he asked. A man had come into sight, walking briskly toward the church, humming quietly and wiggling the fingers of his right hand in time with his private music.

"No, that's Sidney Weguelin, the church organist," Chloe told him. "He's one of us, moved here a couple of years back."

Weguelin reached them, and Chloe introduced Oliver.

"My wife mentioned that she'd bumped into you the other day," Weguelin said, addressing Oliver as he shook hands, rather limply. Odd to think that those flaccid fingers would be powerful enough for toccatas and fugues. He mentioned a wife? Oh, yes, Lesbia, the straight-faced verger of St. Edmund and St. Crispin, she of the black plastic specs and artificial-looking bob.

One of Mallard's former sergeants, now Detective Inspector Welkin, had the peculiar trait that he always reminded people of somebody they knew; Sidney Weguelin had the same effect on Oliver now, although he'd surely have remembered who else possessed poorly cut, crinkly hair and a fussy moustache and goatee. Weguelin's beaklike nose supported unfashionable gold-rimmed spectacles. Oliver always thought too much facial hair was a mistake for the habitual wearer of glasses. It gave a cluttered impression. Even his uncle's disreputable white moustache was pushing the limits. And since most beards are cultivated to disguise a plurality of chins, Weguelin's decision to grow hair on a well-etched jawline seemed even more regrettable.

"He and his good lady must make a strange-looking pair," Oliver commented, after the organist had passed into the church, trading the warm spring sunshine for the chilly interior of the sixteenth-century nave. More people were coming along the lane.

A red sports car threaded its way around the pedestrians and stopped close to the lych-gate, crushing an orange bollard that marked a parking space for the expected hearse. A tall, middle-aged man vaulted nimbly from the seat and, to Oliver's irritation, failed to fall onto his face. The man wore his elegant dark suit and silk tie as if it were a second skin and the funeral an afterthought.

"He's cute, in a rich, well-tailored sort of way," said Chloe. "Which, when you think about it is the best way. I don't know him, though."

"I do," said Oliver, and switched on his most insincere smile. "Mr. Scroop," he cried, as the man strode toward them. "Fancy you making any kind of effort whatsoever to be here!"

Scroop returned a smile of the same quality. "Oh hello, Swithin," he drawled. "I heard these were the very sticks from which you hailed. I have traveled the considerable distance from London—geographically and socially—as the delegate of the Sanders Club, since nobody in the club could conceivably trust you to represent them."

Scroop paused to scrutinize the Latin motto on the breast pocket of Oliver's shabby blazer. He shuddered. "You're lucky I'm here," he continued. "I'm of a class that generally expects more than a nanosecond's notice of a burial. I always associated indecent haste with country weddings, not funerals." It occurred to him that Oliver had a female companion, and his tone softened.

"But my dear Oliver, aren't you going to introduce me to your sister?" he crooned. "You are so remiss in your manners, young man—this isn't the first time I've had to scold you."

Oliver sighed. "Mother, this is Mr. Scroop, who writes books. You won't have heard of him. Mr. Scroop, my mother, *Mrs.* Chloe Swithin, the former Miss Winsbury."

Chloe beamed broadly while Scroop lifted her hand to his lips.

"Ah, Mrs. Swithin," he crooned, "such a joy to meet the only person poor Oliver can count on to read his, uh, works, I suppose I should call them. You do read his books about our woodland chums, I'm sure."

"Oh yes," Chloe replied. "I've read them all. At least I've read one of them. That's the same thing." She withdrew her hand from Scroop's grasp to swat furtively at Oliver, who had pinched her. The top button of Oliver's shirt snapped off and skittered across the paving stones.

"A sad occasion for such a delightful encounter, dear lady," said Scroop. "Frankly, most of us in the club were surprised the old sod was still alive. Dennis told me once, many moons ago, that he'd never expected to make it past seventy-five, so he'd planned all his pensions and annuities to run out five years ago. Goodness knows what he's been living on. Country air and the beauty of his neighbors, I presume." He bowed slightly to Chloe, ignored Oliver, and strutted into the church, stooping unnecessarily in the doorway to imply that he was even taller than his six-foot stature.

"He's very charming," Chloe said, smoothing her close-cropped gray hair, but Oliver's mind was on other matters. If Dennis was out of money, how could he pay a blackmailer? Was that why self-slaughter was his only option when he opened that letter, even before he knew the amount of the vig? Could have been dead for a ducat.

More people were following Scroop into the church, all Synne residents, identified by Chloe:

"Woman who runs the village post office, lesbian but not in a way that would interest you…

"Local gynecologist, also village peeping Tom—well, one of them…

"Retired PR guru, tried to boost Synne's profile by renaming it 'Synne!' Came up with the slogan 'It's the end of the Wold as we know it.'

"Relic of the sixties satire boom. Famous for not being famous. Claims he's the Ninth Python and the Fourteenth Beatle…"

From inside the church, Sidney Weguelin began a meandering improvisation on the organ. Oliver noticed the same small, elderly man he'd seen stepping out of the village shop on Saturday, now observing the church from the other side of the lane. Where had he seen him before?

"Who's that one?"

"What one?"

"The man standing in the street. I know him from somewhere."

Chloe peered across the lane, but the man was gone.

"I didn't see anyone," she said with a shrug.

The arrivals continued, including Davina Bennet as the representative of her clan, accompanied by vulgarian Eric Mormal. A stout woman in her early forties followed them and nodded to Chloe.

"Maudie Purifoy," Chloe whispered. "Art dealer, late-in-life single mother, convinced her only son is a four-year-old genius. One of these women who uses the phrase 'who is gifted' all the time, as if it's the kid's middle name. You know: 'My son, Hugo, who is gifted…Hugo Who Is Gifted…' Never had that problem with my kids. She's in the vicar's writers' group—she's trying to get Hugo W.I.G. to dictate his memoirs."

"Writers' group?"

"A handful of locals, all working on some book or other, meet in the vicarage once a month to critique each other's work. Very exclusive."

The party from the Swithin house came into view over the churchyard wall…Bob striding ahead, Tim and Phoebe Mallard walking with Effie, who'd borrowed a simple black dress from Eve Swithin's closet, and Toby bringing up the rear staring at Effie's. A hearse was also approaching, drifting slowly along the narrow lane, followed by a large, black limousine.

"Hey, there's an idea," said Chloe. "You're a visiting author. Get the vicar to invite you to talk to the group. I think there's a meeting this week."

"Well…"

"Go on, they'd be all over you. Just tell Mr. Edwards you've heard about their activities and you'd like to join in for an evening. He'll be tickled pink, but being him, he'll make it sound like he doesn't want you there at first. Tell him you know what it's all about and that you'd really like to see what they're doing.

Oh, Ollie, it'll be good for you—everyone likes an audience. Effie can spare you for a while, I'm sure."

"I'm certainly getting used to it," Effie said as she reached them. She slipped her hand into the crook of Oliver's arm. He squeezed it with his other hand, but he was watching the limousine, now disgorging the distant kin of Uncle Dennis: a couple of older women, closing in on Dennis's age, whose permed, thinning white hair, blue plastic glasses, frowns, and plain Marks & Spencer raincoats made up the uniform of their years; a middle-aged married couple, the portly husband uncomfortable in his suit, the bony wife uncomfortable in her life; and a slew of their overweight, unruly children, whom the couple succeeded in ignoring almost as expertly as they ignored each other.

The visitors wore their dissatisfaction with the world almost like a proud campaign medal. Were these the guardians of the Breedlove family secret, the insiders to the blessed plot? Was the haste over the funeral just their impatience to find out what was in Uncle Dennis's will—not much, if Scroop is to be believed?

"We'd better go in," said Chloe, as the relatives formed a loose knot behind the coffin. The Reverend Mr. Edwards himself, cassocked and surpliced, passed them in the opposite direction and stepped out into the sunlight to greet the funeral party.

The Swithin family found an empty pew near the middle of the church, giving Oliver a good view of the thirteenth-century doom painting above the altar, a well-preserved decoration that had been carried over to the current building from its Norman predecessor. An emaciated, mildew-stained Christ sat enthroned on judgment day, flanked by the kneeling images of his mother and the Apostle John. Scattered below them were the naked figures of the judged, rising from graves and either being led by angels into a celestial city or getting tortured and devoured by demons. It could have been a scene from a television talent show.

Given that most artists of the day worked for religious orders, Oliver was always intrigued by how frequently their holy subjects gave them an excuse to conjure gruesome images of blood-drenched torment for the damned, plus some well-drawn derrieres. Sex and violence on the church wall, the medieval equivalent of late-night TV. The artistry made him think again of Effie's athletic posterior, moving ahead of him in the moonlight on Synne Common, or as he'd last seen it that morning when she was wandering unselfconsciously through the bedroom, wearing only a tight pink t-shirt.

The previous evening had been yet another sexual washout. Effie was clearly still chafing from his absence during the day, so to help the atmosphere, Oliver had found a radio station playing romantic songs that he'd left on at bedtime. The kissing and casual stroking stage was promising, and he was about to make the next move when the program broke for a news broadcast, ushering in reports of a flood in Bangladesh, wildfires in California, and National Health Service waiting lists for hernia operations. He leaped from the bed and groped in the dark for the radio's off-switch, overturning the bedside lamp and spilling a glass of water over his side of the duvet. But by then, the bounce had gone out of their bungee.

The congregation in the church rose, and Uncle Dennis himself made the slow journey down the nave behind the vicar, who was holding a lit candle. The coffin was placed on wooden trestles, and the Breedlove relatives sidled into a reserved pew in front of the altar rail. Two of the children began a pillow fight with hassocks.

The vicar carried it off well. After prayers and a hymn, he delivered a brief address, making just two approving references to the ancient habit of burying suicides at a crossroads and ignoring the moment when an entire bag of candies spilled out of the front pew, although he did glower slightly as the unmistakable aroma of a McDonalds Happy Meal started to spread through the church. Whoever had briefed him on Dennis Breedlove's life had covered all the salient points that Oliver already knew, but added nothing fresh.

Oliver gazed around the nave. The relatives were too far forward to see their faces, but Breedlove's neighbors showed a mix of solemnity, boredom, and slight amusement. Even

Oliver's mother and her sister wore identical faint smiles, as if contemplating the late author's heavenly reward. Assuming, that is, he qualified for the next round, eschatologically. Nobody was weeping, although Toby would win the prize for the saddest expression.

The service continued, brief, with no eulogies or tributes. After a final series of prayers, the vicar took up a position at the far end of the coffin.

"Lord, now lettest thou thy servant depart in peace…" Edwards began.

There was an odd noise from the opposite end of the church, like a snappish release of compressed air coming from the vicinity of the font. In the solemnity of the moment, nobody dared move. Edwards glared at something and began again.

"Lord, now lettest thou thy servant depart *in peace*," he repeated, but the sound came again—somebody trying to attract his attention with a loud "pssst."

The mourners began to look for the source. An elderly man was tiptoeing slowly down the aisle, adopting that hunched gait that people think makes them invisible, even after fifty pairs of eyes had fallen upon him. He was wearing old, worn clothes, and his trousers were stained with mud.

"Not the best time, Mr. Sowerbutts," said the vicar through clenched teeth, as if, in his turn, a semblance of ventriloquism might persuade the congregation that he hadn't really spoken.

"Sowerbutts, the sexton," Chloe whispered into Oliver's ear.

"Sorry, your worship," said Sowerbutts, stopping in the center of the church. He had removed his cap and was nervously kneading it in both hands. "But would I be right in thinking you're going to stick him in the ground right away?"

It was the genuine local accent of Synne. Shakespeare would have spoken like Sowerbutts—Stratford Will, anyway.

"We are proceeding immediately to the committal, yes," said the vicar firmly, with a glance of apology toward the relatives' pew. A small female occupant said "penis" to him and dissolved into chuckles.

"Ah," confirmed the sexton, but stayed where he was. He smacked his lips. "Any chance of a bit of delay, vicar?"

"A bit of a delay?"

"Well, he's not in a hurry, is he?" Sowerbutts nodded toward the coffin. There were some mild, controlled sniggers. Edwards took a step toward the sexton, but skidded on a candy.

"Is there a problem, Mr. Sowerbutts?"

"I told you, your reverence. It's the grave."

"The grave? What's the matter with the grave?"

"Well, it was fine last night, sir."

Most of the congregation had now given up all attempts to preserve the solemnity of the occasion. Many were pressing handkerchiefs to their mouths.

"I haven't been drinking, your grace," protested the sexton. Some mourners broke into open laughter. Davina Bennet took out her iPhone and began to text rapidly.

Edwards tried to exert some priestly authority by clapping his hand several times. The small children in the family pew picked up the cue and burst into applause, which didn't cover the noise of a beer can being opened by their father.

"But you did dig the grave, Mr. Sowerbutts?" Edwards resumed wearily.

"Oh, yes, I dug it all right, your grace."

"Splendid."

"Ah, but where is it now?" Sowerbutts tapped the end of his nose and winked at his audience.

"What?"

"Old Mr. Breedlove's grave, vicar. Where is it now?"

"Well, where you left it, you idiot!" yelled Edwards, immediately followed by a guilty glance across his shoulder at the picture of Christ in judgment. But the damage was done—every new utterance was now greeted as raucously as if the event were an Eddie Izzard stand-up. Even the sexton's name was a cause of joy with each repetition. Some mourners were leaning against each other in helpless mirth. Maudie Purifoy hastily exited her pew and headed for the church toilet.

Well, thought Oliver, they're weeping at last. Like Niobe, all tears.

"That's just it, your highness," Sowerbutts resumed. "It's gone."

"Gone?" Edwards shrieked.

"Yes, squire. Somebody's stolen it."

Chapter Nine

Tuesday morning (continued)

"Do you think I should call the police, Superintendent Mallard?" Edwards asked nervously. "Officially, I mean. Though I hate to bother Constable Bostar. He gets so cross if you disturb him during his soap operas."

"If you think about a freshly dug grave," pondered Mallard, contemplating the intended site of Dennis Breedlove's last resting place, "it's not a thing." He thrust his hands into his trouser pockets and jingled the loose change. "It's an absence. A hole. Somebody stole a hole. And I'm not at all sure that particular fault is a crime."

"A bit like the Grand Canyon," Oliver offered.

"You can't steal the Grand Canyon."

"No, but every year, millions of tourists trek out to Arizona to see a big, long, deep hole. They don't go there because of what's there, but because of what's not there that should most decidedly be there. A pregnant negative, as Toby would say. Like the curious case of the dog in the nighttime."

Mallard shot him an exasperated glance. "Now, if the earth taken out of the grave had been stolen, you might have a crime," he continued, philosophically. "But there it is."

The three men stared at the pile of soil that Sowerbutts had deposited, a yard or so from the original hole. The hole itself was plainly outlined, a long oblong surrounded by grass, but it had been filled to the brim with dark earth.

When it became clear that the funeral could not continue, Edwards had rapidly blessed the congregation and asked some of his less judgmental parishioners to escort the Hull contingent to one of the village pubs for lunch. Most of the churchgoers had staggered gleefully back to their homes at the same time, leaving Dennis Breedlove's remains alone in the nave. Effie had chosen to walk back with the Swithins.

It was obvious to Mallard what had happened. The way to the grave was an overgrown, brambly path that weaved between the tombstones, tricky for the pallbearers, even harder for a half-dozen trips with a wheelbarrow full of damp earth, and besides, there were no fresh wheel tracks through the grass. But the gravesite was next to the low drystone wall that surrounded the churchyard. If a lorry or tractor had pulled up on the other side, it would have been fairly simple for one or two men to shovel the dirt over the low wall and into the open grave. A clump of dense bushes would have hidden them from the lane.

"A practical joke, I suppose," Edwards remarked. "Someone with an antic disposition. Like those fellows who make crop circles with a plank of wood and hope we'll think they're landing strips for flying saucers. Although there's no reason why a believer should pooh-pooh the possibility of alien visitors outright. There are more things in heaven and earth, as it were, and in fact some people believe the shining angel messengers mentioned in our New Testament are actually men in spacesuits—"

"I'd get your sexton to dig it out again," Mallard cut in. He knew the vicar's conversational style. "Then you can get the burial done before Breedlove's people go back to Hull or Hell, whichever they hail from."

Mallard and Oliver turned away from the grave, or lack thereof, and walked back toward the church. "Well?" Oliver said, once the vicar was out of earshot.

Mallard shrugged without stopping or looking back. "A prank, like the vicar said. Half of the village was here. Great audience. Put the 'fun' in 'funeral.'"

"You don't believe that. If it's a practical joke, why not just dump back the dirt that Sowerbutts dug out? There's more to this. We have a man being blackmailed with a letter that mentions plots and digging up the past. And now here's a plot—*his* plot, his private plot—that's been dug over. Coincidence?"

"They do occur."

"Oh, come on, Uncle Tim. It's evidently a message of some kind. Someone has unfinished business with Dennis Breedlove, which didn't end with his death."

"So you say."

"You don't think the blackmailer's still on the scene? You don't think that's who filled up the grave last night, after old Sowerbutts had gone? You don't think he was sitting in that church, enjoying the mirth in funeral with the rest of us?"

Mallard halted. "Ollie, I have no idea," he said. "And I'm really not concerned. Just because you're bored witless out here in the wilds of Warwickshire, you don't have to drag everyone else into your private fantasies. And incidentally, Hyacinthe McCaw would tell you that a thwarted blackmailer would be too wary and just too bloody embarrassed to turn up at the burial of a victim."

"If you're not concerned, why did you send me to Dr. McCaw?"

"So she could convince you that it's impossible to identify the blackmailer from the text of that first letter."

"Then Dennis's killer gets away with it?"

"Dennis killed himself!" spluttered Mallard.

"So you say."

Mallard took a deep breath and perched on a tilted headstone. "My dear nephew," he continued, plucking burrs from his trousers, "you knew the victim only slightly, you happened to discover his body. That's not enough to spur any dull revenge. Leave the investigation to the excellent Sergeant Culpepper and pay attention to poor Effie instead."

"Effie?"

"She's taken more than a week of her precious holiday entitlement to be with your family, and so far, you seem to have arranged an evening of abuse and embarrassment, left her for two days in the company of an unnecessarily handsome houseguest, and then treated her to a funeral. Not much joy for her."

Oliver realized with sudden dismay that his uncle was right. Poor Effie. "I could take her somewhere nice after lunch," he ventured, after a moment's contemplation.

"She told me she's never been to Stratford-upon-Avon."

"Then I'll show her the sights! The Birthplace. Hall's Croft. Holy Trinity. And we can take a look at Toby's dig."

"You might want to come by the theater. We're rehearsing again this afternoon."

"And have Effie witness the filth that I saw yesterday?"

Mallard laughed. "Oh, Humfrey changed his whole conception of the play again. It now takes place in a nunnery and we're performing it backwards. But you're probably right to skip the rehearsals. Save your applause for Saturday, the big night."

He walked away, not knowing that he had been entirely wrong about the blackmailer's presence at the funeral.

Oliver stood thoughtfully, looking at a double coil of blue columbine that cricked its way up the rusty railings enclosing a ancient chest tomb. (Were the spikes on top to keep intruders out or occupants in?) Yes, he needed to nurture Effie. And there was still the spotless reputation of his teenage bedroom to be besmirched. He sneezed four times.

"Bless you," said the vicar. Oliver hadn't heard his approaching footsteps, muffled in the long grass. "That was in my secular capacity," Edwards continued affably, as they began to walk together toward the church. "The habit of blessing the sneezer probably comes from the superstition that a sneeze can release one's soul into the air and leave it prey to evil spirits. But popular tradition insists on linking it to the bubonic plague. The same misguided belief applies to the children's rhyme 'Ring a Ring o' Roses'—'Ring Around the Rosie,' as they call it in America, but

then they call the 'Hokey Cokey' the 'Hokey Pokey,' so what's
that all about? Sneezes were never especially symptomatic of
the plague, and many variants of the rhyme don't include the
words 'a-tish-oo.'"

Oliver made a mental note to include this misconception in
his book. "Dennis Breedlove wrote an entire book debunking
the myth about 'Ring a Ring o' Roses' and the Black Death,"
he commented.

"That's where I got my information. He and I used to have
some great chats. Ah, Dennis—we have done but greenly in
hugger-mugger to inter him."

"Do you know much about Dennis's life before he came to
Synne?" Oliver asked, sensing the opening. "Religious background, that sort of thing?"

"No, he never talked about that," Edwards responded briskly,
and Oliver found another example of a positive absence, like the
openness of an empty grave: the sudden silence that fell where
the vicar's habitual second sentence should have been. Here
endeth the lesson. Ah, that reminded him.

"I understand you have a book club," Oliver said, as they
stopped by the church door.

Edwards frowned. "We have a writers' group in the village, if
that's what you mean. There are about ten of us. We do take it
very seriously—only people who are working on a manuscript
may join."

"You're writing a book, too?"

"I'm ever hopeful that my weekly sermons will be less
ephemeral."

"And less heretical," thought Oliver. Aloud he said, "May I
join you for your next meeting?" The vicar shook his head before
the offer was complete.

"Oh, no, no, no, out of the question. We couldn't possibly…I
wouldn't dare intrude on your precious family time."

"It would be fun for me."

"Ah, but under your feminine *nom-de-plume* you're the cel-
ebrated creator of The Railway Mice and that paragon of animals,

the sublime Finsbury the Ferret. You don't want to be pestered by unpublished midges."

Why does everyone assume O.C. Blithely is a woman? What had his mother said? *Be insistent. Tell him you know what it's all about.*

"I do know what it's all about," he said.

Edwards fixed his gaze on a fat bumblebee, dithering around an azalea. "You do?" he asked, after a few seconds.

"Oh yes. And I'd really like to see what you're doing."

"You would?"

"Absolutely. Count me in. After all, everyone likes an audience." Chloe's prompts seemed to be working, Oliver reflected.

Edwards brightened a little. "I see we understand each other."

"Then I can come?"

"Very well. We meet at the vicarage tomorrow night, seven o'clock. If you've done this before, I'm sure you know what to expect." He smiled shyly at Oliver. "Perhaps you feel this a little, shall I say, unorthodox? Especially for a man of the cloth."

"Not at all. We do so much of it alone, behind closed doors— it helps to show it to somebody else, from time to time." Oliver remembered his mother's comment about Effie's sparing him for the occasion. But did she have to? "Can I bring my girlfriend?" he asked.

"We don't generally allow couples."

Oliver guessed that Edwards was concerned about Effie's non-writer status. But Effie was a discerning reader and was unafraid to voice her opinions on works in progress, although admittedly, he'd only heard them in the context of the adventures of woodland animals as told for pre-teens; she might be a tad more scathing about four-year-old Hugowhoisgifted's maternally ghosted life story.

"Oh go on, say yes," Oliver pleaded. "It's a chance for her to see what I get up to while she's at work. And she's quite prepared to join in."

"Really? Effie?"

"Yes. She'd never be content to sit on the sidelines and just observe. You may have trouble shutting her up."

"I see. Intriguing. Well, tomorrow then." Edwards brushed some dirt from his white surplice, noticing as he did that the lower part of the vestment displayed the outline of a generous set of male genitals, executed in tomato ketchup. He sighed.

Chapter Ten

Tuesday afternoon

"Suppose Jesus did have children," Effie was saying over a Starbucks latte and an indifferent tuna and corn sandwich. "Then surely *any* of his offspring, male or female, would carry a half-share of God's genes, not just the first-born son."

"I suppose so," Oliver replied. "Maybe more than half. Look at the Swithins. Toby got a heavy chunk of the brigadier's genes, going by appearance. But I get my hair and eyes from my mother."

Effie lay back in the leather armchair she had snagged and stretched her left leg toward him languidly. Her sneaker had the letter "L" drawn on the toecap. She kicked him with it.

"It doesn't always have to come back to you, you know," she said. "Sometimes I get to talk."

"Sorry."

Oliver normally avoided Starbucks; as the great songwriter said, it could be anywhere in a Starbucks. But just once in a while, that's a blessing. Everyone in Stratford-upon-Avon, it seemed, was either serving the Bard, serving up the Bard, or serving those who serve or serve up the Bard, and for a moment, Oliver and Effie had enough of outlets selling souvenir china thimbles of Anne Hathaway's cottage, Droeshout portrait oven gloves, and kilts in the Macbeth tartan. Starbucks had offered a brief haven from the town's relentless Shakespeareanism.

Their conversation had been provoked by a shop that promised tourists their own coats of arms, inviting them to find out if they had any rude forefathers lying in Holy Trinity Church or its graveyard, not far from Will himself. (But not Will himself: Shakespeare's only great-grandchild died without issue.) Effie had contended that even if a present-day visitor from Buttocks, Texas, did find a family name on one of those sixteenth-century tombstones, it didn't prove a direct line of descent, and anyway, after half a millennium, any genetic link would be so diluted as to be homeopathic. This had led to her deflation of the many Jesus-rogered-the-Magdalene theories.

"You just interrupted me with the astounding news that you're the product of two parents," she went on after another gulp of coffee, "which makes you just like, oh, most macroscopic organisms that have ever existed. But let's talk about you, anyway. Now, the brigadier and Chloe each had two parents—your four grandparents. They had parents—your eight great-grandparents, and so it goes, sixteen, thirty-two, sixty-four, the number doubling with each generation as you go back. Got it?"

"Sure."

"So let's assume an average generation lasts thirty-odd years, three per century. How many notional ancestors did you have at the time of Jesus, twenty centuries ago?"

"A pretty big number, I'd imagine," Oliver answered, with a light laugh. Surely she didn't expect him to work it out?

"How many? Take a rough guess."

Oliver swallowed. Damn it, she did. Was there a calculator in his satchel? *I am ill at these numbers.* "Well, thousands. Tens of thousands, maybe."

Effie smiled and took another bite of her sandwich.

"Do you know the old Indian tale of the rice and the chessboard?" she continued. "There was once a king in Kerala, who was addicted to chess. It was known throughout the kingdom that he that plays the king, no matter what his status, can earn a vast reward for a good game. Well, one day, a poor sage turns up to accept the challenge. But he doesn't ask for gold or jewels. No, he asks only for a few grains of rice if he wins—one grain on the first square of the board, then two on the next, four on the next, and so on, doubling up each time until the last, sixty-fourth square. Just like ancestors, doubling with each generation. The king readily agrees to this, as you would have, apparently, you innumerate dullard. A handful of rice seems to be getting off cheap. Well, they play, and the mysterious sage wins, duh. And so the rice is brought in and placed on the board. One grain, two, four, eight, sixteen, thirty-two. By only the twentieth square, they're up to a million grains. Soon, the royal granaries are empty. And if they'd gone on to the end, before the sage called a halt, revealed himself to be Lord Krishna, and issued some smug little life lesson involving compound interest—according to Einstein, the most powerful force in the universe—they'd have needed enough rice to cover India three feet deep."

I love you Effie, Oliver thought. Nobody in your life has ever loved you or does love you or will love you as much as I do right now. I'd eat a box of wasps for you. I'd cook bacon naked for you. Stay with me.

"Now the math for that is two to the power sixty-four, minus one," she was saying happily. "Conveniently, that's also the number of ancestors you're looking for, since sixty-four is roughly the number of generations since the year one A.D. Any ideas now?"

"With or without the minus one?"

"It's eighteen quintillion!"

"I said it would be pretty big."

"Pretty big? That's the number of people who've ever lived multiplied by a number that still has too many noughts for you to get your brain around."

"But…"

"But you were going to say that there clearly weren't eighteen quintillion people alive on Earth in one A.D. Of course not. The world population back then was only about 200 million. So where are the rest of your sixty-second-great-grandparents?"

"Mars? Betelgeuse?"

She screwed up her napkin and threw it at him. "If you draw up a family tree, and you go back far enough, you'll start to see the same names popping up more than once. Your maternal fourth-great-grandfather could also be your paternal fourth-great-grandfather, for example."

"As long as he's not also my fourth-great-grandmother," Oliver said, remembering again that the vicar had thought his pseudonym was meant to be female. An idea struck him. *Travesty!*

"With each generation, you get more and more overlap. Everyone's everyone's cousin at some remove. So sixty-four generations ago, with eighteen quintillion slots in your family tree, but only 200 million people to fill them, you're going to see the same names come up billions of times. By the way, don't try to draw it. If the boxes on that row were just one-inch apart, you'd need a piece of paper wide enough to go to the moon and back…"

"Wow."

"I hadn't finished. To the moon and back over 600 million times."

"You like this stuff, don't you? I think it's the humiliation you inflict on others."

"Anyway," she persisted, "the point is, logically and mathematically, it's more than likely that everybody in the world today—unless they live in a tribe that's been totally isolated since the caveman days—is descended not once but billions of times over from every individual who was living and breeding at the time of Jesus. Including Jesus. So all these secret societies that exist to protect Christ's descendent—Templars, Rosicrucians, Priories of whatever—are going to have their work cut out. By now, everyone on the planet has probably got a bit of the *sang-real*—the royal blood or 'Holy Grail.' Including you and me."

"Then I suppose we can never get married," Oliver joked.

Effie dropped her sandwich and gasped. Oliver thought at first she was choking, but she waved away his concern and stared at him with wide-open eyes.

"Oh, Oliver, this is so sudden," she said breathlessly. "But, yes, of course I'll marry you, you wonderful man, yes." She dabbed at her eyes with a napkin.

"You are so funny," she went on, looking at him with affectionate indulgence. "Sneaking a proposal into a conversation about genealogy, of all things. How perfect, since the Strongitharm and Swithin family trees will be joined in our children. And I want lots of children, Ollie, starting very soon!"

Effie paused suddenly, as if reacting to his expression, her joy replaced by fear. "Oh, Ollie, you *were* serious, weren't you? I haven't let my foolish, girlish hopes get ahead of me" She grasped his hand, squeezing it enough to cause him minor pain. "Please say you mean it. Please."

"Well," he began nervously, hoping he could come up with a loving and fair reply in quick determination. "I hadn't—"

She laughed suddenly. "Psych!" she cried, prodding him on the nose with her forefinger. "Swithin, you're such a pushover. Come on, let's go and see Toby's dig."

She drained her paper cup, watching him with delighted, bewitching eyes. Most people would have said Effie's best feature was her hair, those thick, copious curls. But Oliver knew it was her smile—even when the source of her amusement was his discomfort. But what did it mean? Life can be very confusing.

They took the pedestrian Tramway Bridge to the south bank of the Avon. As they came level with the Royal Shakespeare Theatre across the water, they spotted Mallard enjoying a mid-rehearsal beer on the theater's riverside terrace, too far away to hear their shouts. Cabin cruisers, rowing boats, and the occasional drifting swan passed them, heading downstream with the current as far as the vast chancel window and thin stone steeple of Holy Trinity, the "Shakespeare Church," on the opposite bank. Further progress was blocked by a chain across the river, just south of the church, the visual warning of something they could already hear—the twin weirs, where the calm waters of the Avon suddenly drop several feet, splashing and spurgeoning over two sets of steps that flanked a broad, tree-covered ait. Boats going further south would take the left fork into the Colin P. Witter Lock, for a slow, gentle descent. Swans had to figure it out for themselves.

Toby's college group was working on a small river-island near the lock, recently the site of a Victorian lockkeeper's cottage, which had fallen into decay. This blot on Stratford's pristine landscape had survived so long because a dense cluster of horse chestnuts, hornbeams, and willows hid it from both banks of the river. The town had finally decided to demolish the ruins, but as Toby had said, there was no reason to believe the island held any trace of sixteenth or seventeenth century life. So Oliver and Effie were not surprised to be told by the fresh-faced young student who had intercepted them at the plank bridge that Toby often disappeared during the day, using a small rowboat to cross the river and visit Holy Trinity. He mentioned that the mile-long walk to the church could be avoided by taking a hand-cranked chain ferry across the river, a hundred yards or so back upstream.

As they approached Holy Trinity, along a long avenue of lime trees, Oliver found himself wishing that Toby's wild theory was right, that Stratford Will was a red herring. Because take away the Shakespearean accretions, decommission the sight-seeing buses, fire the pushy, bright-jacketed tour guides, evict the talentless street entertainers in front of the theater, banish the shirtless tourists, and Stratford could easily be one of the most beautiful towns in the world. But on its own merits—not milking a questionable association with a playwright who did his best work somewhere else, which half the worshippers at his birthplace and tomb had never read nor seen.

The interior of the church was bright, with massive stained-glass windows at its east and west ends and a clear-glass clerestory above the Cotswold limestone nave. Holy Trinity has a "weeping chancel," which means it was built out of alignment with the nave by a few degrees. This feature of some medieval churches made the cruciform floor plan even more Christ-like by replicating the leaning of his head toward his right shoulder while on the cross, the way an Englishman surveys a bookshelf.

As they paid their chancel entrance fee to a jovial cassocked attendant, who conducted a brief, apologetic search of Oliver's satchel and Effie's shoulder bag, they spotted Toby, still in his baggy cricket sweater, standing motionless in front of the altar rail. He was at first startled, then pleased to see Oliver. Then he noticed Effie and looked even more startled and pleased, in turn. He tried to straighten his sweater.

"Your colleagues told us that you decamp here at the first sign of a shovel," she reported.

"There are ten of us working on that island. And besides, there's no real digging. It's just trowels and brushes in a couple of inches of soil. So I come here to think."

Oliver looked down at the spotlit array of gray tombstones in front of the altar. Because the occupants were buried with their heads to the east, toward the rising sun, the inscriptions were upside down, but a blue sign and a bowl of cut flowers indicated Shakespeare's last resting place. The gravestone itself had no name or dates, just the famous curse. A framed rubbing of the single verse had been placed at the foot of the grave.

> *Good frend for Jesus sake forbeare,*
> *To digg the dust encloased heare.*
> *Blesse be (th)e man (tha)t spares thes stones,*
> *And curst be he (tha)t moves my bones.*

For Jesu's sake forbeare. Someone had used that expression recently, Oliver recalled. Probably Toby.

"Not his best work," he commented.

"Oh, nobody thinks Shakespeare wrote that," said Toby, still fidgeting with his sweater. "Stratford Will was a lay rector, a special title given to generous church benefactors. It came with the privilege of burial inside the building, closer to God. But our forebears believed in rotating their stock. When the indoor graves were all used, the church simply dug up the bones and stacked them in the charnel house, so they could sell the choicest sites a second time, or a third time. Stratford Will's survivors wanted their money's worth out of this prime real estate—you'll note that his widow, Ann, got the next grave over—so they had this cheap piece of doggerel masquerading as a curse carved on the stone to scare the heebie-jeebies out of some avaricious future sexton. Epitaphs like that are pretty common in the seventeenth century."

"It seems to have worked. He's still here."

"Not because of the curse, but because the London Will industry sprang up within a few years, which meant he didn't have to fight for a plot again."

Toby pointed at the wall to their left. A three-dimensional effigy of Shakespeare from the waist up was fixed to the wall. The statue depicted a full-faced and well-tanned Shakespeare, with moustache and goatee, wearing a red doublet and dark jerkin, clutching a white quill in his right hand and a piece of paper in his left. It sat in a kind of arched booth with miniature blue Corinthian columns on either side. Below it was a base with a Latin phrase and some additional poetry in English that clearly referred to Stratford Will as the famous playwright. Above was a 3-D carving of the poet's coat of arms between two blank-eyed cherubs, blocking the lower part of a window.

"J. Dover Wilson, the eminent critic and biographer of Shakespeare, said this effigy made him look like a self-satisfied pork butcher," said Toby.

"Maybe. But even a waste of space like Catriona Bennet could see that this puts the kibosh on your theory. The man on the wall is clearly London Will, not ten feet from where Stratford Will is lying hearsed in death, no doubt nibbled by a convocation of worms, political or otherwise."

Toby smiled. "Stratford Will died in 1616, as the inscription says. The first reference to any Stratford memorial is in the First Folio of 1623, in a commemorative poem by one Leonard Digges. I think those were the crucial years for the old switcheroo. Until then, zilch. Stratford actually had a ban on theatrical performances in the early 1600s—an odd way of celebrating a local boy who'd already made good by this time."

They paused as a statuesque middle-aged woman addressed a tour group in loud Russian. One man trained a video camera on Oliver long enough to make him uneasy.

"As you can see, the effigy holds a quill and paper, the tools of the writer," Toby continued. "But as late as 1656, the first time anyone drew a picture of it, there's no quill or paper, and the face is quite different, with a longer moustache. A bit like Uncle Tim's."

"Is that the best you've got?"

"Okay, remember what I was saying at supper the other evening, about pregnant negatives? Such as the absence of anything to do with the theater in Stratford Will's will. Here's another example. London Will created some of the most articulate and memorable daughters in literature: Rosalind, Perdita, Innogen, Juliet, Ophelia, Desdemona, Marina, Miranda, not to mention Cordelia and her two Ugly Sisters. Yet Stratford Will's two girls, Judith and Susanna—Susanna's grave's right there—were both virtually illiterate."

Effie wandered away to examine some of the intricately carved misericords in the choir stalls.

"I'll tell you who Shakespeare really was," Oliver said softly. "He was Alan Smithee."

"Who?"

"Alan Smithee is the fake name once used by movie directors when they wanted to disown a project. I think 'William Shakespeare' was the sixteenth-century equivalent of Alan Smithee."

Oliver fixed his eyes on Toby's face. "You see, Tobermory," he continued, "there never was a London Will. 'William Shakespeare' was a pseudonym-for-hire used by anyone who wanted to hide the fact that he stooped to write plays for the groundlings— Bacon, because he was too cerebral, Oxford and Pembroke, because they were too aristocratic, or Marlowe, because he was too dead. William Shakespeare wasn't one of them. He was *all* of them, and more. Surely you don't think the playwright who gave us the hilarious *The Comedy of Errors* was also responsible for the bloodbath of *Titus Andronicus* in virtually the same year?"

"That's ridiculous," Toby muttered. "Where did the name 'William Shakespeare' come from then? Are you saying they just made it up?"

"No. There was a man called Richard Field, born here in Stratford three years before Shakespeare. Heard of him?"

"I know the name."

"Field went to London in 1579 to become a printer, which at that time was synonymous with being a publisher. In that capacity, he would have known many of the most important writers of the day. Isn't it possible that he might have come across, say, the disguised, dead, gay spy Marlowe, still alive and seeking a suitable pen-name? 'I have a suggestion,' Field might have said. 'There's this young buck I used to know back in Stratford called Shakespeare. Don't you think that's a good name for a writer? "Shake speare." Just like "Crapper" would be for a privy-maker. Oh yeah, got any poems you want published, guvnor?' It's the ultimate conspiracy theory. This whole Stratford Will exploitation makes more sense when you realize they're *all* in on it." He leaned toward his little brother. "Doesn't it make sense? That London Will never existed. Doesn't that explain all your pregnant negatives, Toby?"

Toby didn't answer, but his mind was clearly racing through an internal trove of facts, probing and testing Oliver's theory. Oliver stepped back and smiled, enjoying his brother's consternation. The time he'd spent on the bus to Oxford yesterday with one of Toby's books on Shakespeare stashed in his satchel had been worth every second. *Naked maze-running, eh? Touché, Tobermory.*

As Oliver and Effie left the chancel, leaving a discomfited Toby staring at the effigy, the jovial attendant stopped them.

"Pardon me, sir and madam," he asked, "but is the gentleman you were just talking to a friend?"

"He's my brother."

"Ah." The man paused and scratched his head. "A bit… touched is he, if you don't mind my asking?"

"Well…" Oliver began.

"He's perfectly normal," Effie insisted. "What makes you ask that?"

The jovial attendant looked a little less jovial. "Oh, no offense, ma'am. It's just that he's here almost every day. Stands there for hours, not moving, not talking to anyone. We all wonder about him."

"He's writing a thesis about Shakespeare," Effie explained. The jovial man looked jovial again.

"Ah, now I get it. Student. Brainy type. Thinks a lot. For this relief, much thanks, lady and gentleman."

"I heard what you were saying to Toby," said Effie as they walked out of the church. "Why did you have to be so mean? The poor lamb was quite bewildered."

"Oh, there's a flaw in my argument, which he'll spot soon enough. London Will existed all right. He wasn't just a playwright; he was also an actor, in the company of the King's Men, no less. You don't trick James the First into giving the royal warrant to a fictional character. Not if you want to keep your head."

They had wandered through the churchyard to the riverside pathway. The grass around the mottled gravestones was speckled with tiny wild daisies. To the left, the river curved away, weeping willows masking any view of the theater. To the right was the weir. Toby's island site was almost directly opposite, just a little downstream—a short trip for a rowboat, but a good mile distant along the footpaths and across the bridge. It was five o'clock, the sun was still warm. A light breeze came from the water.

Oliver sneezed, his first of the day. As he pulled a tissue from his satchel, it brought a folded sheet of paper with it, which floated across the terrace toward the river. He ran after it. It was the torn page from Dennis Breedlove's Shakespeare, the extract from *Henry VI, Part Two*. He'd forgotten all about it.

"What's that?" Effie asked.

An inner voice begged him not to tell her, not to remind her of the Breedlove investigation after this flawless afternoon (and while you're at it, you dolt, why not really ask her to marry you, here, in this perfect spot, in this perfect weather, with her hair and her Look and her mathematical genius and her karate black belt and her bottom and that smile?)

He stopped, staring at the paper, not looking at the text for once but at the page itself, as if seeing the jagged outline, the absence of margins for the first time. *Dear God, it's the dirt from a grave. What an ass I am!*

"What is it, Ollie?" Effie asked again. He'd have to answer her now. What had he been thinking before the idea came to him?

"It's the Grand Canyon," he answered. "It's what's not there."

◇◇◇

Half an hour later, Oliver and Effie jumped out of her car and ran up the short path to Dennis Breedlove's front door. The pile of dirt in the front garden had been turned into a children's play area, complete with muddy pools of water. The door stood open, yellow police tape still dangling from one side. They rushed into the house without knocking.

One of the older women challenged them first, looking up from where she was rifling through Breedlove's bookshelves.

"What do you want?" she snapped. "This isn't your house."

The large man broke off from searching through the author's piles of research papers and took a long sip from a beer bottle, staring at them mutely. Many of Breedlove's papers had slewed across the floor, and were now covered in muddy shoeprints. One boy was crouching in a small nest of folded paper airplanes. His thin mother was sitting at the bureau fingering a calculator, the dead man's personal documents splayed out in front of her like a Tarot deck.

"Well?" the old woman repeated. Her clone stepped into the room, holding Breedlove's silver hairbrush and glaring at the newcomers. Another child, sticky-mouthed and dirty-fingered, came into view from behind the sofa and put her tongue out at them.

"Police business," Effie announced, without bothering to show identification. She and Oliver ignored the reaction and the rudely shouted questions and headed for the 'S' section of the bookcases. There was one Complete Works of Shakespeare, leather-bound, old and oversized. Oliver lifted it off the shelf and opened it slowly.

As they'd expected, the volume was hollow. The central rectangle from each page had been crudely cut out and discarded—most of them dropped into the wastepaper basket, no doubt. But one, containing a prosaic excerpt from one of the least-performed plays, must have floated across the author's desk and dropped unnoticed into the slim void behind it. Its words were meaningless.

And inside the cavity—what? A typed confession to a childhood crime? A detailed journal? Cash? The last will and testament that Breedlove's kin were clearly hunting?

Oliver lifted out the small book that had been cached in the secret space and showed it to Effie. *Uncle Dennis's Nursery Rhyme Book.*

"That's mine!" snapped a female voice. Again, they disregarded the claim.

The book dated back to Dennis's BBC days. Just a cheap, quick issue of some popular rhymes, a Christmas stocking filler—unexceptional cover art, no commentary, no introduction. Big black-and-white studio photograph of a much younger Breedlove on the back, tinted brown, looking as smug as a man should look who'd probably earn ten times as much from the book as the subeditor who'd assembled it.

Effie held it by its board covers and shook it toward the floor. Nothing fell out, no letters between the pages, nothing hidden beneath the dust jacket. She began to riffle through the pages. Only about thirty rhymes. One rhyme per page, large type, white space. Every third rhyme had a whimsical two-color linocut by an artist fashionable fifty years ago. Nothing else. No writing—no, wait!

She flicked back a page and looked a second time at "Mary, Mary, quite contrary." There were faint, penciled notes in the ample margin. Mainly numbers, not words. She turned the pages slowly. "Twinkle, twinkle, little star," more numbers—dates, amounts of money, a couple of words in capitals, the square handwriting familiar.

She opened the book wide, bending it back against its spine until the binding protested, and held it up in front of Oliver's face. He studied the pencil marks, frowning. Then he met Effie's eyes.

"I think we've identified the blackmailer," she said.

Oliver nodded. "Yes," he replied. "Dennis Breedlove."

Chapter Eleven

Wednesday morning

"So he was blackmailing himself?" said Culpepper, frowning at a photocopy of the letter found on Breedlove's desk. "Had he lost his marbles?"

"He wasn't blackmailing himself!" Oliver snapped, flashing a look of scorn at the tall detective. "That letter was meant for somebody else. He'd written it, but he hadn't sent it."

Mallard cleared his throat. "I think, dear nephew, Detective Sergeant Culpepper is, uh, teasing you with the 'marbles' reference."

"Oh, so we're back to that, are we?" Oliver adjusted the ice pack in his trousers.

"Just a little fun, Oliver," said Culpepper, sipping some tea. "Don't get your knickers in a twist."

"Or your knackers," Effie added helpfully. Oliver bit at a slice of toast.

Ironically, because he was the only person at the garden table who wasn't a police officer, he had sustained his injury the previous evening because he'd been mistaken for one. One of the younger Hull visitors had taken a signed first edition of Oliver's *The Railway Mice and the Fretful Porcupine* to Breedlove's bedroom, where he sat eating crisps and idly adding moustaches to Amelia Flewhardly's delicate illustrations. When he returned to the living room in search of more junk food, he heard his parents and great-aunts grumbling about the intrusion of the police into what they felt was morally, if not yet legally, their private property. And so he followed his native instincts for dealing with the boydem. Bypassing the slender, curly-haired lady, who was clearly well too hot to be Babylon, he ran over to Oliver and kicked him in the groin.

Oliver rapidly lost interest in the Breedlove case, and when he crawled into bed later, it was with a jockstrap filled with crushed ice and a decidedly dampened ardor. Meanwhile, Effie summoned her boss and Simon Culpepper to a meeting the next morning. Chloe Swithin had set up a table for them in a sunlit corner of the Swithins' walled garden.

"The handwriting inside the old book, *Uncle Dennis's Nursery Rhyme Book,* matched the blackmail letter," Effie was saying. "The same squarish block capitals."

"We never thought to check Breedlove's writing," Culpepper confessed. He tore a piece off a flaky croissant and spread it with some of Chloe's homemade damson jam. "So what's in the book?"

Effie blew some crumbs off the book's cover. She had placed several torn-paper bookmarks between its pages.

"Five pages have records of dates and payments written in the margins," she remarked. She pushed aside a basket of muffins and lay the volume open at the first bookmark. "This one seems to be the oldest, the page with 'Tweedledum and Tweedledee.'"

"Is that a nursery rhyme?" asked Culpepper. "I thought it was from *Alice in Wonderland.*"

"Lewis Carroll fleshed out the characters of Tweedledum and Tweedledee for *Through the Looking Glass,*" said Oliver, "but the rhyme already existed. He also used old rhymes as the inspiration for Humpty Dumpty and the Lion and the Unicorn. Interestingly, he hadn't done this for the earlier *Alice's Adventures in Wonderland,* where his character names tended to be personifications of well-known idioms and phrases—to grin like a Cheshire cat, to 'send in' a bill, mock turtle soup, mad as a march hare, mad as a hatter. Did you know that Carroll never calls him 'the Mad Hatter' in the book, just 'the Hatter'? Anyway, back to Tweedledum—the origin of the rhyme dates back to the early eighteenth century. It refers to—"

"Enough," yelled Mallard. "Words, words, words! You're as bad as the vicar. Why couldn't that kid have kicked you in the voice box, instead of the nadgers?"

Chloe emerged from the house, carrying a tray with fresh breakfast supplies.

"Now does anybody need anything?" she inquired, gently stroking the back of Oliver's head. "Sergeant Culpepper, can I press you to a sausage?"

"No thank you, Mrs. Swithin," he replied, half rising out of his seat. "You've already spoiled me quite enough."

She looked down indulgently at her son. "What about you, Ollie?" she asked. "Can I whip you up a couple of eggs?"

"*Et tu*, Mother?"

Chloe smacked him lightly on the head and turned back to the house.

"Breedlove starts with notes about his initial contact with the victim," said Effie. She pointed with the blunt end of a pencil to the open book. "See here 'FIRST LETTER SENT' and the date, about four years ago. There's a second letter, and then the monthly payments begin and are duly logged. In this case, he starts off with £100 a month. After a year, it jumps to £120, after another year £150, then £175. He didn't get around to noting this year's increase."

"And the other pages are the same?" asked Culpepper.

"They all start with a letter sent around this time of year. One shows three years of payments, another two years, and another just one year."

"An interesting way of celebrating May Day," said Oliver through a mouthful of orange-and-raisin scone.

"It's a bit more lucrative than gathering nuts," said Mallard.

"The fifth page has only one line of writing, noting an initial letter sent," Effie resumed. "It was dated two days before his death."

"Then why was the letter still on his desk?" Oliver asked.

"Perhaps he hadn't got around to sending it," said Culpepper, producing a photocopy of the letter. "Or could it be sudden remorse? It's consistent with suicide: Breedlove, ashamed of what he had become, chooses to take his life rather than continue this unpleasant hobby."

"It wasn't a hobby," Oliver said. "It was his livelihood. According to my mere acquaintance Scroop, Dennis was scheduled to run out of income about five years ago, having bet all his annuities on a seventy-five-year lifespan. With only a pittance from royalties for his nonfiction books, he needed alternative sources of money. And what does everyone say about him? That he was easy to talk to. It's quite possible that in a quarter of a century of living in Synne, he'd collected a juicy confidence or two. Time to cash in."

"A big moral jump," said Mallard.

"It was that or starve." Oliver noticed Culpepper laughing. "Okay, Lofty, what testicular pun did I make without intending to?"

"No, it was 'living in Synne,'" said Culpepper. "I'd never thought of it that way."

"That's probably enough for the coroner, right there," said Mallard, stretching. "Dennis Breedlove, blackmailer of four unknown victims, would-be blackmailer of a fifth, takes his own life for reasons unknown, but possibly because he was old, poor, tired, and disgusted with himself."

"Case closed," added Culpepper.

"No it isn't," Oliver snapped. "I've been saying all along that Dennis couldn't have hanged himself without help. Four blackmail victims give us four suspects."

"Suspects for…?"

"Murder. Murder most foul."

"But Ollie," said Effie, "these people were coughing up a hundred quid or more a month, just to keep him quiet about their crimes."

"Or sins, perhaps," Mallard speculated.

"If Breedlove's targets are terrified of public exposure," Effie continued, "they're hardly likely to find the *cojones* to break the world's greatest taboo." She gasped and lifted a hand to her lips. "Oh sorry, darling, that one was unintentional."

"Besides, why now?" Culpepper asked. "The time when a potential victim is most likely to bump off the blackmailer is when he or she is first approached. Which makes this year's appointed King or Queen of the May the most likely culprit. But that initial letter was never sent, despite the entry in Breedlove's book."

"Maybe one of the existing victims found the annual cost-of-living adjustment too much to take?" Oliver persisted. "Maybe they'd had enough of being a cash cow in Breedlove's personal pasture?"

"Look, Ollie," said Mallard, "if it is murder we're dealing with—mind, I said *if*—then we have the same problem we had before. Just as we couldn't identify the blackmailer from the text of that letter, we can't identify his victims from a list of cash payments. And the site of Breedlove's death, up there at the Shakespeare Race, is already too contaminated to get any viable evidence. As for his cottage, presumably his starting point that evening, it's been trashed."

Culpepper poured himself some tea, and Oliver had a sudden vision of the endless al fresco tea party in the first Alice book, posing pointless riddles and going round in circles. Effie would be a curly-haired Alice, Culpepper the lanky hare, Mallard clearly the hatter, even though he'd placed his panama under the chair. Did that make Oliver the Dormouse, with his slow movement and sour mood that morning? About to be stuffed into a teapot by the two detectives?

"But we do have some clues," he protested, grabbing at the nursery rhyme book. "Why did Dennis use *this* to record his income? Why not a ledger book or blank paper?" He flicked through the pages. "He didn't start at the beginning of the book. Or even put the victims in order of their start dates."

"So?" said Culpepper.

"I suggest that Dennis Breedlove, whose life was steeped in the world of children's folklore and fable, chose each page for a reason. There was something about that particular nursery rhyme that reminded him of his victim. He had that sort of mind. It may seem like madness, but there's method in it."

The Dormouse strikes back. Oliver flattened the book at one of Effie's bookmarks, the victim who had first been contacted two years earlier, and read:

> *"Mary, Mary, quite contrary,*
> *How does your garden grow?*
> *With silver bells, and cockle shells,*
> *And pretty maids all in a row."*

"Somebody called Mary?" Mallard offered, checking his watch. He was already late for his *Hamlet* rehearsal, and parking in Stratford was a bugger. "That really narrows it down. I bet it was the most popular girl's name in Britain in the year Breedlove was born."

"Ah, but we're not looking all over Britain. Breedlove rarely left the village. The people of Synne confided in him during personal chin-wags."

"And during one of those chats, one of his neighbors let on that his second cousin on the Isle of Skye was supplying half the Hebrides with hooch. 'Mary' could be five hundred miles away."

Oliver shook his head. "The victims are local. And maybe it's not the name. 'How does your garden grow?' Is somebody in the village raising a crop of marijuana among her runner beans and lobelias, the blossoms of my Synne?" He threw the book onto the table, rattling plates and cups. It almost went into the butter. Culpepper winced and fumbled in his briefcase for an evidence bag.

"Too neat," said Mallard. "Breedlove's not going come across somebody called Tom whose guilty secret is that he stole a pig, or a pervert called Georgie who kisses girls and makes them cry. Yes, when he caught the first fly in his web, four years ago, he probably decided it would be amusing to keep track of the payments in his old book of nursery rhymes. But the victims are who they are, and if his choice of pages has any significance, it'll be something obscure, a contrived and opportunistic fit. You'd need to read Breedlove's mind to get it. And for that, you need a crystal ball. Or two."

Culpepper claimed the book, slipped it into its bag and then into his briefcase, and stood up, brushing croissant flakes off his well-cut suit. Mallard also got to his feet and retrieved his hat.

"So that's it?" Oliver cried. "You're leaving?"

Culpepper snapped the briefcase shut. "Oliver, nothing's changed," he said quietly, without looking up. "I know you feel that when a blackmail victim kills himself, his blackmailer bears a moral responsibility for the death, and I agree with you. But when it's the blackmailer himself who commits suicide, whom can we say drove him to it? I doubt some foul play ever happened."

"If he was murdered, I most powerfully and potently believe that we must find the murderer. That's our duty. No matter what kind of ugly, reprehensible villain Breedlove turned into."

Culpepper finally turned his dark-eyed gaze to Oliver's face. "I still have no evidence of murder," he said firmly. "I have no suspects. Dennis Breedlove is dead and, as of yesterday afternoon, finally buried. Let's leave this investigation with him."

He offered his hand to Oliver. For the first time in his life, Oliver was angry enough to consider not returning a handshake; but he also knew he would never sink that low. Culpepper and Mallard walked toward the kitchen door.

Oliver reached for his orange juice, only to see several unidentifiable things, rank and gross in nature, now floating on its surface. "Why can't I get your pal Simon the Giant to take this seriously?" he asked Effie.

She chose to ignore the lingering hint of jealousy. "Are you surprised? As far as the police are concerned, the only good blackmailer is a dead one."

"But Uncle Tim—"

"Tim has no jurisdiction here. Simon didn't have to be as accommodating as he was. It just shows he's a gentleman."

Oliver sniffed. "Your so-called gentleman friend never wanted to explore the possibility of murder, even when he thought Breedlove was an innocent victim."

"Yes, because that blackmail letter seemed to be a very powerful motive for suicide."

"And now that we have a very powerful motive for murder instead?"

Effie was silent, watching a thrush peck at some early fruit on an espaliered apricot plant growing on the sun-drenched garden wall. A wood pigeon in the horse chestnut began its distinctive call.

"Understand what you're asking Simon to do," she said. "You want him to identify four unknown blackmail victims who, by definition, have very good reasons for not wanting to be found. Then you want him to ask them, one by one, if they murdered an awful little man who may not have been murdered anyway." She shook her head. "No overstretched police detective can give that much time to a case. And that's not a reference to Simon's height."

She rested her clasped hands on his shoulder, and laid her head on top. He could feel the curls pressed against his neck.

"But a police detective who's on holiday can help," she continued idly. It took a moment for him to realize what she meant.

"We're going to keep working on this?" he asked in wonderment. She smiled, without lifting her head.

"Sure. What else is there to do in Synne but look for sinners? But promise me this: that if we don't ravel all this matter out by the weekend—let's say by the time of Tim's play on Saturday night—we leave it and go home. Not a jot more."

Oliver smoothed her hair. "I love you, Effie Strongitharm," he said.

"I love you too, Ollie, even though I probably won't have all those children I'm longing for."

◇◇◇

Five minutes later, Oliver was speaking on the kitchen phone, finger pressed on his right ear to shut out the noise of his mother filling the dishwasher.

"The letter turned out to be irrelevant," he said, having briefed his contact on all that had happened since their last meeting. "Apparently it was never sent, even though Breedlove had logged it."

"You might still try to find out who it was meant for," replied Hyacinthe McCaw from her room in St. Basil's, Oxford. "It does give some village malefactor a get-out-of-jail-free card."

"Uncle Tim thinks Breedlove's victims could be anywhere in the country."

"Then tell him from me he's a tithead. Of course it's local. Breedlove depended on his personal charm and sincerity to wheedle secrets out of people. You have to look them in the eye. What's the set-up there?"

"Synne has less than a hundred homes, say two hundred residents. There's a neighboring village called Pigsneye, a little larger, that may have been in Breedlove's purview, but nothing else for several miles around. That's our known world."

"Then it's positively Aristotelian in its unity of place. And trust me, *mon brave*, your problem won't be finding suitable contenders for a spot of blackmail. It'll be whittling down the list to only four or five."

The dreadful record of Synne.

"But how do I start?"

"Have you ever heard of the old prediction—that if you march up to any door in any town and say 'the game's up, hand over the money,' then half the time you'll actually get something? Most of us just don't bother to ask."

"I find it hard to believe that Breedlove's victims will be clamoring to confess, when it puts them into the frame for a murder investigation." He put his hand over the microphone to muffle the noise of his mother dropping a saucepan into the sink and strained to catch Dr. McCaw's reply.

"Breedlove didn't want his victims to reform. He wanted them to keep up the bad behavior, so they'll keep up the payments. If you want the fruits of my advice, start by talking to the noted gossips of the community. Can you think of any?"

"Oh certainly," Oliver replied, watching his mother hurry out of the kitchen to answer the doorbell. "So do I still play up the sex angle?"

"*Bien sur, mon ami.* We're British. And apart from anything else, fiddling with your neighbor's wife is a lot more interesting than fiddling the company's books. More fun for the neighbor's wife, too. *Au revoir.*"

He hung up as Chloe returned to the sunlit kitchen, followed by Lesbia Weguelin, the grim, black-bobbed verger of St. Edmund and St. Crispin's. Chloe introduced her distractedly and began to fill the kettle. The verger gave him a curt nod.

"We've already met," Oliver reminded her. "The other day near the church."

"Yes. Yes, of course," Lesbia replied, and managed what she must have intended as a tight smile before turning back to Chloe.

In the garden, Oliver found Effie leafing through a copy of *Uncle Dennis's Nursery Rhyme Book.*

"Did you lift that from Simon Culpepper's briefcase?" he asked.

"Tampering with evidence, what do you take me for? No, this is a spare copy that I picked up at Breedlove's house last night, while you were distracted." She gathered her dense curls behind her head, holding them back with two hands, then let them go again. Her hair fell back into place, fanning out around her head like a bird's wings spreading for flight. "So we have to find four sinners in Synne, with only this book to go on."

"Five."

"Why five?"

"Hyacinthe says we should pinpoint all five of Breedlove's targets, actual and intended."

"Why?"

"Purposes of elimination. If we know who victim five was meant to be, we know that he or she isn't victim one, two, three, or four. And in five's case, we have two sets of clues: the content of the letter *and* the nursery rhyme Breedlove chose."

Oliver's mother arrived at the table carrying two steaming mugs. "I say, that Sergeant Culpepper is one tall, dishy drink of ink," she said. She placed the mugs in front of them and turned back to the house. Oliver winked at Effie.

"Mother, if you wanted to blackmail somebody in Synne, who would make a good target?" he asked.

Chloe stopped, without turning to face them. "Why are you asking me?"

"Well, you seem to have the lowdown on everyone in the village."

"Are you implying I'm an old gossip?" Chloe said, taking a seat at the table.

"Yes, of course."

"No."

"No what?"

She looked at him kindly, but he could sense something hardening behind her eyes. "No I'm not going to answer that question about blackmail."

"Now, mother, what's the matter?"

"I know what this is about, Oliver. You want to keep this Dennis Breedlove business going, just to satisfy your curiosity."

"It's a little more than that, Chloe," said Effie gently.

"But you were happy enough to help me at the funeral yesterday," Oliver broke in.

"That was different, dear," Chloe answered. "Then, you were looking for a blackmailer, a bad hat. Now you've found your blackmailer and you're looking for his victims, who may not be bad hats." She stood up. "These are my neighbors, Oliver. These are my friends. Leave them alone."

"But, Mother—"

"We understand completely, Chloe," Effie interrupted, laying a hand on Oliver's arm.

"The lady doth protest too much, methinks," muttered Oliver as they watched her walk away, her white hair as bright as ice in the sunlight.

Chapter Twelve

Wednesday afternoon

On Google Earth, the Shakespeare Race looks like a bull's-eye, a target for a preposterously tardy *Luftwaffe* bomber. Zoom in closer, and you can discern its pattern of recursive, enfolded pathways, like a cabalistic tattoo or a Chinese decoration, its perimeter notched by the shadow of the Synne Oak. And if the photograph had been taken that Wednesday afternoon, you could have made out two figures lying on the green circle at the center of the turf maze. But if you were one of those people who think scrutinizing aerial photography for blurry naked bodies and posting the results on YouTube is a service to mankind worthy of your brief, precious time on the planet, you'd be disappointed to notice that these figures were, on this occasion, fully clothed.

"I wish I'd listened to my mother," said Oliver.

"And what piece of maternal advice are you currently regretting?" Effie asked, tickling his ear with a long blade of grass.

"Not advice. Gossip. Facts. Stories, complaints, jokes about the denizens of Synne. Our weekly telephone calls are full of them. I used to tune most of it out." He brushed away a cranefly. "I was counting on Mother. Most pernicious woman!"

"There's a difference between private gossip and public exposure. Chloe's just drawn a line, that's all."

Oliver didn't answer. He watched a cloud float across the sapphire sky, backed like a weasel, its edges steaming and morphing. The Race was the highest point for many miles, and the views toward the Vale of Evesham were breathtaking. A mild breeze caused the branches of the Synne Oak to groan slightly. He shivered with memory, despite the warmth of the afternoon.

Effie lifted her head and looking around the deserted Race. "How come we're the only ones here?"

"There's a big hole on the main road, something to do with drainage repair. Cars can get by, but the gap is too narrow for tour buses. Should be cleared up in a day or two."

"Let's hope we are, too. Okay, who do you know who lives in Synne?"

"Apart from you and me?" Oliver answered, with a slight snort of laughter. Simon Culpepper was right, it was still funny. Although it didn't apply to their sexless time in the country. No sin in Synne so far. Maybe their luck would change tonight? After witnessing his charismatic guest-star appearance at the vicar's writers' group, Effie was bound to be overcome with lust. And his gentleman's area was starting to recover from the previous day's assault.

"I hardly know anybody," he continued. "A smattering of neighbors and my mother's cronies. The landlord of the local pub. The vicar. Vic, the village voyeur. No, he's the peeping Tom, the voyeur's the other one. Police Constable Bostar, I suppose. The Bennets, if you stretch it to Pigsneye. Eric Mormal, God forbid. But there's a constant influx of professional people who want to escape to the smiling and beautiful countryside. They're the ones most likely to provide fodder for a blackmailer. And they're strangers to me. Although I do have one potential candidate."

"Oh yes?"

"It was an idea that struck me yesterday. Do you recall the vicar introducing us to Lesbia Weguelin, the verger?"

"Vividly. Not much to say for herself. Clearly wearing a wig."

"Ah good, you thought so, too. And did you happen to notice her husband, Sidney, the church organist, at the funeral yesterday morning?"

"Not really. He was already playing when we arrived. Did I get an odd impression of the wrong kind of beard?"

"That's him. Too much facial furniture, like he's hiding behind it. Same with the missus—big glasses, thick makeup."

"You think Dennis Breedlove was threatening to report them to the Taste Police?"

"No," Oliver replied. He swallowed. "I think they're the same person."

"Go on," she said warily.

"Well, first, they seem to be about the same height and weight, which is hard to disguise. Second, they both wear as much stuff on their faces as they can for their gender. Third, notwithstanding the previous point, they have the same-shaped pointy nose and firm jawline. And fourth, Lesbia has a deep voice and Sidney has a weak handshake."

"So Lesbia's a bit butch, and Sidney's a cissy. That's still two people, not one. Does Lesbia have an Adam's apple? Is Sidney taping down a pair of size C boobs under his waistcoat? Where's the evidence?"

"Okay, Lesbia came over to the house this morning, and she acted as though she'd never met me before. Why's she so standoffish, all of a sudden?"

"Because you completely failed to make an impression on her the first time?"

Oliver shook his head. "She/he senses that I'm on to them. Him. Her. Hem. And so was Dennis Breedlove." He tapped the copy of Breedlove's book, lying on the grass between them. "I think they're Tweedledum and Tweedledee."

"I thought you said there was only one of them?"

"That's the point. That's why they fit that particular poem."

Effie reached for the book of nursery rhymes and found the page. She read Carroll's words aloud.

> *"Tweedledum and Tweedledee*
> *Agreed to have a battle*
> *For Tweedledum said Tweedledee*
> *Had spoiled his nice new rattle.*

> *Just then flew down a monstrous crow,*
> *As black as a tar-barrel,*
> *Which frightened both the heroes so,*
> *They quite forgot their quarrel.* "

"Don't see the fit," she said.

"It's possible that Uncle Dennis was thinking of Lewis Carroll's treatment of them in *Through the Looking Glass*—and Tenniel's illustration—as two identical, portly schoolboys."

"But that's still two people."

"Well, Sidney's trying to be two people."

"Two people who are as unalike as possible—a thin bearded man and a chubby woman. Not two people who are indistinguishable."

"Ah, but there's more. Dennis Breedlove was an expert in children's literature. So he would have known about the origin of the Tweedles. It goes back to the early eighteenth century, when a great rivalry developed between the German composer Handel and the Italian composer Bononcini, both working in London. The poet John Byrom, whom most people now think of as a misprint, wrote a satirical epigram about the disagreement from the viewpoint of a tone-deaf Philistine who couldn't hear why one composer's music was so much better than the other's. 'Strange all this Difference should be/'Twixt Tweedle-dum and Tweedle-dee!' He meant those nonsense words to represent the sound of rococo music to his untrained ears, like 'tra-la-la' or 'oom-pah oom-pah.'"

"It's still about similarities, not differences." Effie stifled a yawn and turned to another bookmarked page, the victim who was targeted three years earlier.

> *"Jack and Jill went up the hill*
> *To fetch a pail of water.*
> *Jack fell down and broke his crown,*
> *And Jill came tumbling after."*

"Okay, that could also be Lesbia and Sidney," Oliver cut in. "Jack and Jill, two sides of the same coin, linked forever in their activities—Jack can't even fall down a hill without Jill, of necessity, tumbling after him. It's clearly them."

Effie looked at him silently, and then turned to the next rhyme. "And starting two years ago, we had 'Mary, Mary, quite contrary…'"

"You don't have to go any further," Oliver interrupted. "That must be Lesbia and Sidney. 'Mary, Mary,' the same person mentioned twice—and her contrary nature is emphasized." He laughed complacently. "And Uncle Tim said it would be hard to find the victims from the rhymes."

Effie smacked his head with the book. "Oliver, sometimes you're the pinprick in the contraceptive of life." She lay back and stared at the sky.

"I'll try to accept it, of course," she continued, a slight catch in her voice. "On those days when my friends ask 'Where did Oliver disappear to?' and I'm forced to reply 'He's going to his mother's closet.'"

"What?"

"Well, you're clearly obsessed with cross-dressing. First it was that Oona in Plumley, who was really Barry, and now you want to dress Sidney up as Lesbia. All I ask, dearest Oliver, is that you spare me from public shame. A twinset and pearls I could take, in the privacy of our home. But if I ever find you performing in falsies and a liberty bodice in some seedy Aldgate drag club calling yourself The Lady Vulveeta, it's off."

"Have you finished?"

"Of course, if it *is* off, it'd probably be off anyway."

He launched himself onto her, and there were a few moments of painless, good-humored wrestling, before they lay back again, breathless and happy with each other.

"Okay, what's next?" he asked.

Effie picked up the book again. "One year ago. 'Twinkle, Twinkle, Little Star.'"

"Ah yes, another poem, not a nursery rhyme, with an actual author and several forgotten verses." He sang the first verse to its familiar tune.

"Twinkle, twinkle, little star,
How I wonder what you are!
Up above the world you fly,
Like a diamond in the sky!"

"If you're going to hijack the reading, you could at least get it right," Effie complained. "That third line is 'Up above the world *so high*.' I don't know where you got 'you fly' from."

"My fault." He thought for a second. "Oh, it's from Lewis Carroll's parody, which the Hatter sings during the mad tea party."

"Well, at least you're not trying to make out a case for your new girlfriend Sidney with this one. Just remember that I'd prefer you to ask before you try on my lingerie."

Oliver whispered the phrase "How I wonder what you are!" to himself.

"And our fifth and final entry is, presumably, the victim who never knew that he or she was a victim. It's a finger-play rhyme." Effie put the book down and sat up straight, with her hands clasped in front of her face, fingers interlocked inwards.

"Here is the church."

She lifted her index fingers until their tips were touching.

"And here is the steeple."

She moved her thumbs apart.

"Open the doors."

And then in one movement, she turned both hands palm upward, revealing wiggling fingertips.

"And see all the people."

"Okay, Ollie," she said, looking at her wristwatch and faking a sports commentator's cadences, "you have thirty seconds to find all the transvestite references there. Go! Tick, tick, tick... Church, yes, Sid and Les both work at the church. Steeple, no, no steeple on the parish church, but it's probably a phallic symbol, so we're still in the game. Do it, England! Open the door—an obvious reference to the Weguelins' bedroom, are they hiding in two closets or just the one? See all the—uh-oh—people. People plural. '*All* the people,' not 'both the people,' so it's not just two, we're losing points, the clock is running down, and unless they're in the church to pray for hormone therapy, I'd say the number's up for this plucky little verse. Bzzzz! There's the final buzzer, and once again, England has failed to qualify."

She managed the final sentence between convulsive giggles, because Oliver had jumped on her a second time and was attempting to tickle her into silence, always dimly aware that she could bring the encounter to an abrupt and painful end if she wished. Fortunately, she didn't. They concluded the tussle with a prolonged and intrusive kiss that was just damp enough. Then they brushed the grass and dust from their clothes, and headed downhill in the late afternoon sunshine.

Chapter Thirteen

Wednesday evening

The Reverend Gibeon Edwards met them at the door of the vicarage, an ugly late-Victorian pile charitably screened from St. Edmund and St. Crispin across the lane by a high wall and two stubborn sycamore trees. They were late for the writers' group meeting, largely because Oliver had spent the previous hour loitering outside the Weguelins' small cottage, pretending to exploit a stray hotspot for his iPod.

The vicar was still wearing his long black cassock, but with bare feet showing beneath the hem—a mark of humility, Oliver wondered? He deflected their apologies in his usual manner. "You're by no means the last, and we come and go at will, as the mood takes us, and if we can't celebrate our individuality in this venue, where else can we? Punctuality is surely one of the most overrated virtues, I always…"

He trailed off. A middle-aged man had slipped into the entrance hall. The man stopped when he caught sight of Oliver and Effie, but Edwards drew him forward.

"This is Hartley Vavasoeur, one of our founder members, if you'll pardon the pun." ("What pun?" thought Oliver.)

"This is a little irregular," said Vavasoeur directly to Edwards, although he was gazing at Effie.

"It's quite all right, Hartley," soothed Edwards. "Oliver and Effie are of our persuasion and are most anxious to contribute."

"Actually, this kind of event is new to me, Mr. Vavasoeur," said Effie. "But don't worry, I don't plan to hold back."

Vavasoeur broke into a broad smile. "Then why are we standing here talking?"

"Perhaps you can show our guests the drill," said Edwards, turning to a side table and bringing over a tray. "Do take a glass of wine. Rather a different situation from when I usually present wine to my parishioners."

They each accepted a glass, and Vavasoeur led them into a small drawing room, furnished with closed curtains and low lighting. Upholstered benches stood against the walls, some of them occupied by piles of neatly folded clothes, which Oliver assumed were donations for a jumble sale.

"Is this where we meet?" asked Effie, puzzled that they were the only occupants of the room.

"Oh, no, this is where we get ready for our grand entrance," said Vavasoeur, sitting in a clear space on one of the benches. He indicated a pair of double doors. Faint music could be heard and the odd muffled grunt of appreciation, no doubt for a fellow member's way with words. Vavasoeur began to untie his shoelaces. Oliver and Effie, knowing that the removal of shoes was a gesture of respect in many households, sat down and followed suit.

"So what are you writing, Mr. Vavasoeur?" Oliver asked.

"Writing?" the older man replied, bent over as he took off his shoes followed by his socks. Were bare feet also a requirement? Edwards had been barefoot beneath his cassock.

"Yes. The book you're going to discuss tonight."

Vavasoeur sat up and stared at Oliver. Then a smile crept across his face.

"Oh, you mean my cover. Nice one."

Well, thought Oliver, many would-be authors do plan a long way ahead, but a cover design is a little premature if you haven't yet put a single word on paper.

"Confusables," Vavasoeur stated, removing his jacket. The vicar certainly did have the heat cranked up, Oliver noted, taking a sip of wine. He slipped off his own corduroy sports jacket, somewhat reluctantly, because he felt it bolstered his self-image as the wildly successful yet still humble storyteller. This had the minor advantage of being utterly true; legal action over the illustrations for the Railway Mice series meant his interim royalties were still only a tiny percentage of the books' enormous sales. Effie put her thin cotton cardigan to the side.

"Confusables?" Oliver repeated.

"Yeah. A book for children. Explaining the crucial differences between commonly confused things. Such as an alligator and a crocodile. Or a seal and a sea lion." He undid the top button of his shirt and loosened his tie.

"Oh, I see. That's quite good." Time for Oliver to switch on his role as the established author, generous with ideas. "You could include some very basic things. Such as a bowl versus a dish. A pond and a lake."

"Yeah, that'd do." Vavasoeur took off the tie and unbuttoned the rest of his shirt. He laid them on the bench beside him.

"Or a horse and donkey," Oliver continued.

"S'pose."

"A frog and a toad," added Effie, trying to ignore the obvious fact that Vavasoeur was unzipping his flies and beginning to take off his trousers. She took a large gulp of wine.

"A boat and a ship. A kangaroo and a wallaby," Oliver offered, with increasing apprehension. "A cashew and a penis. A peanut, I mean."

Vavasoeur had removed his underpants and was standing stark naked in front of them.

"Yeah, all good stuff, Chiefy," he said. "Now, if you'll excuse me, I can't wait all night for you two to get stripped for action. Don't be too long, Effie."

He winked at her, picked up his glass, and headed for the double doors. As they opened, the noise level rose briefly, including the sighs of satisfaction with what Oliver was beginning to suspect was not a well-rounded phrase.

He and Effie sat together in uncomfortable silence.

"Oliver," she said.

"Yes?"

"Is it me, or is there something funny going on?"

"Oh, you spotted that too?"

"When you've been on the force as long I have…" She finished her glass of wine.

"Do you think I should find out what's happening?"

"If it's not too much trouble." She reached for Oliver's wineglass.

He stepped over to the doors, took in a deep breath, and opened one slightly. Across the adjacent room, the sweating face of Maudie Purifoy, mother of Hugowhoisgifted, stared back at him. It was clear that one of the piles of discarded clothes he'd noticed earlier belonged to her. A cautious flicker of his eyes confirmed that the other piles were all represented by their former occupants, spaced around the room. He closed the door again slowly and rested his forehead against it. *Well, that explains the pun.*

"Effie?"

"Still here, my love." She hiccupped.

"Effie, I think we've stumbled across a potential blackmail victim."

Chapter Fourteen

Thursday morning

As we've already noted, Synne's isolation—indeed its very pointlessness—makes it look like the perfect destination for disenchanted corporate types longing to escape the pettiness of company culture and the *Loaded* lads, new ladettes, lager louts, looters, and luvvies who haunt their urban streets. But when these burned-out television producers, advertising copywriters, and human resources managers arrive in the middle of nowhere, what can they do with the rest of their lives?

If you're childless, forty-eight-year-old, laid-off widower Hartley Vavasoeur, former brand manager for Toothaker Teas' range of decaffeinated tropical fruit-flavored infusions, and you've blown all your retirement savings on a drafty eighteenth-century cottage facing the Square, you fall back on what you know best. You open a tea shop in your front room.

"Pineapple oolong?" he offered Oliver sheepishly, when the young man turned up on Thursday morning. "Banana Darjeeling? Orange pekoe?"

"Ah, orange pekoe…"

"Not what you think. There's no tea in it. Just orange. Well, orange flavoring." He sighed. "You want a cup of builder's?"

"I think so."

Vavasoeur slunk off and returned a couple of minutes later with a steaming teapot and a plate of chocolate biscuits. "On the house, squire," he said. "With my apologies to you and your good lady for the mix-up."

"Forget about it, Hartley," said Oliver with a forced smile, even though he hadn't been able to forget about it, to the point of letting his brief scan of the vicar's sitting room stifle his sex drive for another evening. Fortunately, the Reverend Mr. Edwards hadn't been in the room at the time, so Oliver could manage to look him in the face when he arrived at the tearoom ten minutes later.

"I can't tell you how sorry I am about last night," Edwards began, after Vavasoeur had disappeared into a sufficiently remote kitchen. He and Oliver were the only customers that morning.

"I don't blame you for that. Crossed wires. I was the more deceived." Oh my God—he'd told the vicar that he might have trouble shutting Effie up! *Mother, you have a lot to answer for.*

Edwards looked at him intently. "You don't think it a sin?"

"If it is, it's hardly original. More honored in the breach than the observance."

The vicar laughed. "Others in the community may disagree, which is why we operate under a cloak of the utmost secrecy. I trust I can rely on your continued discretion?"

"Yes, of course. But in turn, I hope you'll satisfy my curiosity."

"I see." Edwards leaned back in the wicker chair and placing his clasped hands over his stomach. "These are lonely people, Oliver, myself included, I'm not ashamed to say. They gain a little extra spiritual comfort from sharing certain natural, uh, intimacies they would undoubtedly be according themselves privately. I find it brings us closer together—not bodily, of course, we have our protocols—but as part of the Church's greater family. I have often felt that accommodations to one's sensual instincts, far from being frowned on by the Church, should be encouraged as part of our ministry to the community of souls. 'There is nothing either good or bad, but thinking makes it so,' as the Good Book says, which, let us not forget, includes the Song of

Solomon, and even Ezekiel gets a bit racy. Alas, I fear such an opinion would fall on stony ground at the episcopal level, and there is no gain in preaching to stones. I don't want to sound like I'm bashing the Bishop, but—"

"You misunderstand me," Oliver interrupted. Dear Lord, was there nothing Edwards the Concessor couldn't justify, if it suited him? Maudie Purifoy's "spiritual comfort" involved a black-leather teddy.

"I just need some information," he continued. "Did Dennis Breedlove know about your group?"

The complacent smile disappeared from the vicar's face. He almost lost his balance in the chair.

"I know where this is going," Edwards said slowly. He turned to look out of the window. "About three years ago—this time of year, in fact—a blackmail letter turned up, pushed through the vicarage letterbox in the middle of the night. Anonymous. Nebulous. Not making any specific accusations or demands. But unmistakable in its meaning."

Three years ago. That made Edwards the "Jack and Jill" victim. Oliver ran through the verse in his head, but failed to make any connection between fetching pails of water or falling down hills and the writers' group's true *raison d'être*.

"Did the letter come in an envelope?"

"I think so." Edwards helped himself to one of Oliver's chocolate biscuits. "And do you know the irony? It was Dennis whose advice I sought. Naturally, he said I should take it seriously, with that regretful smile of his. I did. A second letter arrived, with specific payment information. I sent the money. A hundred pounds. You can imagine my disgust when I discovered that my antagonist was none other than my affable confidant. One may smile and smile and be a villain."

"How did he find out the truth about the group?"

Edwards sat forward, his face in his hands. "I told him, damn it," he answered. "During one of those lovely, long, meandering, intimate conversations we used to have, before he revealed his true colors. He had a silver tongue, that one, a candied tongue. How could I know it would turn out to be forked as well?"

"A hundred pounds a month isn't too great a financial burden, when shared out among all the members."

"Good heavens, the others don't know about the blackmail!" exclaimed Edwards, looking to make sure Vavasoeur couldn't hear their conversation. "I have carried the burden alone, spiritual and financial. It is my duty."

And had your little troupe of exhibitionists found out that their peccadilloes were, to some extent, common knowledge, it would have spelled the instant end of your group, thought Oliver. Not what greedy Breedlove wanted. Not what you wanted either.

"So where did the money come from? Church funds?" Oliver asked, wondering if Dennis might have missed a second opportunity to blackmail the vicar. Edwards looked offended.

"Trust funds," he corrected. "I can afford this extra subsidy out of my own pocket." He wiped his fingers on a small napkin. "Are we done, dear boy? This is all frightfully embarrassing."

"Just one more thing. The Weguelins aren't part of your group, are they?"

"Our gathering is strictly for singles."

"But since they both work for you, you must spend some time with them, as a couple."

"Well, with one or the other. Lesbia and I handle all the church business between us. I see far less of Sidney—he simply turns up on Sundays and other occasions when music is required and plays the organ flawlessly."

"And Lesbia's there, to hear him play?"

"Actually, she gives the services a miss. Lesbia's a bit of a heathen, you see, but then faith is not a job requirement for a verger. I think we Christians often err in thinking we can learn nothing from our atheist brethren. How dare we insist on mute respect for our beliefs, claiming that any challenge to them is an offense against good manners, when we exploit that privilege to tell the unbeliever he's going to roast in hell? That's just as offensive, if you ask me. Take this Dawkins fellow…"

◇◇◇

Half an hour later, Oliver was gazing at the Weguelins' house with renewed suspicion. He wondered if he should follow Dr. McCaw's advice and march up to their front door, announcing "I know everything!" when it was opened by Sidney or Lesbia, whichever persona was currently inhabiting the cottage or indeed the body. But fearing he would be mistaken for an over-enthusiastic encyclopedia salesman, he chose instead to walk around the property, and was pleased to find a footpath that ran behind the high rear wall of their garden. He pulled himself up by his lean arms, scrabbling his feet on the brickwork, and managed to see over the coping, to be rewarded with the sight of Sidney hoeing in a flowerbed. There was no sign of Lesbia—nor did he expect to see "her"—before his trembling fingertips let go and he fell noisily into the nettles below. He limped back to his parents' house, planning to return under cover of darkness.

Chloe and Phoebe were sitting at the kitchen table looking at some old photographs. It was the first time he'd seen his mother that morning.

"You knew, didn't you?" said Oliver immediately.

"Knew what, dear?"

"About Edwards the Concessor's writers' group."

"Oh, that." Chloe laughed. "Of course, I knew. Everyone in the village knows what goes on there."

"So why did you suggest that I get myself invited?" He jabbed a finger into the air. "You told me specifically to say I knew what it was all about. Insist, you urged."

"Yes, it all worked rather well, didn't it? Effie told us all about it."

"I wish I'd been there to see your face," chuckled Phoebe.

Oliver chose to ignore his aunt. "I repeat, why?" he asked Chloe.

"You were bored, darling. The clouds still hang on you. I just wanted to put a little color into your life."

"But then why do that to Effie?"

"Hey, I told you to go on your own. You're the one who got Effie involved."

"Effie's a big girl," offered his aunt. "She sees worse things than Hartley Vavasoeur's dong in the course of a single day's work with Tim." She nudged her sister. "I say, that didn't come out very well, did it?"

"Everyone knows about it?" Oliver asked, doggedly returning to his theme. "So why has nobody confronted Edwards? He's the vicar, for God's sake. He and his circle of jerks are convinced that it's still a big secret. Are you just laughing at them behind their backs?"

Chloe looked at him intently. "No, Oliver. While they're minding their own business—so to speak—we're minding ours."

"You swore blind that you weren't going to help me in the search for Breedlove's victims. You know right well you did. But Edwards's group is an obvious candidate for blackmail. It's the stuff of the Sunday scandal sheets: 'Vicar of Synne shamed in sex romp outrage.' Why did you lead me down that particular path, then?"

"You may recall, dear Ollie," Chloe said with maternal patience, "that I played my little trick on you before you found out that Dennis Breedlove was a blackmailer." She turned to the pile of photographs and held up a glossy black-and-white picture. It featured a mustachioed stage magician in tails, posed between two skimpily clad young women. "Here, take a look at us when we were your age," she invited.

Oliver studied the photograph, not knowing whether to be more embarrassed at seeing the expanse of his mother's or his aunt's fishnet-stockinged thighs. "Which is which?" he asked.

Chloe took the picture from him and frowned at it. "I have no idea," she concluded, showing it to Phoebe, who shook her head.

Oliver found Effie in their shared bedroom, hunting for a clean shirt. Her blue denim jeans, still unbuttoned at the waist, were the only clothes she was visibly wearing. She looked up and smiled, unselfconscious, caught in a sideways shaft of bright sunlight from the window, which accented the gold in her hair and cast sculptural shadows across her small breasts and muscular belly. Ben Motley would have complained that it was the least flattering lighting for a body shot, raking across every blemish and scar; but Ben wasn't in love with the model, nor therefore with every mark of individuality etched on her flesh.

"Now?" he asked.

"Sorry, not now," she said, reaching for her bra. "I have an interview with the vampire."

"Huh?"

"My contribution to the investigation. This Vampire of Synne chap sounds remarkably mysterious, so I called the manor house and arranged a visit."

Oliver nodded glumly, adding this fleeting chiaroscuro of her body to his list of the ten most erotic sights of his life. It meant demoting one of the few remaining images that predated Effie, but it was worth it. He briefed her on his conversation with Edwards while she continued to get dressed.

"But there's something wrong," he concluded. "Based on the timing, the vicar is the Jack and Jill victim. But that doesn't make sense—I can't get the rhyme to work, not with the situation, the location, the names of the principal players. On the other hand 'Here's the church, here's the steeple, open the doors and see all the people' is tailor-made for a group of onanists in a vicarage."

Effie stood in front of a cheval glass, borrowed from Eve's room, and tried to pacify her curls with a stiff-bristled brush. "Breedlove started to record the vicar's payments three years ago," she said. "He could have used 'Here's the Church' then, but he didn't. So unless he chose the page at random, there must be a reason why 'Jack and Jill' works better."

"And if that reason depends on some association of ideas, known only to Breedlove, as Uncle Tim said?"

"Then you'd better arrange a séance," she concluded, tying the hair behind her neck with a large blue ribbon. She checked her face in the mirror and decided makeup wasn't necessary to meet a man who lived in the dark. She gave Oliver a kiss on the lips, perfectly timed to express devotion without raising expectation, and headed out of the door.

"Don't forget the garlic," he called after her.

Chapter Fifteen

Thursday afternoon

Furbelow Hall, Synne's manor house, was built in the early seventeenth century. At that time, the village was known officially as Lesser Synne, a name that stuck until well into the twentieth century, when Warwickshire County Council finally agreed to drop the "Lesser." The villagers' complaint was not that there was no longer any corresponding Greater Synne to justify the demeaning qualifier, but that there never had been one in the first place.

Synne had narrowly escaped being the site of an early Civil War battle when the young "Mad Cavalier" Prince Rupert of the Rhine stopped at the recently completed Furbelow Hall, eager to try out the confections from its state-of-the-art kitchens. He missed the Roundhead army because, hours later, he was still trying out his host's state-of-the-art privy.

The Hall stood on the main road, about a third of a mile to the west of the village. If it had ever been surrounded by formal gardens, they had long since disappeared under ivy and bracken, but Effie found a cleared brick path from the iron gates to the main door. Like so many Jacobean mansions, the Hall's floor plan was a huge uppercase H, with its principal entrance in the center of the crossbar. As Effie approached the door, the jaundiced yellow and gray stonework of the high, flanking wings seemed to envelop her, even though she was still outside. It was as if she were walking between the outstretched paws of a gigantic cat, crouching like a Sphinx, waiting for a clueless mouse to wander up.

She looked for a bell-pull or doorknocker, but seeing none, pushed against the door, which opened with a satisfying creak into a dark entrance hall. She could just make out an ornately carved wooden staircase, folding itself into the wall to the right, and the dim rectangles of paintings above the balustrade. She took a few paces, her footsteps reverberating across a sea of black and white tiles.

What was that? A noise, like another footstep, distant. It seemed to come from a curtained doorway to her left. She tiptoed across and pulled the heavy curtain aside, revealing a long corridor. A faint square of light at the end—and did she see the edge of a man, tall, sliding out of sight? Maybe it was another curtain at the far end, swaying in a draft.

"Welcome to my house!"

The deep male voice came from the top of the stairs. A monk stood on the landing, holding a single candle in a holder, his face mostly hidden beneath a cowl. He began a stately progress down the stairs, shielding the candle's flame with his free hand, his floor-length black robe flowing over the steps.

"Welcome to my house," declaimed the Vampire of Synne again as he descended. "Come freely. Go safely. And leave something of the happiness you bring!"

"Mr. Snopp?" Effie inquired. The man waited until he had descended to her level, then inclined his head.

"I am Snopp. And I bid you welcome, Detective Sergeant Strongitharm, to my house. Kindly forgive the low light. Follow me."

He led her into the corridor she had just inspected and opened the door to a room on the north side of the H's crossbar. The curtains were closed, letting in only a sliver of daylight, which fell like a stream of pale fire onto a moth-eaten Indian carpet. But with more light than heat, the room was indifferent cold and damp. Snopp motioned Effie to take a seat on a dusty damask sofa. He sat opposite her in a wingback chair, placing the candle on a table beside him. Effie had only the vaguest impression of clean-shaven, middle-aged features, marred by patches of loose, flaky skin.

"My home is not conducive to hospitality," Snopp intoned. "But for days that must be spent in darkness, Furbelow Hall has its charms." He spread his hands, white in the candlelight, the robe's cuffs falling back to reveal the sleeves of a sweatshirt and an expensive gold watch on his wrist. So Snopp was not penniless, she reflected.

"And one of those charms is that it looks better in the dark," he was saying. "As do I, I might add."

His voice was unusual—crisp and well-articulated, but there was a hint of another accent not too far beneath, English regional not foreign. The words seemed to flow easily, as if scripted or rehearsed, perhaps in a thousand imagined conversations during the long, shadowy solitude.

"You've had xeroderma pigmentosum all your life?" she asked.

"All my life. And an unusually long one for someone with the condition. According to the odds, I am presently living on borrowed time."

He placed his hands, powerful fingers curved, like white spiders on the arms of the chair, motionless but as if a sudden claw-like grip could fling him upright.

"You live alone?" Effie continued, when it was clear that Snopp was not going to break the thick stillness with any further comment.

"Completely."

"You must get lonely." And it must have been a curtain caught in a cross-draft that she'd seen earlier.

"I am used to my own company. It never seems to leave me, even though it often tires of me." His thin mouth curved into a small, crooked smile beneath the hood. She still could not see his eyes.

Effie asked him about the van he claimed to have seen on the night of Breedlove's death, but as Culpepper had reported, the vampire's brief impression in the moonlight had only isolated the word "Cooper" on the side of the speeding vehicle, among other writing, and he couldn't even determine its make or color.

"This sighting was early, when I first ventured out," he told her. "Probably before eleven o'clock. It's an habitual route—I walk out of the village and beside the river toward Pigsneye. It was on my return journey, more than an hour later, that I saw the naked women on the Common."

"Well, we don't think there's any connection between them and Mr. Breedlove's death," she said hastily. "Oh, did you hear that Breedlove's open grave was filled in on the day of his funeral? Or rather, the night before."

"How distressing." Snopp did not sound convincing.

"The dirt used to fill the grave was not the dirt that had been dug out of the grave in the first place. Can you think of any reason why?"

Snopp's head inclined forward for a moment, and he moved his hands slowly together. "I fear, Sergeant, that you have let the local legends cloud your judgment," he stated. "I presume you're hinting at the superstition that vampires can only sleep in the earth of their homeland, and so when they travel beyond their borders, a certain amount of soil must go with them to assure them of a haven for the night. But I have only a passing knowledge of this tradition. They call me the Vampire of Synne because of my necessarily nocturnal habits, but I can assure you I have never sought to encourage it."

"Then why were your welcoming words to me lifted straight from *Dracula*? The book, not the old movie."

Snopp's face was immobile, and Effie could guess that his unseen eyes under the shadowy hood were looking intently at her. Then the mouth smiled again.

"Why? Affectation, my dear. Forgive me for underestimating you. Now if we are finished, even this amount of light may cause skin damage if I tolerate it for too long." He stood up and blew out the candle, a wraith of white smoke barely visible in the darkened room. Effie stiffened, wondering if some form of attack was to follow in the darkness, the recluse clearly having better night vision. But there was only that voice, odd and strangely familiar, as if his words were the expressions of thoughts he'd had much earlier.

"If you'll follow me," he invited.

He had turned to go. She stayed in her seat.

"Was Dennis Breedlove blackmailing you because he knew you didn't really suffer from XP?" she asked.

There was silence, then the sepulchral voice again. "What makes you ask that?"

"Is that a denial?"

"Not at all. I merely wanted to know how you found out."

He strode to the door and turned on the light switch. The sudden glare of a candelabrum above Effie's head dazzled her dark-adapted eye, and her reflexes prepared her again for a sudden opportunistic assault from Snopp. But he stayed with his back turned to her, his body entirely hidden by the black monk's habit, those white hands now swathed in the long, wide sleeves.

"For a start, you have no marks of the disease on your hands," she said, "not even freckles, and yet the hands get more sun exposure than most body parts. But mainly, you wear an expensive watch—the kind that is hardly likely to be luminous or have a bulb inside. Not much use for a man who needs to live in permanent darkness."

Snopp laughed, still without turning round. "Excellent. It took several evening strolls with Dennis before he reached the same conclusion. That was not long after I arrived in Synne. Strange that the first man I befriended in my lonely life was a real blood-sucker, while I was merely a mock one."

"Why the pretense though? I assume, despite what you said earlier, that you do, in fact, cultivate the Dracula persona?"

"It fits with the impression I wish to give, that I do suffer from that heartbreaking medical condition."

"But why? Why choose to live this way if you don't need to?"

Effie looked around the illuminated room—it was spacious in the possession of dirt, the dust thick on every surface, and she was sure she'd walked through a cobweb on the way in. She'd need to shower again when she arrived back at the Swithins' house.

"Now there, Dennis was ahead of you, my dear," Snopp answered. "He not only knew what I didn't have. He knew what I did have, and why I still choose isolation. Not the isolation of darkness, perhaps, but the isolation of loneliness. You see, a case of XP and a few mysterious but rather romantic habits may do no more than raise an eyebrow in such a place as Synne." He lifted the hood from his face, slid his bent hands back into the opposite sleeves, and turned to Effie. "But my new neighbors may not be so tolerant if they discovered that in their midst, they had a leper."

Chapter Sixteen

Thursday afternoon (continued)

There was a time when every English schoolboy knew that William Shakespeare—the Stratford one, anyway—died on his birthday, April 23, fittingly the feast day of St. George, patron saint of England. But every English schoolboy could well have been wrong: Holy Trinity's register shows only Will's baptism, on April 26, 1564, and his burial on April 25, 1616. Those patriotic birth- and death-dates are wishful guesswork, examples of the gaps in the record that frustrate researchers like Toby Swithin.

No danger of such vagueness in the present day, when we post, text, blog, tweet, like, poke, and generally Facebook our way through our daily lives in a rhapsody of words, most of them spelled incorrectly. Andy Warhol famously said that everyone would be famous for fifteen minutes; with the New Narration of social networking, Oliver had heard—and wished he'd said first— that instead, everyone will be famous to fifteen other people.

Sitting on a bench on the village green with a dog-eared gazetteer, a list of neighbors' names extracted from Hartley Vavasoeur, and his laptop connected to the nearby pub's Wi-Fi, Oliver had spent a productive hour or two investigating some of the newer villagers who'd left their smutty fingerprints all over the Internet. The children's book publisher (not Oliver's) who visited Thailand at least three times a year. The human resources director whose expense claim for his cat's aromatherapy had been featured in *Private Eye*. The theater composer whose Barbican bedroom was rumored to be made entirely of black leather. The sexagenarian MP for Pigsneye, whose overpaid, nubile research assistants were reported to have bust sizes that rivaled their IQs. Admittedly, all this was already in the public arena. But was it merely the tip of an iceberg of sin? We know what we are, but know not what we may be.

Damn it, why did Oliver still care about the old so-and-so's death? The one victim he and Effie had identified so far had fallen into their lap—perhaps literally, if Oliver had stepped into that room in the vicarage. Maybe the police were right, let just desserts be eaten.

He picked up a pair of binoculars, which he'd stolen from Toby's window ledge, and trained them on the Weguelins' house on the main road, where half an hour earlier he'd watched Lesbia return home after a brief visit to the post office. All he could see now was the small, elderly man he'd noticed while waiting for Breedlove's funeral to begin two days earlier. The man seemed to be looking back at him, so he hastily switched direction. The sudden magnified image of Effie, approaching from the house, almost provoked a coronary.

She'd clearly showered and changed since her return from the vampire's lair; some drips of water were still clinging to the ends of her damp hair, and her bare arms and shoulders had that freshly bathed aura. Her feet were also bare, and she walked toward him in the sunlight with a gentle smile, uncaring that the grass might make them dirty again. How like an angel. If her thin-strapped cotton dress wasn't the only article of clothing she was wearing, it was unmistakably one of only two. It was another top-ten erotic moment, the second in the same day, and it easily displaced the current tenth-place memory of his college girlfriend, Lorena Random, peeling carrots in her underwear and hiking boots.

"I found Twinkle," she said, after he'd kissed her as boldly as he dared for the location.

"Huh?"

"I found the Twinkle Twinkle victim. The Vampire of Synne was certainly a sucker, but he was also one of Breedlove's donors."

It took Oliver a second or two to register the news. Then he hugged her again. *Back on track!* Two victims pinpointed in two days, Sidney and Lesbia almost in the bag, and only halfway toward the Saturday deadline! And the interim is mine.

"They call it Hansen's Disease now," he said after she had briefed him on her meeting with Snopp. "Nobody's really sure if it's the same leprosy mentioned in the Bible. But it's treatable. Why was Snopp so badly affected?"

"It was a perfect storm of bad luck. Only one person in twenty is susceptible, but he's one of them. He thinks he picked up the infection when he was working in Africa, but he was late seeking treatment, and then the condition was misdiagnosed. By the time the appropriate medicines were given, he'd suffered permanent disfigurement to his face. He's as pale as his shirt, and there's considerable scarring."

"But not on his hands, as you'd have expected with XP."

"Yes, but in this part of our bat-and-mouse game, he was one jump ahead of me. I didn't notice until the lights came up that he was wearing white surgical gloves. Mind you, a melanoma or even a batch of freckles would still have shown through the latex."

"Why the gloves?"

"He's beginning to lose sensation in his fingers. The gloves offer him some mild defense from an accidental scrape or scalding, which he might not notice because he wouldn't feel the pain."

The shadow of the memorial obelisk was creeping toward them across the grass. Effie shivered slightly, a reminder that English spring was not yet English summer.

"Dr. McCaw will be disappointed, though," Oliver commented, gathering his equipment. "This is one blackmail situation with no hot love on the wing. But why does Snopp choose to live in extreme isolation? Admittedly, the words 'leper' and 'leprosy' can still startle us, just like the word 'plague,' but society has moved on from the days when he'd have to tinkle a bell and yell out 'unclean!'" A new idea struck him. "Ah, tinkle. Sounds like Twinkle. Could that be the connection to the verse? Although it's more likely to be that sentiment in the second line: 'How I wonder what you are!' But that could apply to anyone."

Effie had already strewn the mental breadcrumbs so that she could find her way back to Oliver's original question.

"Right or wrong, Mr. Snopp is unshakably self-conscious about the stigma. And, despite what he says, I think he rather enjoys the Nosferatu alter ego."

"Could he have killed Dennis Breedlove? Could he have carried that little man up to the Synne Oak and dropped him into the noose?"

"I think so. He seems fit enough. It doesn't mean he did."

"Let's go indoors and have a cup of tea before our guests arrive." Oliver glanced across the street. The elderly man was still there, peering into the window of Hartley's tearoom.

"I know I've seen him before," Oliver murmured.

"Who?"

"Tea!" he exclaimed.

"Yes," replied Effie, with exaggerated patience, "we're going indoors to have tea, don't worry." She'd noticed he referred to the Swithin house as "indoors." He never called it home.

"No, it's the twinkling of the tea," he said. "The Mad Tea Party. Lewis Carroll. *Alice's Adventures in Wonderland*. The Hatter's song at the concert for the King and Queen of Hearts—that parody of 'Twinkle, Twinkle, Little Star.'"

"Go on."

"It goes 'Twinkle, twinkle, little bat, how I wonder what you're at!' *Bat!* Like you said. Fits the Vampire of Synne perfectly!"

Effie absorbed the information. "So should we be looking for famous parodies of the other rhymes?" she asked. "Is there a variant of Jack and Jill that applies to a bunch of pope-pleasers in a rectory? 'Jack and Jill required a thrill…'"

"I don't know. But it proves that the rhymes can connect to the blackmail victims. At least in this case."

Breadcrumbs, thought Effie. "Who did you say you'd seen before?" she asked again, as they walked to the house. Oliver looked around, but the man had gone.

"He was standing across the street. Seemed familiar."

"I didn't see anyone."

Oliver shrugged. "It's probably nobody."

◇◇◇

The man who had been studying Oliver in the reflection of Hartley's window had slipped into the tearoom. As he stood by the door, unsure if he should sit at one of the empty tables or go on waiting for his host to notice him beside the potted ficus, he was asking himself a similar question: where had he seen Oliver before?

He would have been astonished to find out that it *was* a similar question. Underwood Tooth had long ago assumed that nobody ever remembered meeting him. That's because Underwood was the world's leading expert on being ignored.

Or used to be.

Underwood had no idea that he had superpowers. Throughout his sixty-seven years, he had assumed that everyone spent hours of their day on hold, on line, on order, on the sidelines. (But always on time: Underwood was never late for a disappointment.) He was quite unaware that he possessed a unique combination of inoffensiveness, timidity, and drabness that rendered him virtually invisible. Like a gray ghost, he drifted through the spaces between people, blindly bumped into and unrepentantly trodden on, never advancing from the back of the queue, never getting through to a live operator, never catching a bartender's eye. Underwood might have been the patron saint of waiting rooms.

But then, just three months earlier, his life changed forever. He opened an Internet account.

He would never forget that extraordinary morning when he'd logged on to check the weather, and a wondrous strange male voice from his computer said those three little words he'd longed all his life to hear: "You've Got Mail." He opened his mailbox to see a message from a Pertinence Q. Sanctimony offering him a free sample of Viagra. "No thank you," he typed back. But the next day, Pertinence had returned, making the same generous offer (judging by her name, from a Quaker pharmacy).

Underwood had never been badgered before in his life; he found it refreshing. He began to answer every piece of junk mail, usually with a polite no, although he was a little firmer at declining the racier enticements from young ladies in former Iron Curtain countries—not so much for the services they sportingly offered, but for the spelling. He wondered for many hours what made a girl "sluty," and he eventually gave up on the phrase "skank hos," although he guessed that it was Lithuanian for "thank you."

Emboldened, Underwood moved on to newsgroups, those bulletin boards for enthusiasts of every complexion, especially blushing. It is common for the younger sort to lack discretion, he reflected. But he found a literary group devoted to Robert Browning, his favorite poet, and lurked for many days, watching with fascination as the threads of conversations cascaded down the screen and invariably deteriorated into pseudonymous name-calling and inane, long-distance threats of physical violence. And then some cheeky wag mentioned he'd like to see a nude picture of Elizabeth Barrett Browning. Another poster had replied "me too." Underwood was suddenly struck by what he thought was an original and witty response. Tentatively, he typed "me three" and hit the reply button. Fifteen people flamed him within the hour. He responded to each of them, analyzing each insult and explaining why it applied more to the writer than to himself. And so, immune to identity theft, "UTooth" gradually become an online presence, bold and witty, his quips quoted and requoted across the Usenet.

Underwood assumed that this newborn fame was what had attracted the email from a mysterious organization known only by its initials "P.S." It didn't seem like spam or a scam, and it mentioned his full name, spelled correctly, which is more than his credit card company had ever managed. He was sufficiently intrigued to attend the meeting, in a McDonald's near Finchley Central Underground station, where he first encountered the massive, white-haired monk, morosely eating a Quarter Pounder. He seemed to have trouble sitting comfortably.

"Are you familiar with sin?" the pale-skinned man had seemed to demand, in a thick French accent. A quailing Underwood had just begun to confess the time he'd accidentally Googled the word "erotica" when he was looking up Beethoven's third symphony, when the monk interrupted him.

"I speak of Synne, a small village in your War-wick-shire," he said, crossing his legs with a wince. Underwood had to admit that he had never heard of the place.

"This is to the good," the monk continued, nodding. "For it is better that Synne is not so, how you say, notorious." The man leaned forward across the table and lowered his voice. "I represent an ancient society, the Priory of Synne. We are guardians of a great truth, an unbroken line of servants to an ancient secret. The Secret of...Synne." He burped. Underwood held his breath—and not just because of the wafts of garlic—spellbound and only slightly conscious that staring back into the bulky monk's purplish eyes was like being menaced by a large white rabbit.

"And we have chosen you, uh…" The monk paused, consulted a small notebook, and continued. "We have chosen you, Underwood Tooth, to join our brotherhood."

It was a pivotal moment for Underwood, diminished a little by hearing his name pronounced "Toot." He listened to the tale of a secret society that had been founded at the time of Shakespeare to protect an astounding fact about the insignificant Cotswold village, sustaining the community through the centuries and providing clandestine funding at times when its inhabitants might have abandoned it in search of better prospects in the towns and cities. He learned that he was to become one of only four Grand Masters of the order: the monk and another man in France and two men in England, only one of whom ever lived in Synne.

"Do you accept this 'oly task, Underwood Tooth?" the monk asked, squirming again on the plastic bench. Underwood agreed and inquired meekly after his companion's comfort.

"It is nothing," the monk boomed. "My cilice is particularly mortifying this morning, that is all. You will hear from us only when it is required."

He rose awkwardly. Underwood asked when he would learn the secret, and the monk slapped a hand to his broad forehead. "*Mon dieu*, I'd forget my name if I hadn't carved it into the living flesh of my torso as a penance for existing," he muttered and handed Underwood an envelope. Then he left, forgetting to clean up the table.

Underwood was surprised when, only a few weeks after his accession to the P.S., he received a call from the other Grand Master in Rennes-le-Chateau, who informed him that the long-serving G.M. in Synne, a man called Dennis Breedlove, had died. Underwood's task was to go to Synne and find a replacement. Underwood had little idea how to choose a suitable Grand Master from a village of strangers. Yet once again, his anonymity became his strength, because he found that he could sit unserved and unobserved in tearooms and coffee shops and pubs, soaking up the imprudent remarks and gossip until he felt he knew them all—certainly well enough to exclude that shameless vicar as a candidate for a post of the highest discretion.

He was surprised to see some familiar faces in Synne. He recognized Lesbia and Sidney Weguelin, a couple he'd often seen shopping together in his local Asda in Finchley before they decamped to the country two years earlier. And he kept seeing that fair-haired young man with the curly-tressed girlfriend. Now he remembered! They'd chatted in a police station waiting room last Christmas, before the days of the Priory of Synne. How could he have forgotten such a rare event as a conversation? Well, if the young chap lived in the village, would he be a suitable Grand Master? The thought occupied him as he left the tearoom half an hour later, still thirsty, and walked out into the cool dusk.

Chapter Seventeen

Thursday evening

Dennis Breedlove had died under the full moon. Six days later, the moon's face was nearly half in shadow, but it was bright enough for Oliver to find his way around the side of the house without a flashlight. It was eleven o'clock, after a dinner with all the Swithin houseguests that, despite the presence of the brigadier, had been prolonged and raucous. Oliver had almost abandoned his plan to haul the borrowed stepladder to the rear wall of the Weguelins' house and try to get proof of his two-are-really-one theory—oddly, the precise opposite of Toby's Shakespeare thesis. Still, he'd give it ten minutes and then go back and do naughty, naughty things with Effie.

It would also give him a quiet moment to refine his theory of MindSpam, as he'd decided to call it (no space, no hyphen, uppercase *S*, with a little *R* in a circle).

Oliver had already noticed that MindSpam seemed to have two distinct and rather contrary attributes. First, it's irresistible—the facts snag onto the memory, as clinging as the last wet hair that sticks to your finger when you're cleaning a bath.

But then once there, they hunger for freedom again, as if a little knowledge, a dangerous thing according to Alexander Pope, had to be regurgitated from its host. So they spy through the fabric of social intercourse, searching for a tear to leap through, blurting like a telemarketer at the slightest opportunity, even though you know from their glazed eyes and weak smiles that your audience is already well aware of these dubious factoids, having themselves been infected years earlier. ("Factoids" does sound like a medical condition.) And that's why you find yourself compelled to declare, "Oh, since we're talking about Australia, did you know the water runs down the drains counterclockwise?" and "Apropos of nothing, I've heard that the Great Wall of China is the only man-made structure that can be seen from the moon, and roast goose is very greasy, and the initial letters of the Beatles' "Lucy in the Sky with Diamonds" are

It's not the pain, it's the unexpectedness that throws you off, he reflected, sprawling across the metal ladder, which he'd dropped when he fell. Oh well, no matter how much he'd like to stay down here, now that he'd processed the last three seconds, he decided that it made more sense to get up. In case that black-clad figure hit him in the head a second time. Ah no, the attacker was aiming a kick at his kidneys, fortunately only making contact with the ladder.

Oliver struggled to his feet, but a gloved fist again bounced off the side of his head, dislodging his glasses. He landed a weak blow in the attacker's stomach, reliving the impotent weakness of fights in dreams against too, too solid flesh.

The figure seemed unhurt, but didn't follow up with another punch. The two faced each other.

"Stay away," the figure hissed through the mouth opening of the ski mask, the voice strained and unidentifiable.

"No, you stay away," Oliver riposted, impressed with the wittiness of the retort, given the circumstances. His left ear was numb and was singing to him about it. He touched it. His fingers felt wet, but he dared not take his eyes off his blurry attacker. Where's a rush of adrenaline when you need one?

"I mean stop poking your nose into other people's business," the figure added with a tone of impatience, which Oliver found rather impudent.

The next punch came straight, but Oliver's cricket-honed reflexes were fast. He caught the fist in his hands, before it made contact with his chin. But he forgot about his attacker's other fist, which caught him on the cheek. He fell back, letting go. Another slap struck him on his bleeding ear. Oliver punched again, hitting the attacker's breastbone. He heard a sudden exhalation of pain. The figure dropped back, tripping slightly on the ladder and falling against the kitchen window.

Oliver felt a surge of sympathy, never truly wishing to hurt anyone. He didn't have the soldier's ruthlessness that his father would have learned and taught, dehumanizing the enemy as Hun, Bosche, Gooks, Charlie, towel-heads. His opponent was a human being: a single hard, bare-knuckled blow could cause an injury that might never go away, not like the shaken-off punches of television fights. Despite the pain and the blood, Oliver still found himself thinking more in sorrow than in anger.

Then the figure braced his hands against the window ledge and aimed a rapid kick toward Oliver's recovering groin, and the adrenaline dam broke.

Oliver leaped sideways, slamming into the brick wall of the house. Now it was personal, which made it impersonal. This bugger buggered up my ear, he screamed silently as he flung himself toward the advancing attacker, climbing into the cage of flailing arms, slicing fists hard into sides. *You don't do my ear that violence and get away with it.*

He smashed his forehead into the woolen ski mask. His opponent pushed back, and they found themselves locked like two tired boxers, scuffling for advantage. If only Effie were here to play referee, to call out "break!" Or better still, to knock the sod arse over tit with a karate chop. Could nobody inside the house hear the commotion?

Effie! Of course. She'd talked about just this situation—incident readiness, she called it. There were ways to win a fight quickly and decisively. First of all, keep your head, don't be passion's slave. Go for the vulnerable parts, one of which was always exposed in the tango of combat. She'd taught him an acrostic: HOMES.

So it's Head, then Ovaries, then, uh, Medulla Oblongata…

No, hang on, that's the acrostic for the Great Lakes: Huron, Ontario, Michigan… Shoot, not now, Ollie.

Oh wait, it's SING. Solar plexus. Instep. Nose. Groin.

Okay, solar plexus, currently pressing against mine—rather too intimate frankly, even if the man was a friend, and he clearly isn't. A friend, that is, not a man. It had to be a man.

Instep, yes, but is that the bit on top of the foot or on the shin?

Nose, nebulous beneath the cushioning mask, but I could probably make a good guess.

Groin—see solar plexus, worryingly.

And one more thing: Don't hit anything hard with your fist. As any Saturday night emergency room nurse will tell you, you'll break your own fingers first. But there's another body part you can use.

Oliver's foot scraped down his attacker's shin and stomped hard on top of his boot. The figure recoiled slightly. Oliver rapidly slid his bent right arm into the space between their bodies and straightened it sharply. The heel of his hand smashed into the underside of the attacker's nose. Oliver clawed at the mask, which tore but did not come off as the other man careered backwards into the inky cloak of nighttime, whimpering. He did not return.

Chapter Eighteen

Friday morning

Despite its sexism, Emily Seldom secretly liked her job title, "Subpostmistress of Synne." If she blotted out the first two syllables, it conjured appealing fantasies of an alternative life to that of a middle-aged village shopkeeper and the uneasy celibacy that went with it.

Sensing her loneliness, the vicar had dangled the diversions of his writing group before her, but like Lewis Carroll, who said nude boys "always seem to need clothes," the strictly sapphic Emily thought the naked male body, especially as it approached her age, to be ungainly, unhygienic, and slightly ludicrous (a sentiment also shared by the majority of heterosexual women). She longed for love, but unless the woman of her dreams walked into the post office and asked for a copy of *Jazzwise*, she had no idea where she'd find it.

The dark-haired woman currently hovering outside the shop, beside a wire carousel of postcards of Synne, was certainly attractive in a curvy, Italianate way, and when she glanced up in Emily's direction, revealed astonishingly large brown eyes. But she was less than half Emily's age, and probably straight, even though it taxed the imagination to guess what she saw in her companion, a short, beady-eyed, long-nosed young man who looked like a puffin with low self-esteem. Tourists, Emily thought, blinking in a sudden flash of rainbow-edged sunlight that reflected off the music CD they were inspecting.

Odd to carry CDs rather than use mp3 files, thought Emily, but with some approval for the girl's preference for lossless music. Odd to use over-the-ear headphones rather than convenient earbuds, but the sound quality is better. Odd to carry a portable CD player when they must have arrived by car. Emily guessed they were motorists, because they were not burdened with parkas and bloated backpacks, which inevitably knocked items off her crowded shelves.

The bell on the front door jangled, and the young man and woman came into the shop, midway through an argument, apparently about the CD.

"'Land of Hope and Glory,'" insisted the young woman.

"'Rule Britannia,'" bleated her companion.

The woman shook her head. "You're totally wrong as always," she said scathingly, then turned a dazzling smile on Emily that, in tandem with her low-cut sweater, made the incognito Mistress of Synne feel a little better about life. "Hello, do you have any bottled spring water?" she asked, while the young man walked over to the magazine rack opposite the counter.

Emily pointed out the water. "Just visiting?" she asked.

"Something like that," the girl replied. She turned to study her friend's back. "The naturist magazines are on the top row," she called. "I'll lift you up if you can't reach. And it's 'Land of Hope and Glory,' you tone-deaf wombat."

"'Rule Britannia,'" he mumbled back with subdued defiance, pretending to be fascinated by a kayaking magazine.

The girl switched her attention back to Emily. "Do pardon this unseemly burst of patriotism, but my fellow-citizen and I are having a mild difference of opinion. He thinks he isn't an ignorant, pig-headed, beaky-nosed prat, and I happen to disagree on all counts. I say, do you know anything about music?"

Further along the shop's single aisle, Sidney Weguelin stopped looking at Emily's meager stock of birthday cards and seemed to pay attention to the conversation.

"I am something of a classic jazz aficionado," Emily remarked.

"Oh, how splendid. I'm partial to a little hard bebop myself." She ignored the pointed snigger that came from the young man's direction. "Only we're having a bit of a debate about this CD of East Coast hip-hop music."

"I'm afraid I don't know much about hip-hop. East Coast? You mean from New York City?"

"Er, no. It's actually an English rapper who comes from Clacton-on-Sea. Calls himself Masta DJ T-Bot, but his real name's Trevor Bottomley, and he's a fourteen-year-old Young Conservative. The tune of the time is called 'Why Doesn't U Stand Up 4 the National Anthem?' You see, he's sampled the orchestral introduction to a patriotic song, but we never get as far as the big theme. I think it's the opening of 'Land of Hope and Glory,' but the sniveling idiot over there insists it's 'Rule Britannia.' I have a pint of Bishop's Finger riding on it."

"And you know what I always say…" the young man began.

"Yes," said the girl quickly.

Emily giggled. "I'd know the main themes, of course," she said. "But as to the introductions…" She noticed Weguelin. "Sidney, could you possibly spare a moment to help these young people?"

The church organist, who had been following every word, glanced up with an expression of feigned distraction, the same look of humble wonderment adopted by opera divas when they emerge for a curtain call, as if they'd been sitting backstage with a cup of tea and decided to see where all that clapping was coming from.

"Tell you what," said the young woman, "why don't you listen to it?" She flipped open the cover of the CD player and removed the CD that was inside.

"Here," she said, tossing it to Sidney, "hold that for a moment." Sidney grabbed at it mutely, while the girl loaded the other CD into the player. Then she passed Sidney the headphones.

"Let me help you," said the young man. "They adjust to fit, you know." He reached over and fiddled with a slider, but only succeeded in trapping some strands of Sidney's crinkly hair.

The player whirred softly, and Sidney listened to the music for a few seconds.

"This appears to be a lamentable love song called 'Why Did U Leave Us, Maggie?'" he informed them.

"Oh sorry, wrong track." The girl tried to find the appropriate button on the player, which had the effect of tugging Sidney, still reined by the headphones, sharply toward her cleavage. The headphones came off completely, taking several hairs with them. Sidney yelped.

"Young lady," he said, after the headphones had been restored and he'd listened to the correct track, "what this barbarian has stolen for his neo-Fascistic posturing is not 'Rule Britannia,' written by Thomas Arne for his masque *Arthur*, but the opening of the Pomp and Circumstance March No. 1 in D major, composed in 1901 by Sir Edward Elgar. Its trio section later gained words implying that England is a 'Land of Hope and Glory,' a sentiment with which I am rapidly losing faith. Good day."

He thrust the headphones and the spare CD at the young man and pootered out of the shop, tripping slightly on the threshold. Emily giggled again but then recovered herself, regaining her prefixes.

"Thank you, dear," the girl called out after Sidney, before turning to her friend. "You see, Geoffrey, I always said you didn't know your Arne from your Elgar."

Chapter Nineteen

Friday morning (continued)

"I'm fine, Mother," Oliver said for the fourth time in five minutes. "It's just a few bruises and a cut on the ear."

"I still say we should get you to a doctor," said Chloe. "And we should call the police."

"The house is full of police already." Oliver was lying on a couch in the Swithins' sitting room, while his mother fussed over him.

"It's appalling!" Chloe was muttering, rearranging the piled-up cushions behind his head and tucking a throw over his knees. "People coming onto our property, assaulting members of the family. Who knows what would have happened if he'd actually got into the house?"

"You think I surprised a burglar then?" He hadn't told her about the assailant's hissed warning.

"Of course," she answered, kissing him on the forehead, "that's why I want to call in Constable Bostar."

Oliver knew better, and the last thing he wanted was Bostar—or Culpepper or even his uncle—swooping in and shutting down his investigation when he was evidently getting closer to the heart of the business. (Not that the bone-idle Bostar had ever swooped in his life.) Word had clearly escaped that he was asking pertinent questions about Breedlove's death, and one of the blackmailer's victims wanted to stay undiscovered. In fact, Oliver was convinced the figure in the nighted color was Sidney Weguelin, who must somehow have perceived that he was being watched.

Finally persuaded there was nothing more she could do for her firstborn, Chloe slipped out of the room. At least her ministering angel act had been more tolerable than his father's brief visit, half an hour earlier. "I hear you gave a good account of yourself," the brigadier had grunted, a rare smidgen of paternal pride. "Can't wait to tell Timothy that you saw the bugger off." Fortunately, Mallard hadn't heard about the attack; like the other houseguests, he'd gone to bed before Oliver had stumbled indoors and had slipped out that morning before the household woke, heading for Stratford for another all-day rehearsal.

Effie's head appeared around the door. "You up for a visit?" she asked. Oliver pulled the throw up to his chin.

"I think so." He shuffled further upright, with an exaggerated flinch and coughed a couple of times. "I believe I'm feeling a little better," he whispered, laying a hand limply across his forehead.

Effie smiled. "He's ready for you," she called. The door opened, and the two guests who'd arrived the previous afternoon, Oliver's London flatmates and longtime friends Susie Beamish and Geoffrey Angelwine, burst noisily into the room.

"Mission accomplished," Susie caroled, oblivious to Oliver's suffering, real or fake. "It went like a charm."

"You should have seen us, Ollie," said Geoffrey. "If I say so myself, I gave a standout performance as a downtrodden, cack-handed nonentity. Wasn't I good, Susie?"

"You had me totally convinced. But Ollie, darling, if that was Sidney the Organist you thumped last night, he must have a nose of iron. There wasn't a mark on him."

Geoffrey passed Effie a paper bag containing the spare CD that he'd given to Sidney to hold. She lifted out the disc and breathed on its shiny surface. "Okay, there are some good prints here. I hope none of them are yours, Geoffrey."

"I held it by the edge, as instructed. I'm not a complete prat."

"Not yet, dear, but we have high hopes for you," said Susie.

"I can compare these with the bloody fingerprints we found on the kitchen window," said Effie. "Good job it didn't rain during the night."

"Not the only thing that didn't happen last night," grumbled Oliver.

Geoffrey passed over a second paper bag, and Effie withdrew the headphones. "There are several of his hairs stuck in the adjustable sidepieces," he reported.

"As long as I get the root." Effie carefully detached the hairs with a pair of tweezers and dropped them into another paper bag. "Okay, I'll get them to the lab, in case the fingerprints aren't good enough. We can compare the DNA in these hairs with the attacker's blood. Ollie managed to keep a sample of it isolated from his own blood."

"How long's that going to take?" Oliver asked.

"Normally, several days. But I know a young man in the Birmingham crime lab who'll do anything for me. We can get the beginnings of a PCR test going in a few hours, and he can probably give me some preliminary results tomorrow. If Sidney isn't the attacker, we'll know immediately. If he is, it'll take a bit longer to get incontrovertible proof." She collected the paper bags. "I'm going to put on a short skirt, and drive to Birmingham. An hour to get there, an hour letting young Tyler gaze at my hair across a café table, an hour driving back—I should be home again mid-afternoon. I'll get Tyler to goose up the prints on the CD at the same time."

"I'll keep you company, Effie," said Susie, following her to the door. "But should I change for Tyler, too? Do these jeans make me look fat?"

"They don't need to," Geoffrey murmured, although Oliver noted that he'd waited for the door to close before making the comment. "Okay, Ollie, where does it hurt?"

"I took a couple of big punches to the side of the head, and my ear's still ringing a little. Oh no, wait—that's your voice. Otherwise, the soreness is evenly spread all over, like butter."

"You spread butter on your body?"

"No, like butter on a slice of bread. I drew my metaphor from sandwich-making. Who spreads butter all over their bodies?"

Geoffrey was silent, thinking of a forfeit at his PR agency's Christmas party a couple of years earlier. The front door opened and closed. Oliver pulled off the throw and ran to the window, in time to see Effie's car reach the main road and turn right.

"Come on," he said, "let's go for a walk."

◇◇◇

Half an hour later, they were sitting on a stile on a small rise behind Furbelow Hall. The view wasn't as expansive as the three-county panorama that could be enjoyed from the Shakespeare Race, but they could see much of the village, straggling away along the single main road, with the pale green Common shimmering on the horizon beyond it. The squat tower of the church poked above the tree line. The field in front of them, like most open land in the area, had been left to pasture, and although only a few bemused sheep could ever be seen around the village, the grass was always mown when it reached knee-level. The economics of farming always puzzled Oliver, but Synne farming—or the absence of it—required its own branch of the dismal science.

"You seem pretty certain that your pummeling last night was the work of Sidney-slash-Lesbia," Geoffrey commented, sucking a long stalk of grass. "He didn't look tough enough to me. And as Susie said, there were no signs that he'd been in a fight. Or should I say she?"

"He," Oliver said flatly. The idea of striking a woman hard enough to potentially break her nose was not to be entertained.

"Getting up in drag, though," Geoffrey continued, "it seems a bit tame for blackmail." He took a deep, satisfying breath of the clean air, enjoying the undiscovered country.

"If Sidney Weguelin were just a transvestite, I doubt that it would be a big deal, not even in Synne. Especially not in Synne. But I'm convinced he's one person pretending to be two, Sidney and Lesbia, and that makes all the difference. Whatever the reason, it's exactly the kind of secret that Breedlove could wheedle out of him."

"What if the secret is that Sidney bumped off the original Lesbia and is now pretending to be her to cover up her disappearance?"

"If Sidney were a murderer, Breedlove would have thought twice about blackmailing him. Kill once—"

"Shame on you," Geoffrey chimed in, exhibiting his habit of finishing other people's sentence, usually inaccurately. Oliver glared at him.

"I was going to say 'kill once, and you can kill again.'"

The midday sun was bright and warm. A car rolled along the main road below them, the only sound on the windless air.

"So you have two victims formally identified, and Sidney and Lesbia as a third," Geoffrey said. "Any other suspects?"

Oliver reached into his pocket for a small notebook and squinted at his spidery handwriting. "I've done some modest research. There's an actuary who moved into the old Forge. He used to be an accountant, but he found the work too exciting."

"That's an old joke."

"No, he was an accountant for Hezbollah. And there are a couple of other prospects worth sniffing around. But my best bet is the local MP, who lives—"

"In Synne. That's funny."

"He lives in Pigsneye," Oliver continued firmly, "but I suppose that's in Breedlove's catchment area."

"That reminds me. Didn't you inveigle Ben Motley into some fancy dinner party in Pigsneye last week?"

"Yes. Why? Was he complaining?"

"Quite the reverse. Ben thought it was the funniest evening he'd spent in months. But he asked me to give you a message. Let's see: 'I told you Mormal's arse looked familiar.' Does that mean something? He wanted me to show you a website."

"Okay, we'll check it out when we get back."

Oliver sat silently, watching a distant kestrel hook itself onto the air and wait, flapping, until the sudden abseil down the sky, swift as quicksilver, into the poppy-splashed grass far below. This time, the shrew or vole that had caused the infinitesimal quake of a stalk escaped. Watching birds was one of the few consolations of being away from his London home; he regretted it was still too early in the year to enjoy the spectacle of swallows reenacting low-level *Star Wars* dogfights over the Square.

The black car he had noticed earlier had come back into view, parking behind the manor house. A figure emerged, dark and elongated through the heat haze, and went into the building.

"So do we assume that last night's show of violence was provided by the murderer?" Geoffrey asked. "If so, you got off more lightly than Uncle Dennis."

"The attacker told me to stay away, so it wasn't one of the blackmail victims Effie and I have already identified. But he didn't have to be the killer. It could have been someone who wants to keep his secret safe, now that Breedlove is dead, and has somehow heard about my interest in the case."

"So the attacker's not necessarily the murderer, and the murderer's not necessarily the attacker. Hardly worth your getting black and blue. What I don't understand, though, is why any of Breedlove's established victims would suddenly turn on him."

"Neither do I."

"Then this year's new victim still seems the obvious suspect. Are you sure he didn't know he was about to be blackmailed?"

"The letter was lying on Breedlove's desk, presumably undelivered. It was folded, but hadn't been put into an envelope yet."

"Did you find an envelope?"

"No."

"Odd. People don't generally fold letters until they have the envelope ready."

"Breedlove's annotation in the nursery rhyme book said the letter was dispatched two days before he died. We assumed he'd got a bit ahead of himself, or had second thoughts. But it's not as if the recipient is going to bring it back and deliberately leave it at the scene of the crime when he kills Dennis."

"Why not? You said the contents were pretty cryptic. You're no closer to guessing who it was meant for, are you? Does it work for Sidney?"

Oliver shook his head. "Sidney and Lesbia's situation doesn't fit the letter or the new victim's nursery rhyme, 'Here's the church, here's the steeple.' On the other hand, that rhyme works perfectly for the vicar—'open the door, see all the people.' But going by the timing, the Reverend Mr. Edwards should be 'Jack and Jill went up the hill.' Only it doesn't work."

"Sure it does," said Geoffrey absently.

"Why?"

"Because that's what those groups are called." Geoffrey looked at his friend with surprise. "Didn't you know that?"

"Didn't I know what, damn it?"

"Oh. Well, when men and women get together to, uh, air their differences, it's known as a Jack and Jill club."

Oliver stared at his friend for a moment. Then he slipped down from the stile and performed a brief jig, before he remembered that it would cause him pain. He limped back.

"Oh my God, it works!" he cried. "It works! Geoffrey Angelwine, you're a pervert and a genius."

Geoffrey smiled, happy to see his friend happy. "Oh, not really a genius," he disclaimed.

"No, not really." Oliver searched in his pockets. "I should call Effie, but I've left my phone at the house. Let's go back. I am too much in the sun, anyway. And we can look at that website of Ben's."

◇◇◇

"Double-you, double-you, double-you, dot doctor dash peeper—no spaces—dot com," said Oliver, copying the URL from Geoffrey's scribbled note into his laptop's browser. A home page filled the screen, dotted with several thumbnail images of couples engaged in sexual activity.

"You didn't tell me it was a pornographic website," Oliver complained to Geoffrey.

"Did I hear you spell out Doctor-Peeper-dot-com?" asked Toby from his chair by the fireplace. He had been reading a book quietly when Oliver and Geoffrey ran into the sitting room and claimed a socket for the laptop. "You do know that's Eric Mormal's website, right?"

"I didn't, but I'm not surprised," said Oliver, squinting at the pictures and clicking around the page. It always led to the same pop-up screen, demanding a password or a payment to a company called 740 Ventures, no doubt so that, unlike Doctor Peeper, it wouldn't raise any blue flags when wives scrutinized their husband's credit card bills. "What does he have on it?"

"I have no idea," said Toby. "Eric won't tell me, and he said he won't let me join. Not that I'd ever try. I mean, I know online porn is a multibillion dollar industry, but there's so much free stuff out there, only an idiot would pay for something like Doctor Peeper."

"Yeah. Geoff, what's your Doctor Peeper password?"

Geoffrey leaned over the keyboard and sheepishly tapped a few keys. "It's for research purposes," he said.

The screen changed, and an organized menu appeared on the left side of the page, while the remaining space became the frame for a video. Geoffrey clicked over a line of text saying "Most recent" and the blank frame snapped into life. Toby put his book aside and joined them.

They were looking down on a bedroom from a high camera angle, which seemed fixed and unchanging. Most of the picture was the surface of a bed, but a bedside cabinet supporting a lamp and a television set on a low cupboard showed around the edges of the frame.

"That looks like Eric's bedroom," said Toby, peering over Oliver's shoulder.

As the three men watched, a man and a woman came into the room and climbed onto the bed. Over several minutes, they removed each other's clothes, pausing to pay attention to selected body parts as they were denuded. None of these actions involved looking up toward the ceiling—quite the reverse—and so their faces were never clearly picked up by the camera. But they looked young, the blond man much thinner and spottier than the dark-haired woman, and seemed to be enjoying the encounter. Eventually they were both naked, and in what is known as the missionary position.

"I think that was the bum that Ben recognized," Oliver said. "So I'm assuming our host here is Eric Mormal himself."

"Never mind Eric," said Toby. "Look at the girl."

The dark-haired woman's face could be clearly seen at last beside the back of Mormal's bobbing head. There was no mistaking Davina Bennet. Oliver stopped the playback.

"Is there an archive?" he asked Geoffrey, an idea dawning. Geoffrey mutely clicked on a link that listed dozens of other available videos, distinguished by their dates, which went back more than two years. Oliver selected one at random. The same overhead picture of Mormal's bedroom came into life. This time, his visitor was blond, although the activities proceeded in much the same order. And this time, she was clearly Clarissa Bennet.

"Cheeky bugger," said Toby with a bitter laugh. "He's recording every sexual encounter and charging people to watch them. What a world!"

"But do his partners know their most intimate moments are being splashed all over cyberspace?" Oliver asked softly. "There doesn't seem to be any awareness of the camera."

He stopped the video too late to ever forget what Clarissa's naked body looked like beneath the Lanvin dress—an intrusive knowledge of blemishes and the uneasy truce between breasts and gravity.

"How many girls are there, Geoffrey?" he asked.

"Half a dozen. Ten at the most, maybe. The same ones keep coming back for more. Look, I thought it was a setup," he continued. "I thought it was a professional series, using established porn actors. Only the gimmick was to act like it was a purely amateur affair, caught on a fixed hidden camera, in order to appeal to the voyeur in all of us. That's why I showed it to Ben a couple of weeks ago, to see if he recognized any of the models." He swallowed. "I didn't know it was real. It looked too genuine to be real."

"Ben did say the Bennet girls seemed familiar to him," Oliver said. "I guess it wasn't from the pages of *Tatler*. Well, we have two Bennets out of five—do we dare complete the set?"

He began to click through the archive methodically, fast-forwarding to the earliest point when the female's face was in view and ending the playback as soon as she could be identified. All the Bennets, apart from the youngest, Lucinda, had given in to Mormal's rough-trade charms, most of them frequently and appreciatively. There were also appearances by other girls, whom Toby recognized as old school-friends or workers on the cooperative farm in Pigsneye that employed Mormal during the day.

"'And pretty maids all in a row,'" Oliver quoted to himself. His mobile phone rang, displaying Effie's number. He turned off the computer, giving him an abrupt reflection of his own features in the polished screen, flanked too closely by the mesmerized faces of Toby and Geoffrey.

"What are you doing?" she asked.

"Watching Internet porn with the guys."

"I wish you'd waited for me. But I never had you pegged for an enthusiast."

"I'm not. I didn't see my first dirty movie until I was twenty. I was quite enjoying it until someone gave away the ending. But listen, I think I've found—"

"No, you listen," Effie interrupted. "I'm about to get into the car for the drive back. Sorry, Ollie, but I regret to inform you that your attacker last night was not Sidney Weguelin. The prints don't match."

"You're sure?"

"I'm afraid so. We don't need to bother with that DNA test. So you'd better take care, my poppet. Because somebody else is out to get you."

Chapter Twenty

Friday afternoon

Toby was leaving for the Stratford dig when Oliver hauled him into the sitting room.

"Listen, Toblerone," he whispered, "don't mention what we saw on that website."

"If you're trying to protect the good name of Les Bennettes, you're shutting the stable door a little late. Not that I'm comparing them to horses. Although…"

"I mean don't tell Eric we know about his foul practice. I don't want him making himself scarce until Effie and I ask him a few questions."

Toby nodded. "You think Uncle Dennis found out about the girls' being such, uh, good sports?"

"It would explain something Eric said at dinner last week. When I mentioned that letter, he exclaimed, '*He* was being blackmailed?' The emphasis sounded as if it contradicted something he already knew—that Dennis was himself a blackmailer."

"If Scotland Yard knew about you, Olivia, they'd surely snap you up. Oh wait—they do, and they haven't." Toby shifted the strap of his bulky shoulder bag. "So you want me to suppress all my loyalty to my childhood friend?"

"If it's not too much trouble."

"Oh, no trouble at all." Toby grinned. "Serve the puffed and reckless libertine bloody well right. The only risk I can see here is Eric's embarrassment, two words that have never appeared together in an English sentence before. Feigned obliviousness coming right up."

Not a stretch for you, Oliver thought with affection. "Why is Eric helping you at the excavation anyway?" he asked. "Didn't you say it was only sifting through the topsoil?"

Toby stepped across to the door and closed it. "Listen, Ollie, can you keep a secret?" he asked.

"No."

"I'll tell you anyway. We found something unexpected when we started to dig. There's a hidden cellar beneath the foundations of the old house. That was a bit of a surprise, given the seepage problem on a river island. It needed baling out, and because there were only three us on the project at the time, I asked Eric if he could lend a hand. He's stayed with us ever since."

"Did you find anything down there?"

"No, after all that, it was empty. But the cellar was interesting in itself. There's an odd sort of alcove in the wall, and if the house was older, I'd have said it was a priest hole, but it was only built a couple of centuries ago—certainly not from Shakespeare's time. Probably meant for cold storage, from the days before refrigeration."

"Why all the secrecy?"

"Because if we'd reported the discovery, the Town would have tossed us out and taken over."

"And you didn't want others to dig up the past?"

"Not till we've had our turn."

◇◇◇

Effie arrived back from Birmingham with Susie half an hour later, spent ten amused minutes surveying Mormal's website over a cup of tea, and then drove Oliver to the Stratford excavation.

"Four of the five Bennet girls are on Doctor Peeper," he told her, as they sped along the southern approach to the town. "No Lucinda."

168   Alan Beechey

"Perhaps she's the one who got the good taste in men," Effie suggested. "Having met the Honorable Donald, I know that's hard to believe, but everything's relative."

"Maybe. But do you remember what you said to Ben after that dinner party?"

"Of course not. I was plastered."

"You told him off for using the 'you look familiar' line on the Bennets. But they did. Ben was remembering the time a few weeks earlier when Geoffrey showed him Doctor Peeper."

"Ben's a portrait photographer. He's probably the only man who'd notice that the girls had faces."

"Exactly. But here's the thing: He said on Saturday that they *all* looked familiar."

"Ah, the plot thickens."

"I called Ben just now, but he wasn't in. However, there's another clue. The website belongs to a company called 740 Ventures, presumably named by Eric. Did you notice at dinner that the girls were wearing fancy initial pins?"

"Covered in diamonds. If you're thinking of buying me anything that crass for Christmas, don't. I'd prefer a book. But not one of yours this year."

"And that's why I love you, Eff. That and the hair. Well, it's probably a coincidence, but each of the sisters has a name that begins with a Roman numeral: Davina, Catriona, Clarissa, Xanthe, and Lucinda. DCCXL, in birth order. That's—"

"Seven hundred and forty."

"Exactly. But you need Luce. Without her L for fifty, it would be—"

"Seven hundred and ten," Effie confirmed, as they drove into the riverside park where the dig was located. "I don't know, Ollie—it sounds too cerebral for Eric Mormal."

They heard Mormal before they saw him, his voice carrying over the low-frequency chugging of a cabin cruiser in the neighboring lock and the constant static of the downstream weir. He was pushing a wheelbarrow across the plank bridge from the island, yelling back over his shoulder.

"Listen, Giles or Miles or Niles or whatever-your-name-is, you Oxford prats are so bleedin' effete, you think manual labor is a Spanish wine waiter." He walked on along the path, chuckling to himself.

"Doctor Peeper, I presume," Oliver said. Mormal looked startled, made an involuntary assessment of who else might be listening, and set down the wheelbarrow. They could see that it contained a few ancient bricks and a sports bag.

"Blimey, Olls, you're a bit bashed about the old phizog," Mormal said, noticing Oliver's scratches and bruises. His own face was unmarked.

"The website, Eric…" said Effie firmly.

Mormal let his eyes drift down Effie's body, clearly appreciating the skirt she'd put on for Birmingham Tyler. He seemed to reach into his sports bag for something, but his hand was empty when he withdrew it.

"So who told you about Doctor Peeper?" he asked Oliver. "That mate of yours, Geoffrey Angelwine? Or 'Flackstud,' to use his site ID."

"Isn't membership anonymous?" Oliver asked.

"Not to the man who collects the credit card payments. How many Geoffrey Angelwines do you think there are? So, Effie, are you here to take down my particulars? I should warn you, my lawyer tells me I'm doing nothing illegal, because I'm shooting my little dramas on my own property." He winked at her and picked up the wheelbarrow. "Come up and see me sometime, I've got a good part for you."

He began to trundle the barrow swiftly across the grass, and Oliver and Effie had to hurry after his bony form.

"Do the Bennet girls know they're on the Internet?" Oliver asked, panting.

"Of course not!" Mormal scoffed, without stopping. "You know Davina. She'd die if she found out that an immodest percentage of the male population has studied her tan lines."

"Then aren't you afraid someone will recognize her?"

"Not really. Most of my members wouldn't know her from Adam. And who looks at the faces, anyway?"

And that's what makes it pornography, thought Oliver: you don't care who owns the body. When you do, it becomes eroticism.

They had reached the parking area where they'd left Effie's Renault. Mormal set down the wheelbarrow behind his van—or more appropriately, the van that belonged to Pigsneye Organic Cooperative Farms. He opened the rear doors and began to throw the bricks into its empty, dirty interior.

"Dennis Breedlove was blackmailing you, wasn't he?" Oliver said.

Mormal paused, feeling the heft of a brick in his palm.

"Don't deny it, Eric," said Effie.

Mormal remained silent. He let go of the brick, placed his sports bag on the grass, walked around to the driver's side door of the van, and reached inside. After a moment or two, he emerged with another bag, which he handed to Oliver.

"Toby left this in the van," he said sourly. "He was in such a hurry to piss off to that church that he left it behind. Now I know what the rush was all about. Tell the old mole he'll have to cadge a lift home with one of his poncy friends." He looked from one to the other of his accusers. "All right, I'll give you five minutes."

"How long have you been paying Breedlove?" asked Effie.

"A couple of years."

That ties in flawlessly with the "Mary, Mary" victim, thought Oliver, "pretty maids all in a row." Three out of five, then, and he was still counting on Sidney Weguelin as Tweedledum. And if we identify the four existing victims, do we need to figure out who that undelivered letter was supposed to go to—to dig up the past?

"So Dennis saw the website and knew it was you?" he ventured.

"Nah, this all began long before the website. He just discovered that I was, shall we say, servicing more than one of the Bennet girls."

"How did he find out? From one of the girls?"

Mormal was already shaking his head, prodding his sports bag gently with his foot and moving it a few inches away from where he was standing. "I'm afraid it was me, boasting of my gifts that have the power to seduce. A moment of sympathetic bonding with an old man who seemed wistful for his romantic past. He got me. He got me good, that smiling damned villain." He laughed sharply. "No, I don't think Davvy or Xan or Cat or Clarrie are proud enough of their association with me to fess up to a third party. I do know what I am, Effie: I'm a bit of rough who's prepared to give some man-hungry but plain young ladies secret sex on a weekly basis. I'm the nasty skeleton in their closets, and I make it easy for them to keep its doors closed, especially from each other. That's how it works."

"Very altruistic of you," said Effie. "Although with the website, there's clearly more in it for you than a regular supply of fornication."

"Well, I wouldn't discount the fornication. But then my pleasure grew into my business."

"Which would never have started if Dennis Breedlove had told the girls they were sharing what, for the sake of this conversation, I'll call a 'lover,'" Oliver commented. "Isn't that what he threatened?"

Mormal stared at Oliver with amusement. "You don't get it, do you? What's the worst that could have happened? Oh, the girls would get all huffy for a while, but they'd privately crawl back into my bed for that little touch of Eric in the night. Every dog will have his day. If it's Tuesday, it must be Clarissa." He leaned toward Effie with what he thought was a seductive expression. "I'm hard to get over."

"So's a yeast infection," she replied.

"Then why *did* you pay Breedlove?" Oliver inquired, distracted by the continuing hum of the weir, which he thought was too far from the car park to be audible.

"Because of their mother."

"You think she'd be scandalized?"

"Well, at first I think she'd be jealous."

Oliver looked about to speak, but Effie placed a hand on his arm.

"No," she said. "Just don't go there. I don't want to know."

"You see, Dennis wasn't expecting *me* to pay," Mormal continued. "I didn't have any money back then. Dennis thought I could get Wendy Bennet to cough up a bob or two, rather than see the tabloid headlines of 'Shame of f-four debs in the single bed.' But I had my own reasons for keeping Wendy in the dark. In every sense."

"So you commercialized your sex life in order to pay for his continuing silence," Oliver said.

Mormal laughed. "You *really* don't get it, Olls. Dennis wasn't blackmailing me, at least not technically. He was my business partner."

"What?"

"You didn't know, did you? Yeah, that was my stroke of genius. Dirty old Dennis liked to make money out of sin in Synne. So instead of blackmail payments, I offered him fifty percent of the new Doctor Peeper website."

"Surely Doctor Peeper doesn't pay much?" Effie commented. "When it's the same girls, in the same place, doing largely the same things with the same man, for want of a better word?"

"In the world of cyberporn, Effers, that's a winning formula. The Bennets are popular with the punters, because they're genuinely posh, genuinely amateur, and genuinely unaware of the camera. And they're clearly real sisters, which adds to the piquancy. Horses for courses. All I need is a few hundred obsessive sads around the planet coughing up their monthly £12.95 and we're in clover. I'd give Dennis a hundred quid or so a month in pocket money, as arranged, but there's more than fifty thou in the bank that's rightfully his, and his shares could be worth fifty more."

"And now he's dead, you get to keep it all for yourself." *Do we have a motive for murder?* Oliver wondered.

Mormal looked hurt at the insinuation. "That money isn't mine. I've already notified those relatives of the secret part of Dennis's fortune. Not telling them how he earned it, of course."

"Won't they figure that out?"

"No, the shares are in a holding company, which Dennis insisted on setting up. He called it 740 Ventures—some private joke of his own. He liked private jokes."

Tell me about it, "Mary, Mary," thought Oliver. "Do you think the girls would still forgive you if they found out about Doctor Peeper?" he asked.

"No, I don't. But why should they find out?"

"Because somebody's bound to recognize them sooner or later. Ben Motley did. I did. It only takes one slumming *Tatler* reader to spot demure Davina Bennet, her chaste treasure open, in flagrante delicto with a local yahoo. No offense, Eric."

"Oh, none taken, Foureyes." He gently nudged his sports bag again. "But let's do a test. Do you want to tell your friends, the Bennets, that you stumbled across them while visiting Internet porn sites, Oliver?"

Oliver was silent.

"Effie," Mormal continued, "are you going to be the one to tell the girls their private parts are available for public viewing, knowing they'll never recover from the humiliation?"

It's a temptation, thought Effie, but she knew her limits. "You have it all figured out, don't you, you little shit?" she said.

Mormal seemed unconcerned. "We let sleeping dogs lie, don't we? And incidentally, just because I've been forced to make a few quid off these dogs, it doesn't mean I don't really care for them. I love them. Truly. Some more than others, admittedly."

"Including the lissome Lucinda?" Oliver asked.

"Lucinda? Luce was never part of Doctor Peeper. She's practically engaged to that prick Quilt-Hogg."

"Bullshit," Oliver riposted. Now he knew that the trickster Breedlove had come up with the name, he was confident that 740 Ventures did indeed stem from the initials of all five Bennet girls, converted into Roman numerals.

Mormal swallowed and seemed to reconsider. "All right, fair play, but I've taken down all her videos. And Luce was always legal."

"For sex, maybe," conceded Effie, "but not for pornography. Gotcha." Mormal didn't speak.

"Why did you take her off the website?" Oliver asked. "Were you afraid that Dennis would trade Doctor Peeper for a fresh crack at the Bennet family fortune, once he heard that Luce was a potential Countess of Yateley?"

"No," said Mormal quietly. "I was afraid that somebody would recognize her and tell the Quilt-Hoggs that Luce was no virgin bride, and then we will have no more marriage. My courtesy to Wendy Bennet may not extend to keeping my hands or indeed my glands off her daughters, but it's quite another thing to ruin her heart's desire. Your five minutes are up."

He carefully picked up his sports bag. It seemed to Oliver that the noise of the weir changed tone slightly, from a hum to a whirr.

"Just a minute," he said and snatched the bag from Mormal's hand. Mormal tried to grab it back but he found his thin wrist being gripped tightly by Effie.

"That's mine!" he shouted. "You have no right to take it!"

"So sue me," muttered Oliver, unzipping the bag and peering inside. He reached in and pulled out a camcorder, still running, its red recording light masked with black electrician's tape. Inside the bag's dark interior, a makeshift cradle of short bungee cords had held the camera more or less vertically, peeking through a thin mesh wafer that covered a hole in the bag. The arrangement would have let the camera record anything that was immediately above it.

Effie let go of Mormal, took the camera, and calmly removed the small DVD that was storing the images of her thighs and underwear.

"You're well out of order," Mormal continued to protest. "I'm in a public place here, I've a right…"

Effie snapped the disk in half and handed the camera back to Mormal without speaking. This merited more than the

Strongitharm Look, thought Oliver. But Effie seemed only thoughtful and a little embarrassed. She stepped away, breaking the disk into quarters, trembling slightly. Oliver knew this was the emotional self-control of the martial arts expert and police officer who dared not lose her temper in case she lashed out and broke Mormal's neck with the side of her hand.

"It's all part of the Doctor Peeper expansion," Mormal stuttered. "Up-skirts, down-blouses, all original, all anonymous—none of this lifted off the Internet and recycled schmutter. It wasn't just you on there, Effie—when those twenty-year-old Oxford girls bend over to trowel through the foundations—"

"Eric," said Oliver, holding the open mouth of the bag toward him. "Put away the camera."

Mormal opted to pay attention to the soft, unexpected menace in Oliver's voice. He placed the camera in the bag. Oliver slid it into the back of the van, removed his glasses, and slipped them into the breast pocket of his shirt.

"Now defend yourself," he said to Mormal.

"What are you talking about?" Mormal asked with a mocking laugh, with the result that his mouth was still wide open when Oliver's fist slammed into his cheekbone. The momentum spun him around and into the open rear of the van, leaving only the lower half of his body in daylight. The protruding posterior was a tempting target, but Oliver believed in fair play.

"Respect," Mormal spluttered around his swelling tongue. "Massive."

"Never mind that. Get up."

But only Mormal's legs began to move, like a toad's, squirming to find a firm grip on the ground and then edging his body further into the darkness of the van. Oliver slammed the doors closed. A few seconds later, the engine started up.

"That's interesting," Oliver said as he watched the vehicle drive away, leaving the empty wheelbarrow. Effie, who had been staring at him in astonishment, reached for his hand and kissed his stinging knuckles one by one.

"Didn't I tell you that's a good way to break your fingers?" she scolded. "You never listen to me." She leaned against him, closing her eyes as he put his arms around her shoulders and letting the fragments of the broken disk drop onto the ground.

"I don't need you to defend my honor, you know," she whispered, slipping her arms around his waist.

"I wasn't. That was entirely for my benefit."

She smiled. "I'm so glad you don't know how to lie," she said.

Chapter Twenty-one

Friday afternoon (continued)

If Toby's hard-working colleagues thought of Shakespeare's tomb as the bourn from which no traveler returns, they wouldn't have been referring just to its occupant. Toby's truant disposition meant that Oliver and Effie faced another trip to Holy Trinity to return the shoulder bag he'd abandoned in Mormal's van. The chain ferry across the Avon wasn't operating, so they were forced to take the much longer route over the bridge. At least Toby's bag seemed empty.

As they passed the Gower memorial statue, they found their path suddenly blocked by a Shakespearean character. It was a male figure in a tall capotain hat with a dyed-green ostrich feather, a large cartwheel ruff like a gigantic coffee filter, and a tooled, tan leather jerkin worn over a scarlet doublet. Below the waist, it wore yellow and orange pumpkin breeches, saggy purple hose, and high-heeled shoes with oversized silver buckles. The codpiece was pink.

Oliver first thought it was a garish waxwork, dragged out to entice tourists into some sideshow of famous scenes. They began to move around it, when it spoke.

"Oliver!"

Oliver started and looked again, taking in eyes that were staring angrily at him and tightly pressed lips beneath a rakish white moustache.

"Uncle Tim." Oliver's heart was thumping. "It must be nice to know the old uniform still fits after all these years."

"Never mind the funny, what's this I hear about you getting roughed up?"

"Oh, that."

"Yes, that. I check my phone messages about half an hour ago, and what do I hear? The brigadier exploding with pride because his firstborn, who writes about furry animals, apparently fought off a whole cohort of bashi-bazouks in the dead waste and middle of the night. I eventually got little Angelwine to the phone, who told me where you were." He took a step closer to Oliver. "Why wasn't I told about this attack when it happened?"

"It was nothing…"

"Bollocks it was nothing! You wanted to hide it from me, didn't you? Because you're still going round the village asking questions about Dennis Breedlove. Well?"

"Well, what?" Oliver replied sullenly.

"Well, are you hurt?"

"Just a few bruises. I'll live."

"That's for me to decide," Mallard said, masking his relief. He switched his attention to Effie. "And you! This is how you let your own discretion be your tutor, huh? I hope you like moonlighting as a private eye, Frances Erica Strongitharm, because you may need a new job."

Effie bit her lower lip and stared at the pavement, but she kept hold of Oliver's hand.

"Look, Uncle Tim, doesn't this prove there's something to the case?" Oliver asked. "Somebody's trying to frighten me off. Isn't this something more than fantasy?"

Mallard prodded Oliver in the shoulder. "Don't start all that again. This is the very coinage of your brain. I told you to leave it to Culpepper—"

"What's this from?" said a voice. Mallard, in full choleric flow, took a second to register that the interruption had not come from his nephew or his shame-faced sergeant. A small crowd was forming around the group.

"What?"

"What play is this from?" the questioner persisted, a balding American tourist in a pastel tracksuit and bright white sneakers.

"It's not from a play," said Mallard brusquely.

An American woman spoke up. "I think he's Henry the Fifth and these two are the little princes in the tower." She was also wearing a tracksuit and rather a large amount of gold jewelry. She nudged the man. "Harry, get my picture with him. Make him pretend to strangle me."

Despite the temptation, Mallard remained polite. "Madam, if you don't mind, this is a private conversation."

"Then who are you supposed to be?" asked another passerby, in an Australian accent. Mallard sighed.

"If you must know, I'm dressed as Osric, from *Hamlet*. Now if you'll excuse me—"

"I've never heard of an Osric," proclaimed a female English tourist, as if her ignorance merited praise, "and I've seen all of Shakespeare's films." She smiled proudly.

"So why's he dressed that way?" the Australian asked, still addressing Mallard.

"He's a fop," Mallard explained, wondering why he'd been shifted to the third person. More people were stopping to listen to the conversation.

"What's a fop?"

"A dandy, a popinjay—a man who spends too much time fussing over fashion." Mallard surveyed the crowd, but there was a marked absence of good examples. Quite the reverse.

"Fashion, you may call it…" muttered the English woman.

"So he's a poofter, then?" the Australian continued, with growing interest. "Like Shakespeare himself."

"Osric's sexual orientation is irrelevant," Mallard began. "These stereotypes don't—"

"Now just a moment," cut in the American woman. "My husband happens to be president of our local school board. I think if Shakespeare were…well…I would have been told."

"Oh come on, lady," said a young man with a Scottish accent. "It's a well-known fact that half of his sonnets were written to a man."

"Oh yeah? What about 'Shall I compare thee to a summer's day?'" Harry's wife persisted. "That's one of the greatest love poems ever written."

"Colin Firth recited it to Renee Zellwegger in *Bridget Jones's Diary*," said the older English woman conclusively.

"Exactly." Mrs. Harry leaned toward the young Scotsman. "You can't tell me that was meant for a man."

"Actually it was," said Oliver. "But it's not a love poem."

"Huh?"

"On the surface, it's a poem about poetry, and the way it may confer immortality on someone long after his earthly beauty has faded, and even after his death. But it comes in a sequence of the early sonnets in which Shakespeare is urging his patron to find a wife and start breeding, no doubt because his patron's mother wants some grandchildren."

"I can totally relate," declared Mrs. Harry, nudging her husband again.

"So we have the brilliant ambiguity in the phrase 'eternal lines to time' which can mean both lines of poetry but also bloodlines, carrying the patron's beauty generation-by-generation into the future. But a declaration of romantic love—no."

Oliver had stepped in to deflect attention from Mallard, but the audience seemed appreciative. He chose not to mention his own literary qualifications, although there was a good chance that more of the crowd had heard of Finsbury the Ferret than of Froth or Fortinbras. Meanwhile, Mallard had slipped away from the center of the group to a more removed ground, tugging Effie with him.

"I have to get back," he whispered. "We've made Ophelia's grave straight, but we haven't finished burying the rest of the play. The rehearsal breaks for dinner at five. I'll meet you in Synne at six. You're going to tell me everything that's been going on or you'll be back in uniform and doing crowd control at Millwall home games. I may be the light relief in *Hamlet*, but in real life, I'm not joking."

He strutted back toward the theater, his green ostrich feather bouncing in the sunlight.

"No, I know you're not," she said miserably.

Chapter Twenty-two

Friday evening

There was enough loneliness, disillusion, and alcoholism in Synne to sustain two pubs, both on the main road—The Seven Wise Virgins at the western end of the Square's hypotenuse, and The Bear Without A Head, close to the Swithins' house. The tourist trade divided itself evenly between them, according to whether needing a drink was the initial reaction to arriving in Synne or the final desperate act before departing.

Like many traditional pubs—indeed, like England itself— The Bear Without a Head was divided by class. A frosted-glass screen separated the comfortable "saloon bar" at the front from the chilly "public bar" at the rear, with its own entrance and more spartan furnishings for soiled farm laborers and self-deluding Tory candidates. So when the landlord of the Virgins tried to gain a slight edge by installing a karaoke machine, the Bear's tight-fisted counterpart had fitted his little-used "public" with some secondhand track lighting from a car boot sale in Edgbaston, and announced that from now on, Friday nights were stand-up comedy nights.

"I've always thought I'd be good at stand-up," said Geoffrey. Mallard's inquisition was taking place in the saloon, but the PA system was broadcasting that night's performance at a low level to the entire pub.

"You?" exclaimed Susie. "You can't tell jokes."

"Oh yeah? Well, stop me if you've heard this one…"

"Stop!" said Oliver.

"But you don't know what it was going to be," Geoffrey complained.

"Be quick, then."

"Right, well, the Pope, the Dalai Lama, and—"

"Stop!" said Susie.

"Oh, you've heard it?"

"No, I just want you to stop. I'm being cruel to be unkind."

Geoffrey grabbed the beermat that Oliver had been idly flipping and catching in one hand, and began to scribble some notes on the back. Mallard smiled faintly, checking the change from the second round of drinks, which Oliver had just fetched from the bar. His afternoon anger had faded now that he knew Oliver hadn't been seriously hurt. But the midnight assault was no fiction, and he needed to find out more. And he had no idea what to do about Effie. True, she had been insubordinate. But he also trusted her nose for wrongdoing, and surely the previous night's bloodshed had confirmed that something was indeed rotten in the state of Synne. During the first round of drinks, he'd made the quartet report on their activities over the last two days—the two days, he reminded himself, since he'd forbidden any further inquiries into Breedlove's death.

"Right," he said. "I've got twenty minutes before I have to get back to Stratford. So let's suppose that Oliver was attacked by one of Breedlove's victims, because he or she…"

"He," muttered Oliver.

"…didn't want to be found out, even though Breedlove is dead. Who could it have been?" Mallard took a gulp of lemonade and referred to his notebook. "First up, Tweedledum and Tweedledee."

"We know it wasn't Sidney who attacked me," said Oliver.

"Might have been Lesbia," said Geoffrey.

"There *is* no Lesbia! And I didn't hit a woman."

"Sidney and Lesbia, big question mark," Mallard dictated to himself, stabbing the final dot into his notebook with a flourish. "Now, what about number two, the vicar's Jack and Jill group, a vile phrase."

"Even the open-minded Mr. Edwards would be hard put to rationalize the beating of a parishioner," said Oliver. "Besides, I already knew his secret."

"How about one of the other members of his club?" suggested Susie.

"Edwards swore they didn't know about the blackmail."

"Has anybody seen Edwards today?" Mallard asked. "Does he look as if he's been in a fistfight? For that matter, is there anyone in the village sporting cuts and bruises, apart from Oliver?"

There was no response.

"Then on to Mary, Mary, Quite Contrary—Eric Mormal, number three."

"I think of him as number two," grumbled Effie, breaking a long silence. "What a piece of work. As far as I'm concerned, you can lock him up right now and throw away the key."

"So you think he's the attacker?" asked Susie.

"The what?"

"Eric wasn't the attacker," said Oliver. "There were no marks on his face. At least not before I punched him this afternoon."

"Oliver," said Geoffrey, reaching for another beermat, "you keep making the questionable assumption that you're capable of hitting somebody hard enough to leave a mark."

"Ollie drew blood," said Effie loyally.

"So can a mosquito. Ha! Improv."

Oliver ignored him. "However, I spotted something when Eric drove off this afternoon," he told them. "He works for a co-op farm. That's spelled with a hyphen, or it'll be read as 'coop,' a place where you keep chickens. Of course, you might find coops on a co-op farm."

"Is this going anywhere?" asked Mallard, looking again at his watch.

"Sorry. But when we use the full word, 'cooperative,' we drop the hyphen."

"So?" asked Susie.

"The name of the farm is painted on the side of Eric's van: Pigsneye Cooperative Organic Farms, with 'Cooperative' in larger letters than the rest, because they like to flaunt their socialist credentials. The first two syllables of the word 'Cooperative' can be read as 'Cooper,' which is the word that registered with the Vampire of Synne when a van flashed past him on the night of Breedlove's murder—a van that could easily have been on its way to or from that service road that leads up to the Shakespeare Race. At the very time the suicidal and octogenarian Breedlove was supposed to be dragging his stepladder up the steep slope of Synne Common."

"And?"

"I suggest he was stuffed into the back of Mormal's van for the trip instead, alive or pre-deceased. Culpepper confirmed that Breedlove's clothes were dusty and soiled. The back of Eric's van is dirty, because of the farm produce he carries."

"Ingenious," said Geoffrey.

"Thank you, Geoff."

"And totally wrong."

"What?"

"Breedlove died a week ago tonight, right?"

"Yes, May the first, Friday night."

"Then even if it was Eric Mormal's van that your vampire saw, Mormal wasn't driving it. He was driving Davina Bennet at the time."

"I think you'd better explain," said Mallard.

Geoffrey gathered the beermats he'd been annotating and tapped them on the table, as if straightening a pack of playing cards. "Last Friday, I came home from work and decided to check on Doctor-Peeper-dot-com," he reported. He'd been forced to admit to his online activities during the earlier part of the conversation. "Eric started broadcasting live with Davina at about eight o'clock, and they went on for well over three hours.

And before anyone starts judging me," he added swiftly, "may I remind you that was the time when all of you, minus Susie, plus Phoebe, were prancing around the Shakespeare Race in the buff."

"You're sure it was Davina?" asked Oliver.

"I didn't know her name then, but it was definitely the one you said was Davina. She's the only sister with dark hair."

"How do you know it was live, not a recording?"

"Their television was in the shot when they started. I'd been watching the same program."

"And this went on for nearly three hours?"

Geoffrey nodded. "It was quite a marathon session, even for Doctor Peeper. They did it three times. After each bout, Davina seemed to get cross about something, and they both got dressed and left the room. But then he persuaded her to come back, and they undressed and started all over again."

"He's so leisure," snorted Effie.

"Hang on, we're missing something," said Susie, turning to Geoffrey with astonishment. "You stayed in all evening and watched the same two people boink three times in a row? Have you no life whatsoever, young Angelwine? Why not just sit in a lawn chair and shout at traffic?"

"I will not be disparaged by a woman whose best skill at university was to disguise herself as an unmade bed," Geoffrey retorted. "Honestly, there was nothing she wouldn't show you for a half of shandy and a Nuttall's Minto."

"Virgin," Susie muttered, with a suppressed grin.

"Slapper," Geoffrey shot back.

"Let's move on," Mallard cut in wearily. "Okay, victim number four, Twinkle, Twinkle, Little Star. Mr. Snopp, the Vampire of Synne. Had he the motive and the cue for passion? He's already fessed up to Effie about his true condition, believing that she was on official police business. Which she wasn't. Why would he then choose to send Oliver a message about keeping away?"

Effie, the only member of the group to have met Snopp, shrugged without speaking.

Mallard dropped his notebook onto the table. "Well, Ollie, I have to congratulate you. You did it. These are the players. But now you don't think any of them had either the opportunity or the guts—or both—to beat you up. Is there anything to be gained from identifying that fifth victim?"

"I don't think we need worry about that now," said Oliver. "The letter was never delivered."

Effie stared at him, but he didn't meet her eye. "Didn't you say your Dr. McCaw wanted you to identity all five?" she asked.

"That was when we didn't know who the other four were. Now that we do, we can leave number five in peace. Because no matter who attacked me, one of those four must have murdered Breedlove."

"If being blackmailed was the motive," said Geoffrey.

"If he was murdered," said Mallard.

"We're not certain about Sidney and Lesbia," Susie said. "If they're never seen together, it may not be because they're the same person. They may just hate the sight of each other. Like Geoffrey and me."

"There aren't too many other candidates for the Tweedles," Oliver sighed. "Breedlove started to blackmail them four years ago, which rules out a lot of potential sins." He gulped some beer. "Potential sinners, too. The way people move in and out of this village, it's hard to find residents who go back that far. After only ten years, my parents are almost the village elders. I was just saying that to Mr. Tooth."

"Who?" asked Susie.

"Mr. Tooth. Old acquaintance of mine. You remember, Eff, we met him in Plumley last Christmas. Nice old chap."

Effie shook her head.

"Mr. Tooth's the man I've seen around the village in the last couple of days," Oliver continued. "He was waiting to get a drink at the bar. Hope you don't mind, Uncle Tim, but I treated him to a slimline tonic out of your twenty. Apparently, he's trying to locate residents who are committed to staying in the village, but everyone seems to be either just arriving or planning to move on. It's the one way Synne is like Manhattan. Well, that and the skyscrapers."

"Skyscrapers?" Geoffrey asked.

"A surreal joke, Geoff," Oliver explained. "The point being that Synne is completely unlike Manhattan in the vertical architecture department. There isn't even a steeple on the church." He took another sip from his glass.

"I don't get it," Geoffrey admitted.

"Ah, Geoff," sighed Susie, "I always feel that there's less to you than meets the eye. You have hidden shallows."

"Well, I still insist that you leave Breedlove's death to the capable Culpepper," said Mallard. "But Oliver's attack is another matter, and this Snopp chap seems the most likely suspect to me." He looked over his notes. "Snopp can't decide if he's a vampire or a cancer survivor or a leper, he lives in a dark, gloomy mansion disguised as a monk… There's something a little too Stephen King about this lazar-like existence." He glanced at his watch again. "Effie, you're going to pay another visit to Mr. Snopp, unannounced, and this time I'm coming with you."

It was the first time for several minutes that he had addressed her directly.

"I thought I was supposed to be off duty," she said, looking up. Mallard's face was expressionless, his eyes unblinking behind the spectacles.

"That didn't stop you interviewing Snopp the first time," he said quietly. "Or using a regional crime lab for unofficial business. But if you suddenly want to go by the book, Sergeant Strongitharm, your leave is suspended as of tomorrow morning, nine o'clock sharp, until we're finished with Mr. Snopp."

"You think I need supervision, Superintendent Mallard?"

They held each other's gaze, but Mallard was satisfied that he saw apprehension as well as defiance in Effie's cold eyes. "I think you need company," he said. "And I need to satisfy my curiosity. Clear?"

She swallowed. "Clear. Sir."

Mallard drained his glass and got to his feet, already regretting the flare of displeasure that had forced him to publicly remind his adored Effie of the gulf between their ages, ranks, and experience.

"Meanwhile, Oliver," he continued, glaring at his nephew, "you can stay safe by cutting out the midnight voyeurism. It cannot come to good. Synne already has two peeping Toms. They don't need the competition. Work on that trivial book instead."

"Ooh, I thought of one earlier," Susie interrupted. "Eskimos have thirty-seven words for snow. Everybody seems to want to tell you that."

"Good night, ladies, good night, boys," Mallard said with a brusque nod and headed for the pub door. A second or two after they'd seen his figure stride past the front window, Effie's mobile phone rang.

"Have you heard the one about the—?" Geoffrey began, as Effie listened to her caller.

"Yes," said Oliver.

"Understood," Effie said with a small smile.

"That's not fair! I didn't get the chance to tell you what it was."

"Okay, what is it?"

"It's the one about the duck who goes into the library."

"Heard it. Anyway, it's not a duck, it's a chicken. Susie's right, you can't tell jokes."

"Then I'm going to the toilet," Geoffrey muttered.

"Careful, that's how Elvis Presley died," Susie shouted after him. She chuckled. "Hey, is that another example of your Mind-Spam, Ollie?" she asked, reaching for her drink.

"Yes, and for once, it's true. A lot of people died on the toilet. Elvis. George II. Lenny Bruce. Catherine the Great, it is thought."

"Oh, but I'd heard…"

"No. On the toilet."

Susie seemed disappointed. "Have you figured out why people remember these things?" she asked.

Oliver settled back in his chair. "I think the goal is to know as little as possible about as much as possible. And that extrapolates to knowing one fact about every conceivable topic. Russian history? Catherine the Great's demise. The Inuit peoples of the Arctic regions? Lots of words for snow. Marine biology? The shark has to keep moving forward or it will die. Egyptology? Ancient Egyptian mummifiers would use a metal pick to pull the deceased's brains out through his nostrils."

"Ew!"

"Ew, maybe. But everyone wants to tell you about it. A lot of MindSpam seems to be about death, and not just deaths on the toilet. Everyone remembers—and wants to tell you—that Mama Cass choked on a ham sandwich. That Sweden has the highest suicide rate. That Walt Disney's head is cryogenically preserved somewhere in California. None of this is true, incidentally."

"Truth seems to be an irrelevance."

"Thus runs the world away."

"Geoffrey's taking a while," Effie commented, tuning in late to the conversation. She had been thinking about the phone call and Mallard's crisp instruction to make sure no harm came to Oliver.

There was a wail of feedback from the performance room in the rear of the pub and a smattering of applause. Like many rock singers, the landlord never believed that a microphone could pick up his voice unless it was pressed against his uvula, so they could hear his fuzzy introduction from where they were sitting.

"Now we have a new lad here to entertain us, so give him a chance, ladies and gentlemen, give him a chance. He says his name is Geoffrey Angelhair, like the pasta I suppose, if you like that foreign muck."

He stopped. "Wine?" the voice resumed. "You say you want some wine? Don't blame you, mate, we've a tough crowd in tonight." A longer pause, then, "Okay, I'm sorry, people, he now says his name is Angelwine. Wish he'd make his mind up. Hey, let's see if you whine after hearing him, eh? Ha, ha, he's not the only one with the jokes this evening. Once again, give it up for Jerry Angelwine."

Oliver, Effie, and Susie jumped up from the table, but by the time they'd squeezed through the partition into the rear bar, all the chairs had been taken, and Geoffrey was into his routine.

"…said the frog," he was concluding, and beamed around the room, meeting total silence, apart from the odd, embarrassed titter. His smile faded, and he felt in several of his jacket pockets until he brought out his deck of beermats, which he looked through swiftly.

"Ah, I see. It should have been a chicken, not a duck. My fault." He shuffled the beermats again. "Ah, here's the Superman joke, you'll like this one. My boss told me it. There's this rooftop bar in Manhattan, which is apparently just like Synne only with skyscrapers." He paused, noticing the stillness. "I told Oliver that wasn't funny," he mumbled. "Okay, there are these two men…"

"Oliver," whispered Susie, "can't you get him off the stage? He's going to be totally humiliated. That's my job."

Oliver shrugged helplessly as Geoffrey blundered on.

"So the second guy jumps over the parapet too, falls hundreds of feet and splat!"

He slapped his hands together for the sound effect, forgetting he was holding his beermat collection. Many made it to the side wall before they stopped rolling. The audience began to laugh.

"Never mind. Where were we? Anyway, that's when the barman turns to the first guy and says, only I can't do the accent, 'You know, when you get drunk, Superman, you can be a real arsehole.' 'Asshole,' I mean." He paused, pleased that the joke was getting a better reception than the first. A thought seemed to strike him.

"That would probably have been funnier if I hadn't already told you it was about Superman." He bent over and picked up the nearest beermat. "'Rocket to the sun'?" he read. "Ah yes, I remember. There were these…" He stopped suddenly, motionless, his mouth poised to issue the first syllable of the next word.

"Oh no," said Oliver.

"What now?" asked Susie.

"Geoffrey's just remembered that this joke requires an ethnic group notoriously less intelligent than your own. Several years of corporate sensitivity training have just kicked in, and he doesn't know what to do."

But Geoffrey had seen his friends at the rear of the room, and a glimmer of inspiration seemed to strike him. "I have this friend called Oliver," he began again. "And he's really stupid."

"He's on his own," said Oliver.

"How stupid is he?" an audience member chanted. Geoffrey was still a little slow to react.

"Erm, well, I was just going to tell you how stupid he is. He told me the other day he was going to build a rocket to go to the moon. I mean the sun. The sun. So I said, isn't that dangerous? Aren't you worried you're going to, you know, burn up? Because the sun is hot, you understand, and in reality you couldn't possibly…Right. Well. But Oliver said, 'No, it'll be okay, because I'm going to travel by night.'" Before the audience could react, he rapidly corrected himself. "By day," I mean."

He relaxed, enjoying the polite, largely uncomprehending laughter. Then a look of consternation came to his avian features, and he shot back to the microphone. "No, I was right the first time, it *was* by night."

The flashes of merriment continued, partly genuine as some members of the audience decoded the humor buried beneath the stumbles, partly sadistic at Geoffrey's expense, and partly knowing, from some avant-garde types who thought they were witnessing ironic performance art.

"That was quite amusing, actually," said Susie.

"Amusing?" snapped Oliver. "There aren't too many Olivers in this village—they'll know he means me."

She prodded him in the back. "Oh, lighten up, Swithin. It's just a bit of fun."

"And then there's my friend, Susie," Geoffrey picked up. "What a slapper!"

"We're leaving," said Susie instantly. She grabbed Effie's hand and began to push her way out of the bar. Oliver followed, hearing Geoffrey's voice all the way.

"Eyes you could drown in and a nose you could ski off. She told me just now that the Eskimos have thirty-seven words for snow. Which is odd, because Susie doesn't have even one word for 'no'! The closest she gets to it is 'Wait till the choir's gone past the end of the pew....'"

Chapter Twenty-three

Friday evening (continued)

"So, Oliver, I hear you got into another fight today."

Oliver stirred his lentil soup moodily, without looking up. Two pints of bitter before dinner hadn't been a good move.

"I'd rather not talk about it, Aunt Phoebe," he muttered.

"No, dear, this is your mother speaking."

This time he looked. Chloe and Phoebe were flanking the brigadier at the far end of the dining room table—all three staring at him. Effie was the only other diner that evening: Susie had rushed tearfully to her bedroom when they arrived back from the pub, Geoffrey was missing, and Toby was working late at the dig, as he'd informed Oliver and Effie that afternoon when they finally reached Holy Trinity and passed on his empty shoulder bag.

"What's that?" grunted the brigadier. "Young Oliver got into a scrap again?"

"I heard it from Wendy Bennet." Chloe seemed to be addressing the brigadier and her sister, but her eyes never left Oliver's face. "Oliver took a swing at that friend of Toby's, Eric Normal or whatever his name is. Slimy piece of work."

"Oh, I wouldn't say that about Oliver," protested Phoebe.

Chloe smiled. "Wendy says Eric bit his tongue badly and can't use it. A step in the right direction, I'd say, but for some reason, Wendy seemed to think it a disadvantage."

Oliver glanced up again and caught the twinkle in his mother's expression. *Was there nothing this woman didn't know about the seedy underbelly of the Cotswolds?*

"Good show, old chap," said his father, beaming down the table. He wiped his mouth on his napkin. "Sounds like you're getting a reputation as a man to be reckoned with, eh?"

That could be the first time the brigadier had ever called him a man. "It was just a passing moment, Father," Oliver said. Effie contributed nothing.

"Always thought you'd make a useful boxer," the brigadier continued. "Let's see, you'd probably be in the middleweight class now, but with a bit of training, we might get you up to light heavyweight. When your mother met me, I was regimental champion, welterweight. Remember that, old girl?"

"I certainly remember some bobbing and weaving from those early days, dear," Chloe remarked, passing a small pot of caviar to the brigadier.

After dinner, Oliver and Effie found themselves alone in the sitting room. Effie subsided onto a sofa and kicked off her sandals. She had changed out of her short skirt before the meeting in the pub, and was now back in the thin cotton dress that had found its way onto Oliver's erotic top ten list on the previous afternoon.

"Are you okay?" he asked.

Effie looked up, ice-blue eyes like a winter night. She nodded. "Tim was right," she said. "I should have left this case to Simon Culpepper."

"Then are *we* okay?" he asked anxiously, after a pause, sitting beside her. If he still hoped to turn his teenage bedroom into a love nest, there were only two nights left, and tomorrow was the Theydon Bois Thespian's *Hamlet*, so how much of a buzzkill would that be?

She leaned her head against his neck. Her curls tickled, smelling faintly of apple-scented shampoo.

"Yes, of course, we're okay, you silly pillock," she said. "And in spite of everything, you've hooked Tim. You know—the rendezvous with the vampire tomorrow morning? Although it

may be a solo jaunt for Tim if I don't get to bed fairly soon."
She yawned.

Uh-oh.

"Since we're going to bed," he began, reaching for her hand.

The door was flung open abruptly, and Geoffrey half stumbled into the room.

"Not quite the segue I was aiming for," Oliver complained, as his friend hurried past them and dropped onto an armchair.

"Women!" Geoffrey exclaimed, folding his arms crossly.

"I'll explain what they are later," said Oliver. "First, where the hell have you been for the last three hours?"

"In the pub. They wouldn't let me go. Kept making me tell more jokes." He smirked, despite his bad mood, in a way that made Oliver want to grab his nose and pull hard. "Apparently, my performance was a huge hit."

"How? You were messing up every time."

"That's just it. They said it made it funnier. They thought it was my gimmick." He pointed at Oliver. "You may laugh…"

"I sincerely doubt it."

"…but they've asked me back next week."

"Good for you, Geoff," Effie remarked, with an admonitory stare at Oliver. "Then why are you so peeved with my sex?"

Sex, Oliver thought mormally.

Geoffrey lifted a throw cushion onto his lap and punched it. "It's the Beamish creature. Chloe said she'd gone straight to her room when she came in, so I went up and knocked on the door, to give her the news. Susie told me to do something that's basically impossible unless you're a well-endowed and limber hermaphrodite."

"Well, dear, what did you expect? You identified her in your act as a slut. The poor thing was mortified."

"But she *is* a strumpet," Geoffrey exclaimed, reaching for another throw cushion to hit, only to discover it was a cat. "We've always joked about Susie's flexible morals. I thought she'd be flattered, as if she were a Muse, or something." He smiled again. "You should have been there—I did ten minutes of jokes about her cleavage alone. Comedy gold."

"You don't know much about women, do you, Geoff?" Oliver commented, shaking his head. Effie also tried to say something, but Oliver could only make out the odd words "kettle" and "black" through her laughter.

"Of course I don't," Geoffrey confirmed. "Nobody does." He turned to Effie, who was catching her breath. "I mean, I did twenty more minutes of Stupid Oliver jokes after you'd gone, and it brought the house down—you don't see Ollie getting all huffy about it."

"You did what?" Oliver asked.

"Never mind that for now," Effie cut in. "Susie's upset, and you need to make it right. So tomorrow morning—"

"No," Oliver interrupted, striding up to Geoffrey and pulling him to his feet by his lapels. "Not tomorrow morning. Now. Geoffrey Angelwine, you go back up to Susie's room and apologize for your malicious mockery. You identify yourself as the most abject item crawling between heaven and earth. You beg her forgiveness and ask what you can do to make it up to her. Don't botch the words up. Is that clear?"

"Yes, but—"

"I haven't finished. Then, you'll listen to her. You won't interrupt. Even if her wild and whirling words last till breakfast. You won't leap into the conversation with witticisms or off-color remarks, not even if she says something that reminds you of a Susie's cleavage joke."

"Don't worry, I'm not to touch that one."

"Good."

"But I might give the other one a quick—"

"Geoffrey!" Oliver snapped. "Don't. Even if you work out how many Susie's cleavages it takes to change a lightbulb. Even if you know why Susie's cleavage did cross the road. Well?"

"Well, what?"

"Well, why are you still here?" Without waiting for an answer, Oliver propelled Geoffrey toward the door. A second or two later, they heard his slow footsteps going up the stairs.

"Swithin," Effie purred, stepping toward Oliver, "your machismo is showing. I want you."

"This isn't one of those wind-ups like the proposal business the other day, is it?"

"Does this answer your question?" She slid a hand behind his neck and kissed him very firmly, twice.

"No," he gasped. She chuckled and broke away.

"No, you're right, it was a wind-up. But I feel like taking pity on you anyway."

She picked up her sandals and led him to the door.

Five minutes later, he hurried back from the bathroom with washed hands and freshly minted breath, but stopped in his bedroom doorway, heart thumping. The light was off in the room, and Effie was looking out of the window, her shadowy figure a dim collage of grayish-blue and silvery skin in the faint moonlight. She had waited for him before undressing, he noted gratefully. So would she now lift the dress up and over her head in one swift, practiced move, raising and spreading her untamed ringlets like a Japanese fan? Or would she slip off the shoulder straps, reach back and unzip the bodice, and then let the material cascade around her to the floor, stripped by the attractive power of the very planet itself? (And in either case, had she taken off her underwear first?) His heart continued its loud, rhythmic tattoo, almost as if the sound was truly perceptible in the room.

"I thought I heard something," Effie said quietly, without turning around. Oliver caught a faint shriek in the distance.

"There it is again," she said.

"If it's that bloody vixen, I'm going to campaign to bring back fox hunting," Oliver muttered, stepping over to her and beginning to kiss her bare shoulders.

"I don't think it's coming from outside," she answered, ignoring his attentions. "And can you hear a sort of banging?"

So it wasn't just his circulatory system. He paused and listened. The regular, percussive beat seemed to be coming from the ceiling, and there were more vocalizations, louder, more frequent, and clearly human. Dear Lord, was someone being attacked again, this time inside the house? It sounded like Susie's voice, and her screams were gaining in volume and intensity. Had Geoffrey snapped? There were words, a phrase shouted over and over. Was it "Help me?" Something "me," anyway.

"Oh, my God!" Oliver exclaimed. "They're…"

Effie burst into laughter. "It sounds as if your advice worked," she said, switching on the bedside lamp. "I think you can say they've reached a rapprochement." She gathered the top cover from Oliver's bed and headed for the door.

"Where are you going?" he asked.

Effie paused and glanced up at the ceiling. "I'm not staying here with that soundtrack."

"It's not our fault. We shouldn't be driven out of our own room because someone else beat us to the nookie."

"Then you go upstairs and tell them to stop," she replied, yawning one more time. "I'm going to sleep on the couch downstairs. If you come with me, I'll share the duvet."

"Okay, but does this mean we aren't… ?"

She stopped and looked at him tenderly. "I'm afraid so, darling. The public rooms of your parents' home are off-limits to the four-footed frolic by sheer definition."

"But when Geoff and Susie are finished…?"

"Who knows when that will be?" she said, with another wary glance upwards. "I have to get up early. Besides, if the walls of the Chateau Swithin are that thin, I'd prefer to wait until we get back to London."

Oliver stood still, dejected, glaring at his still-unnotched headboard. It certainly sounded as if Geoffrey and Susie's first close encounter was going to be a long one. Geoff may have been a novice in the art of love, but he'd put himself in the hands, arms, and presumably other body parts of an expert.

"Thank you, Geoff," he grunted—or something fairly close phonetically—and followed Effie out of the room.

Chapter Twenty-four

Friday evening (continued)

Oliver went downstairs to find Effie cocooned on the sitting room couch, already dozing, with the opportunistic cat furled beside her. He doused the lights and took the *Guardian* crossword to the kitchen, hoping to catch Toby. After half an hour of waiting, he decided instead to defy his uncle and continue the surveillance of Sidney and Lesbia. Effie may have fallen into line, but Mallard wasn't *his* boss. Some must watch while some must sleep. He let himself out the kitchen door and strolled around the side of the house.

He stopped dead when he saw the black-clad figure, crouched over the stepladder he had planned to use. The intruder hadn't heard his approach. Oliver looked around for a weapon, saw nothing in the moonlight. But in the last twenty-four hours, hadn't he proved he could take care of himself? Two victories, no defeats, after all.

On the other hand, fighting hurts, even if you win.

He slowly removed his glasses and placed them on the nearby window ledge. The man was still unaware that he'd been seen. The readiness is all. Oliver tapped a blurry body part that he hoped was a shoulder, then shifted his weight back, ready to land the first punch.

The intruder spun around with a low whimper, dropped backwards, and sat on the ground.

"Lawks-a-mercy!" he exhaled. "It's you, Oliver. Oh, you did give me a turn."

Oliver put on his glasses. As he'd guessed from the voice, the intruder was Vic Flimsy, the Peeping Tom from whom he'd borrowed the stepladder a week earlier. Flimsy was a middle-aged man, with an untidy growth of caramel-colored hair and eyes that were too small for his face by precisely the same percentage that his nose was too big for it.

"Good evening, Mr. Flimsy," said Oliver. "My apologies for the scare. Doing us tonight?" Had Flimsy heard the top-floor fornication from the street, like a dog whistle?

Flimsy shook his head and got to his feet, a pair of binoculars swinging from a strap around his neck. "Oh no," he chirped, "I have much too much respect for your dear parents. They're church people. No, I'm visiting the Crumbs, in the Close— they're Baptist heathens. Their youngest is just back from a fortnight in Ibiza. That's why I need my ladder."

Oliver nodded, half-remembering that the Crumbs' resident daughter, Clodagh Crumb Maxwell, was a morose divorcee in her early forties who never closed her bedroom curtains. Do peepers and exhibitionists complete each other, he wondered? Or does it deprive the voyeur of the thrill of the hunt? He didn't feel inclined to discuss this with the unsavory Flimsy, who was now struggling to balance the long stepladder on his shoulder. But then a thought struck him.

"Mr. Flimsy, you have your ear to the ground in Synne," he said. *And your eyes to the keyholes.* "May I detain you for a second?"

"That's all right, sir. Clodagh won't start without me."

"Have you heard any rumors about the late Dennis Breedlove?"

"That he was a blackmailer, you mean? You're helping the police clear that up, aren't you? I assume that's why you borrowed old Bessie here." He patted the stepladder affectionately with his free hand.

Oh, great, Oliver thought. If the village grapevine knew about his investigation, then last night's attacker could have been anyone in Synne with a balaclava and a guilty conscience. (And surely a broken nose, today?)

"In your, uh, research, have you come across anything that might have whetted Breedlove's appetite?"

Flimsy sucked on his teeth. "Well, there's the vicar, obviously—we all know what his book club's really about." He lowered his head sadly. "Shameful business, on church property. I have more self-respect than to sully my binoculars on the vicarage curtains. And you might want to keep an eye on that kid Eric from Pigsneye. Not Normal."

"No, he certainly isn't."

"No, I mean his name's not Normal, it's something like it. Norman? Mormon? Moron? Anyhow, I've noticed him in Stratford, mixing in with the young lady tourists, working the camcorder-in-the-bag gag. Bleedin' amateurs, relying on this newfangled technology—where's the skill, where's the craft? They have no technique to fall back on. Oh, and there's something very fishy about that chap who moved into the manor house last year. Keeps odd hours, men coming and going at night. Not that I've given him any of my services. I'm strictly heterosexual, as you know, Oliver. Old school."

"Yes, you are."

"I'm what?"

"Old school."

"Eh? No, I meant you could check out the old school. It's just been converted into a dwelling. Couple from the Smoke. Rich, not gaudy. Wifey used to manage a hedge fund, hubby makes bloody pottery, we don't care."

Newcomers, Oliver thought. Breedlove wouldn't have got to them yet. But why hadn't he thought of consulting Vic Flimsy before? This is golden.

Flimsy had stopped, distracted by a light that had just come on in a second-floor window across the Square. Bessie seemed to shiver, as if straining at a leash.

"One last question," Oliver ventured. "I don't suppose you've peeped in on Mr. and Mrs. Weguelin?"

Flimsy stared at him censoriously in the moonlight. "How dare you!" he exclaimed. "Sidney and Lesbia are pillars of the church. The very idea of subjecting them to my vile attentions! I'm surprised at you, young Oliver."

He hoisted Bessie higher on his shoulder and marched primly away. Oliver followed at a distance, relieved when the voyeur walked past the turning that would have taken him to the Weguelins' back garden.

An hour later, Oliver was holding his position behind the Weguelins' house, in the fading hope that they hadn't retired for the night, although all the rear-facing windows were dark. The high wall had been a challenge without Bessie, but once he'd jumped and established a handhold on the coping, he found he could wedge his foot onto a slightly projecting brick. He'd fallen only twice, first onto a pile of earth that someone had dumped behind the wall, and the second time into the soft, familiar, welcoming bed of stinging nettles.

It was well after midnight by now, and the half-moon was close to setting. A light breeze brought a sweet gust of night-scented stock from the Weguelins' garden. The air was filled with the odd metallic hum of insects. A badger snuffled past in a nearby field. A hand clamped onto Oliver's shin.

"I thought I told you to stay out of this," came a voice, alarmingly close. Oliver risked a look down. The beam of a flashlight met his eyes, blinding him.

He kicked back wildly with his free foot like a donkey, toward the place he thought a head should be, and was satisfied when his shoe made contact with something other than air. There was a grunt of pain and the man—oh, let it be a man—fell backwards. But he kept hold of Oliver's leg. Oliver was pulled from the wall, and both men plunged into the nettles. Oliver landed two punches into the stranger's stomach, which felt annoyingly well-muscled. The hand let go.

Oliver rolled and got to his feet first, blinking away the snake-like afterimages of the flashlight bulb. Amazingly, his glasses had stayed on. He adopted a fighting stance, bent forward, center of gravity low, and waited for the first sign of a fresh assault.

The dark-clothed man was breathing hard, trying to speak. He rolled cautiously onto his side, but still made no attempt to stand. Oliver took a step nearer, trying to see his opponent's face in the deep shadows. The flashlight lay a few feet away, illuminating a patch of fleabane.

Suddenly, Oliver was tipping. The man had hooked one foot around Oliver's ankle, and now pushed with his other foot against Oliver's knee. Oliver tumbled backwards, over the edge of a drainage ditch. He landed hard on its slope, wheezing and flailing for support.

The man rose to his feet and, from Oliver's point of view, failed to leave off the ascent where most people would. He recovered the flashlight and shone it again on Oliver's face. Oliver closed his eyes to the blazing glare and prepared for the *coup de grace.*

"It's the purple trainers that are the giveaway," said the man breathlessly. Another familiar voice, this time with a thick Brummie accent.

"Simon?" Oliver ventured.

"A piece of him."

Oliver scrabbled at the grass around him and tried to climb out of the ditch. Culpepper offered him a hand. The two men found themselves standing together in the darkness, in an awkward facsimile of a handshake.

"I guess I'm under arrest," said Oliver, letting go and tugging his wet trousers away from his skin.

"Frankly, I wouldn't know where to start. Assaulting an officer, public nuisance, trespass, interfering with an ongoing investigation, wasting police time…" Culpepper straightened his tie. "Fortunately for you, Oliver, your uncle called me earlier and told me about last night's assault. So despite the bruises and the nettle stings, I'm inclined to excuse your belligerence."

They subsided onto a patch of grass on the bank, side by side, still breathing hard.

"Did you just happen to be passing?" Oliver asked.

"Not at all. Sidney Weguelin called a short while ago and claimed that someone was peering at them over the back wall. They've been hiding inside with the lights off."

"Why you? Why not Ernie Bostar?"

"I left my phone number with the Wegeulins when I interviewed them about Breedlove's death. As it happened, I was in the area. I'd better call Sidney and tell him it was all a mistake. You should clear off." He produced his mobile phone from a pocket and began to search through the list of recent calls.

"Hang on," said Oliver, frowning. "You said you interviewed 'them.'"

"Yes, last Sunday afternoon. The day after I first spoke to you and Effie. Just routine."

"But you saw them separately. At different times."

"No. I went to their house and spoke to them together."

"Together? Together in the same room at the same time?"

"Of course. Why?"

"Are you sure there wasn't a big mirror in the room, and one of them only sat sideways to you? Was Lesbia on a closed-circuit television from a different room? Or did Sidney seem very stiff in his movements, like a big ventriloquist dummy?"

Culpepper switched off his phone without placing the call. "And offer me a gottle of geer while Lesbia drank a glass of water?" He gave a sharp laugh. "So that's why you've been spying on them. You think Sidney and Lesbia are the same person and Breedlove was blackmailing them to keep quiet about it. Which of the rhymes was that brainwave supposed to apply to? Jack and Jill?"

"Tweedledum and Tweedledee," Oliver mumbled.

"Well, it fits, in the sense that we just had a battle." Culpepper prodded his stomach and grimaced. "But no, I can confirm that there are two of them. By the way, Sidney told me that he suspected it was you at the bottom of his garden. You're not good at being furtive, are you, Oliver?"

"I suppose that's a sort of compliment."

"Maybe. Now bugger off before Sidney comes out to see what's been going on."

Oliver hurried away along the lane and back to the deserted main street. He stopped in the bus shelter, catching his breath and straining to read his wristwatch in the darkness. Bollocks! Now he needed a new candidate for Tweedledee and Tweedledum, the Oldest Member of the Breedlove Blackmail Club.

There was a slight movement to his left. Without shifting his body, he turned his head. A man in dark clothes was leaning against the village memorial, watching him. At least, he supposed it was a man. These figures usually were.

He knew he'd been seen. His fair hair was too conspicuous in the moonlight. But the watcher said nothing, no evening greeting, no genial comment to a passing stranger about the lateness of the hour. That couldn't be good. After two false starts, was this finally the reappearance of yesterday's attacker? The stranger's head was certainly covered in something dark.

Oliver pretended he hadn't noticed the figure and started slowly back across the Square toward his parents' home. The edge of the obelisk's broad stone plinth came between him and the silent watcher. He abruptly reversed course and tiptoed directly toward the memorial, flattening himself against the stonework and cautiously peering around corner.

The stranger had gone, vanished.

Oliver paced forward, clockwise around the obelisk, lowering his feet quietly on the grass. He craned his neck to view the street side of the memorial. Again, no sign of the stranger. But he couldn't have escaped. If he'd gone along the main road, his footsteps would have been audible. And if he'd crossed the village green, Oliver would have seen him.

Advancing cautiously, like a child in the last round of musical chairs, he looked around the next corner. Nobody. Oliver completed his circuit. Still nobody. Either the stranger had vanished, or he'd been circling the memorial, too, always keeping it between him and Oliver. In which case…

Oliver spun around. The dark figure was standing behind him.

With a cry of battle, Oliver snatched off his glasses and lunged forward.

The next moment, he was airborne and upside down. He landed flat on the grass, without the relative softness of the nettles to break his fall this time, but aware that hands gripping his sleeves had expertly controlled his descent. Winded, he decided to lie still for a few seconds and enjoy the clarity of the stars. Was that Cassiopeia?

Above him, his opponent's face loomed into sight, upside down from his vantage point. He watched fascinated as the figure used a free hand to remove a tightly tied black headscarf. The dark, round outline of the head abruptly transformed into a more trapezoidal shape as a mass of light curls sprang out. And Oliver knew he was going to recognize this voice, too.

Chapter Twenty-five

Saturday morning

"A young Shakespeare scholar named Toby,
Is no expert on Melville's *Dick, Moby*,
But his inquiry proper
Contains such a whopper
You'd say it's very like a whale."

Oliver opened his eyes. "You might have rhymed," he said aloud, but the shadow of a dream was already slipping from his short-term memory, like soapy fingers trying to turn a doorknob. He tried to remember, knowing that this waking rehearsal would soon be all that he'd recall, a shadow's shadow. Finsbury the Ferret, dressed as Hamlet, declaiming the limerick from a stage set up in the middle of the Shakespeare Race, then telling him to jump.

Oliver had looked around, but it hadn't been one of those dreams that left him teetering on a precipice. "Jump?"

"Jump upon this bloody question."

Question?

It was ten o'clock. Morning sunshine streamed through the east-facing window. Oliver turned, but he was alone in his bed. Effie must have left for her appointment to revisit the vampire with Mallard. Memories of real life rushed back: Effie angry that she'd woken to find him missing; angry that she'd had to throw on dark clothes and a headscarf to scour the shadowy village; and angry—he presumed—because he had so quickly and brazenly flouted Mallard's warning, knowing that she was constrained by loyalty to her disgruntled boss. (Oliver had no idea that this masked a deeper anger with herself for breaking her private pledge to Mallard to keep his nephew safe.) Despite the occasional giggle from the floor above, they'd returned to his bedroom and lay parallel in bed and in silence until sleep took pity on them.

Oliver assessed the effects of last night's violence on his body—inflicted by supposedly friendly members of the police force, he noted. Had Effie taken a perverse pleasure in finding an excuse to flatten him on the grass? He'd certainly hoped to end the night spread out and exhausted because of her efforts, but under different circumstances.

To be or not to be.

That dream. It had been about the phantom fifth victim, the most and least likely killer—most likely, if he or she had just received that final blackmail letter; least likely because it was never sent. The Schrödinger's Cat of suspects. Unless, for some peculiar reason, the addressee took it back to Breedlove's cottage to wave in the face of the blackmailer, and in the excitement of the rash and bloody deed that followed, left it on the desk. Who would be that clumsy?

The fifth victim was unique in another way: Oliver knew both the contents of the initial blackmail letter *and* the nursery rhyme that Breedlove had chosen as his private *aide memoire*. But where was the overlap? The letter spoke of history and plots and, notoriously, a family secret. But the rhyme was church, steeple, door, people. It seemed to indicate some involvement in church life, but the vicar was Jack and Jill, the sexton and organist were…well, could they still be Tweedledum and Tweedledee, despite Culpepper's revelation?

Breedlove was finicky, selecting only one new victim a year, like an Incan sacrifice. With the income from Doctor Peeper, he clearly didn't need a victim this year—and yet he chose one. No doubt it was now a ritual, a game, a foolish celebration of a little old man's power over his sinning neighbors, an old man being twice a child. How many wheedling tête-à-têtes with unsuspecting villagers would it take for him to pinpoint a suitable target for that dubious annual honor, now chosen for sheer sport? Even dim-witted Cat Bennet had fallen under Uncle Dennis's spell.

Ah, maybe those references to "history" and "family" had something to do with the Bennet fortune, supposedly flowing from their grandfather's groundbreaking laxative. Or did Cat blab about the hoped-for blue-blood betrothal for Lucinda, officially a virgin? Breedlove knew better, and he knew whom to target. Frailty, thy name is Wendy.

So was "hiding your history" a reference to removing an activity record from a web browser? Was Luce the "little family secret"? Did the nursery rhyme's "Open the doors and see all the people" refer to that society wedding?

But then was it worth slaying the lucrative bird in the hand of Doctor Peeper for the two in the Bennets' bush? Probably not. The Mormal was right—making Dennis a partner in porn was a stroke of genius.

Tobe or not tobe.

Cat wasn't the only person at the Bennets' dinner table reporting heart-to-hearts with sweet old Uncle Dennis. Finsbury hadn't lied in his limerick: Oliver was secretly worried that that this year's target was his own little brother.

Admittedly, the letter referred to something that had happened in the past, and Toby wasn't old enough to have a past. He said that he and Breedlove had discussed Shakespeare. But had he unwittingly passed on tidbits about the rest of his family—about his parents, those regular churchgoers who might well fit the last nursery rhyme? Oliver was unaware of any Swithin family secrets, although he knew little enough about his father's military service. Or would "family" include an uncle by marriage, opening up the long career of Detective Superintendent Timothy Mallard to some scrutiny? The blackmail letter's "blessed plot," the little

family secret that might be revealed by digging up the past…
was that why Chloe had clammed up? To protect the brigadier
or Uncle Tim?

Toby or not Toby?

That was the question.

And if, as Oliver hoped, the answer was that his brother was
innocent, why was Toby so obviously lying about his thesis?

Oliver swung himself out of bed and dressed as quickly as
he could, using his time-honored method of brushing his hair
by pulling on a sweatshirt.

Downstairs in the kitchen, Susie and Geoffrey were sitting
close together at the counter, feeding each other muesli from
the same bowl and giggling with every mouthful. Oliver filled
his mug at the coffeemaker.

"We have something to tell you, Ollie," said Geoffrey, with
a smirk.

"Do your worst."

"Susie and I have, uh, buried the hatchet."

"The hell you say," Oliver replied, sipping his coffee. He saw
the self-conscious amusement in Susie's dark-brown eyes.

"I'm sorry if we disturbed you last night, Ollie," she said.

"Think nothing of it," Oliver said, with a gallant gesture. He
picked up the morning newspaper and scanned the headlines.

"Does that mean you heard something?" asked Geoffrey.

"Every squeak and gibber."

"I say, being overheard, that makes it all a bit embarrassing," Geoffrey remarked, not entirely convincingly. "But it
does remind me of a joke I could use in my next performance.
Did you hear the one about the—oh, let me get this right—the
dyslexic…agnostic…insomniac? He used to lie awake at night,
wondering if there was a God."

"Dog," Oliver murmured, not looking up from the paper.

"What?"

"Dog, not God. He's dyslexic."

"Dog," repeated Geoffrey. He kissed Susie tenderly and stood
up, without letting go of her hand. "Darling Susie, I need to

use the bathroom. This is the first time in twelve hours we'll have been apart."

"I'll be waiting, sweetie," said Susie, ignoring Oliver's mime of incipient nausea behind Geoffrey's back. Geoffrey reversed out of the room and blew her a kiss at the door. Oliver dropped the newspaper.

"So what's it all about, Susie?" he asked.

Susie wiped her mouth with a napkin. "Geoffrey came to my room last night to apologize. He said all the right things and, well, one thing led to another."

"And another and another and another."

She laughed. "I've always said that Geoffrey was fucking hopeless. But not vice versa, as it turns out."

Oliver gulped some more coffee. "So do you think you'll become an item?" he asked, slightly warily. He had just remembered that Geoffrey's room was directly above his in the Holland Park house they shared with Susie and Ben. Maybe those floors were thicker.

"It has a certain rightness to it. But it's also odd, our being best friends already. I know I have a reputation for kissing more than my fair share of frogs, but what if your Prince Charming is already in your life?"

"Are you implying that Geoffrey is *not* the amphibian he so closely resembles?"

"Why do we do that, Ollie?" she continued, as if he hadn't spoken. "Why do we let Love's blind, meretricious chemicals fool us into believing that strangers may be soul mates, when surely friendship is the better guide? I never thought of Geoffrey 'that way' before. But this morning, I woke up outrageously happy. All trembly and heart-thumpy and fixated."

"And off your food?"

"Let's not get carried away."

"Well, I wish you the best. But I don't recall your ever describing Geoffrey as your best friend. In fact, you've tended to imply that you loathe him."

Susie shrugged. "Hate and love. They're often the same thing, aren't they?"

"No."

"Well, there's always an element of competitiveness in relationships, isn't there?"

"No."

"No? You ask Effie if she agrees. And don't be so judgmental about my love life," she added, flicking at him with her napkin. "You had your chance with me."

"When?"

"When we were at Oxford. You were three sheets to the wind in your college buttery, and you said you wanted to make love to me very badly. Because I thought you probably would, I demurred."

They heard rapid steps on the stairs. Geoffrey slipped into the room again and reclaimed his place beside Susie.

"Miss me, darling?" he asked.

"Not in the slightest," Oliver answered quickly. "Have either of you seen Toby?"

"He left for Stratford about ten minutes before you came down," Geoffrey informed him. "One of his college friends picked him up."

"Eric Mormal hasn't forgiven him, then?"

"Apparently, Eric's taken to his bed since you decked him yesterday," reported Susie.

"Blast. I really need to talk to Toby. And Effie's not here to drive me."

"Geoff and I were going to Stratford this morning for a little sightseeing. We can take you. Can you be ready in about a quarter of an hour?" Geoffrey whispered something into her ear. "Actually, make that forty-five minutes," she added, as they both hurried from the room.

Chapter Twenty-six

Saturday morning (continued)

A hundred yards beyond the Jacobean hulk of Furbelow Hall, a gap in the drystone wall, marked for some reason by a pile of earth, gave access to a small lane, shaded by dark Scots pines, which led to the back of the manor house. Mallard eased his Jaguar onto a rough gravel parking area. Tire tracks showed that other vehicles had used the space recently.

The Hall's rear entrance was at the end of one of its long projecting wings. Effie reached for a bell-pull, but Mallard stopped her.

"Let's not be in too much of a hurry to announce ourselves," he said, with a brief grin.

It was a hint of their usual working relationship, and it made her want to sing. Mallard pushed at the door, and they stepped into a small entrance hall and listened. Not a mouse stirring. They set off cautiously down the long, dim corridor, occasionally shining a flashlight into empty side rooms. The corridor was oak-paneled, but bare of the paintings, stuffed deer heads, and sentinel suits of armor often found in period houses. Its flagstones were uncarpeted.

They reached the crosspiece of the house's H-shaped plan, the corner where Effie thought she'd glimpsed a man during her earlier visit. They turned left, past the closed door to the room where she'd conducted her interview with the Vampire of

Synne, and through the heavy curtain that brought them into the main entrance hall.

"Mr. Snopp!" Effie called, following Mallard's nod. There was no answer. She took a few steps across the checkerboard tiles and called again. Mallard stepped back into the shadows. They could hear hasty footsteps from the upper floor. Then, slightly breathless, the cowled figure of a monk seemed to materialize on the landing high above their heads. He made no attempt to descend the stairs.

"Who is it that disturbs my tranquil and solitary life?" Snopp intoned, in his odd, richly layered voice. As before, his hands were pushed into the opposite sleeve openings, creating the impression of a single arm that looped from shoulder to shoulder.

"It's Detective Sergeant Strongitharm, Mr. Snopp."

"Of course," Snopp replied. He paused, like an actor unsure of his lines. "You choose an odd hour to visit a nocturnal wanderer. And this time, you come unannounced."

The reproof was clear. The vampire still held his position at the top of the stairs, upright but a little fidgety, hood low over his face, so none of his disfigured skin could be seen.

"I apologize for that, sir, but I have a few additional questions about the Breedlove case. Just routine you understand."

Again, a long pause. Snopp seemed to be weighing the situation. "It shall be so," he said at last. "Pray find your way to the same chamber in which we held our brief conference on Thursday. I will join you in a matter of a few moments."

The hooded head turned to one side. "And yet I see you are not alone, my dear," he crooned. "Who is it that hovers in the shadows beyond? Kind sir, will you come forward and declare yourself, that we may embark in a true spirit of forthrightness and candor?"

Mallard took a couple of steps across the tiles and stood beside Effie, looking up at Snopp.

"Hello, Reg," he said. "I thought you were dead."

The Vampire of Synne threw back the hood to reveal a beaming, middle-aged face, without a trace of a scar. "Mr. Mallard!" he cried, in a strong west-London accent. He spread his arms, the loose sleeves of the robe waving like brown wings. "I'm undead."

Chapter Twenty-seven

Saturday morning (continued)

Oliver found his brother once again among the tourists in the chancel of Holy Trinity, gazing at the Shakespeare burial site with its doggerel curse.

"Will's will," he said in Toby's ear.

"Will's will's what?" Toby seemed sleepy and irritable. His clothes were muddy from the dig, and he pulled awkwardly on the oversized cricket sweater he insisted on wearing despite the warm weather.

"You know what I'm talking about," Oliver went on in a low voice. "The last will and testament of William Shakespeare of Stratford-upon-Avon, which you brought up the other day. It mentions a famous second-best bed and quite a lot of other things. Including the crucial evidence that links Stratford Will to London Will. Evidence that you claim doesn't exist."

"Go on."

"London Will had three great friends, his lead actor Richard Burbage and the actors John Heminges and Henry Condell, who assembled the First Folio of his plays after his death."

"What about them?"

"They're mentioned in Stratford Will's will!" Oliver's voice echoed off the stone walls. A group of Japanese tourists looked at him with curiosity. He continued quietly. "He left them each twenty-six shillings to buy memorial rings. You must have known that. It completely undermines your thesis that there's nothing to connect Stratford Will to the London playwright."

"Contrariwise, it's a key piece of evidence that supports it."

"Explain."

"That bequest was written into the will between the lines, in a different handwriting and at a later date. It wasn't initialed by Stratford Will or by the witnesses, which was the usual practice. As you say, these were London Will's greatest friends—the actor who first played Hamlet, Lear, Othello, and Richard III, and two men who devoted themselves to preserving his Complete Works for posterity. And they're merely an afterthought, in a will made just a month before Shakespeare's death? Isn't it more likely that this is yet another clumsy postmortem attempt to dress the upstart Stratford Will in London Will's feathers?"

Oliver could not resist a glance up at the memorial on the wall. The polychrome effigy of Shakespeare, quill in hand, gazed into the mid-distance.

"And I'll tell you something else," Toby added. "The will has another late bequest. Hamnet Sadler's name was written in, replacing the name of another man. Now, this Sadler was a friend of Stratford Will's parents. Will had known him all his life and even named his only son after him. Sadler was also a witness to the will. So you'd think Will, of all people, would know how to spell the name Hamnet. But in the addition to the will's text, it's written as 'Hamlet.' Rather a crude and, if I may say, obvious attempt to forge a connection to the playwright."

"Yes, but in that First Folio of London Will's plays, there's a poem by Leonard Digges. It mentions this memorial, to Stratford Will." Oliver pointed to the effigy. "Doesn't that prove that Heminges and Condell knew the author of the plays came from Stratford?"

Toby laughed softly. "No, the only question is what did Heminges and Condell know and when did they know it. Digges, interestingly, was the stepson of one of the will's overseers."

"Are you suggesting they were *all* part of the conspiracy to elevate Stratford Will?"

"Maybe it suited their purposes, for some unknown reason."

"Careful, you're getting perilously close to my Alan Smithee theory."

"As if I wouldn't remember that London Will was real enough to be a Groom of the Chamber to King James," Toby snorted. "Along with Burbage, Heminges, and Condell, incidentally."

Oliver gazed down at the tomb. A rope barrier swagged across the chancel a foot or so in front of the altar rail. Toby's shoulder bag was slumped against a brass pole at one end.

"Why didn't you mention the suspicious amendments to the will at the dinner party?" he asked.

"What am I guilty of now—précis? You remember the audience that night. Most of them couldn't follow your little essay on bananas."

"Did you discuss these issues with Dennis Breedlove?" Oliver continued, hoping to make the transition sound casual.

"Yes. He didn't keep interrupting the way you do."

"When you had these chats, did Dennis ever ask you anything about the family? Mother, the brigadier, Uncle Tim, or Aunt Phoebe? Even me?"

"Sorry to disappoint you, Olivia, but I don't remember your name coming up. Nor any other relative."

"So Breedlove didn't get you to admit something that, in retrospect, you wished you'd kept quiet?"

"Nothing that he'd blackmail me for, since that's clearly where you're going with this."

"But there was something he got out of you?"

Toby glanced around the chancel. There were no tourists within earshot, apart from an old, balding man with his back to them, who was studying the choir stalls. Toby didn't seem to notice him.

"The last time I spoke to Uncle Dennis," he whispered, "we'd just discovered that priest-hole in the cellar across the river. I may have let it slip that we were keeping it a secret from the Town

Council. But if he'd threatened to sell us out, we'd probably have called his bluff. Today's our last day on the project anyway, and we haven't found anything interesting." He pulled ruefully on his muddy cricket sweater. "As you can see, I've been doing my fair share of digging the dust."

What had the blackmail letter said? Oliver asked himself. *You don't want others to dig up the past....* It fits, but as Toby said, scarcely worthy of blackmail. And where, then, is the "family secret"?

Chapter Twenty-eight

Saturday afternoon

The long room on the upper floor of Furbelow Hall never received direct sunlight, but any hint of gloom had been chased away by a warm, light-toned décor, bright upholstery on the sofas and armchairs, and several well-positioned lamps. A massive flat-screen television hung over the seventeenth-century stone mantelpiece, trailing wires that led to a satellite box, a Blu-ray player, and several types of video game consoles. An iPad had been left on an ottoman. Glass-fronted bookcases were well stocked with recent best-selling thrillers and DVDs. In one corner of the room was a small dressing table with a lighted mirror, strewn with boxes and tubes of theatrical makeup.

"Not quite how I pictured Dracula's lair," Effie remarked, after "the vampire" had ushered them merrily into the room and disappeared again with promises of a "nice cuppa tea." She dropped onto a window seat. "Who is he?" she asked.

"His name's Reg Thigpen."

"That's the name of the bus driver who was shot during the Undercroft Colliery strike," she said with a frown. "A couple of years ago in Derbyshire. Well, you knew him. You'd had him for burglary, years earlier. You're not telling me you know two people called Reg Thigpen?"

Mallard shook his head. "Just the one."

"But Thigpen's dead! He's probably the most famous dead person we've had in this country. Angus Snopp, alias the Vampire of Synne, can't be Reg Thigpen. Unless…"

She stopped, horrified by the words she was about to utter.

"It was a con," she breathed. "His death outside that mine was faked. And now he's hiding out here in Synne."

"That's the way it's looking."

Thigpen came into the room, carrying a tray crammed with tea-making equipment and plates of snacks. Over tea, he was perfectly happy to tell his story, as if he relished an audience. How after a lifetime of petty crime in the London area, he had left prison for the fourth or fifth time and was looking for a job ("bent or straight") when one day, a well-dressed man approached him in the street and invited him to lunch at a nearby, expensive restaurant.

"My first thought was 'Hello, what's your game?' Still, I was hungry. And then over lunch, he asked me if I wanted a whole new life—basically, I could live anywhere in the world, at his expense. Well, I was more convinced than ever that he was a sausage jockey with a taste for a bit of rough, pardon my French, Sergeant Strongitharm. So I was going to give him the bum's rush, prawn cocktail or no prawn cocktail. But it turns out he just talked that way because he was a toff."

"And what would you have to do for this life of ease?" Mallard prompted.

"What I did, Mr. Mallard. Stop being Reg Thigpen for the rest of my life. Well, I was all on my own, no close family. Hadn't seen most of my friends for years, because I'd been inside. And one more thing. Something I have in common with Inspector Mallard here."

"I'm a superintendent now," Mallard told him, leaning back in the comfortable sofa. "And I know you won't take this the wrong way, Reg, but I can't think what we might have in common."

Thigpen grinned. "Acting!" he declaimed. "We both like a touch of the old theatricals, don't we? I remember we had quite a chat about it, that time I was handcuffed to you in the back of the police car. So last time I was in the Scrubs, I joined the theater group. Me and ten harry hoofters, doing *Follies*. Happy days!"

"And this 'toff' wanted you to perform the role of a man being shot in the head?"

"Not just that one gig," Thigpen protested. "I had to *be* a scab bus driver for several weeks. That took some preparation, I can tell you. It goes against my true nature to stand counter to my brothers in the union, Mr. Mallard."

Mallard sipped his tea, suppressing the observation that Thigpen was unlikely to have ever been a member of a trade union, since he'd never worked a day in his life.

"And your performance continues, as the Vampire of Synne," Effie said.

"Yeah, I do like doing that posh voice," Thigpen said excitedly. He let his Cockney-ish accent slip away and resumed the deep tones of Angus Snopp. "I bid you welcome to my dank and unworthy abode, Sergeant Strongitharm. Of course," he added, back in his true voice, "they had to write me some brainy lines for the character. I didn't know they'd 'alf-inched a few from Bram Stoker, as you pointed out. Can't trust anybody these days."

"Yes, who are 'they'…?" Effie began.

"But why are you here, Reg?" Mallard interrupted. "Still in England, I mean, where you may be recognized? Aren't you supposed to be in Punta del Este, flashing your *pesos* and surrounded by tanga-clad *chiquitas*?"

Thigpen looked uncomfortable and took a bite from a slice of Battenberg cake before answering. "Yeah, that was the idea. But when Captain C—he's my minder—started listing all the places I could go, I realized I couldn't speak the lingo, and I didn't like the food. Eventually, I said I wanted to stay in England."

"Didn't that throw a spanner in the works?" asked Effie.

"Oh, it was too late by then. I was already dead and in hiding, in a safe house in Chiswick."

While Thigpen's attention was drawn to Effie, Mallard emptied his teacup into a potted plant. "Could I get some more tea, please, Reg?" he asked. Thigpen reached for the teapot.

"Maybe a fresh pot?" Mallard prompted.

"I'll put the kettle on again." Thigpen headed out of the door.

"We could be in trouble here," Mallard said, prowling around the room and peering into vases and under lampshades. "That's why I stopped you asking who's behind this."

"The company that owned the colliery, I suppose," said Effie, watching him with curiosity. "A clever plot to turn public opinion their way and get what they wanted: the closure of a money-losing pit, without union resistance. That surely leaves them with deep enough pockets to promise Reg a life of luxury."

"Maybe. But remember, that was what the government wanted too. That U-turn of public opinion after Reg's murder helped them win an election. And here's old Reg talking about 'safe houses' and 'minders.'" He ran a finger around the edge of a picture frame. "Let's not forget, Eff, faking a very public death requires a lot of inside assistance. No, this smacks of Whitehall. I just don't know which Ministry." Mallard paused in front of the window, noticing a black car parked beside his Jaguar. *How long had that been there?*

Thigpen returned with a steaming teapot.

"Are we bugged?" Mallard demanded.

"Not at all."

"Then how come we have company?"

Thigpen glanced out of the window. "Oh, that'll be my minder, Captain C. I called him when you first showed up." He grinned. "You'll like him, Mr. Mallard. He's very tall."

There was a brief rap on the door, and without waiting for an answer, Simon Culpepper stepped into the room.

Chapter Twenty-nine

Saturday afternoon (continued)

Chloe's bicycle had twenty-one gears, but none of them could get Oliver out of a ditch. Which was ironic, because fiddling with the gears had caused him to ride off the road in the first place.

Susie had thought of pitching the bike onto the roof-rack of her car, so Oliver had a way to get back to Synne as soon as his meeting with Toby was over. He'd agreed, not admitting that it had been years since he'd attempted to cycle anything more challenging than the half-mile along Kensington High Street to the Harrods food hall. Still, the ditch incident had provided some amusement for the trio of overheated workmen in the large hole across the road, who had paused to lean on their spades and make insulting comments.

The hole they were standing in was the reason why buses hadn't been passing through the village for a week or so. Most tour companies had been warned about the obstacle—only one or two fifty-foot motor coaches had been forced to beep their way slowly backwards for two miles along the dusty Synne road to its junction with the A3400.

Oliver mounted the bicycle again, determined to complete the last half-mile of his ten-mile journey without any further loss of dignity. Arriving at the Swithins' house, he drank several glasses of water and then went upstairs to collapse onto his vestal bed. He was just considering, in his own mind—as well as he could, for the hot afternoon made him feel very sleepy and stupid—whether the pleasure of guzzling a lunchtime beer would be worth the trouble of getting up and going downstairs to the fridge, when suddenly a Jefferson Airplane ringtone began to play close by him.

It was Effie's phone, on the bedside table. She must have forgotten to take it with her. Oliver reached over and checked the identity of the caller—a Birmingham telephone number. He was going to explain that Effie wasn't there, but the squeaky voice started before he could speak.

"D.S. Strongitharm? This is Tyler, in the crime lab. It's urgent."

Oliver swallowed. Did he dare? "Yes, Tyler?" he said, in a soft falsetto.

"Sergeant Strongitharm?" Tyler hesitated. From his voice, Oliver could tell that he sported a bad haircut.

"Yes," Oliver said again. He felt guilty—he was, after all, committing a crime by impersonating a police officer—but he reflected it was only like taking a message.

"I'm sorry, ma'am," said Tyler, "but I think I've made a big mistake. You remember that those two sets of prints you collected didn't match?"

"Yes." Keep it short, Olive thought, and I may get away with this. Tyler was referring to the fingerprints taken from Sidney Weguelin and Oliver's midnight attacker.

"You said that wrapped up the case. But I forgot to cancel the DNA test. The preliminary results just came back. Only I think I've got it wrong. We have a perfect initial match between the specimens."

"What?" *Oops, dangerously low.*

"Bless you, ma'am. Yes, but that can't be, can it? I must have accidentally analyzed the same specimen twice. I'm sorry."

"That's all right, Tyler. Better luck next time."

"Erm, Sarge?"

"Yes?"

"I hope your boyfriend's recovering from the attack. From the way you spoke about him, it's clear he's a great guy who means the world to you."

Oliver paused, wishing now that he'd left the phone alone. Love is a mystery, but as long as Effie loved him, it was a mystery that could remain unsolved. "He's doing fine," he said huskily.

"I only hope when I get to his age that I can still inspire the same sort of adoration. There can't be too many wheelchair-bound men in their late fifties who…"

What? "Yes, thank you, Tyler, heck of a job," Oliver spluttered. So Effie had charmed young Tyler by implying that she might be back in play as a merry widow, huh? He let his voice rise to a comically high level. "Are you still there?"

"Yes, ma'am."

"Next time I see you, dear boy, I'm going to give you a great big sloppy wet kiss! You hold me to that. Goodbye."

Oliver closed the phone and dropped it as if it were on fire. It had to be a mistake, of course: Sidney and the attacker couldn't possibly have different fingerprints but identical DNA. That doesn't happen.

Does it?

He sat upright, thought for ten seconds, and then ran out of the room, down the stairs, and out of the house. It took thirty more seconds to traverse the Square, curvet onto the main road, and sprint the hundred yards or so to the front door of the Weguelins' house. He hammered on the door.

Footsteps inside. The door opened. Sidney—silly beard, bad haircut, pointy nose, glasses. No bruises.

"Mr. Weguelin," Oliver gasped. "I know everything!"

Sidney stared at the young man panting on the doorstep.

"You'd better come in then," he said.

Chapter Thirty

Saturday afternoon (continued)

"I'm an onion, that's what I am, Mr. Mallard," Thigpen announced, lying back in the armchair. "I have layers."

"And he makes me cry," said Culpepper.

"It was all my idea," Thigpen continued, addressing Effie. "All them diseases. So I could use the makeup, you see. I'm a master of disguise. Man of a thousand faces."

"If you'd just gone to South America or South Africa," sighed Culpepper, nervously pacing around the room.

"We know why you didn't go abroad, Reg," said Mallard, "but how did you wind up here?"

Thigpen shot a scathing look at Culpepper. "You've heard the expression 'Be careful what you wish for'? In exchange for not being Reg Thigpen, the Captain's mob promised me any life I wanted. So I said I wanted to stay in England and be a 'Lord of the Manor' somewhere. They found me Furbelow Hall. But then they told me I couldn't leave it in the daytime." He sniffed. "That's why *I* invented the Vampire of Synne."

"You couldn't just have plastic surgery, like anyone else," muttered Culpepper.

"Hey, it was my cover story, and it worked. Layers, as I said. On top, the vampire, attracting attention maybe, but that layer's easily peeled. Underneath, you find the poor XP sufferer, enough for most people in the village to say 'what a pity' and ask no more questions. But then, for the persistent, we have yet another layer, that of the unlikely modern-day leper. A *triple* bluff, which trapped Dennis Breedlove like a fly in...what's that oozy stuff?"

"Treacle?" Effie suggested.

"Amber." Thigpen looked more closely at the large bruise on Culpepper's cheekbone. "You been in the wars, Captain C?" he asked. "And what's all that pink stuff round your neck?"

"Calamine lotion," grumbled Culpepper. "For nettle rash." Effie smiled.

"Thought you'd been at my makeup." Thigpen waved an arm in the direction of the dressing table. "It only takes a few minutes. Mainly dried rubber cement and flour, with a lot of Leichner number five greasepaint. I pretend to need surgical gloves because of my condition, but it's really so I don't have to make up the hands as well."

"Is there any chance that Dennis Breedlove got through that last layer and discovered your true identity?" Mallard asked.

Thigpen shook his head. "That's the beauty of the onion. Old Uncle Dennis was so pleased with himself at reaching the leprosy level, it actually stopped him probing any further. Even he couldn't pluck out the heart of my mystery."

"So I take it, *Captain* Culpepper, that Mr. Thigpen is in some form of witness relocation program?" Effie asked.

"Something like that."

"They don't do a bad job, though," Thigpen piped up. He spread his arms. "They done up this whole floor nice—this room, bedroom, a little kitchen, bath. And Captain C does take care of me. I only have to snap my fingers and he's round, with a bag of chips or a new video. It's like having your own Jeeves."

"I must say, though, Cap'n," Effie remarked to Culpepper, who was glaring at Thigpen, "that letting your prime charge wander around the countryside at night dressed as Friar Dracula isn't my idea of keeping him out of the public eye. It certainly attracted the attention of the local blackmailer. Who's then found dead in suspicious circumstances. Is that why you were demoted to a mere sergeant?"

Culpepper lowered himself onto the ottoman. "I was a copper for several years, Coventry CID, before my department recruited me. When Breedlove was found dead, we didn't want too many questions about the Vampire of Synne, so I was asked to resume my role of a local police investigator and manage the situation. It all went through official channels."

Effie glanced at Mallard, but he signaled his lack of knowledge of the arrangement.

"Did you 'manage' Breedlove up that tree with the skipping rope?" she asked. Mallard growled a wordless caution.

"Effie, you have my department confused with some other government entity," Culpepper replied. "If we had the ethical laxity to actually kill British citizens for our purposes, Reg would have died for real in that Derbyshire bus and none of this charade would be necessary."

"Oi," protested Thigpen.

"But this is not a matter of national security," Culpepper persisted. "This is politics, and my masters don't want blood on their hands."

Effie looked past him, gathering her thoughts as if he hadn't spoken. "I mean, this whole business seems to be about subverting a general election, telling lies to win the ruling party another five years of power. Everything is bent for England. Yes, you may spare Reg's life to achieve your ends, but what's the life of one inconvenient eighty-year-old blackmailer when there's a national scandal to keep under wraps?"

"That's enough, Sergeant," Mallard interjected, but Culpepper raised a hand, like a priestly blessing.

"It's okay, Superintendent," he said calmly, never taking his dark-brown eyes from Effie's face. "Nobody from my department had any involvement in Breedlove's death, Sergeant Strongitharm."

"But you'd known for a year that he was a blackmailer?"

"Obviously."

"Did you know he had other victims?"

Culpepper shrugged. "We never tried to find out. We just needed him to keep quiet about Angus Snopp, so we paid him. And then we left him alone." He placed his long hands on his knees. "His murder has been a distinct inconvenience."

Effie's eyes narrowed. "Then he *was* murdered? Oliver's been right all along?"

"Yes, your boyfriend was right," Culpepper conceded, after a brief hesitation. "Breedlove was murdered. It was impossible for him to hang himself like that. In fact, the pathologist is pretty sure he was dead before he was hauled up that tree. Throttled first, then hanged to cover it up. But I wanted the world at large to think it a suicide."

"After all, Uncle Dennis was only a filthy blackmailer, he's better off dead," Effie snapped, remembering Oliver's anger when he thought he was facing the same official indifference. "The killer's a hero, doing us all a favor. So who cares if this murder is unsolved? Does that account for the law's delay, in this case?"

"You didn't let me finish. I wanted his death to be seen as a suicide until we had the murderer under lock and key. A public investigation risked drawing too much attention to Reg, as you and Superintendent Mallard have already proved."

"That's why you told Oliver to stay out of it. You knew it would make him even more determined to find Breedlove's murderer, while you hid in the background and waited for an amateur detective to do your job for you."

Culpepper was already shaking his head, amused at the outburst. "No, I told Oliver to stay out of it because I wanted him to stay out of it."

"Then why did you show him that letter?"

"Having the body discovered by two Scotland Yard detectives presented a challenge. I couldn't risk your getting too involved in the investigation. The letter was vaguely worded, like so many blackmail notes, and didn't name names. I thought if I could convince you and Mr. Mallard that it was written *to* Breedlove and not *by* him, then you'd believe he'd topped himself and leave everything to me. I was really showing the letter to you, Effie. The inquisitive Oliver just happened to be there."

"So who was it sent to?"

"It wasn't sent. I really did find it on Breedlove's desk."

"But you hid the envelope. You know who it was really meant for."

"There was no envelope." Culpepper studied his long fingers. "Look, I apologize for deceiving you, but it was necessary."

"Well, more fool you anyway, because despite your attempts to wrong-foot him, Oliver still got to the truth about Breedlove."

"Has he identified the murderer?"

"He's found all the blackmail victims, which is more—"

"Has he identified the murderer?" Culpepper repeated, holding her gaze with his dark eyes.

"No," she admitted.

"Then maybe this is as good a time as any to remind you and Mr. Mallard that, as serving police officers, you're bound by the Official Secrets Act. And if ever there was an Official Secret, this is one." He leaned forward. "You can't tell Oliver anything."

Effie took in the instruction, already aware of a growing urge to shout this particular official secret to the entire world. "Was it you, then, who attacked Oliver outside the house?" she asked.

"No. And I don't know who did. Honestly."

Mallard stood up, buttoning his jacket. "Since Breedlove was murdered, Captain, do you have any idea yet who was responsible?"

Culpepper seemed relieved that Mallard had shifted the focus of the conversation. "We got some prints off those cut-off skipping rope handles, although we haven't found a match yet. But I'm not convinced that one of the blackmail victims would suddenly turn on Breedlove after steadfastly paying up for two, three, four years. And I can personally assure you that Reg is innocent."

"That's the first time I've heard that from a copper," said Thigpen.

"He's not a copper," said Effie, stone-faced. "'Captain Culpepper' sounds more like a pirate."

Culpepper smiled. "I've been following some other leads," he continued. "Dennis Breedlove was a member of a shadowy organization known as the Priory of Synne."

"Really?" said Mallard, checking his watch.

"There are reports of its existence as far back as sixteenth-century France. Perhaps Breedlove ran afoul of some ancient protocol and was, uh, suspended. There's something a little ritualistic about being hanged from an ancient gibbet, after all. We believe one of the Priory's present-day operatives has been in the area recently, although nobody seems to know the man's name or what he looks like. They choose their people well."

Effie had guessed from Mallard's fidgeting that he was running late for his last rehearsal before that evening's performance. She stood up, ignored Culpepper, and extended a hand to Thigpen. "A pleasure to meet a true historical figure, Mr. Thigpen."

"Yes, Reg," said Mallard, "it's been nice seeing you again."

"You haven't seen the last of me today, Mr. M. Or should I say I haven't seen the last of you. Captain C told me you were performing at the RSC tonight, so I insisted he get us tickets. Front row!" He smiled graciously at Culpepper, who scowled in return.

"I know every word of *Hamlet*," Thigpen went on. "Hey, maybe I should have that plastic surgery, after all. If I looked a bit more like Laurence Olivier, I could take to the stage and leave Angus Snopp behind."

"A consummation devoutly to be wished," muttered Culpepper.

Chapter Thirty-one

Saturday afternoon (continued)

Oliver followed Sidney Weguelin into a small sitting room, with curtains drawn and the lights on. Another person was sitting on a couch, watching television. It wasn't Lesbia; it seemed to be a man. In fact, it was Sidney. Another Sidney, albeit a Sidney with, mercifully, no moustache or goatee or glasses, but with a large surgical dressing taped across a swollen and discolored nose.

"He found out," said the first Sidney.

"You idiot, he's bluffing," snarled the other Sidney.

"No," replied Sidney One, turning off the television and looking at Oliver. "He knows."

Sidney Two didn't answer, but glared at Oliver. There was an awkward silence.

"Is it broken?" Oliver asked.

"It bloody hurts, that's all I know."

"Sorry. Have you seen a doctor?"

"How could I go to a doctor? If I'd stepped outside looking like this, you'd have been waiting with your binoculars and your notebook and Christ knows what else. Then you'd know it was me who'd attacked you."

"I said I was sorry." Oliver leaned in and showed the side of his head. "Look, you bruised my ear. It's still ringing a little."

"Good. I was only trying to warn you off, you know." Sidney Two sighed. "It doesn't matter anyway, since you seem to have rumbled our little secret. All that spying finally paid off, did it?"

"No. Until a few moments ago, I was still convinced there was only one of you, playing two roles."

"Then how did you find out?" asked Sidney One, cautiously removing the goatee and moustache and placing them in a small pouch. The organist looked surprisingly younger.

"Oh, I was given a conundrum," Oliver explained. "How can two people have different fingerprints but identical DNA? The answer: because they're identical twins. We happen to have a set in the family."

Sidney One let out a brief laugh. "But you were right, Oliver. Today, I *am* both Sidney and Lesbia. At least while my sibling is indisposed. I've just come from organ practice as Sidney, and according to the timetable, Lesbia is due to meet with the vicar in about half an hour to discuss the annual fete. So you'll have to excuse me. My real name's Robin, by the way."

Oliver was left to the malignant glare of the other twin.

"So, blackmail," said Sidney Two at last, with disgust.

"Blackmail," Oliver confirmed. "I'd have left you alone otherwise."

"You're very professional. And very persistent."

"Thank you. I will, of course, be the soul of discretion. Nobody in the village need ever know. You two can just carry on doing…whatever it is you do."

The injured organist let out a snort of mirthless laughter. "That's the way it works, is it? All right, how much do you want?"

"What?"

"How much money do you want?" repeated Sidney Two impatiently.

"I don't want any money," protested Oliver, puzzled by the reaction.

"What kind of a blackmailer doesn't want money?"

"Blackmailer? *I'm* not a blackmailer."

"Oh, you may choose to call it something less distasteful, but blackmail is what it comes down to. You're here to arrange payments. Am I wrong?"

"No!" Oliver cried. "I mean, yes, you're wrong. I'm not here to blackmail you. You're already being blackmailed!"

"No, we're not."

"Well, not now, but you were. Do you deny that Dennis Breedlove was blackmailing you?"

"That old coot who hanged himself last week? He wasn't blackmailing us."

"Yes, he was."

"No, he wasn't. Nobody's been blackmailing us except you!"

"But I'm not blackmailing you."

"Not yet, you're not."

"But you're Tweedledee and Tweedledum!" yelled Oliver, and stopped, breathless. "You must be," he added softly, as Sidney Two stared at him with incomprehension. Of course, Oliver considered, the Weguelins may still deny being Breedlove's victims, because they don't want to be suspects in his murder. But from what he could see of the face staring back at him, around the bandages, the bafflement seemed genuine.

"Tweedle—?" Sidney began and then broke off to laugh. "This is all because you thought—?" the organist cackled between gasps for air. "But then we thought—" Again, convulsive laughter ended the sentence. And Oliver joined in.

"My name's Kim," said Sidney Two, stretching out a hand. "I shouldn't laugh so much, it hurts my nose."

"Yeah, I'm really sorry—"

"Oh, no hard feelings. Sorry about your ear. Do you want a drink?"

As they entered the kitchen, Lesbia spun around from a mirror propped on top of a counter—or rather, it was almost Lesbia, complete with cassock and thick cosmetics, but without the black-framed glasses and shiny wig. Kim reported what Oliver had revealed, and Robin joined them in the general merriment, punctuated by the opening of three bottles of beer. Free from their fears, the twins were friendly and good-humored, a marked contrast from their characters of Sidney and Lesbia, about whom Oliver was hearing.

"It's performance art," explained Kim. "We're identical twins, Kim and Robin Essiss, playing a prissy married couple, Sidney and Lesbia Weguelin, the verger and organist in the Cotswold village of Synne. Life imitates art imitating life."

"But there are two of you," Oliver noted. "Why has nobody seen you together?"

"Plenty of people have seen us together," said Robin, sliding the wig into place. "But we do minimize our joint appearances, in case someone spots any similarities. At parish meetings, we sit on opposite sides of the room."

"So normally, you, Kim, are Sidney, and Robin is Lesbia?"

"Oh no," said Kim. "We swap regularly. It's an artistic statement about the malleability of human identity in modern life. Of course, we have to keep each other briefed, so that if I'm Lesbia one day, I'm not caught out by something Robin learned when playing Lesbia the day before."

"Then when I first met Lesbia, coming out of the church…"

"That was me," claimed Kim. "And that was me, too, as Sidney at Dennis Breedlove's funeral."

"But when I saw Lesbia next, in my parents' kitchen, she reacted as if she had never met me before. Because that was you, Robin?"

Robin, now almost fully Lesbia, nodded. "Kim hadn't fully informed me about Sidney and Lesbia's earlier encounters, but I still should have improvised better. That's what makes this performance so much fun."

"You keep this up full-time, then?"

"Well, not once we're home and behind closed doors," Robin continued, swigging from the beer bottle and stuffing some folders into a large purse, which had been used to hold the mirror up. "Our impersonation of a married couple doesn't go all the way to the bedroom."

They both chortled at the idea, and Oliver was relieved. It would be hard to think of a term for a pair of incestuous gay transvestites, an unlikely threefer.

"How on earth did this all start?" he asked Kim, after Robin/Lesbia had scurried out of the front door.

"With our mother. She treated us identically, dressed us identically, made us go everywhere together. When we showed some musical talent, she couldn't wait to parade us out onto the concert platform in identical costumes, playing four-handed pieces on the piano."

"It's not unusual for parents to dress twins that way, even if they're nonidentical."

"Yes, but Mother went further. She simply refused to accept that we were two different people, separate souls. And so as we got older, Robin and I would joke about how we could make ourselves look as different as possible. For a start, one of us would change sex. One of us would keep our slim build, while the other would pad up, and so on. And we'd always be ready to swap roles, which made it fun. Thus were Sidney and Lesbia born, two characters as unlike as we could make them. Originally, it was a routine we did to amuse our friends. Then, as an experiment, we tried to set up a household in Finchley. And then one day, we both decided we wanted a break from London and our jobs as professional musicians, and, well, here we are, living in Synne. Next year, we're getting a film crew to make a documentary about the project."

"I should have guessed that there was an element of fantasy about your lives," Oliver said, with a smile. "After all, who's called 'Lesbia' in real life?"

"Our mother," Kim informed him. "Another beer?"

Chapter Thirty-two

Saturday afternoon (continued)

"Can you believe what we've just heard?" Effie fumed.

"Unfortunately, yes," said Mallard, opening the passenger-side door for her.

"I'm speechless."

"No, you're not," he assured her.

"And we're supposed to walk away and do nothing, say nothing, with the certainty that our present government connived with the permanent Whitehall Mandarins to keep themselves in power? By callously manipulating public opinion."

"Isn't that what 'spin' is?"

"Here's what spin isn't, Tim," she stated, pacing along the gravel like a caged tiger, ignoring his invitation to get into the car. "Faking a murder and spending the taxpayer's money on the cover-up, while accusing union agitators of crimes they haven't committed. It smells to heaven."

"There's nothing you can do about it. Unless you want to lose your job, never work for a public entity again, and probably be prosecuted for treason."

"Treason?" she yelled. "Winning a general election on the back of a blatant, calculated, deliberate lie, that's treason! The people should know. The press should know."

"Not from us." He grabbed her elbow to keep her in one place. "Like it or not, Effie, when you became a police officer you did indeed sign the Official Secrets Act."

"So you're siding with him." Effie shook herself free from his gentle grip. "With Long John bloody Simon bloody Culpepper. Mr. James sodding Bond and his official secrets." She kicked the tire on Culpepper's adjacent car.

"Wrong government department, I believe. Simon wasn't obliged to be so frank with us. It was perfectly clear he was not in sympathy with the morality of the exercise."

"Yeah, he was only doing his job," muttered Effie. "Only obeying orders."

"That's a little unfair—"

She spun toward him, eyes blazing. "But remember what he told us—Oliver isn't covered by the Act. If his amateur investigation were somehow to lead to the truth about this strange eruption to our state, independently of any hints we might drop, I bet we could get it into the newspapers."

"Leave Oliver out of this. Captain C wasn't giving us a hint, he was giving us a warning. As far as Oliver's concerned, this morning we visited Angus Snopp, leprosy sufferer, who demonstrated, beyond all doubt, that he's innocent of Breedlove's murder. End of story."

Effie stared at her mentor. "Where's the outrage?" she demanded. "You don't seem shocked at all."

"Oh, I'm shocked," Mallard replied. "But I'm not surprised. And I do know that if you use Oliver to channel your anger to the public, you can probably say goodbye to his freedom and possibly his life."

He walked up to her and hugged her tightly, pulling her head into the crook of his neck and bending forward to whisper through her curls. "Simon's department doesn't work with single spies," he told her. "We're all going to be under some scrutiny now, because of what we've discovered. You and Oliver are both very, very dear to me, and I want to keep you. So for once in your life, Effie Strongitharm, play by the rules. Okay?"

She didn't answer, but he could feel a slight relaxation of the resistance in her body, and it was enough. He let her go and opened the car door again.

"No, I'll walk," she said. He nodded. As he drove away, Effie looked up at the Hall's bilious brickwork, unsure which of the mullioned windows were Thigpen's apartment but certain that Culpepper was watching her through one of them. She found a footpath through the overgrown gardens and made her way back to the main road. In five minutes, she was skirting the Square, noting the village landmarks. The Seven Wise Virgins, with its dilapidated dovecote. The post office. The ugly bus shelter. The pointless memorial obelisk. The Square's single bench, with Oliver asleep on it…

"Are you still cross with me?" was his first croaky response to being woken with a firm shake.

"I'm cross with everything," she told him. "But I missed you." She sniffed. "Have you been drinking?"

"A couple of beers with my new friends, the Weguelins," Oliver admitted through a yawn. "Sat here to think. Must have dozed off."

"Come on," Effie said, hauling him upright. "Let's go for a walk."

They headed for Synne Common, but this time they kept going along the main road, a single lane between shoulder-high hedgerows. Despite his grogginess, Oliver was still riding on the elation at his success—finally—in getting to the truth about the Weguelins. The unrelieved sexual frustration, the variety of bruises, rashes, and muscle strains, the prospect of three hours of amateur Shakespeare directed by a nitwit that evening… these things shall pass. The next day would return them home to London, the panacea, the remission of Synne.

Effie was only half-listening, her mind still privately festering with anger and frustration over Reg Thigpen, and to Oliver's relief, she barely reacted to hearing about the intercepted phone call from Tyler. By the time he finished, they were approaching the bend in the road where the workmen were digging.

"And so we have our complete set, at long last," he concluded. He became aware that the workmen had paused to study him.

"Look who's back!" he heard one of them say.

"Including number five?" Effie asked him at the same time.

"And look what's he's brought back with him!" The speaker gave a low wolf-whistle.

"I had convinced myself it was Toby," Oliver said, trying to ignore the workmen's comments, "but what could Breedlove threaten him with? Closing his dig a day or two early? There's no long-term source of revenue in that. And I still don't get that 'family secret' reference. Toby couldn't possibly have a family secret—that kid's been an open book to me since he was born."

"You reckon Crystal Tipps there's his girlfriend?" asked the third workman.

"And Toby denies knowing anything about blackmail?"

"Nah, he'd never get a looker like that," said the first workman who had spoken. "She must be his nursemaid."

"So do the Weguelins, for that matter," Oliver replied. "That's their prerogative." He noticed that Effie seemed unconcerned by the background observations. Perhaps she had long ago accepted this humiliation as the common lot for any young woman passing road works or a building site.

"Or his nanny." The workmen laughed raucously.

"The deadline for your investigation is looming," said Effie. "What are you going to do with the information?"

"She can sit me on her naughty seat anytime!"

"Hand it over to Simon Culpepper and tell him to pick the killer," Oliver said. Should he say something to the workmen and be prepared for another fight? He should probably wait for signs that the boorish running commentary was bothering Effie. "Maybe I'll hold Toby's name back."

"Miss! I need a good spanking, Miss!"

"I wouldn't worry about Toby," said Effie. "Simon doesn't think Breedlove was done in by any of his blackmail victims."

"Miss, did you put too much starch in my nappy or am I just pleased to see you?"

"I know," said Oliver. "He still believes it was suicide."

"Miss! I need to sit on your naughty seat, Miss!"

"No, I meant he *does* now think Breedlove was murdered, but that it had nothing to do with blackmail."

"I already did that one. You never pay attention when we're harassing women."

Oliver frowned. "This is new. Simon didn't say anything about that last night. Was he visiting your vampire as well this morning?"

"Is it me now, or did Kevin miss a turn?"

"No, no, he wasn't there." *Shut up, Effie,* she said to herself, *don't let Ollie connect Culpepper to Snopp, alias Thigpen.* "We passed him on the road," she improvised. "Stopped for a quick chat. Simon says he thinks Breedlove was murdered because of his connection to some peculiar secret society. The Priory of Synne or something like that." *Good, get him to bite on that.*

"Yeah, you can cut my bread and butter into soldiers and dip them in my soft-boiled egg any day. Sorry, that one didn't make sense."

"How cheerfully on the false trail they cry," said Oliver, with another nervous glance toward the braying workmen. "How did Uncle Tim take to the Vampire of Synne?"

"Hey, sugarlips, kiss *this* and make it better. Oh, by 'sugarlips,' I meant the girl."

Bugger, he's back on the vampire. "There's nothing to tell you," she lied. "Tim and I both agreed that Snopp couldn't possibly have murdered Dennis Breedlove. Excuse me a second."

She turned from Oliver and walked a few paces toward the digging crew, who, having finally gained her attention, resorted to delighted, nonverbal animal impressions. She stopped and studied them for a moment. The noises ceased abruptly, and each man became oddly obsessed with his feet.

"Now tell me one more thing about the Weguelins," she said, returning to Oliver's side as if nothing unusual had happened. "They're identical twins, right?"

"Yes. Just like my mother and Aunt Phoebe." He glanced over at the workmen, puzzled.

"And identical twins are always the same gender?"

"That's right."

"So when they're playing Sidney and Lesbia, one of the pair has to drag up and one doesn't."

"Exactly."

"Which?"

"What?"

"Which one is in drag, the one playing Sidney or the one playing Lesbia?"

"The one playing Lesbia, of course."

"So in real life, they're male."

"Yes."

"Are you sure?"

"Oh, they're male, all right," Oliver said with confidence. "I saw them both without their disguises."

"And how could you tell they're male?"

"They had Sidney's short hair. And I'm pretty sure that Robin had to add the boobs to become Lesbia."

"Women can have short hair, or so I've heard. Women can be flat-chested, too—I'm not far beyond that state myself. Certainly, Geoffrey isn't going to be telling any jokes about *my* cleavage walking into a bar. And Lesbia's the plump one, so wouldn't she have to wear extra padding anyway?"

"Yeah, but their names—Robin and Kim—they're…oh." He thought back over the earlier meeting. "They…they use masculine pronouns to refer to each other. Or wait, do they?"

Oliver stood still in the road, baffled. *That should take his mind off the vampire,* Effie thought and kissed him on the cheek. There was only respectful silence from the audience in the hole. "Call yourself a detective?" she said wickedly. "Come on, let's go and prepare for this evening's entertainment." She walked away, heading back toward Synne.

"They have to be men," Oliver called after her desperately. He was about to follow, when he felt a hand plucking at his sleeve. One of the workmen had sidled up to him.

"Er, is that lady your girlfriend?" the man asked, clutching his cap tightly.

"Yes."

"Ah. Good for you, John. Then on behalf of the lads, may I offer my profoundest apologies for our dreadful behavior. I am sick at heart. We truly appreciate your considerable restraint in not setting to and giving us all a damn good thrashing, which is no less than we deserve."

"No problem," said Oliver, making to leave again.

"No, no, fair do's. You're a gentleman, Chief, that's plain as a pickle. Anyway, me and the lads had a bit of a whip-round, and we'd be grateful if you'd use this money to buy her some flowers, on our behalf."

He handed over some dirty pound coins, keeping his head lowered so that he wasn't tempted to look at Effie walking away from them in her tight jeans, as if he feared the seductive vision might turn him into a pillar of salt.

"I'll do what I can," Oliver promised. "Now, if you'll—"

"Duchess, is she?"

"What?"

"Is she a duchess? Or some member of the Royals? Because they're different, aren't they? We all felt the magic when she looked at us."

"Ah," Oliver responded, understanding. "No, she's not a duchess. She's a police officer."

"A police officer?" repeated the workman, brightening. "Maybe she can help us with our stolen hole."

Oliver stopped. "Your what?"

Chapter Thirty-three

"How big was the hole?" Effie asked, glancing over the photo-copied cast list. The performance was due to start in about ten minutes, and the Royal Shakespeare Theater was, surprisingly, beginning to fill up.

"About the size of a grave."

"Sounds familiar."

"Yes. They finished the work on the drains yesterday. They only had to come back this morning and fill in the hole. Somebody beat them to it overnight."

"Makes their job easier, I suppose."

"Not really. They had to dig it all out again."

"Why?"

"Health and Safety. It was the wrong type of dirt. But they're done now, and the road is finally open again to all traffic. We'll be going home to London just before Synne fills up with tour buses again."

Home to London, Oliver thought with satisfaction. Although with a murder unsolved. He glanced around the theater. Quite a good turnout for the Theydon Bois Thespians, whose audiences usually had fewer members than the cast list, even when the players were trebling the parts, like his uncle's Polonius, Grave-digger, and Osric. Oliver supposed that the play had attracted a number of tourists, foolishly trusting that any Saturday night performance in Stratford's main theater might merit the three or four hours of their lives they'd never get back. His uncle had reserved the fourth row of the stalls for the Swithin party, and Oliver and Effie had taken the two seats closest to the aisle. The row behind them was filled with the same party of Japanese tourists he'd seen in Holy Trinity. He nodded to them.

"Peculiar story, eh?" he said.

Effie laughed humorlessly. "Not for these parts, it seems. Look at Breedlove's list. Cross-dressing identical twins pretending to be a married couple. A vicar who runs a masturbation club for lonely parishioners. An online pornographer who's seduced five deb sisters *and,* it seems, their mother. And a vampire who's genuinely back from the dead."

"Back from the dead?" Oliver echoed, puzzled.

Uh-oh. "I mean, he wasn't expecting to have survived leprosy for this long." *Hmmm. Not the best recovery, Eff. Move on, though.* "No wonder the late, semi-lamented Uncle Dennis had a field day when he turned to crime."

"Yes, but only two of the four were about sex. Dr. McCaw overestimated. And if victim number five had been Toby, I can guarantee that would reduce the McCaw Sexual Ratio to a mere forty percent."

He glanced to his left. A sullen Toby was sitting in the same row, separated from him by their parents and Aunt Phoebe, who were sharing a box of chocolates. Toby seemed distracted, and not just because Susie and Geoffrey, in the seats next to him, were necking as if they were in the back row of a cinema. Ben Motley, who had driven up from London to see the play, was sitting beyond them. Perhaps Toby's gloom was separation anxiety from the Bard's grave, Oliver wondered. Well, maybe during the intermission—*oh please, let there be an intermission*—he could treat his brother to a drink—*oh please, let there be time for a drink*—from the bar on the outdoor balcony, where Toby could enjoy the stunning view along the river toward Holy Trinity's slim spire, visible above the weeping willows.

"Now add to that a pair of peeping toms," Effie was saying, "a work-shy village policeman, a disputatious sexton, a funeral that's more like a stand-up routine, a stand-up routine that's more like a funeral…the list goes on. I've seen everything. No, wait."

The tall, elegant form of Simon Culpepper passed the end of their row, accompanying a shorter man—well, most people would be shorter than Captain Stretch, Effie reflected—dressed in full Scottish garb, including kilt, sporran, and tam o'shanter, and clutching a serpentine walking stick. There was so much wild hair on the Scotsman's face that it almost obscured the broad wink he gave her. Effie turned nervously to Oliver to see if she needed to explain Thigpen's greeting—she'd already dismissed the idea of identifying him as Culpepper's father—but Oliver seemed thoughtful and hadn't noticed the newcomers, who took seats in the front row.

"Okay, *now* I've seen everything," she concluded, but then spotted the unfashionably on-time arrival of the entire Bennet clan—mother Wendy in the vanguard, a single file of daughters dressed as if for a court appearance (royal, not legal), inoffensive multimillionaire father, Lafcadio, bringing up the rear. With a susurration of silk and taffeta, they sidled into a row across the aisle, just as the lights in the auditorium began to dim.

Humfrey Fingerhood stepped onto the stage to applause from the largely unsuspecting audience. Effie watched the slight figure with fascination; it was the first time she'd seen anyone attempt to bow using only his hands.

Humfrey raised his eyes to the follow spot. "It is with the most abject and profound humility of an undeserving treader of the boards that a humble Humfrey Fingerhood—that's Humfrey with an *f*—and his devoted troupe come before you in this hallowed shrine of the buskin and motley. We are, naturally, unworthy of the honor bestowed upon us this evening. But when Humfrey Fingerhood is called from the ranks of mummery to stand up and be counted for the Swan of Avon, to use Sam Johnson's mellifluous epithet for his departed comrade of the the-ah-tah, Humfrey Fingerhood becomes erect…"

After five more minutes, Humfrey reluctantly ceded the stage, and the production began with a blackout and the recorded sounds of a dark and stormy night. When the lights came up again, they revealed the silhouette of a crenellated battlement, with a steady snow falling—actually soap flakes shaken straight from their packages by the backstage crew up in the fly tower—and Humfrey still trying to grope his way into the wings. He collided with the edge of the proscenium, resulting in two loud, distinctive knocks.

"Who's there?" said Barnado, starting the play, to considerable laughter.

"Nay, answer me," responded Francisco, but his next line was drowned out by several audience members chanting "Nay-answer-me who?" in unison. Unfortunately, this flash of originality was not only unintentional, it was unique. Humfrey had despaired of coming up with any fresh interpretation of the play, and so the performance progressed in a straightforward and flavorless manner, little more than a text reading—literally so, for the actor playing Claudius, who carried his Penguin *Shakespeare* with him at all times.

It was at the beginning of the second scene, a long, boring speech from Claudius about Denmark's dispute with neighboring Norway, which Humfrey didn't have the wit to cut, that Oliver sat upright.

"Got it!" he shouted.

Ignoring the protests around him, he stood up and leaned as far as he could across his parents and his aunt, beckoning frantically to Toby and scattering chocolates across the floor. Behind him, the row of Japanese tourists stood up simultaneously. Toby grudgingly got to his feet and sidled after his brother, who was also nudging Effie ahead of them. The three reached the aisle just as Mallard, as Polonius, had his first speech.

"He hath, my lord, wrung from me my slow leave," he began, distracted by the noise from the auditorium and visibly offended when it seemed that his first lines had caused his two nephews and his sergeant to storm noisily out of the theater.

Oliver propelled Toby into the daylight, with Effie following. It was still two hours before sunset. The three marched across the theater's parking area until they reached the river's edge.

"What the f—" Toby began.

Oliver grabbed him by the shoulder and made him face the river. He pointed at a white bird, floating serenely on the water.

"What's that?" he demanded.

"You dragged me out of *Hamlet* for ornithological advice? It's a swan. Did you know a full-grown swan can break a man's arm?"

"Shut up!" Oliver kept pointing at the bird. "And what's it swimming in?"

"A river, duh."

"Which river?"

"The Avon."

"Exactly. So it's a Swan of Avon."

Toby seemed relieved. "Ah, I see. Yeah, Humfrey said that epithet was coined by Samuel Johnson, but he meant Ben Jonson. I guess we're lucky he didn't say Boris Johnson." He sniggered.

"Ben Jonson," Oliver repeated. "Shakespeare's old friend and fellow playwright. Who memorialized him in the introductory verses to the First Folio as the Swan…of *Avon*. That river there. Which runs through Stratford. Stratford-upon-*Avon*."

"Is this going somewhere, as the bishop said to the—?"

"You claimed there's *nothing* in the historical record that connects London Will, bosom buddy of said Jonson, to Stratford Will, dweller beside the Avon."

"Ooh, Toby," said Effie, "you got served."

"Unless you're now adding Ben Jonson, acclaimed playwright and the nation's first poet laureate, to your expanding list of conspirators?"

Toby was silent.

"You tell everyone that you think Stratford Will is an irrelevance," Oliver continued, "but you moon over his gravesite like a bereaved puppy. You tell us the island has no connection to Shakespeare, but you and nine other Oxford postgraduates take weeks out of the academic year to dig there." He prodded Toby in the chest. "You know what I think?"

"If I say 'yes,' you're still going to tell me."

"I think this thesis of yours is really a big chunk of misdirection. Because you don't want anyone to know what's really going on at that dig."

"I already told you, we uncovered a Victorian cellar."

"That's the half-truth you told me, to fob me off. And that's what you claim you told Breedlove, but as you said, he wouldn't resort to blackmail over something as trivial as that. And you *were* that fifth blackmail victim, Toby."

"I don't have to stand here and listen to this!" shouted Toby, standing there and listening to it.

"The fifth victim's payments would have been logged beside a nursery rhyme about a church with a steeple," Oliver said. "There's no steeple on the Church of St. Edmund and St. Crispin in Synne. But look down the river—Holy Trinity, where you seem to live these days, has a steeple!"

"That's your proof?" Toby began to bluster, but Effie held up a forefinger.

"I don't think Oliver's finished talking," she said amiably, "largely on the grounds that Oliver's never finished talking."

"Every time I've seen you recently," Oliver went on, "you've been wearing that baggy cricket sweater, despite the weather. Yesterday morning, when you were leaving for Stratford, you were carrying your shoulder bag as if it contained something heavy. But when Eric gave me the bag later, it was empty. You'd taken something out of it and hidden it under your sweater before you went into the church, because all bags are searched at the chancel entrance. Something small but heavy that you wanted to keep secret."

"Oh, Toby, it's not one of those ludicrous ghost-hunting devices, is it?" Effie asked.

"I think it's an RFID," said Oliver. "A radio frequency identification device, souped up so that Toby's position can be read over a short distance, even through walls and solid earth."

"But why does anyone need to keep track of Toby?" Effie wondered. "He always seems to be in the same place."

"It's not Toby they want to pinpoint. It's what he's standing in front of."

Effie nodded slowly. "Shakespeare's tomb."

"Think about the blackmail letter," Oliver said. "The 'whole blessed plot' it mentions could refer to Shakespeare's grave, using his own words. But it's no longer 'covered up forever,' because somebody's going to 'dig up the past.'"

Oliver moved in front of Toby, forcing him to make eye contact. "Your island may be ten minutes from the church on foot, but it's less than a hundred yards away as the crow flies. Or the swan swims. Or should I say as the 'old mole' digs? Because that's what you and your friends have really been doing for the past three weeks. That was no priest-hole or larder you found in the cellar of the old house. It was an old tunnel under the river. And you decided to explore it, guided in the darkness by your infernal machine."

He grabbed Toby's shoulders. "'Open the doors and see all the people,'" he quoted. "You're trying to dig your way into Shakespeare's grave!"

Toby opened his mouth to speak, so Oliver and Effie were both caught off guard when he bolted instead, running away along the towpath toward the boat basin. They watched him hurtle across the footbridge that spanned the lock gates and disappear from view.

"I was just getting interested," said Effie. "Correct me if I'm wrong, Ollie dear, but weren't you the one who said he couldn't possibly have any secrets?"

"He won't go far."

They found Toby a few minutes later, sitting disconsolately on a low step in front of the Gower Memorial. He didn't react as they sat quietly on either side of him.

"He stopped, Ollie," Toby said at last, with a backward nod toward the figure of Shakespeare, seated high on the plinth behind him. "Words, black as blood, dripping from the end of his quill, roared from the mouths of the finest actors of his time, moving a queen to laughter and a king to tears. He was so great that he *must* have known his greatness. And he just stopped. By 1613 at the very latest, not even fifty years old. He left the stage and the city of London, the center of the universe, and came back to this footling market town where he merely happened to be born. He stayed here in obscurity until he died. Silent. A man who *had* that muse of fire, now content to see out his days as a petit bourgeois. *Without writing another line.*" He took a deep breath of evening air. "There were no manuscripts, no plays, no poems discovered after his death. Nothing passed on to the Widow Anne or to Susanna or Judith, the daughters he never taught to read. Nothing mentioned in the will. It's never made sense."

"Perhaps he was sick," Effie suggested. "Perhaps those illiterate daughters threw out all the papers with the old bed linen."

"Perhaps he just wanted a rest," Oliver ventured. "He'd written getting on for a million words. Thirty-seven plays. Thirty-nine, if you allow for those last collaborations."

"Do you know of any other writer who didn't keep on writing to the end?" Toby asked. "All those unfinished works—*Sanditon, The Mystery of Edwin Drood, Sunset at Blandings, The Salmon of Doubt.* Writers write. Writers can't *not* write. But Shakespeare, the greatest of them all, stopped."

He lapsed into silence again.

"You think he didn't stop," Effie said. "You think there may have been manuscripts after all, which were buried with him when he died."

"I'm not the first person to consider that," Toby said. "Nor am I the first person to try to look inside the grave to see. Well, when I found that forgotten cellar and the century-old beginnings of a tunnel, I knew what I had to do. I had to finish the job."

"Surely paper wouldn't survive burial for four hundred years?" Effie said.

"Parchment might," said Toby. "I had to see. Even if we don't find anything intact, just some hint that there was something, once. A lump of sealing wax, the remains of a leather wallet. Then at least we'd know. I just wanted to know."

"Which is why your initial team of two or three earth-sifters mysteriously blossomed to ten, no doubt including a couple of civil engineering graduates. How far did you get?"

"We've mostly been tunneling through gravel, although there are one or two spots where we had to go through sandstone. But it's agonizing work—most of the digging is by hand, in a very confined space. The toughest challenge, though, is keeping the noise down. Luckily, we could put the pumps and generators we needed down in the cellar. We haul the earth out in sacks, then winch them up through the cellar opening. Our first thought was to dump it straight into the river, but we were afraid it would clog up the lock."

"And that's where Eric came in?"

"At first he was there just to help bail out the cellar. But when we found the tunnel and I called in the rest of the team, he was very keen to stay on. I didn't even have to pay him. Every night, close to midnight—and presumably after he'd finished humping whichever Bennet sister had drawn that day's short straw—he'd meet me at the island, and we'd fill up his van with the dirt we'd dug out that day. Just a few wheelbarrow loads at a time, across that rickety bridge. He'd drive me home, then go off and empty out the van. I don't know where."

I do, thought Oliver. Wherever it took his fancy. Into road works or country lanes or any other holes opened up by Synne's gardeners, ditchers, and grave-makers.

"What happens to the tunnel when you're finished?" Effie asked.

"It's rigged to collapse," Toby told her. "Set off some minor charges on the key props, and the whole thing comes down. A tiny tsunami on the Avon that nobody will notice, a brief tidal bore that dissipates when it reaches the weir. Nobody will know we were there."

Oliver scrambled to his feet and offered a hand to Toby.

"Let's go," he said brusquely. Toby stayed where he was, looking up at his brother quizzically.

"Where?"

"To the island. If there be any good thing to be done, we're going to collapse that tunnel now. Hide every piece of evidence, before it's too late."

Toby stared at him. "Why are you so angry about this?" he asked.

"Because who knows how many laws you've already broken, little brother."

"Why, Ollie?" Toby asked again.

Oliver ran his hands through his lank, blond hair. "Because it's dangerous, Toby," he said, with sad affection. "You could be buried alive down there. And you know that Mother would blame me."

Toby looked down, wrapping his arms around his knees. "I wasn't, though, was I?" he said, his voice muffled. "Buried alive, I mean. You see, we're finished. We broke through to the grave this morning. I got the call just after you left the church."

"And?" Effie whispered.

Toby shook his head, still hiding his face. "And all for nothing. Just human remains. The whole escapade's been a waste of time."

"No parchment?"

"No parchment."

"Never mind the parchment!" Oliver exclaimed. "Toby, you saw him! You saw Shakespeare. What was that like?"

Toby looked up. "As you'd expect. Old, old bones, nothing more. No epiphanies, no magic. I didn't swoon on the spot with the significance of it all. William died, William was buried, William returned into dust, the dust is earth." He stretched and stood up slowly.

"But it was Shakespeare's dust. The quintessence!" said Oliver breathlessly.

"It's not really the place for a mystical experience, Ollie. You're wearing breathing equipment and overalls and a flashlight on your head, you're toting night vision cameras and radio equipment, it's cramped and dark and dirty and hot and claustrophobic and very, very wet, and you're worn out by the time you get there, and all the while you're wondering if you even have the strength to get back out again."

He started to walk around the memorial, from Hamlet clutching Yorick's skull toward the draped form of Lady Macbeth, dreaming of washing her hands. The others kept pace, rapt.

"The coffin was pretty well rotted away," Toby continued, "but the space was still there. We got our geophysics right. We came in from the side, near the head, just intrusive enough to snake in the fiber-optic night vision camera and let it take a good look around. There was nothing. At least, nothing that the worms had left us."

He turned the corner and headed toward Falstaff.

"What about the curse?" Oliver asked. "You didn't forbeare to dig the dust, as instructed. Aren't you scared now?

"'Cursed be he that moves my bones,'" Toby quoted. He laughed indulgently. "I told you, Ollie, it was a piece of anonymous doggerel, added so that Will could hold on to his prime real estate. But we didn't move his bones. Not because of the curse. Because of respect. And then we collapsed the tunnel."

"What?" Oliver and Effie exclaimed simultaneously.

Toby leaned on the jovial bronze Falstaff, turning to face the others with a similarly amused expression. "Yes, Oliver, there's no need to play Big Brother and bury my mistakes for me. As soon as we'd found out what we needed, we got our equipment out of the tunnel and set off the explosives. Tomorrow, we'll finish cleaning up the site as if nothing had ever happened."

"Something did happen though," Oliver commented, pinching his upper lip. "Dennis Breedlove tried to blackmail you."

"That again? I told you, I never received any blackmail note. What could Dennis have got out of me, anyway?"

"Had you found anything in that grave, it would have been worth a pretty penny."

"None of us was in it for what we could make."

"Oh yes, you were. What you could make was a name for yourselves. Hide the tunnel, get your cover story straight, and your little team becomes world famous as the discoverers of Shakespeare's missing plays. That's what you all dreamed of, deep inside. That dream may be dead now, but it was very much alive last week when, out of nowhere, a letter arrived threatening to reveal what you're up to unless you pay up thirty pieces of silver. And then what did you do, Toby? Pay?" He leaned forward. "Isn't it safer to track down the blackmailer and kill him?" he hissed.

"I didn't get any letter," Toby protested. "And I certainly didn't kill Dennis."

"But he did wheedle the whole story of this foolhardy expedition out of you?"

"Yes, but—"

"And you've been known to drive Eric's van, which was seen going by the Common on the night of the murder, very near the time it must have been committed."

"I only—"

"And the damp earth from your dig was dumped out of that van into Breedlove's front garden, to make room for the body of an old man and a stolen stepladder."

"You can't—"

"Even though Eric himself was apparently despoiling Davina at the time."

"No he wasn't."

"Yes he was. Geoffrey was watching him till nearly midnight."

"The time is out of joint," Toby said. "Eric was at the dig by ten o'clock that night, earlier than usual. I was going to ask him why, but then he got a text and hurried off."

"Must have been another night."

"No, it was definitely the night of the murder. Don't you remember? I had to hitchhike home. I told you the next day."

The brothers continued to stare at each other. Effie watched in silence.

"Ollie, I didn't—" Toby began again, imploringly.

"Didn't kill Dennis Breedlove?" Oliver reached out and straightened Toby's collar. "Of course you didn't, you whingeing little clotpole. I never thought you did. You just needed that smile knocked off your face. Come on, we have an alibi to break."

He turned away abruptly, heading for the car park.

Chapter Thirty-four

Saturday evening (continued)

Getting no answer to her knock, Effie effortlessly picked the lock of Mormal's flat in Pigsneye, and they trooped into the bedroom, already familiar from DoctorPeeper-dot-com. They found the camera on top of a wardrobe, its lens poking through a hole in an old cardboard suitcase. Beside the wardrobe, just out of the camera's range, was a small desk, on which Mormal had stacked a computer and several external hard drives. Effie flicked on the computer and found a list of passwords and IDs in an untidy drawer. Within a few moments, she had located the video that Eric and Davina recorded on the night of Breedlove's murder and left Oliver and Toby watching in fast-forward while she prowled around the cluttered room, opening more drawers and sniffing inside containers.

At sixteen times the normal speed, the convulsing pair seem to change position every three seconds, but Oliver was still surprised at how much time they spent in post-coital pillow talk. Then they jumped out of bed and dressed. The screen went blank.

"It's over," he announced.

Effie was peering distastefully into the wardrobe. She shut the door rapidly and checked her watch.

"It can't be," she said, returning to the desk. "Geoffrey claimed they were at it for three hours." She pulled her curls back behind her head, snapped an elastic band around them, and started to click her way into the DoctorPeeper logs. Oliver glanced around, noting the odd sensation of seeing the same bed he'd just been watching on the screen, similarly tousled but now unoccupied.

"Okay, here's what happened," Effie said. "You just saw the live broadcast, which started at about eight o'clock. It lasted an hour and ten minutes. At that point, Eric paused the transmission, uploaded the recording he'd just made to the website's server, and set it to replay continuously. It was turned off at 11:44 p.m. exactly, which is when he must have come home." She swiveled to face the others. "Pornography is, of course, predictable and repetitive," she remarked. "That's part of its charm. But you'd think that even a simpleton like Geoffrey Angelwine would notice that he'd witnessed the same performance three times in a row!"

"So where was Eric between 9:10 and 11:44 p.m.?" Oliver said.

"He turned up at the dig at about 9:30 p.m.," said Toby. "He stayed for about an hour, and then got a call or a text and pissed off. He normally doesn't arrive until elevenish. It looks like Davina cut him off early. She did appear a bit cross in the recording."

"Geoffrey mentioned the same thing."

Effie played the closing moments of the video again, this time at normal speed. She froze the playback on Davina. But the camera set-up offered her no close-up, and the young woman's face was distant and indistinct.

"I wonder what caused her to get so angry?" she said.

"Perhaps it just occurred to her that she'd been shagging Eric Mormal?" Oliver suggested.

Effie let the video finish, Davina storming from the room, Eric stealthily approaching the off-screen computer, presumably to stop the recording and arrange to broadcast the replay. Again, Oliver was struck by the dislocation between the real and the recorded. He couldn't help glancing behind him, and recoiled as he came face-to-face with the real Mormal, who had crept into the room without their hearing. Mormal leaped backwards even further.

"Don't you hit me again!" he whined. "You're a bleedin' menace, you are, Oliver Swithin." Mormal's still-swollen tongue gave him a mild lisp—the last word came out as "Thwithin." "Oh hello, Tobe," he continued. "Do you need the van again?"

Toby shook his head. He swallowed, uncertain how to play the new situation. "Not anymore, Eric. We're all done with the tunnel. Just this afternoon."

"Anything come out yet?"

"No. It was—"

"Hang on, I'll put the kettle on. Won't keep you." Mormal slipped out of the room and went into his small kitchen. Toby shifted a pile of dirty clothes from the only armchair and sat down. Effie stayed at the desk, writing. Mormal came back a minute later, throwing his car keys and phone onto the bed. "Spent the day in bed, thanks to this bully," he explained, with a nod toward Oliver. "First time I've been out—nipped into Shipthton-on-Thtour for a latte."

"You don't seem surprised to see us," Oliver noted.

Mormal pointed to his bruised jawline. "Thought you were back to gloat over your handiwork. Either that or you're sniffing for free samples from Doctor Peeper. Give Effie a thrill."

"You can thrill me by telling us who killed your business partner," Effie murmured, without turning round.

"What are you talking about? Dennis committed suicide."

"You know he didn't, Eric," said Oliver. "Because you were there that night. You went to Dennis's house from the dig. You dumped out the earth you'd collected into his front garden, you slipped down the lane to get the church stepladder, and then you drove him up to the Shakespeare Race."

Mormal took a deep breath and sat on the bed, lying back on his elbows. "Wow!" he said slowly—and successfully, since the word was free of s's. For a moment, the scratching of Effie's pencil was the only sound in the room.

"Okay, Thyerlock, you got me," Mormal continued unexpectedly. "That's all true. My, um, business with Davvy had ended a little sooner than expected, so I went round to work at the dig early and loaded up the van with the day's dirt. And then I realized it was the first of the month, and I needed to pay Uncle Dennis his monthly stipend. So I popped in on the way home. But get this: *He was already dead when I got there.*"

Mormal waited a second, gauging the reactions in the room. They seemed to please him. "Thtrangled," he resumed. "With a thkipping rope. Gave me quite a turn, I can tell you." He shook his head. "Who can have done this? I asked myself. And right then, I saw there was a letter on his desk, just like the letter I got when Dennis started blackmailing me. It was clear to me that it was all about Toby's Shakespeare project. I assumed that Toby had received the letter earlier that day, rushed over to the house clutching it, and killed Breedlove."

"I didn't!" Toby shouted, but Oliver signaled him to be quiet.

Mormal grabbed a tissue from a box beside his bed and blew his nose. "I didn't want my dear old school chum to get arrested, so I tried to cover up the murder. I thought if I strung the body up using the same rope, it might hide the strangulation marks and look like he'd hung himself."

"Hanged," Oliver murmured.

"Hanged? Really? Well, hanging made me think of the old Synne Oak, the village gallows. A good place to leave him, a long way from the real scene of the crime. But in the fuss, I left the letter behind, just like you did, Tobe. Still, I thought, nobody else could connect it to dear my old mate, Toby Swithin." He sighed deeply and loudly. "Sorry. I reckoned without your smartarse big brother. Can't choose your relatives, eh?"

"I was at the dig on the evening of Breedlove's death," Toby said, glaring at Mormal, "before you arrived and after you left. The others will vouch for me."

"Ah, Toby, Toby, I can see what you're doing there. But trust me, mate, it won't stand up as an alibi. Any smart lawyer could sow doubt. 'Oi, Lord Snooty, are you sure it was the first of May you're remembering, or was it the second or the third?'" Mormal slipped into an overwrought impression of one of Toby's fellow Oxford diggers. "'Oh I say, m'lud, now you mention it, one's brain does get so bleedin' fluffy over dates when one's been sluicing Chateau Lafitte all night, what, what, what?'" He laughed, not caring that the others didn't join in.

"Eric's right, Toby," Oliver said suddenly. "Breedlove was killed because he'd found out about the tunnel. That letter *was* sent, just as his ledger shows. And the next day, he was dead."

"But—"

"But you didn't kill him. I know. Because even if you had opened the letter, you couldn't have known who sent it. In fact, if you think about it, the only people who could have identified Breedlove as the author were his previous victims, who'd have recognized the style and the handwriting." (*The vicar, the vergers, the vampire, and the vulgarian*, Oliver thought.)

"Yeah, but I told you," Mormal cut in nervously, "I never saw that letter until I went to Breedlove's house that night. And he was already dead."

"Of course you saw it. If Breedlove had stuck to his usual habits, he'd have dropped that first letter through our letterbox after dark on Wednesday night, exactly as he recorded in his secret ledger. It was probably on the doormat when you came to pick up Toby for an early morning session at the dig. You recognized it for what it was, you opened it, and you kept it."

"Why would Eric do that?" Toby asked.

"Oh don't be so bloody naïve," Oliver snapped. "Your problem, Toby, is that you're too honorable, too trusting. Somebody else in this room thinks so too."

"Effie, you mean?"

"Eric, I mean."

"Oh."

"You're one in a million, Tobe," Mormal piped up. "A diamond."

"Why do you think Eric's been providing his haulage services for nothing?" Oliver continued. "Because from the moment you found that tunnel, Eric's been planning to make off with whatever came out of the grave. Who knows what that potential treasure trove might have been worth—ancient manuscripts, forgotten plays? And you and your merry band of tomb-raiders could hardly protest as he heads off into the sunset with your swag. So the last thing Eric wants is for you to get a guilty conscience and shut down the dig, before the tunnel is complete. And so he took the letter, to keep you in the dark."

No reaction from Mormal this time.

"But how did it get back to Breedlove's house?" asked Toby.

"Breedlove is killed. That changes everything. Now, Eric needs to frame someone for the murder, and who better than you, the newly minted blackmail victim?"

"But the letter doesn't mention me."

"True. In fact it's so obscure that we started out thinking it was sent *to* Breedlove—a little bonus misdirection that I don't think Eric intended."

"Then what was the point of bringing it back?"

"Just to let the police know that a letter existed—that a fifth victim was in play. Remember, Eric doesn't know about Breedlove's secret ledger. And then he disposes of the body at a local landmark called the Shakespeare Race, another subtle pointer to the obsessions of his old school friend, Toby Swithin."

"But none of that is enough to identify me, even with the nursery rhyme."

"Of course not. As I said, Eric still needs you to finish that tunnel. But once it's completed…"

"Then what?"

"Come on, Toby, what's missing?"

Toby thought for a second. "The envelope?" he ventured.

Oliver smiled. "The concomitant envelope, which will mysteriously turn up when the work at the tunnel is all done. And its addressee, Master Toby Swithin of Oxford and Synne, gets hung out to dry."

"Hanged," murmured Mormal.

"Darling, did you work all that out by yourself?" asked Effie, looking around from the desk. "Just you and your brain?"

"Well, yes."

"Oh, well done, you." She beamed at him, unable to console him with the news that the "bonus misdirection" had come from Simon Culpepper. She held up a sealed envelope, torn across the top edge. Oliver could see the odd, penciled capital letters in the address. Toby's name.

"How long ago did you find that?" he asked.

"About three minutes after we got here. Top drawer, left hand side, when I was looking for Eric's passwords."

"Never underestimate the methods of a police officer," Oliver muttered.

"Not just any police officer," Effie prompted.

"A police officer with naturally curly hair."

"Good boy," she said. "Eric, you're just not very good at this, are you?"

"You put that there," said Mormal. "Police, planting evidence."

She swiveled on the office chair and glared at him. "Oh, no, you did *not* just go there."

"It's your word against mine," Mormal maintained. "And your discovery process is hardly kosher."

"Your process of discovering what women are wearing under their skirts is totally legit, is it?"

"I have my rights," he snapped, jabbing a forefinger toward her face. *Including the right to throw us out, long ago*, Oliver thought, but he hasn't. *Odd.*

Effie held the envelope up to the overhead light. "Then if what you say is true, Eric, you've never touched this envelope, and so these grubby fingerprints can't possibly be yours, right?"

Mormal paused, finger still raised. Then he snatched the envelope from Effie's grasp, screwed it into a ball, and stuffed it into his mouth, wincing as he tried to accommodate both the dry paper and his swollen tongue. Effie leaned back in her chair, momentarily startled. They watched with fascination as he chewed and champed.

"I think that answers your question, Effie," said Toby.

Mormal tried to respond to Toby, but the words were incomprehensible. He attempted a swallow, coughed, and spat out a bolus of soggy paper onto the bed.

"I said it still doesn't prove a thing," he gasped.

"I agree," said Effie, "especially since you've just chewed up a blank envelope I found in your drawer and wrote Toby's name and address on." She waved another envelope, identical to the first. "This is the real one, and I wouldn't recommend your trying to take it, Eric, on the grounds that I don't wish you to."

Mormal glared at her, but chose the path of discretion.

"You're wrong," he said with a sneer. "I didn't steal the letter from the doormat. Dennis gave it to me to deliver. He didn't drop it off at the house, because he was afraid that someone else might open it by mistake. He didn't know that I'd joined Toby's team of tunnel-diggers and so had a vested interest in *not* delivering it. Well, what am I, a fucking postman?"

Oliver whispered something in Effie's ear. She nodded.

"Are you going to arrest Eric?" Toby asked Effie.

"What for?"

"Breedlove's murder, of course."

"Oh, Eric didn't kill Dennis Breedlove. He just tried to cover up the murder, exactly as he said."

"Who for?"

"For Jesu's sake, forbeare," said Oliver.

"Well, it's an obvious question, there's no need to be rude."

"'For Jesu's sake, forbeare.' It's part of that curse on Shakespeare's tomb. Davina used the phrase the other day. An odd expression, unless you've been talking about graves and bones and curses." Oliver stepped over to the bed and leaned his face into Mormal's. "She knew all about the tunnel, didn't she?"

Mormal seemed to make a calculation. "Yeah, I told her," he admitted.

"Why would you tell Davina?" demanded Toby. "You were supposed to keep it secret."

"I love her, Tobe," Mormal said, with uncharacteristic sincerity. "I'll always tell my Davina the truth. Well, apart from the bit about bonking her sisters and broadcasting it live, of course."

"And they say romance is dead," said Effie.

Mormal ignored her. "I'm sorry it had to be you who got screwed over, Tobe," he said. "But if that grave holds what you think it holds, we'll be rich, Davina and me. Really rich."

"Davina's already rich."

"*Richer,* then. And now. Not beholden to her moody Daddy's checkbook or to trust funds that don't mature before menopause. I'll be able to buy her anything she wants. We can get married."

Effie revolved in the office chair, clicking the mouse to summon the final minutes of Eric's dalliance with Davina.

"I think you can actually pinpoint the moment when you tell her that Breedlove has found out about the tunnel," she said, as the naked figure of Davina stiffened and then turned angrily toward Mormal. "What a falling off was there. Don't think we need a lip-reader to see how that went down."

They watched again the silent, irate conversation and the decisive departure of Davina from the bed. She pulled her clothes on, elegant even at low resolution, and rushed from the room, while Mormal approached the desk and stopped the recording. Effie turned off the playback and clicked another control on the screen.

"We know Eric went straight to the dig at that point," Oliver said. "But we haven't asked where Davina went. She's angry. And about an hour later, Eric gets a text and he hurries off, leaving Toby stranded in Stratford. It was from Davina, telling you to come to Breedlove's cottage, wasn't it, Eric?"

Mormal nodded.

"Davina knew that even if Toby could be kept in ignorance of the blackmail, Breedlove still had to be reckoned with."

Mormal nodded again.

"But she didn't go to negotiate terms, did she?"

Mormal shook his head.

"I expect she tried at first to threaten him—with exposure, with disgrace, with social ostracism, even with physical violence, before she realized that none of these could keep a shameless old man quiet."

Mormal nodded.

"There were only two ways to stop him. Pay him or slay him."

Mormal shrugged.

"And Davina wasn't prepared to part with a penny."

Mormal shook his head.

"So when Uncle Dennis wasn't looking, she took that priceless Victorian skipping rope from his display case and strangled him with it."

Mormal glanced at his watch.

"And then she texted you to come over and clean up for her. Which you did, picking up Toby's blackmail letter on the way, in case it came in handy. Or perhaps that was her idea, too. And the business of taking the body to the Shakespeare Race. No wonder she was so matey with you at the dinner party on the following evening. Private jokes, conspiratorial glances, a marked desire to avoid talking about the recent death. You scored a lot of brownie points with the divine Davina. But what's she going to say when she finds out you just pinned the murder squarely on her?"

"She's not going to know, is she?" Mormal replied, looking around in triumph. "Because this conversation ain't happening. It has no existence in legality. Effie didn't read me my rights. You shouldn't be here without a search warrant. Everything's hearsay. Nothing's gonna stick to me or Davina. I'm bleedin' Teflon."

Another example of MindSpam, thought Oliver—that Teflon was a byproduct of the space race. He wisely chose not to mention it.

Mormal laid his index finger against the side of his nose. "But even so," he continued, "you'll notice that on the matter of who killed Dennis Breedlove, I haven't spoken a word. So who's to say I accused anyone?"

"Currently, about four hundred puzzled perverts out there in cyberland, probably waiting for something interesting to happen," said Effie, reading a statistic on the monitor. She

268   Alan Beechey

gestured casually to the camera on top of the wardrobe. "We've been broadcasting for five minutes."

◇◇◇

Ben Motley woke suddenly from his doze when his telephone began to play the sound of Doctor Who's Tardis materializing. Mallard glared in his direction from the stage. Still only in Act II. Ben answered the phone quickly.

"Effie? Wait, I should take the call outside."

"No, stay there. Listen, do you remember which of those Bennet creatures is Davina?"

"Yeah, dark hair, short, current possessor of the only family brain cell. Looks a bit Scandinavian."

"Hardly."

"No? I think she has a face like a Norse."

"Cut the gags. Can you see the Bennets from where you're sitting?"

Ben looked to his left, across the impinging heads of Susie and Geoffrey. "Yep, pretty maids all in a row. Plus their mother. But minus Davina."

"What?"

"She got a phone call or something about twenty minutes ago. Hasn't returned yet. When are you lot coming back?"

But Effie had rung off.

◇◇◇

She looked thoughtfully at Mormal, who was sitting on the bed, muttering about seeing a lawyer. Then she made a sharp grabbing motion toward his crotch. He rolled instinctively, and she picked up the cell phone he had been sitting on and flicked it on.

"You people just don't respect a citizen's rights!" he yelled, trying to seize the phone back. Oliver pushed him away.

"He sent a text," Effie reported. "It must have been just after he arrived, when he slipped out to the kitchen. It says: 'There thru. Dont w8 4 me.'" She pushed some additional keys. "And that number belongs to... Davina Bennet."

"But the tunnel's gone," breathed Toby. "We collapsed it."

"What?" shouted Mormal. "You didn't tell me that! You said you hadn't taken anything out yet."

"Because there was nothing to take out!"

For Jesu's sake, forbear. . .

Effie hit the redial key. She heard the ringing tone several times before it flipped to Davina's mailbox.

"Come on," said Oliver, heading for the door. "We've got to go back to Stratford. Now I know why Eric didn't throw us out. He was stalling, trying to buy time for Davina to get to the tunnel. Only by now, there is no tunnel."

"Where do you think you're going?" demanded Effie, as Mormal tried to follow Oliver.

"I'm coming with you, of course."

"I don't think so, buster." There was a flash of silver in her hand, and Mormal found his wrist suddenly encircled in metal, one loop of a pair of handcuffs. Effie looked around and then snapped the other end to the cast-iron bed frame.

"Won't you need them if we manage to intercept Davina?" Toby asked, admiring Effie's professional technique.

"Those aren't mine," she told him. "I'm off duty. I just got them from a box in the bottom of Eric's wardrobe."

"Hey, I don't have keys!" Mormal shouted, tugging at the handcuffs.

"Then I'll tell Sergeant Culpepper to bring bolt-cutters," Effie called from the doorway, pushing Toby ahead of her. She came back into the room, pulled something shiny from her pocket, and placed it delicately on Mormal's pillow. It was a piece of chocolate, wrapped in foil.

"Here, compliments of the management."

She blew a kiss to the camera and ran out.

Chapter Thirty-five

Saturday evening (continued)

The hole was the size of an open grave, opaque in the dusk. Toby pointed his flashlight down into the opening. Its round beam reflected off a layer of still, black water.

"How deep is it?" Oliver asked.

"Only a few inches," said Toby. He dropped to his haunches, steadying himself on an aluminum ladder, which led down into the cellar.

"But if the tunnel collapsed, wouldn't the water be level with the river by now?" Effie asked.

"If the tunnel filled with earth, it would act like a plug."

Oliver looked around. A few patches of flagstone and some dusty shards of broken blue tiles remained to show where the river-island cottage had once stood. The old trees surrounded the clearing, waiting impatiently to move in. He could hear the constant roar of the Stratford Weir, a few yards downstream.

"Where's all the equipment?" he asked.

Toby pointed toward a dim pile at the edge of the clearing. "What's left is over there. We had to get the big stuff—pumps, generator, lights—out of the cellar before we set off the charges. Some of it's already been carted away. No time to lick our wounds. That's odd."

"What?"

"I got this flashlight from a portable locker, where we keep the more valuable tools. I just realized it wasn't locked."

Effie walked toward the stack of wheelbarrows, buckets, lengths of rope, and the battered locker, scanning the ground in the fading light.

"Toby, give me some light," she called.

Toby pointed the flashlight in her direction, making the object she held glitter and sparkle. A long pin with a diamond-covered head in the shape of a letter D.

"She picked the lock," Effie said.

"Probably trying to see if we'd stashed the only surviving copy of *Cardenio* in a Portakabin for the night," Toby said. "She'll be disappointed."

"Has anything been taken?"

Toby inspected the open locker. "There were six of these expensive flashlights. I've got one. One's missing."

Oliver and Effie both turned and looked solemnly toward the hole. Then they looked back at each other. Oliver nodded.

The water in the cellar was cold around his feet and ankles, and was already soaking into his rolled-up trouser-legs. He shone his flashlight around the small chamber, scattering wild reflections off the glossy tiles and rippling water. The air was dank, thick with the smell of mold.

Effie came down the ladder, clutching another flashlight under her arm. Toby stood at the top, shining his own bright beam directly down into the cellar, silhouetting Effie's wild curls. She stopped on the rung above the water's surface.

"You don't have to come," Oliver said.

"And what if she needs help?" Effie asked. She reached behind her back, undid the zip on her dress, and, balancing with difficulty on her bare feet, hauled it over her head. *That answers that one*, thought Oliver. He'd already removed his jacket and left it by the locker above, beside his shoes and socks.

Effie passed the dress up the ladder to Toby. His beam of light seemed to tremble.

"Oh, calm down," she sighed. "Haven't you seen a woman in her bra and pants before?"

"He probably hasn't," said Oliver, wading toward the dark entrance to the tunnel in the middle of the cellar wall, his voice echoing off the tiles. He trod on what he thought was a python but made himself think better of it.

The opening was about a yard in diameter, more or less circular but slightly flatter on the bottom. A steady trickle of water dribbled over the rim, leaving a brownish-green stain on the wall. The inner surface of the tunnel was covered with the same glazed tiles, like the passages in the London Underground, but Oliver's flashlight beam showed that they stopped after a few yards, and the bore beyond was lined with pale, sweating concrete. The tunnel stretched away, perfectly straight. There was still no sign of Davina.

Oliver looked up at Toby, shutting his eyes to the bright, white light. "It doesn't look like it's collapsed," he called.

"You wouldn't see it from here. We only covered up our own tracks."

"How far in is that?"

"The old tunnel goes in about a hundred feet. We dug out another two hundred."

"I wonder why the first diggers stopped?" said Effie, peering into the gloom.

"Perhaps the Shakespeare curse got them," Oliver muttered.

"Our extension was narrower," Toby continued, "and not so high, held up with timber. We didn't hit any serious rock, so we managed about fifteen to twenty feet a day—about a grave's worth of dirt. We're below the level of the riverbed, but the gravel's very porous, it was like sitting in a stream while we—"

"Shut up!" hissed Effie. "What was that?"

They listened carefully. Small waves slapped against the cellar walls. The weirs could still be heard, faintly. There was no other sound.

"Turn your torch off," Effie said. Oliver pressed the button.

Only Toby's column of light behind them held off the suffocating blackness. They waited for the after-images to fade.

They both saw it. A pinprick of light, far down the tunnel. And a faint, exhausted cry.

"I'll get her," said Oliver, snapping the flashlight on again. It flickered for a second.

"I should go. I'm the cop."

"Once again, Effie, you're underdressed for a Bennet family social occasion."

He started to climb into the tunnel entrance.

"Wait!" she cried and splashed back to the base of the ladder. "Toby!" she shouted up into the light. "Bring me some rope."

"Are you planning to tie her up?" Oliver asked.

"I want to put a safety line on you."

Toby reappeared, passing down a length of rope. Effie tied one end firmly around Oliver's waist.

"Be careful," she said.

"It's only Davina."

"She's a killer."

"She's still only Davina."

She kissed him and pushed him into the tunnel.

Oliver tried to move in a low, loping crouch, but his back scraped against the roof. He dropped to his hands and knees, tucked the flashlight into his waistband, and scrabbled forward at a slower pace. The rope was getting heavier as he dragged more of it with him, soaking in the shallow channel of water that ran along the tunnel floor. Breathing was hard.

A hundred feet. The lined passageway ended abruptly, as if the Victorian engineers had lost interest. Or was this all the work of one single, fanatical, Bard-obsessed digger, who had grown too old or sick or mad to continue? Oliver stopped, gasping for fresh air that wasn't there. Behind him, he could see the disc of Effie's flashlight, bright enough to be visible but not bright enough to give any illumination, like the stars on a moonless night. Could she still see him or just a skein of rope vanishing into the darkness?

He clambered on, into Toby's bore, which was square and narrower, with no room to turn around. The walls now were dark compacted earth, cold and damp to the touch, shored up every few feet with timber props.

Which were still standing.

He crawled now across wet dirt, like a commando. The rope was still following. But what if Effie came to its end before he reached Davina? Would she hold it to stop him going any further? Or would she let it be dragged out of her hands and into the blackness of the tunnel? Had that already happened? Damn it, they hadn't arranged any signals.

His flashlight flickered again.

Oliver shook it. It went out. Darkness. He shook it harder. It struck a prop on the side of the tunnel and bounced out of his hands. He groped around sightlessly, feeling only loose, wet earth.

He tried to sit up, but hit his head on the unseen planks above him and fell back onto his hands and knees again. He could still see nothing ahead of him in the darkness. Should he leave her to heaven? What the hell is the point of going on?

Oliver went on, reaching ahead, trying to find his way without his eyes. His hand closed on something that was clearly not his flashlight. It was a human foot.

He let his hand continue over the well-toned calf and a short way along a slim thigh until it ran into something other than skin—the hem of a dress. He dragged himself forward into the tight gap between the body and the wall, until he was level with the girl's head.

"Davina." He shook what he hoped was her shoulder. She groaned in the darkness, and he knew her face was only inches from his. He could feel and smell her breath. She shifted slightly. Then he was blinded.

"Oh, hello, Ollie, darling," she said huskily. "Fancy seeing you here."

Reaching into the red world beyond his eyelids, he covered her hot flashlight with his hand and prized it from her grip, turning it away from his face and back along her body. She was on her stomach, with her left arm raised and holding on to a wooden prop. She was wet and filthy, and there were several streaks of blood on her bare legs. The expensive dress in which she'd strutted into the theater an hour earlier was torn in several places, and on the opposite side to him had ridden up almost to her hip. She wore no underwear, at least below the waist.

"Are you hurt?"

"No, dear. I'm stuck."

She shook her left arm. He trained the flashlight on it. It seemed to be attached to a damaged prop. He needed a closer look. With a curt apology, he shifted himself onto her back. She exhaled noisily.

A long tapering spike of the splintered prop had caught in the gap between Davina's wrist and her wristwatch. Her skin was uncut, but shards of wood had impaled the links on the steel bracelet.

"Take your watch off," he ordered.

"I can't," she gasped. His weight was pushing her down into the sodden earth. "It's a Cartier Tank Americaine."

"You'd rather stay here and die than be parted from your fancy wristwatch?"

"No, silly. It has a folding clasp, which goes on over my hand. I'm trapped."

Oliver propped the flashlight against her neck. He wrenched away the sharp splinters that had pinioned the clasp and gently slid Davina's hand out of the luxurious manacle, oddly taking care not to scrape the healing burn she'd attributed to an ironing mishap at that dinner party, a century ago. He rolled off her. She raised herself up on her elbows, rubbing her wrist.

"A minute longer and you'd have to marry me."

Oliver wasn't listening. He trained the light again on the fractured prop, noticing the charring and the traces of gaffer tape. This had to be the prop that was rigged to collapse, the first domino to be toppled. The small explosive charge had gone off, although it hadn't severed the wood completely. But it couldn't last much longer. Davina's struggles to free herself, his tearing away the wooden shards—had they hastened the process?

"Davvy, we have to get out. Quickly. You'll have to trust me that there was nothing in the grave."

"I know."

"What? How?"

"I've been there."

The dress riding up. The impaled watch bracelet. Davina had been crawling backwards, blindly returning along the narrow tunnel that offered no turning space. And this was after she'd made it to the end while dressed for a night at the theater, a trek Toby had only managed with protective clothing and breathing equipment. They breed those Bennets tough. It wasn't so hard to imagine her garroting an old man, a pointless murder, as she'd just discovered. That burn on her hand wasn't from an iron, he now knew. It was torn there by Alice Liddell's skipping rope, pulled taut around Breedlove's throat.

He slithered down her body and set off backwards along the tunnel on knees and elbows, holding the flashlight in one hand and gathering the wet rope under his chest with the other. Davina began to move, too, the grimy, cracked soles of her bare feet in his face. Loose earth dropped from the walls as they brushed past.

The floor of the tunnel became hard again, and he knew he was back in the older section, at least a foot wider and higher. He pressed himself against the side wall and let Davina back out into the space beside him.

"You can turn around here," he told her, noticing that she was cradling something in one arm, close to her stomach. It was her pantyhose. She slumped against the side of the tunnel facing him, trying to fill her lungs with air that was only marginally fresher. Scraped, dirty limbs protruding further from her ruined dress than its designer ever intended, sweaty face, tangled hair. And those feral eyes in their shadowed sockets, assessing him warily. In the narrow beam of the flashlight, she looked like the hideous gamine figure of Want in *A Christmas Carol*, grown to terrifying womanhood. What was it Clarissa had said about Davina's vanity? She'd sooner die than be caught with a hair out of place.

"How did you know the grave was empty?" she asked.

"Toby got there this afternoon."

"This afternoon? That fucking prole Eric Mormal sent me here an hour ago."

"And he speaks so highly of you. He didn't know that they'd made it all the way to the end."

"He just can't get anything right. You do know that it was Eric who killed Dennis Breedlove?"

"Save it for the police. We need to get to safety."

He untied the rope. It would be easier to move without it. He shifted into position to lead the way out, but Davina stayed sitting, watching him.

"So he shopped me, as your little lady-friend might have put it?"

"It wasn't like that," Oliver said, but wondered if it was. "The word 'love' came up."

"Oh, Jesus Christ. As if." She looked away.

"We have to go," he said.

Davina sighed noisily.

Another noise, alarmingly unlike an echo, answered her from the darkness—like a firecracker, followed by a soft rain of dirt.

Domino?

"Now, Davvy!" He grabbed her bony arm and pushed her ahead of him. They began to crawl toward the dim circle of light a hundred feet ahead of them, each moving on three limbs, Oliver playing the flashlight's beam low along the floor, Davina still clutching the bundled pantyhose. Their tortured breathing bounced off the concrete walls, filling his ears. He looked down at the rope, lying in the central channel of muddy water.

Effie was at the other end of that rope. He'd never wanted to see her more.

The channel deepened, rapidly. A wave of cleaner water overtook them, pushing ahead in the race for the tunnel's outlet, spreading across the width of the tunnel floor. His knees and hands were now splashing in cold water. And louder than their breathing, sounds from behind them, a halting bass rumble, the treble counterpoint of sudden, high-pressure streams of liquid.

He trained the flashlight back along the dark tunnel. Its beam hit a flailing curtain of water, racing toward them, the Avon leaping and careening inside its newfound escape route. He flung himself onto Davina, locking his arms around her waist.

The river wrapped them before he could warn her, tearing off his glasses and wrenching the flashlight from his grip. His knuckles grazed across the harsh concrete. Davina whimpered, but was silenced when the water filled her mouth.

Once chance. The bitter cold water was already deep enough to cover them. Oliver dived and began to swim, sightlessly, working his legs frantically, still clutching Davina. He was sure the flow was moving him, but it was also buffeting him against the concrete walls. He raised his head for another breath, but the water had reached the roof.

His chest muscles began to pump instinctively, craving new supplies of air. How much further? There was a searing pain behind his eyes now. He flailed on sightlessly, disoriented. In five seconds, he would have to breathe out.

His hand closed around something moving underneath him. The rope. The rope that Effie thought was still tied to him, that was now being hauled in faster than he could swim, that might be pulled beyond his reach at any second.

He held on, still moving his legs, trying to keep away from the abrasive tunnel walls. And then he gave in to his reflexes and filled his lungs with half a pint of the Avon.

Ten seconds later, Oliver and Davina tipped out of the tunnel's mouth into the dimly lit cellar. Effie and Toby dropped the rope and dragged them away from the cataract of river water. Oliver struggled to his feet, coughing and gulping the fetid air.

"Get up the ladder," Effie commanded. "The water's rising fast."

Oliver started to obey, but the cellar was a blur. He could only vaguely register the shape of Davina rising out of the dark pool near him, shivering and still hunched over. He reached out to steady her, his hand brushing the pantyhose. She still hadn't let go. Was this some atavistic urge to restore a degree of decency as soon as she was out of the tunnel?

He found the ladder by touch and pulled himself up, followed by Davina, and then Toby, also drenched but even now distracted by finding himself sandwiched between a half-naked woman swathed in wet silk and his brother's girlfriend in soaking underwear.

Oliver staggered in the vague direction of his jacket. So he was several yards away, groping for his spare glasses, when he saw the outline of Davina shake off Toby's arm and begin to whirl something in air, like a sling. It swung over Toby's head once, but gathering speed in its second orbit, caught him on the side of the head.

There was a sound like a temple block being struck, and Toby crashed into Oliver, who had stumbled blindly toward his little brother. Before Effie reached the top of the ladder, Davina pushed her hard, causing her to fall back into the cellar. There was a deep splash.

Davina scuttled off through the trees, in the opposite direction to the bridge. Oliver let her go, scrambling across the sandy flagstones of the ruined cottage until he could lean over the cellar opening, calling Effie's name. He grabbed Toby's dropped flashlight and shone it downwards. It lit up Effie's face as she surfaced from the underground pool.

"I'll get her for that," she vowed, climbing the ladder again. Oliver turned back to Toby, who was sitting up, cautiously testing the side of his head.

"What did she hit me with?" he asked.

"Her pantyhose," Oliver said, finally locating his spare glasses.

"How thick are they, four billion denier?"

How did Toby know so much about pantyhose? "She must have hidden something hard in them, a rock or a piece of wood."

"Which way did she go?" demanded Effie. She picked up her dress.

"The wrong way," Oliver said, pointing along Davina's escape route.

"Okay, Toby, get up and block the bridge. She's trapped, unless she fancies another swim."

"Or unless…" said Toby.

"If she tries to swim for it, she's going to be pulled over the weir," said Oliver.

"Good. But be quiet, Ollie, we're missing something. Unless what, Toby?"

"Unless she was planning to take my dinghy. She seemed to be running toward it."

They sprinted to the riverbank. In the twilight, they could clearly see the outline of Davina, rowing the small boat toward the opposite shore, struggling hard against the current.

Chapter Thirty-six

Saturday evening (continued)

"Where will she go?" Effie asked Toby.

"The church has the nearest landing spot."

Effie picked up her purse, which she'd left beside Toby's locker, and thrust it at Oliver.

"Take my car and try to head her off. I'll follow her."

She ran toward the bridge, pulling her dress on over her wet hair. Oliver and Toby grabbed the clothes they had discarded and followed, heading for Effie's scarlet Renault, which they'd left on the riverside path.

Oliver had found the keys and clambered into the driver's seat before something occurred to him.

"I can't drive," he admitted, as he started the engine. "At least, I never passed my test."

"Just get moving," Toby yelled.

Oliver went through the motions he was still learning. Clutch down. Shift into first. Release handbrake. Depress accelerator. Bring clutch up gently. Stall car with a lurch.

He tried again. This time the car moved forward gradually. Oliver got it into second gear and they cruised along the path at about fifteen miles an hour. He was gripping the steering wheel, praying that he could avoid piloting the vehicle into the river in the darkness. Then he remembered to turn on the headlamps.

"There's Effie!" cried Toby, as they drew level with Holy Trinity across the river. She had commandeered a kayak that had been left on the bank and was rapidly paddling after Davina, who had almost reached a mooring slip downstream of the church.

"We're not going to get there in time," said Oliver grimly.

"Not at this speed," said Toby. He stamped down on Oliver's bare right foot, at the same time turning the steering wheel sharply to the right. The Renault accelerated across the grass of the riverside park and began to bounce alarmingly on the uneven surface, screaming for a gear change.

"Don't brake!" shouted Toby, "I'll steer." He swerved to avoid a dog-walker who had appeared in the headlights, sending up a spray of mud and shredded turf. The car fishtailed over the grass. Oliver slammed the gear stick into third and ignored the metallic shriek it provoked.

They veered left onto the narrow but mercifully empty road through the Recreation Ground and then skidded onto the main road. Oliver braked sharply to make the left turn onto the bridge, then ploughed ahead, ignoring traffic lights, yields, and other cars—Bridge Foot, through the Bridgeway merge without stopping, onto Bridge Street, unavoidably wondering why the birthplace of the most prolific word-coiner of all time couldn't come up with some less prosaic street names.

Another left, onto Waterside, the straightest route toward Holy Trinity. The façade of the theater came into sight, looking like a 1930s grammar school. How long since they'd left? An hour and a half, maybe. The play would still be in progress.

"There she is!" shouted Toby.

Ahead of them, in the middle of the lamp-lit road, the bedraggled figure of Davina was sprinting toward them, carrying her pantyhose under her arm like a rugby player. About fifty yards behind, Effie was gaining.

Oliver slammed on the brakes. The car slewed sideways across the road and mounted the curb. Davina saw them, stopped, then ducked out of sight around the back of the Swan Theatre. Toby was first out of the car and chased after her. Oliver grabbed his shoes and followed Toby across a small courtyard and through a black metal door, into a world of darkness and silence.

He halted, disoriented. Toby was also motionless a few paces ahead of them. No noise of footsteps, but Davina's bare feet wouldn't make much sound on the firm floor. The door behind them opened again, and Effie came in, gasping for breath. Then they heard a woman's voice, thin and electronic: "But long it could not be till that her garments, heavy with their drink, pull'd the poor wretch from her melodious lay to muddy death."

They were backstage in the main theater. The unseen loudspeaker was transmitting the action on the stage, and, dear God, they still hadn't finished Act Four—an entire act still to go.

Oliver's eyes adjusted to the weak illumination from Exit signs and table lamps. Tall brick walls covered with pipes and wires, leaning ladders, abandoned scenery, unused lighting equipment, large trunks that probably held costumes. He glanced up. The ceiling was high, lost in the darkness.

They stepped forward cautiously. It was a warren of potential hiding places for Davina, with makeshift rooms and changing spaces constructed from flats covered in black velour. Effie let Toby creep a few paces ahead, and then reached for Oliver's hand.

"For a moment, I thought I'd lost you," she whispered, "I shouldn't have let you go in after that murderous bitch."

"You're not the boss of me."

"We'll discuss that later."

"See?"

"See what?"

He tightened his grip on her hand. "There'll always be something for us to talk about."

A brief female scream came from the gloom ahead of them. They ran forward. A group of figures seemed to be scuffling. Toby launched himself on the nearest, pushing the person to the floor.

"What the hell's going on?" it cried, in a voice that was instantly recognizable, and not merely as not belonging to Davina. The man, who was dressed in a peasant smock, got a grip on Toby and dragged himself to his feet.

"You!"

There were several unseen demands for silence.

"Sorry, Uncle Tim," Toby whispered. "I thought you were a woman in a dress."

Mallard glared at his younger nephew, then pushed him away. He spotted Oliver and Effie.

"I don't want to know," he snarled. "Who knocked into me, what this is all about, why you left, why you're back here…I don't want to know. I'm supposed to be going on. Gravedigger." He stalked away and took his place in the wings, untying a bundle, ready for the start of Act Five.

They turned to other person to come out of the melee, the actress playing Gertrude.

"I just came off and went to my little changing area back here," she reported. "A girl shot out, caught me by surprise."

"Did you see where she went?" Effie asked.

Gertrude shook her head. They pressed forward and emerged into an open area in the wings, lit only by a couple of closed-circuit television screens broadcasting the action from the stage. A few rows of rush-bottomed chairs were lined up, some of them occupied by members of the cast in various stages of slumber or catatonic boredom. Effie rapidly checked another row of changing spaces. All empty.

"We need backup," she said.

They spotted the sleeping form of Humfrey Fingerhood, sprawled across two chairs. Effie checked his jacket pockets, extracting a phone.

"Okay, Toby," she said. "Go back and make sure she doesn't find a way out through the Swan Theatre."

Toby saluted, turned, and instantly crashed into a stack of brooms.

Effie placed a call. From the hushed auditorium, they heard the faint sound of Doctor Who's Tardis. On the monitor, Oliver watched Mallard, now onstage, dry for a moment and scowl into the audience.

"Ben," Effie said urgently. "No, I know Davina didn't come back. But she's somewhere in the theater. Get Geoff and Susie and cover all the exits from the auditorium. Well, throw a bucket of water over them. Don't let Davina get away. Because she killed Dennis Breedlove, that's why."

She snapped off the phone. She knew that Simon Culpepper was sitting disconsolately in the front row, beside the heavily disguised Reg Thigpen, but she refused to give him the satisfaction of asking for help. Instead, she used her Scotland Yard credentials to call for a police presence at the theater. Oliver continued to watch Mallard on the screen, noticing his reaction when several more members of his party left their seats and walked out of the theater as he was speaking.

"Should we stop the performance?" he asked.

"She could slip away in the confusion. It's better to wait until we get the plod surrounding the building."

They made another search of the backstage area, checking each changing area again, looking under tables, behind stacked scenery, up at the catwalks over the stage, even inside the huge metal costume trunks, but always keeping the return route to the loading dock in their field of vision. All the time, the play limped toward its conclusion—the gravediggers, Ophelia's burial, Mallard's lightning quick-change into his elaborate Osric costume, the insincere reconciliation between Hamlet and Laertes. But Davina eluded them.

The last scene began, with its duels and deaths. Oliver and Effie watched from the wings, silently accepting the likely truth that Davina had escaped. The grand drape hadn't been lowered between Acts Four and Five, but she could easily have slipped across the stage during the blackout and escaped the building through the unguarded exits on the river side of the theater.

A single flake of fake snow, left over from the opening scene, fluttered languidly down into the intensely white stage lighting, landing on Hamlet's head while he was in the *en garde* position. Even a sliver of soap wanted its one moment in the limelight, Oliver reflected.

Then he stiffened. He looked up, above the stage, shielding his eyes from the blinding spots. He nudged Effie.

"Somebody's up on that gantry," he said, pointing up. "That high one, up in the fly tower."

They scanned the walls. Effie caught sight of the spiral staircase, immensely tall, half-hidden in the shadows. She patted Oliver on the cheek.

"You stay here," she said. "This is my turn."

She began to climb the staircase, watching with every coil the changing perspective of the dazzling stage and its cage of curtains and lighting rigs, shrinking beneath her.

Effie stepped onto the dizzying catwalk. Her first confrontation with Davina had been as a nervous, underdressed guest facing a catty socialite hostess. What a difference it makes to your self-confidence when you're a cop facing a criminal.

Even if the criminal has armed herself.

Davina had nowhere to hide, certainly not behind the unused bags of soap flakes abandoned by the stagehands as soon as their snowmaking duty was over. She no longer had her pantyhose flail, so she'd picked up some sort of grappling hook and was now waving it at the approaching policewoman.

"Davina Bennet," Effie began.

Davina lifted the weapon above her head with both hands and brought it down with all her strength onto the point in space where Effie's head had been half a second earlier, before she'd skipped lightly backwards. The catwalk shuddered and swayed.

"I arrest you for the murder of Dennis Breedlove."

Davina swung wildly at Effie. The hook smashed onto the handrail, raising sparks.

"And for assaulting a police officer."

Davina slashed again through the air in front of Effie's stomach.

"And for assault occasioning actual bodily harm to my boyfriend's little brother."

Davina heaved the hook upwards for another swing at Effie's skull. Effie scooped up a handful of soap flakes and threw it into Davina's eyes. She howled, and the spiked end of the hook buried itself into a sprinkler pipe just above the gantry. Water gushed over her, soaking the remains of her tattered dress and tipping her onto a pile of loosely coiled ropes, legs flailing. The hook stayed embedded in the mangled pipe.

"And for indecent exposure, come to think of it."

Davina scrabbled backwards and kicked a bag of soap flakes at Effie, who batted it aside with ease. It struck the edge of the gantry, splitting and snowing onto the stage far below. Effie gracefully sidestepped the stream of water from the broken pipe and continued to advance on the murderer.

"You do not have to say anything…"

Davina jumped up. She pulled a length of rope tight between her hands and lunged at Effie's neck. Effie tripped her.

"…but it may harm your defense if you do not mention when questioned something which you may later rely on in court."

Effie picked up some of the rope and made a loop. Davina tried to drag herself to her feet again, but skidded on the wet, soapy surface. She clutched onto the handrail and aimed a wild kick into Effie's face. Effie caught her ankle, making her hop on the slick catwalk.

"Anything you do say may be given in evidence."

She discounted the scream that Davina made as she tipped over the edge of the handrail and plunged toward the stage eighty feet below.

Chapter Thirty-seven

The Guardian
Monday, May 10, 20—

Theatre Review
by Threepwood Gallimaufry

Hamlet
Theydon Bois Thespians
Royal Shakespeare Theatre, Stratford-upon-Avon

To the weary, stale, flat spirits among us, director Humpty Fingerhood's production of *Hamlet* on the Royal Shakespeare Theatre's main stage might seem the quintessence of dull. Indeed, the breathless incompetence of this uncut, four-hour performance of Shakespeare's longest play drove many less-enlightened audience members into the public houses of Stratford as early as Act One. However, those of us blessed with greater discernment soon divined Mr. Fingerhold's darker purpose in filling the stage with such excruciating tedium.

For like Steiner, Stanislavski, or Meisner before him, this outrageously gifted director has created his own school of acting. The Fingerhand Technique, if I may coin the phrase, is drama for our time, *of* our time; nothing less than an anti-intellectual haddock slapped into the sweaty faces of those purists of the theatrical world who worship the false gods of Quality and Adequacy.

Starting with the amusing fiction that we are witnessing a suburban amateur theater company (the risibly named Theydon Bois Thespians), the entire tragedy is a constant barrage of boredom and banality. Brechtian touches abound, such as actors frequently forgetting their parts, audible prompts from the wings, and the constant display on the stage of the text itself, a truly stunning example of post-modern self-referentialism. When lines are remembered, there is no attempt to convey the meaning or poetry of the words—indeed, it is the triumph of Mr. Fingerhole's Method that his well-schooled troupe succeed with breathtaking credibility at suppressing any indication that they understand the first thing about the play. He has clearly scoured the nation's drama schools and repertory companies to find actors skilled enough to appear so convincingly clueless.

(Alas, it behooves this critic to single out veteran performer Timothy Mullard, who demonstrated considerable presence and intelligence in his diverse and colorful triple-turn as Polonius, the Gravedigger, and Osric, utterly betraying the artistic vision of his director. Mr. Fingerhoop should consider recasting these parts with a trio of actors who are better at masking the slightest hint of talent.)

But to quote Derrida, as you often find me doing, "It's such a fine line between stupid and clever." For just as we stagger to the end of this monotonous presentation, the director drops his bombshell, confirming one's faith in one's prized perspicacity.

Since you, dear reader, were not sufficiently prescient to obtain tickets to this necessarily one-time offering—we privileged few will dine out on our fortune for many a year to come—I feel I can describe the production's last-minute surprise without hearing your distant, green-eyed cries of "Spoiler!"

We have reached the final tableau. The duel between Hamlet and Laertes commences with swordplay of an incompetence that approaches genius, and the histrionic deaths of the main characters follow in sequence—well done, Claudius, for a full minute of convulsions on the banquet table.

The doomed Hamlet, expiring in Horatio's arms, hears the approach of Fortinbras (excellent sound effects from above the stage), and as he speaks his last words—"the rest is silence," as we all well know, or should—snow begins to fall inside the castle, turning to rain, the significance of which I don't need to explain, I'm sure.

Ah, but the rest is far from silent. There is a piercing shriek, and a woman is lowered head-first from the top of the stage—a barely-clad wench, dirty, ragged and soaking wet, hanging by her ankle from a long rope. She swings wildly, screeching and cursing and waving her free leg around in such a display of "country matters" that we must conclude she is no angel winging the sweet prince to his rest, but none other than the vexed and tormented spirit of the drowned Ophelia. And one—well, this one—instantly comprehends the excruciating monotony of the production: to lull us into a state of complete habituation, so this shattering *coup de theatre* has its greatest possible impact.

Meanwhile, the actors below attempt to go on with the scene in the continuing heavy downpour, on a stage that is now rapidly filling up with soapsuds, an obvious nod to Artaud's Theatre of Cruelty. When Horatio slips and disappears beneath a cloud of froth, unable to continue, a heavily bearded Scotsman leaps onto the stage from the front row of the audience and picks up the speech "So shall you hear of carnal, bloody, and unnatural acts, of accidental judgments, casual slaughters…" but seeming to forget the lines, switches to "It is a tale told by an idiot," thus confirming what I had instantly intuited, that he is meant to represent that other tragic hero, Macbeth. An enormously tall black man, no doubt portraying Othello, also rises from the front row and attempts to drag Macbeth off the stage again. Oh, the significance!

In the chaos of a deepening sea of foam—Tzara! Beckett!—Macbeth accidentally collides with another character (I think it was Osric), which mystifyingly strips him of his wig and false beard. The denuded Macbeth falls off the stage into the lap of an older man in the audience. (Lear? I regret that I remember little of this performer's appearance.) (*Editor's note.* See story on page 1 "Anonymous blogger proves scab driver death a hoax. Government resigns. Who is UTooth?" Also pages 2, 3, 4 and 17.)

At this point, a sudden horde of actors in police uniforms—a clear *homage aux* Les Keystone Kops—rush in through the auditorium, many of them joining the melee on the stage. It is, naturally, the final key to Mr. Fingerfook's conception of the play: Hamlet is completely sane; it is the rest of the cast who are mad. Like *The Cabinet of Dr. Caligari*, the entire play takes place in a madhouse. Only while Hamlet lived could the lunacy be held in check.

And we, the theater audiences of today, are now revealed as no better than those middle-class doctor-peepers of yesteryear who sought their entertainment in touring the bedlams of England. As we are herded from the auditorium, our ears and cheeks now aglow with much-deserved shame, as we walk voyeuristically past the young couple kissing passionately in the foyer (I'd seen the same actor at a local comedy club, doing a stunningly Fingerhoodian portrayal of a second-rate stand-up comic), and as we are patted down with delicious intimacy in the evening air by young men dressed as policemen, who pretend to take our names and addresses (call me, Trey), we feel duly and deliciously abased. Positively degraded, in fact.

Thank you for that, Hymfrey Fingerhook—genius.

Chapter Thirty-eight

Saturday evening (continued)

"You know, Tobias," Oliver reflected, "it was the Mikado who wanted the punishment to fit the crime. That's comedy. Shakespeare lets the punishment fit the criminal. That's tragedy."

Oliver and Toby were back in the fourth row of the otherwise empty auditorium, still damp, but draped in blankets scavenged from the RSC's props department. They had just watched as Davina Bennet was lowered headfirst to the sudsy stage, freed from the noose around her ankles, and led away in a blanket and handcuffs by several detectives.

"The odd thing is that she killed Breedlove because he was blackmailing me," Toby reflected. "She never knew that she had been one of his victims for years."

Effie was standing stage right, in earnest conversation with Simon Culpepper, who seemed partly distracted by the fidgety Scotsman hovering beside him. The smaller man had reapplied his wig and beard.

"I bet that tall chap plays basketball," said Toby. "Who is he?"

"That's Detective Sergeant Culpepper. He's supposed to be in charge of the Breedlove case. He and Effie started out as bosom buddies, but somewhere along the line he must have blotted his copybook. Never a good move with Eff. Apparently, he was convinced that Breedlove's murder had something to do with a peculiar outfit called the Priory of Synne."

Toby flinched, but said nothing.

"You've lived in Synne since you were a kid, Tobe—don't make the joke—have you ever heard of such a thing?"

"Never," Toby answered quickly. Oliver turned in his seat and looked at his brother closely.

"You're lying," he said. "I've always been able to tell when you're lying, ever since that time you vehemently denied stealing Eve's first training bra, but I had the videotape of you wearing it as a World War II flying helmet."

Toby shuffled uncomfortably. "Okay, but you have to keep this to yourself. I'm actually a member of the Priory of Synne."

"Since when?"

"Since this morning. Do you remember that little man who was sitting in the front row? Wee Jockie McSporran over there landed in his lap during the final fracas."

"You mean Mr. Tooth? You see him, too, do you?"

"What do you mean, 'see him'?"

"Nothing. It's just I was beginning to…No, nothing. Never mind."

"I wasn't in the theater for all that malarkey, but I bumped into Mr. Tooth as he left, and he told me what had happened. He seemed quite charged about it—kept muttering something like 'Thickpin' or 'Pigpen.' Anyway, he'd turned up earlier today at Holy Trinity, just after you left and just before I got the call about the tunnel. Apparently he's some kind of recruiting officer for this Priory of Synne. It always has one member who lives in the village, and he thought I'd be a good choice, since I am native here. I was in a bit of a rush, so I said yes."

"What are you supposed to do?"

"Nothing really. Just protect the Secret of Synne."

"And that is?"

Toby looked shocked. "I couldn't possibly tell you, Ollie."

"After all I've done for you in the last week?"

"I was sworn to secrecy!"

"Come on, Tobe. Let this be our little family secret."

He stopped. The phrase echoed in his mind.

"Oh, very well," Toby glanced around and brought his voice to a whisper. "Synne is French."

"French for what?"

"No, really French. Mr. Tooth gave me a handout with all the details. You see, Synne started out up in the Middle Ages as a small settlement on a plot of land that a nearby French Benedictine priory had kept to sneer at. This expatriate community of monks was ruled by the Abbots of Brest in Brittany, and at some point, one of these Abbots decided to name the village 'Sein.' That's French for breast."

"In the nurturing sense of the Madonna feeding the Christ-child?"

"No, it was in bile-soaked retaliation for all the sniggering double-entendres that the Abbot of a place called Brest had to endure when visiting his English outpost. Anyway, a few decades later, Thomas Cromwell undertook the Visitation of the Monasteries, basically casing the joint for Henry VIII. But he failed to notice that the Benedictine possessions included a straggle of hovels and their impoverished English occupants. Twenty years later, Bloody Mary was to lament the final loss of Calais, which was England's last corner of France. Little did she know that, because of a clerical oversight, there was one tiny part of England that was still legally French. And still is to this day. The village of Sein in Warwickshire. Or, as it is now known, Synne."

"French!" said Oliver, aghast.

"When you think about it, it does explain a lot."

"French," Oliver muttered again. He got up to join Effie, who seemed to have finished with Culpepper and the mysterious Scotsman.

"Toffs nil, workers one," he said, stepping up onto the low stage and prodding the long, swaying rope, still attached to the gantry far above them. "But did she fall or was she pushed?"

Effie smiled. "The silly girl did seem determined to rock the boat up there, so I tied a bowline around her ankle, in case there were any unfortunate accidents. She fell only a couple of feet before the rope stopped her. But it turned out to be a good way to keep her out of mischief until the cavalry arrived. Simon should be able to match her fingerprints to the ones found on the skipping rope. That reminds me, Simon's on his way to Eric's flat with some bolt-cutters. I ought to warn him what to expect when he gets there."

"Why?" Oliver asked. "Eric's handcuffed to the bed frame. He's not going anywhere."

"True. And that could be the problem. I left a chocolate on Eric's pillow."

"A kind touch."

She screwed up her face. "Yeah. But the thing is, Ollie, I found it in one of Eric's desk drawers. It was a free sample of the Bennet family's laxative."

She skipped away, trying to avoid the shallow, iridescent puddles of soapy water. Mallard emerged from the wings, still wearing his multicolored Osric costume. To Oliver's surprise, after the disastrous finale, his uncle seemed blissfully happy.

"Er, great performance, Uncle Tim. At least what I saw of it."

Mallard laughed, threw back his shoulders, and stared around the empty auditorium. "This is the place to be, isn't it? The greasepaint. The bright lights. The codpieces." He bounced lightly, as if testing the springiness of the boards beneath his feet.

"Ollie," he continued, his voiced hushed. "Something happened to me tonight. I've made a decision, and I'm telling you, even before I tell Phoebe and the others. I'm sixty years old—half my life is over already. So I'm going to take my long-overdue retirement from the Yard and become a full-time actor."

"What brought this on?"

"I've always been a little stagestruck, as you may have noticed. But earlier this evening, I had one of those transcendent moments."

"It was certainly an Osric to remember, Uncle. Distinctly foamy, but a palpable hit."

"It wasn't Osric. It wasn't even Polonius. It was when I was the Gravedigger. You remember I'd been complaining about the Styrofoam skull I had to use for Yorick? Well, the props manager came up with a much better skull, right at the last minute—brown with age, jawbone missing, decayed, a bit whiffy—but it looked as if it had just been taken out of the ground. I found it on the props table, tied up in an old pair of tights for protection."

His eyes looked up dreamily to the distant dress circle.

"It may sound crazy, but just holding this skull seemed to transform my performance to a level I've never reached before. I felt the words coming from my mouth as if they had just formed within my brain. It was almost as if Shakespeare himself were out there on the stage with me."

Oliver listened in silence, trying to resist a certain growing suspicion. It would explain why Davina hadn't tried to escape the building, but hid on the high gantry instead, waiting for the theater to empty to recover the spoils she'd dropped.

"What, uh…what happened to the skull?" he asked.

Mallard gestured vaguely around the stage as he strode away. "Oh, it's here somewhere."

◇◇◇

It was half past eleven. Oliver was tucked in his teenage bed in his teenage bedroom, the beneficiary of a long, hot shower. He lay still, thinking, waiting for Effie to finish in the bathroom, toying with the events of the last few days, trying to ignore the aches and the flecks of soreness. Little family secrets…

Effie swept into the room, wearing a short blue-silk dressing gown, tied loosely at the waist.

"It's very quiet," she said, sitting on the end of the bed and rubbing her hair with a towel.

"Well, Toby got Ben to drop him off in Oxford on the way back to London. And the entire older generation is out to dinner in Stratford."

Effie pointed at the ceiling. "I meant our upstairs neighbors," she said. "Have they run out of energy at last?"

"Ah, that's interesting. I was chatting to Geoff and Susie at the theater about the wonders of making love by moonlight in the middle of the Shakespeare Race. They seemed very keen to try it, so they're on their way up Synne Common as we speak, stripped and ready for action."

Effie laughed. "Let's hope they don't find any dead bodies hanging from trees."

Oliver looked thoughtful. "No, not bodies. Not *dead* bodies."

"What have you done, Oliver?"

"Do you remember that very pleasant group of Japanese tourists in the row behind us this evening? I merely happened to mention to their guide that a midnight visit to the Shakespeare Race is a splendid diversion for jet-lagged travelers. And that since the road is finally open to motor coaches again, tonight would be an excellent night for such an expedition. I recommended flashlights and video cameras, to capture the wildlife."

Effie got up and draped the damp towel over the back of a chair. She turned to face him. "Do you want to know what it is?"

"What what is?"

"What it is I see in you. You asked me last week, in the Race."

He propped himself up on his elbows. "Yes, I think I would like to know."

"Most of the time, you get it right."

"And by 'it,' you mean…?"

"Whatever it is. You usually get it right, Ollie. And even when you don't, you try to."

"Ah. Doesn't that apply to most of us?"

Effie shook her head. "You'd be surprised how rare it is. That's what makes you a keeper." She looked down. "This is our last night here, and we seem to have the place to ourselves. Do you want to make love?"

Oliver considered. "Well, in recent days, I've been kicked in the cobblers, set upon three times in the village, stung by nettles, scraped up, bruised, nearly buried alive, virtually drowned, and shot out of a drain like a pea from a peashooter."

"Is that a yes, then?"

"Of course it is." He swallowed. "Is that robe all you're wearing?"

"Yes."

"Are you going to take it off, then?"

"No." She lifted her head and let her pale, bright eyes meet his.

"No?" he echoed.

"No. You are."

Chapter Thirty-nine

Sunday

"I always loved Prussian blue," said Oliver, peering into his mother's box of watercolors.

"As a child, you used to eat it." Chloe washed the raw sienna out of her brush, turning the clear tumbler to the color of cider.

With the Sunday morning church service over and with most of her guests departed for London, Chloe Swithin had put on her wide-brimmed straw hat and taken her easel and paint box up to the heights of Synne Common. Oliver had volunteered to carry the rest of her equipment while Effie was packing.

"You can't see the village from here." He looked out over the countryside. The sun was still high in the cloudless sky.

"Not your usual tagline about that being a good thing, dear?"

"My wit's deceased. So's my hay fever, incidentally. And I'll admit that Synne is very beautiful." He sat down in the long grass beside her, watching a buzzard wheel around the top of the Synne Oak. They were only a few yards from the Shakespeare Race.

"Even when the church organist attacks you at night?" Chloe remarked.

"How did you find out it was Sidney?"

She dabbed some red poppies onto the foreground. "He apologized to me privately this morning. That was quite a bashing you gave him."

She noticed that her tumbler of water was speckled with drowned midges and tipped it out onto the grass. Oliver refilled it for her from one of the jugs of fresh water that she'd stationed beside her campstool. *So Kim finally emerged from isolation,* he reflected. And will now have to stay as Sidney until the swelling goes down. Unless, by some peculiar coincidence, Lesbia sustains an identical injury.

"The odd thing is," Chloe continued, "that attack happened on Thursday night. I could have sworn I saw Sidney on Friday, and there wasn't a mark on him." She sat back and scrutinized the painting.

"Do you want to know why?"

"Not really."

"Let's just say that 'Tweedledum and Tweedledee' fits them very well. So it's a shame, in a way, that they weren't Dennis's Tweedle victims."

Chloe lowered her brush and peered around the easel, surprised to find he had been looking steadily at her. "But you were convinced—"

"Yes. But I've been missing something obvious. Something you told me first, incidentally."

"You should always listen to your mother. What was it?"

"The Weguelins moved to Synne about two years ago. Dennis Breedlove started blackmailing his Tweedles *four* years ago. So if we *really* want to complete our set of victims—just for neatness, you understand—we need to find somebody else who fits the rhyme. Somebody who *was* living in the village four years ago."

And he waited. He'd allow her a few stumbling denials if she wished, and then he'd counter with his observations. Not evidence maybe, but impressions. The brigadier's report of her intense dislike of Dennis Breedlove, backed up by her indifference to his death. Her initial assistance when Oliver mistakenly thought Breedlove was himself a blackmail victim, followed by her peevish opposition when he realized the truth about the old man. And Breedlove's odd and fatal change of habit, when he'd asked his stooge Eric Mormal to hand-deliver Toby's first blackmail letter, fearful that if it landed on the Swithin family doormat, it might be opened by somebody else in the house who'd recognize that square penciled handwriting.

Chloe laid her brush and palette aside. Then she sat up straight on her stool and fixed her eyes on the horizon.

"All right, I admit it. Dennis was blackmailing me."

Oliver stood up. "Let me guess. You revealed a great secret to Breedlove in a confessional moment, because he convinced you he was someone you could trust?"

She let out a short breath of laughter at the memory. "Exactly. We'd had him to dinner. We often did back then. I felt sorry for him, living alone, no family. And he was always cheery, a thoughtful guest, a good raconteur, an even better listener. Bob had gone off to bed, as he does. Dennis and I stayed at the table, finishing a second bottle of a rather good St. Emilion. I revealed something amusing from the past, thinking my secret was in safe hands. Oh, he was most apologetic when he later demanded money for his silence. He'd fallen on hard times, apparently, and blackmail was his only source of funds. My sins may even have inspired him to start." She took the sheet of paper from the easel and screwed it savagely into a ball. "I suppose you want to know what it was all about."

"Not if you don't want to tell me," Oliver lied. But he did want to know. It was the ultimate solution to that mystifying line in the blackmail letter, Breedlove's in-joke that Toby's capitulation would turn out to be a "little family secret," even if the blackmailer himself was the only one to know why. That the son had joined the mother in his panoply of victims. Dennis's private plot.

Chloe tore a fresh sheet from her tablet and clipped it into place, tilting the easel away from her.

"I'm not Chloe Swithin," she announced.

"You're not my mother?"

"Of course I'm your mother, you dull ass! But my name isn't Chloe. It's Phoebe. Phoebe Mallard." She picked up a wide brush, and started to apply a faint blue wash to the white surface. "And Phoebe is really Chloe. We swapped identities."

A bee landed on Oliver's shoulder. He ignored it.

"Why?"

She looked toward the sun, closing her eyes. "Do you remember the story about my meeting your father? We'd taken the magic show to Cyprus, to entertain the troops. It was my turn to eat in the officers' mess that night, while Phoebe had to stay hidden in the civilian guest quarters in Episkopi, to maintain the pretense that there was only one assistant. According to family legend, I met Bob and fell in love on the spot with this handsome, confident, charming captain in his early thirties. Well, that's all true. Chloe did. But I wasn't Chloe then. I was Phoebe. *I* was the one who spent the evening holed up with the latest Tom Sharpe novel and dinner on a tray. My twin sister, the real Chloe Winsbury, met Bob first. And fell in love with him.

"Of course, we had to let Bob know there were two identical Winsbury sisters. When I met him, I could see why Chloe had been so taken with him. I found Bob very attractive too, but Chloe was my sister—she and Bob were soon engaged—and there are rules you don't break."

"Let me be clear," Oliver cut in. "We're talking about Brigadier Bob, right? The foul-tempered old misanthrope who can barely manage a conversation with his children unless it treats of violence? He managed to charm not one, but two sisters?"

"Don't be cynical, Oliver." She removed her straw hat and briefly fanned her face with its broad brim. "He was a different person in those days. And he's still an honorable man."

Oliver snorted. "Go on with your story."

"Well, I was the one who first met Tim Mallard—I'm still Phoebe at this point, remember? Tim and Bob had a lot in common back then. They were both good-looking, both kind and intelligent and considerate, both courageous when they had to be. Tim asked me to marry him, and knowing by then that I could never have Bob, I agreed. The four of us had a summer double wedding."

"This isn't going to get kinky on the honeymoon night, is it?"

"Do you want to hear the story or not?" She started to add new colors to the landscape, wet in wet. "One day, perhaps thinking that marriage had carried us to safe ground, your aunt privately confessed to me that she'd been very impressed with Tim when I first brought him home and may perhaps have chosen him over Bob, if she'd met him first."

"It *is* going to get kinky."

"No, dear. Well, we talked. I mentioned my constant fears for Tim's safety, she seemed almost to relish the excitement of his stories of the London criminal classes. In turn, she complained of the uneventfulness of life on an army camp, I said how I envied the quiet predictability of peacetime life. And eventually, we both confessed we were more attracted to each other's husband. So we decided to swap places."

"Just like that?"

"There and then. On the spot. I became Chloe Swithin. My identical twin sister became Phoebe Mallard. It was the best thing we ever did."

"When was this?"

"Oh, very early on. Only three or four months after the wedding. Before your time."

"What about the Brigadier? What about Uncle Tim? Surely, they noticed the difference?"

"They each ended up with a wife who loved them more than before. If they detected anything in those newlywed days, it was only that it suddenly became even better."

"But Breedlove threatened to spill the beans."

"Yes. He was going to tell our husbands that for more than a quarter of a century, they'd been, well, 'living in sin' without knowing it. So I paid up. Anyway, now you know what he knew. Your aunt and I are the interchangeable Tweedledum and Tweedledee."

Oliver stood still with his hands in his pockets, attempting to redraw the family tree in his head. His mother looked down the hillside ahead of her, spotted something, and reached for a pencil.

"Wait a minute!" he cried.

"Yes, dear?" she answered, focused on the picture.

"Me!" he said. "My birthday!"

"No dear, it's not your birthday. This is May, and your birthday's in August. You'll just have to be patient."

"Exactly," he spluttered. "My birthday is in August. One year after you got married!"

Chloe added a tiny daub of ultramarine to the painting. "Well?" she said eventually.

"What if you were already pregnant when you swapped places!"

"Oh, you spotted that, did you?"

"Which means that, unlike Eve and Toby, I may not be the offspring of Brigadier Bob. My father could be my uncle-by-marriage Timothy Mallard! And Brigadier Bob…"

"Bob's your uncle." She smirked. "It does explain a lot, doesn't it?"

"Oh my God! I'm not really Oliver Swithin. I'm a bloody Mallard!"

"You'd better duck."

"This isn't time for a joke!" He stood in front of her, blocking her view of the landscape. "When were you planning on telling me this, Mother? If that is your real name."

She put down the brush. "There may be nothing to tell you. I didn't know I was pregnant until I was happily ensconced with your father. The brigadier, I mean. Yes, Tim could be your birth father, if you were a late arrival. But so could Bob, if you were early."

One idea surfaced from the boiling stew of implications. "Does Brigadier Bob know he may not be my father?" Oliver demanded. "Does that account for his coldness to me?"

"Oh no, he doesn't suspect a thing. He just doesn't like you very much. It's nothing personal."

"And this was the man you preferred to Uncle Tim?"

"I love Bob. And you owe him your respect—he did play his part in nurturing you."

"Uncle Tim had more to do with me when I was growing up than Bob Swithin ever did."

"Then this should be good news. Besides, darling, think what would have happened if you'd been Oliver Mallard. They'd have called you 'Quackers' at school."

Chloe reached out to take his hand, but he stepped away and began to pace a circle around her.

"Oliver," she said, "you've just discovered that a man you've never had time for might not—I say *might* not—have been your biological father. Meanwhile, the one man who's acted like a surrogate father to you all your life could well be your real father too. Tim and Bob have the same blood group, so you'd need a DNA test to find out the truth. But what difference does the truth make, when you've already reaped its benefits?"

"What difference?" Oliver patted his chest with both hands. "I want to know whose DNA runs through my body. I want to know if Swithin is my bloodline, my ancestry, my descent, or if it's just an arbitrary label, with no more meaning for me than, than… my pen name, 'O.C. Blithely.' I want to know who I take after, who I look like. These are all things that make me *me*. I'd say it makes quite a difference."

Oliver stopped, staring over his mother's shoulder at the picture on her easel. A tiny figure had been painted in, a woman in blue, far away down the hill. He looked up into the real landscape. Effie was halfway up the slope, her blue dress bright in the afternoon sunlight.

"I was going to ask her to marry me," he whispered.

"About time. You'll never do any better, although God knows what she sees in you. Just make sure she isn't really Tim's daughter, no matter how much he treats her like one."

"You don't get it," he said, shaking his head again. "How can I ask her to have me when I don't know who I am?"

He waved to Effie. She waved back, smiling that smile of hers.

Notes

My thanks to my friends in the South Shore Writers Group, who patiently and insightfully reviewed this book at the speed it emerged, and especially to the group's founder Maureen Amaturo and my fellow founding member Suki Van Dijk.

Thanks to Linell Nash Smith and Frances Smith, daughter and granddaughter of the extraordinary Ogden Nash, for their kind permission to use his limerick as an epigraph.

Special thanks, too, to Dr. Thomas MacDonald, associate professor in the Environmental Management department of the University of San Francisco, for advice on the challenges of tunneling under rivers. If the scene rings true, it's because of Tom's generous help; if there are errors, they're where I blatantly ignored his expert suggestions.

Of the many books about Shakespeare and Stratford-upon-Avon that I read in researching this story, I particularly want to express my indebtedness to the late Samuel Schoenbaum's masterly and fascinating *William Shakespeare: A Compact Documentary Life*, published by Oxford University Press.

At the time of writing this novel, the Royal Shakespeare Theatre in Stratford is undergoing major reconstruction. Since we can't have *Hamlet* performed on a building site—although Humfrey Fingerhood has undoubtedly considered it—the reader is asked to imagine the story taking place in a parallel universe in which the old theater was allowed to stay up a little longer.

Every piece of information that Toby presents to support his Two Shakespeares theory is true, but I held back one fact. The written-in bequest to Heminges, Condell, and Burbage was certainly a puzzlingly late addition to Will's final will, which was drawn up about a month before his death—probably not, at age fifty-two, because of any fatal premonition, but to add specific protection for his daughter, Judith, who'd just married a complete rotter; but the annotation was already in place when the will was transcribed for probate, a matter of days after his death. If Toby is right, any attempt to forge a posthumous connection between the two Wills must have begun much earlier than he implies. There have been other interpretations of these oddities, of course—many of them leading to even more unlikely claims about the true identity of the author of *Hamlet*, a play that has enriched our language like no other.

To receive a free catalog of Poisoned Pen Press titles, please contact us in one of the following ways:

Phone: 1-800-421-3976
Facsimile: 1-480-949-1707
Email: info@poisonedpenpress.com
Website: www.poisonedpenpress.com

Poisoned Pen Press
6962 E. First Ave. Ste 103
Scottsdale, AZ 85251